NO BREAD TOMORROW

No Bread Tomorrow is a haunting chapter in Serbian history, leaving a lasting and painful impact on descendants who may still carry the weight of ancestral trauma from their parents or grandparents. In order to give this astonishing story of human courage and bravery the respect it deserves, and to ensure the truth remains intact, it is vital to handle this narrative with grace. No one should ever know or experience hate in such a way— ever again.

NO
BREAD
TOMORROW

MILA EVANOVICH

For my parents
Miloš and Jelena

LIST OF CHARACTERS AND THEIR PRONUNCIATION IN ENGLISH

Family:

Zora Brković: *(Brr-ko-vich)*Married to Peda Brković. Born November 14,1902.

Predrag (Peda) Brković: *(Preh-draag, Pe-da)* Born June 26,1899.

Goran Brković: *(Goh-ran)* Zora and Peda's oldest child. Born January 21,1922.

Lenka Brković: *(Len-ka)* Zora and Peda's oldest daughter. Born May 16,1923.

Neven Brković: *(Ne-ven, rhymes with seven)* Zora and Peda's third child. Born October 21,1924.

Stana Brković: *(Staa-na)* Zora and Peda's fourth child. Born August 16, 1925.

Vukašin (Vuk) Brković: *(Vuk-a-shin)* Zora and Peda's fifth child. Born March 7,1927.

Čedomir (Čedo) Brković: *(Che-doh-mir, Che-do)* Zora and Peda's sixth child. Born November 7, 1930.

Aleksandar (Aco) Brković: *(Ah-lek-san-dar, Aat-zo)* Zora and Peda's youngest child. Born December 18,1932.

Baka Cveta Čudić: *(Baa-kaa Sve-ta Chu-dich)* Zora's maternal grandmother. Born in what is now Croatia on June 9 (or thereabouts), 1856.

Baka Milica (Mima) Nikolić: *(Mil-lee-tza Me-maa Nick-o-lich)* Zora's mother. Born December 20,1878.

Deda Zoran Nikolić: *(Dead-ah)* Zora's father. Born September 20,1876.

Dušica Živković: *(Du-shee-tza Zhiv-ko-vich)* Zora's eldest sister. Married to Marko Živković. Born April 27,1899.

Marko Živković: Dušica's husband. Born October1,1899.

Stefan Živković: *(Steh-fahn)* Formerly Steven Levine, Dušica and Marko's oldest child. Born February 21,1938.

Andrej Živković: *(Ahn-drey)* Formerly Andrew Levine, Dušica and Marko's second child. Born July 19, 1940.

Nada Vamavakos: *(Nah-da Vahm-ah-vaa-kos)* Zora's middle sister. Resides in US. Married to Bobby Vamavakos. Born July 24,1900.

Bobby Vamavakos: Nada's husband. Born January 11,1898

Jelisaveta (Sava) Ivković Ph.D.: *(Yell-lee-sa-veh-ta Iv-ko-vich)* Zora's youngest sister. Married to Vlado Ivković. Born October 31,1907.

Vladimir (Vlado) Ivković: *(Vlaad-a-mir, Vlaa-do)* Sava's husband. Born October 20,1877.

Friends:

Kosta Lazić: *(Cos-ta La-zich)*
Luka Lazić
Dunja Lekić: *(Duhn-ya Leh-kich)*
Tomislav (Toma) Tatalović: *(Tome-ih-slav Ta-towel-o-vich)*
Conductor Boško Matić: *(Bosh-ko Mah-tich)*
Života Pavlović: *(Zhee-voh-ta Pav-lo-vich)*
Đuro Grubičić: *(Juh-ro Gruh-bi-chich)*
Božidar (Božo) Momčilović: *(Bohz-i-dar Bohz-o Mom-chil-lo-vich)*
Jovica Ristić: *(Yo-vee-tza Ris-tich)*
Čiča Draža Mihajlović: *(Chee-cha Draa-zha Me-haj-lo-vich)*
Abbess Mother Katarina: *(Ka-taa-reen-a)*
Sister Simonida: *(Sim-o-knee-da)*

City:

Kragujevac: *(Cry-goy-yeh-vatz)*

CHAPTER ONE

ZORA

Kragujevac, the Kingdom of Yugoslavia
January 07, 1941: Božić

CZECHOSLOVAKIA — POLAND — DENMARK — NORWAY — the Netherlands—Belgium—Luxembourg—France. Hitler's ambitions seemed interminable, and his next target was unmistakable. Zora felt the looming threat in her very bones, an uneasiness that pervaded the air. The newspapers and radio broadcasts painted a grim picture: Adolf Hitler, and the Third Reich's insatiable appetite for conquest, had set their sights on the Kingdom of Yugoslavia. The thought of war, and its brutal possibilities, haunted her. Clutching the wooden spoon, Zora tightened her grip until she noticed her hand tremble. She placed the spoon on the kitchen table.

Her family, especially her two older sons of fighting age, weighed heavily on her mind. The latest news about the atrocities in France at the hands of the Wehrmacht heightened her fears. Like many who followed the tumultuous political climate in the Yugoslav Parliament, she anxiously awaited the inevitable.

Initially, Zora had considered sending her sons to her youngest sister's summer home in the English countryside should war erupt; however, the Luftwaffe's blitzkrieg aerial bombings across England had quashed that idea. She and Dušica had devised a new plan, one that Dušica's husband intended to propose to Peda after dinner tonight. Zora prayed her husband would be receptive and open-minded.

Despite the turmoil, Zora busied herself with preparations for their Božić dinner, checking that her trays of savory cheese pita, hearty casserole of prebranac, and pots of sarma and chicken noodle soup were to her liking. With these tasks accomplished, she turned her attention to making Česnica, their cherished Christmas bread, wishing she had remembered to borrow Dušica's radio from upstairs. While she baked, she liked listening to Radio Belgrade for updated war reports.

In the tranquility of the early hours before dawn, when the world around her slept, she burrowed her long fingers into the deep mound of sticky dough. Each squeeze and fold of the dough awakened memories of the many women who had come before her—generations who lovingly nurtured these unwritten recipes, passing them from mother to daughter. These culinary traditions flowed from her great-grandmother to her Baka Cveta, then to Zora's mother, Mima, and now to Zora and her three sisters.

The feeling of the soft texture between her fingers transported her back to her youth under Baka Cveta's tutelage. Her grandmother, a beacon of wisdom, had emphasized the importance of honoring their sacred holidays—Božić, Vaskrs, and slava. She spoke of these traditions, illuminating how each one would one day become punctuation marks in her life. As a young child

Zora had not understood what her sagacious grandmother meant, yet as time passed, she embraced its importance. This understanding, this reverence for their customs, fueled Zora's dedication, compelling her to prepare this feast for tonight's Christmas dinner.

She punched and kneaded the dough one last time before sliding it into the oven, then poured herself a cup of coffee, the morning silence broken by the howling wind.

Daybreak unveiled an unexpected layer of ice covering their street. Thick, spiky icicles hung from her neighbor Mitza's slanted roof, resembling sharpened swords lined in strict formation, ready for battle. "Please don't let him attack our weakened country," she whispered.

Zora glanced at the bowls and measuring spoons still on the table, her thoughts soaring across the Atlantic to her middle sister, Nada, nestled in her kitchen in Pennsylvania. Somehow through the four-thousand-mile distance, Zora found comfort knowing their time-honored recipes—a legacy of their heritage—bridged the miles. The pang of missing her sister ached something fierce. "One day, I'll visit your Pennsylvania with its rolling hills and sprawling farms."

"Mama, who are you talking to?" Neven's voice, lined with curiosity, floated into the kitchen as he crept in, his eyebrows furrowed.

Caught off guard, Zora felt the flush crawl up her neck. "You caught me," she admitted with a sheepish grin, dabbing her tears with the corner of a tea towel. "It's the holidays, and your mother always turns into a sopping mess."

"Not you." Neven chuckled, his maturity shining through. At seventeen and a half, he stood as her mainstay among her seven children, always exuding an air of grace that belied his years, reminding Zora of a sophisticated British gentleman. "Were you up all night cooking?" he inquired. "I smelled it in my sleep."

Smiling, she moved to the old stove, warming a splash of milk in a saucepan. She then poured it over slices of day-old bread. "*Mir Božiji! Hristos se Rodi, voljeni sine.* Enjoy your breakfast."

"*Vaistinu se Rodi*, Mama," Neven replied, planting a kiss on his mother's cheek before taking the bowl she offered him. His gaze swept briefly over the vacant space in his parents' bed, the unspoken question hanging in the air. "Everything smells wonderful; as soon as I'm finished, I'll head into town to fetch the paper. Need anything else?" He slid his eyeglasses up his nose.

"No, thank you." Zora marveled at how he seemed to have grown taller overnight, nearly as tall as his older brother, Goran. What were the chances? She knew her brilliant son missed nothing and was confident he'd seen the empty bed in his parents' room yet was too respectful to comment on his father not returning home from last night's festivities.

She worshipped each of her wildly different children and pondered their safety amidst the war engulfing Europe. Her conviction that Hitler posed a real threat to Yugoslavia stood in stark contrast to Peda and other family members' disbelief.

Placing the empty bowl in the sink, Neven reached for his jacket on the hook and unwittingly let in a gust of freezing air. Immersed in a chill, Zora exclaimed, "Neven, bundle up. Please don't catch a chill. Remember—promaja." She pointed her finger in warning.

"Really, Mama? Even on Božić, you're cautioning me about getting sick because of our silly, ancient superstition?"

Waving him off, she shut the door, remembering her mother indicating that promaja went beyond logic, yet it conjured up tangible fear in the Balkans, positioned around the belief that drafts, or going outside with wet hair, caused colds.

Blowing the stray wisps of hair from her face, Zora winced as a sharp pain shot through her wrist—a stark reminder of how she had gotten to this point in her marriage. She remembered Peda's charismatic smile that night at the Grand Hotel Gusić, a smile that once lit up the room, now overshadowed by the harsh reality of their twenty years together. Misgivings about her marriage continued to haunt her; nevertheless, she found solace in the faces of their seven children, each a beacon of hope in the fractured world Peda had created with her.

Glancing at the time, Zora calculated she could squeeze in a two-hour nap before the demands of the holiday beckoned her. She also did not want to miss hearing Stana sing the glorious Molitvami Bogorodici with her choir this morning during Divine Liturgy.

Suddenly, the back door to the kitchen swung open, shattering her peace. Peda staggered in with a stale mix of late-night kafana smoke and the bitter tang of sweat that clung to his faded brown corduroy jacket.

"Aren't you going to wish me Merry Christmas?" he slurred, leaning heavily on the wall for support.

"*Hristos se Rodi!*" She refused to meet his bloodshot eyes.

"How about some breakfast?" Peda moved gingerly toward the table and pulled out one of their cracked and yellowed vinyl chairs and clumsily slid in. Lighting a cigarette, he stared at her, waiting.

His commanding tone irked her; it was worsened by his being out all night. He was sweating, and she noticed bruises and blood on his knuckles, an indication of a night spent doing something troublesome. What had he gotten himself into?

"Whash wrong?" he asked noisily.

"Shh, you'll wake the children."

He mocked her, his sneer cutting through the tension. "Don't shush me."

Recognizing the telltale signs, Zora suggested, "Why not lie on the bed while I finish your breakfast?" She sent up a silent prayer that he would fall asleep.

***

The scent of warm apple strudel wafted from the kitchen to greet her parents, Zoran and Mima Nikolić. "Goodness, everything smells heavenly," Mima said before being engulfed in hugs and kisses from her grandchildren.

Zora approached her parents with reverence, kissing them on one cheek, then the other, three times, followed by their traditional Christmas greeting: "*Mir Božiji! Hristos se Rodi*," echoing the depth of their faith and heritage.

Mima surprised everyone by responding in flawless English, the invisible threads connecting them across the continents. "God is born! Indeed, he is born!"

"Baka Mima?" Goran questioned his grandmother. "I never knew you spoke English so well."

"Of course. Your grandmother is no dummy." Mima's eyes twinkled. "Your aunt in America, Tetka Nada, taught me good English."

The family convened in Zora's small kitchen, now metamorphosed into a bustling hub of holiday preparations.

Zora's keen eyes caught the telling signs of Peda's swollen eyelids and puffy face as he lay on the couch, which was layered with a slipcover to hide the wear. A cigarette stuck from between his fingers.

Dušica and Marko shredded cabbage, Goran and Neven poured the soup into bowls, and Mima sliced the roast. Stana and Lenka were positioned at the sink washing the mountains of pots and pans. The absence of her sister and brother-in-law, Sava and Vlado Ivković, hindered by the icy roads in Belgrade, was a sharp twinge in Zora's heart. Once she placed the round Česnica on the overflowing table, it became the focal point for her children's eager eyes; she knew how much they loved this Christmas tradition of tearing this particular bread apart.

Mima's lighting of the tall Christmas candle with its symbolic blue, white, and red band wrapped at the bottom was a poignant reminder of their customs. Making the ubiquitous Troitsa, the sign of the cross in the Serbian Orthodox religion, she recited the Lord's Prayer. "*Oče naš, iže jesi na nebesjeh…*"

Bowing, Zora's family pressed their thumbs, index, and middle fingers together to make the sign of the Troitsa across their bodies in the Holy Trinity. Zora whispered to Lenka, "Please help your little brothers."

"Like this." Lenka demonstrated to Aco how to place three fingers in a pattern reflective of the Father, Son, and Holy Spirit. Serbians were commonly known to do things in threes because of their sacred Troitsa.

After the blessing, Stana glanced at her mother, sticky with perspiration, and whispered, "Everything's perfect. Where did you find the meso?" Stana shopped regularly and meat was seldom on their list.

"Your tetka." Zora lowered her head, slightly ashamed by how much she depended on her sister and Marko's support. Living upstairs in the shared duplex had been an incomparable blessing and underscored the steadfast bond of her family's continual support. Bright and caring, Dušica, although disappointingly unable to conceive, had the most extraordinary capacity for love. She was the sister who most resembled her, with their similar lanky frames. The only difference was Dušica's shorter, pixie-like haircut, and a prominent dark mole above her upper left lip.

Zora beckoned her family closer. "Please everyone, dinner's ready." She handed the large, round bread to Peda. As head of the household, he opened the Božić holiday by gently turning the Česnica round and round. This allowed each of their children to touch the bread before everyone broke it apart with their hands in a ceremonial gesture. The children hungrily searched for the coveted possession—the prized silver coin buried inside. With tiny crumbs dropping onto the hardened soil of their floor, they continued ripping through the Česnica until someone found it. Legend held that whoever found the silver would have good fortune throughout the year, and today, Goran was the lucky recipient.

The younger boys jumped up and down, unable to contain their excitement. "*Hristos se Rodi, Goran, Hristos se Rodi!*"

Knowing her older children were on the cusp of significant changes in their lives and having everyone squeezed around the table made Zora's heart swell. Feeling jubilant about the abundance of food on the table, she asked her husband, "Peda, did you notice the meso?" It had been a while since they last had meat, an extraordinary treat.

Nodding, Peda kept his head bent as he ate.

Zora worked hard to keep her shock from showing on her face. Why would he ignore her sister's kindness and the effort she had put into making all this food? Drawing a measured breath, she momentarily closed her eyes, willing herself to let go of the deluge of emotions threatening to overshadow the joy of the day. Christmas was intended to be joyful. With deliberate care she passed the platters of food and made sure each of her children tried a slip of the roast infused with garlic and baked in its own juices for hours until it fell off the bone, a taste of the paprika-infused prebranac, and the freshly churned kajmak. Her aim was to provide her children with a sense of normalcy and warmth, against the undercurrent of tension threaded through their home.

Luckily, the conversation turned lighter, so Zora felt comfortable when she cheekily asked, "Lenka, where's your handsome fiancé? Will he join us later?"

"Simo felt we should spend our last Christmas before we're married with our own families, so I'm here all evening." Zora heard her daughter's tone of resignation.

"But what do *you* think, Lenka?" interjected Stana.

Hesitating for a fraction of a second, but not before her mother witnessed the doubt across her face, Lenka said, "Now that we're engaged, Simo makes all those decisions."

Stana, ever the free spirit, could not hold back. "Ohh boy; he's starting already," she muttered under her breath, accompanied by an eyeroll.

"Watch it, missy." Zora's warning was swift and firm yet twinged with understanding. "Everyone's entitled to their opinions. Sometimes it is wiser to keep your free-thinking ideas to yourself." In a home, and a society, where the traditional male ascendancy was displayed like proud badges pinned to their chests, Zora did not fault Stana's serious-mindedness over how women in the Balkans were treated. Zora's struggle was twofold: her doubt over why women remained voiceless in Yugoslavia, and her hope that her rebellious daughter would one day find a partner who valued her mind as much as her passion, a union similar to her youngest sister Sava and Vlado's, built on mutual respect.

The moment was interrupted by Goran, his voice cutting through the familial din with a gravity that demanded their attention. Standing with his hands folded over his chest, he faced his parents, his handsome, chiseled cheekbones more pronounced in the candlelight. "I have something important to share. With my nineteenth birthday approaching, I've made a decision. I've enlisted in the Royal Yugoslav Army and leave for training in three days." Goran's eyes shone as he sought his grandfather's and father's approval. "Since you both fought in the Great War, you know how much I've wanted to be a soldier."

"That's good, Goran; training will help," said his Deda Zoran.

Peda's fingers flexed then curled into fists, his voice laced with sarcasm. "Well, it seems I have my own news to share."

Blowing out sharp breaths of air, Zora glanced at the fat jug of rakija situated squarely in front of him, and with a surge of apprehension, she leaned forward, her expression a mix of disbelief and confusion. "Peda, Goran has dreamed of being a soldier his entire life. Please let him share his plans with us. These pivotal moments in his young life will undoubtedly shape his future. Surely, he would love your support, if not your blessing." Her plea hung in the air as her heart raced. She was gripped with thoughts of the peril her son might face. God forbid if something happened to him. Goran's news dislodged an unpleasant feeling in Zora, an awareness of danger lurking that caused her to shiver.

Peda's reaction was fast, accompanied with a storm of indignation which swept across his features. His hand crashed down on the table, causing the plates to jump to attention. "Zora—don't you dare speak to me in that tone, in my home, and especially not on Božić. Do. You. Understand?" His words were interposed by his towering presence as he leaned on the table, his scowl menacing.

Tears threatened to spill as Zora's body shook. Around the table, expressions of shock were mirrored by her family, tension tearing through the room. She attempted to blink the tears away, but not before noticing her father clutching his chest, a silent alarm that caused her breath to hitch.

In that moment Goran rose, his stature dominating the small room. Standing over his father, his presence was both a challenge and a plea. "Tata, I am not seeking your permission; I've already made my decisions. But I hope for your blessing."

"Is that so?" Peda's response was one of scorn laced with incredulity. "So, you think you no longer need my guidance?" His loud voice indicated to Zora this might not have been his first drink of the day. "Enough," Peda bellowed, his gesture dismissive, not just of Goran's admission, but perhaps of his son as well.

Rubbing her collarbone, Zora nibbled anxiously on her bottom lip. With the exchange between father and son came a foreboding of a deep rift in their relationship, a steep price her husband might one day pay for botching it up, likely causing irreparable damage between them.

Then, quite unexpectantly, Peda's tone softened. "I—ah… yesterday, I lost my job."

Zora's head whipped around. "What…?" she stammered as the rest of her family sat in complete disbelief. Her mother sat upright in her chair, her finger inconspicuously tracing the prominent scar against her hairline, indicative of a youthful fall from a tree. Dušica's reaction was instantaneous as her gaze turned toward Zora, communicating volumes without a single word spoken. Everyone else seemed to be dazed.

"It was a bit of a scuffle with a coworker." Peda's lips began to curl upward in an attempt to lighten the mood.

A swarm of questions arose as Zora recalled the fresh abrasions she had noticed on his knuckles this morning. No wonder he had stayed out all night, he was avoiding a confrontation, yet it was perplexing, nonetheless. It was puzzling why neither she, nor her sister, had heard anything about this, despite their employment at the same vast Military Technical Institute, which dominated the preponderance of Kragujevac's workforce, including her husband. Zora exchanged a look with Dušica, who offered a shrug as if to say, I know nothing.

Zora observed Marko's discomfort as he stood too quickly, his sudden movement causing him to wobble, his limp more pronounced. "Gentlemen, perhaps we should adjourn to the other room for a more relaxed Christmas toast," he suggested.

Wringing her hands, Zora recognized Marko's intent to shield her from the uncomfortable stink her husband was creating. Her gratitude toward her brother-in-law deepened, appreciating his tactful intervention. Marko's family had been a cornerstone in the lives of the Nikolić family, embodying the ethos of honesty and hard work through their modest farming in the lush, fertile landscape of Šumadija. His union with Dušica was a source of joy for their family, a stark contrast to the apprehension that clouded Peda's proposal to her. Marrying a man with a family they knew little about had set off alarm bells for Mima, who felt history and familial bonds were most important.

Hers was a big, noisy family that worshipped and protected one another with unwavering support. Zora's parents had raised their four daughters in a home full of love. Rooted in core values and faith, Zoran and his ancestors had thrived in the quintessential region of Šumadija, resplendent with narrow, two-lane roads that meandered onto grassy orchards of apples and plums. Farms burst with a profusion of wheat, vegetables, and cornfields, where brightly colored yellow, pink, or powder-blue houses nestled in. This area supplied a monstrous amount of the food for export to Germany, embodying its nickname of the breadbasket of Yugoslavia. Šumadija was indeed the heartland of Serbia, and where people stuck together in tough times.

Overwhelmed by Peda's outburst, Zora sought solace with her mother and sister in the warmth of her kitchen. Savoring her coffee before she cut the strudel for dessert, she instructed her teenagers, "You'd better get busy on those dishes. They will not wash themselves."

Mima slid her chair closer, reaching for Zora's slender arm to pull her in for a much-needed embrace. "Thank you for the delicious dinner. It was really lovely. You outdid yourself, *dragi moj.*"

Her mother's praise was a balm to her frazzled nerves. "Thank you, Mama. I appreciate you not saying anything at the table, you know, to Peda."

"Ahhh, Zora…why provoke an angry dog?" Mima asked, arching an eyebrow.

CHAPTER TWO

PEDA

Kragujevac, the Kingdom of Yugoslavia
January 07, 1941: Božić

AFTER THE GRAND FEAST, Peda needed a nap. Drained from his previous night's outing, he longed for everyone to go home, yet he was trapped in the living room with his least favorite person—his brother-in-law, Marko Živković. Irritation washed over him as he realized any hope of a pleasant ending to his holiday was dashed. The snores of his father-in-law underscored his predicament: he was stuck making tedious conversation with Marko. Stretching his neck and shoulders back, he waited.

"Peda, what happened at work?" Marko inquired, cutting through the silence.

"Could you give me a minute?" Peda refused to tell him the truth behind his dismissal. It wasn't just an altercation with a coworker. It went much deeper. The coworker had accused him of drinking on the job. Given the frosty relationship with Marko, Peda refused to reveal any of this to him. Their relationship had soured the moment he and Zora first started renting the downstairs unit of the duplex on Gružanska Street owned by Marko and Dušica. The house, cushioned in the heart of the Kolonija Gate district of Kragujevac, was a dream for Zora but a constant source of contention for Peda.

Marko was incessantly nitpicking over home repairs— whether it was a window rattling, a faulty furnace, or water dripping in the bathroom, he believed Peda should deal with it promptly. After a tiring day at the factory, the last thing Peda wanted to do was more maintenance work at home. Brushing his thick black hair back, Peda offered a vague response. "Eh, I'm not sure…Another coworker and I got into a bit of a tumble." He knew the loss of his job would not gain a more favorable position with his in-laws, and Peda was no fool. He sensed their disdain.

He raised the glass of rakija to his lips. The tense dinner, his son's impending enlistment, and the judgmental atmosphere already overwhelmed him. Goran's announcement had blindsided him, and sudden tears leaked from the corners of his eyes.

"Any chance you could have a word with management about reinstating you?" Marko asked.

"Afraid not." He lit a cigarette and exhaled the smoke through his nostrils. How had he gotten here? He used to keep his emotions tucked in, but lately…not so much. Sucking in the last draw, he stubbed out the cigarette and shut his eyes.

"What about the leather or canning factory in town?"

"Sure." Peda opened his eyes. He knew once word got out of why he'd been let go, no company would touch him. Zora's family had seen the cracks and fissures in their marriage, and frankly, he was worn down. Mima's critical gaze during dinner only added to his burdens. He gave her credit though, she was staunch in her dislike of him from the get-go, never wanting her daughter to marry him.

Lighting another unfiltered cigarette, Peda raised his glass to clink Marko's bottle of Nikšićko pivo. "To Yugoslavia—long live the Monarchy."

"Živeli!" Marko took a small swig from the dark bottle of beer Peda noticed him nursing. Marko leaned forward; his look was intent. "Peda, have you heard the talk in town concerning Hitler?"

"Of course, Hitler was on everyone's mind. You would think those men at the newsstand were authorities on our country's politics the way they blather on."

Pressing his lips together, Marko shrugged. "Well, I grew up with some of them, and they're sharp. The consensus stands: if Prince Regent Paul does not stop associating with Hitler and his inner circle, we could be in an incredible amount of trouble. With the escalating situation across Europe, his actions have alarmed many."

Dismissive of the threat, Peda's reaction to the squabbling ideologies was to confront them head-on and aggressively. Sliding the bottle of homemade rakija toward Marko, he began. "Marko, Marko…we've known each other for what, twenty-odd years? How often have we seen Yugoslavia ripped apart, then patched back together, only to be blown apart once again, eh? But you're suggesting this time it's different?" Peda waved his hands in the air as a question. "I don't agree with you, or your friends. Hitler needs us and would be a fool to attack Yugoslavia. We're his country's biggest supplier of food, so why would he be stupid enough to jeopardize our good relationship?"

As he leaned against the chair, which was slip-covered to hide the wear, Peda crossed his thick arms across his chest, glowering. "According to yesterday's *Glas Šumadije*, we've shipped tons more barley and oats to Germany. Hell, they'd starve over there without us." He slammed the glass down harder than necessary, and the amber liquid sloshed on the ground.

"Need I remind you my family has been farming this area for centuries? We're aware of the crops we produce; however, you're missing the true mark of Hitler's appetite. He won't be happy until he's conquered the entirety of Europe." A V formed in the intersection on Marko's forehead between his wiry black eyebrows. "Remember the BBC broadcast you and I listened to a few weeks back about Hitler squeezing Hungary and Czechoslovakia to join his Axis Powers?"

Peda nodded, but he clearly could not recall the broadcast.

"Well, he's pressuring us, like he did to King Carol in Rumania last summer." Marko stood and edged toward the doorway. "The cruelty he's inflicted on the Jews in Germany and Poland…by God, it's outrageous. There's been multiple articles in the *Politika* detailing the anguish he's caused."

Peda's face flushed. The newspaper. Unable to read, he waited for his children to read the newspaper aloud to him. Rolling his eyes, Peda flexed his fingers before working them into fists. "Damn it, Marko. Can you, for one second…stop?"

Marko blinked twice. "Peda, I beg your pardon." Flipping his hands, he said, "I understand, it's a lot to take in. We're only getting snippets of information. Take, for instance, Dušica's friend, Martha Levine."

"Who?"

"Dušica's dear friend Martha. Surely you remember her, they've been friends forever. Her parents, who moved back to Berlin years ago, exposed in their letters the gut-wrenching stories about countless Jews and Serbians, like them, unexpectedly removed from their homes and sent to live in a ghetto. The last letter Martha received from her mother was two months ago. She described the way the SS stormed their home, forcing them out. They received few food ration cards, and the authorities restricted their movement, which resulted in them being cut off from the outside world."

Marko finally took a breath and Peda wished he could be anywhere but there. "Is there more?"

"Martha's story's eerily similar to Kosta's."

"Kosta?" Peda's head spun around. Every time he heard Kosta's name, it incensed him. "Not him again." He crushed his cigarette in the ashtray more emphatically than necessary. Simmering with resentment, he thought about the loss of his job and how he could manage to support his large family. "You're suggesting I turn my concern to the plight of people I know nothing about, including my wife's first boyfriend?"

The shouting woke Zoran, prompting him to say, "I'm going to the kitchen for coffee."

Peda knew all about Kragujevac's adored son, Kosta Lazić, breaking his wife's youthful heart. But why did her family persist in welcoming him? Where was their loyalty and respect for him as their daughter's husband?

Marko squeezed his eyes shut. "Peda, we've been over this before…countless times. We all grew up with Kosta, and his sister. He's my closest friend, and his sister Iva in

Berlin has gone missing. Iva was quite close with your wife so, no, Peda, they're not strangers."

Peda gave Marko a sideways glance, but he was listening.

"There's one more thing—Dušica and I have a little money saved that we'd like to give you, so you could purchase two boat tickets for Goran and Neven's escape from Yugoslavia. Unfortunately, it's too late for Goran, but perhaps Neven and Vuk could go?"

Caught off guard, Peda was left speechless. "W—what are you saying…?"

Marko tried to explain. "We're all terribly uneasy about the war, and we should have spoken to you sooner." Breathing heavily, Marko let out a ragged sigh. "If only we had, we might have prevented Goran from signing up. Our concern is for your boys facing the hostilities associated with war, so we wrote to Nada in America. In her response, she conveyed her excitement at the prospect of housing any of your children until the war subsides."

"Scheming behind my back?" The cords in his neck pulsated. "To be clear, dear brother-in-law of mine, I would never, ever ship any of my children off to America." Peda's staunch refusal underlined his denial of the looming war in the Balkans.

A palpable stillness suspended between them. Peda knew Marko felt he symbolized someone with a strong dislike for change. It could be the consequence of his excessive time in kafanas and inadequate anticipation of Hitler's actions. Peda also surmised Marko felt he existed in a world of denial, primarily with regards to Hitler. But he wasn't in denial; he just did not believe Hitler would bite the hand feeding him.

Tension mounted and Marko apologized to Peda, his ears reddening. "We're only offering out of love, and a way to protect your older sons from the cruelty associated with fighting a war. Trust me; neither Dušica nor I intended to intervene between you and your family." Bowing his head, Marko said, "Forgive me, Peda."

He wasn't done, he was revved up. "Marko, Marko... fear's a funny thing. It might help if everyone stopped being influenced by those idiots at the newsstand, because they're full of doom."

Wincing, Marko looked down.

Peda was just getting started. "We're echoing our past. A country at war, with too many miserable stakeholders with their hands out." Pausing, he allowed the rakija he'd swallowed to glide down the back of his throat, enjoying how it still burned. "The Croatians have a powerful desire to be separated from us. Then, the Communists—"

"Please, Peda. I understand our history."

Peda could see him squirming. Good. "Last, there's those of us who markedly wish to preserve Yugoslavia. Where do we fit in, Marko? It seems to me we have far too many dancers on this stage. So, am I still not understanding, Marko?"

"No, Peda, you have a solid understanding of politics. Again, my apologies." Marko moved away from the big Montenegrin to go upstairs. The Christmassy atmosphere in the Brković home plunged several degrees.

Dušica stopped drying dishes and moved to embrace Zora. "Don't worry, dušo, we'll figure something out."

Frustrated, Peda came through the kitchen, snatched his jacket from the peg, and slammed the door as he left. The chilly air helped cool him. Walking toward the kafana, his thoughts swirled. He'd screwed up tonight. He knew how dramatically his life had spun out of control. At other get-togethers, he'd experienced his mother-in-law's confusion, then disdain over something he'd done…but tonight, he knew Mima had witnessed his anger.

Rubbing his sweaty palms down the sides of his pant legs, Peda pushed through the front door of Stara Srbija, scrunching his eyes to adjust to the haziness of the smoke-filled bar room. Winding around, he plopped onto an open barstool beside his good friend. "Hey Đuro, *Hristos se Rodi.*"

"*Vaistinu se Rodi.* Was it a good Christmas, Peda?" Đuro Grubičić peered more closely at him, his ruddy complexion and bulbous nose indicative of a man older than forty-eight years. Shorter than Peda, he was stout, and his face appeared shinier tonight. Peda wondered if he had been here all day as he double-tapped his knuckles on the scratched wooden surface, signaling the bartender for a drink. "Miško, over here."

Đuro was a coworker from his old railroad days when he'd first arrived in Kragujevac, named for the kraguj bird of prey, the cinereous vulture that lived in the neighboring forests of the Rudnik and Gledić Mountains. Đuro enjoyed these wintry months when railroad construction halted and he could fill his days at Stara Srbija Kafana, where everyone knew him well.

"So, how was the big dinner with your in-laws?" Đuro asked, lighting an unfiltered cigarette.

Peda drained the double shot of slivovitz and slammed the chunky glass onto the bar with more force than necessary. He groaned as he remembered his argument with Marko…about shipping off his boys. God, his hands were shaking. Peda knew the ferocious toll this past year had taken on him; hell, it was more the last twelve years that had caused the most turmoil. He was agitated, his moods were frequent and stormier, and he wasn't sure how much longer he could hold this anger in.

"Everything all right?" Đuro asked, his glassy eyes looking at him.

"Yeah, I guess. The wife…"

"Women," Djuro snorted. "Mine was a nuisance."

"It's the brother-in-law, who thinks he's the only one who understands Yugoslavia's politics. He said Hitler's gunning for us next."

Đuro jerked his head around so fast it almost snapped. "Peda, you don't actually believe—?"

Peda tried remembering Marko's exact wording, but everything was jumbled. Marko was wrong. "Despite the turmoil in other parts of Europe, I don't think Hitler's going to attack Yugoslavia."

"Are you sure about that, my friend?" Đuro's eyes opened wide.

"Why?" Peda asked.

"According to the newspapers and Radio Belgrade, we're in his direct line of fire."

Peda shook his head, refusing to accept that the guy sitting next to him, one of his closest friends, might share views akin to Marko's. Stunned, he tried to regroup. "I guess I'm a true patriot, like my family in Montenegro. Our loyalty to the Karađorđević Monarchy has led us to believe they will solve any problem we encounter."

He'd never forgotten the times he'd had to go searching for his mother, and when he found her, begging her off the bar stool to come home so they could eat. Eleven children, home alone, starving and staring at the empty shelves. Peda never forgot the hunger. Or the bitterness. Or the dilapidated shack they had called home.

Patting him on the back, Đuro grinned awkwardly. "When King Alexandar was alive, that may have been the case, but now, I'd say it's best to be prepared for war, especially since you have two or three young boys within fighting age, right?"

The Božić dinner roiled in his belly.

CHAPTER THREE

ZORA

Kragujevac, the Kingdom of Yugoslavia
January 1941

THE ONLY SOUND IN the stillness of the night was Peda's deep and uneven snores, casting a stark contrast to the turmoil in her mind. Awake at the kitchen table, Zora found herself again questioning her life. The man she had married—charming, handsome, and full of promise was now a stranger consumed by a simmering resentment. Had it been festering, only to erupt in a torrent of anger? As darkness wrapped around her, she found herself adrift. The confrontation with Marko not only exposed the fissures in their marriage but showed how they'd widened.

Frustrated by her husband's indifference to their sons' safety, she grappled with the prospect of navigating a future in a country that confined women to the margins, pigeon-holing them into subservient roles. Zora was unable to grasp when Peda's priorities had shifted so drastically, placing his own pride above the well-being of his teenaged sons, and she feared the worst. With the precarious tightrope of

Hitler's looming presence over Yugoslavia, Peda's decision not to act on Marko's generous offer had likely set the course for Neven and possibly Vuk. She was also flummoxed by his dismissal from the Technical Institute, the senseless fight with a coworker, and now his clash with Marko—each incident a puzzle piece in a jigsaw she could not complete. The most troubling aspect was her husband's swift dismissal of sending their boys abroad for their safety. His resolute rejection shattered something within her. How far would his decisions end up shaping their world?

***

The nightmare jarred her awake, trembling. Clad only in a sweater, she saw the frost on the windows as she tiptoed to the bathroom, the packed surface floor freezing beneath her bare feet. Grateful for Peda's uninterrupted sleep, the haunting image of him in a Nazi uniform lingered in her mind, demanding interpretations. Where had she placed her mother's dream book?

After she had ensured Čedo was not running a fever, her heart warmed at the sight of tangled limbs and arms in the bed. Five growing boys in one flimsy bed was ridiculous, but where else would they sleep?

Following breakfast, she ascended the stairs. She *had* to talk to her sister to right a wrong, and hopefully square things between them. Drawn by the unexpected sugary scent of cinnamon that promised comfort, Zora walked into her sister's home and immediately into Dušica's opened arms. Large, fat tears rolled down her face.

"Shh, it's all right." There was something soothing in Dušica's voice as she stroked her thin back. She hoped her sister wouldn't mention how slight she'd become. She ate less so her children had more, but recently, she was feeling woozy, likely from her persistent hunger.

"I owe you an apology. He was awful," Zora sniffled. "He didn't behave this poorly in our earlier days, so why now?"

"Who knows?" Dušica contemplated, nibbling on her lower lip. "If I were to speculate, I'd suggest it happened more frequently in situations involving alcohol. Remember how mean old Ljubo was growing up? Mama warned us to stay away from him because he drank so much. Is Peda facing a similar type of trouble? But darling, look. I am glad you're here; I made krofne and Srpska kafa and planned on bringing it down to you." Dušica's chocolate-brown eyes were lively and optimistic.

Touched, Zora sank into the warmth of the kitchen, vividly recalling the day Dušica and Marko purchased this two-story duplex twelve blocks west of the center of town. They'd imagined filling it with children, and when that didn't materialize, Zora watched them conceal their sorrow by pouring their energy into their home. Marko dedicated his skills to crafting and designing the furniture, while Dušica expertly sewed the upholstery and drapery. They took immense pleasure in painting their walls in shades of azure and cerulean blue. Anchored in the center of the room was their honey-colored table, which Marko had sanded till it shone, and where the Nikolić women held their most tight-lipped conversations.

From the moment Dušica set the plate of krofne in front of her, Zora was transported to a time with her mother and Baka Cveta in Croatia drinking coffee, eating krofne, and singing their beloved music. Those Serbian songs, cherished by many, were older than dirt. Never forgetting, Zora remembered it all—even the funerals and tombstones. Memories surfaced of idyllic summers frolicking in the open fields of Kušići, her family's village tucked next to Ponikve, where her mother was born. It was in this vibrant land of farmers and peasants that Zora had discovered her rich Serbian traditions. Amidst the cows, chickens, and baby lambs, it was here where Zora felt most centered.

Standing on a wobbly wooden crate in her grandmother's kitchen, she'd experienced the delightful feeling of soft dough in her small hands for the first time. In her mind's eye, Zora imagined the tall, rusted metal canister holding the flour in the corner, and Baka Cveta's round face wrinkling into a smile. Baka had imparted a great deal of knowledge about the intricate process of bread making. On those hot, summery days, she had shown them how to make sweetened egg bread, pogača, braided kolach, and the renowned Česnica with the silver coin tucked inside of it. Whenever Zora folded, kneaded, or pinched the dough, she was reverentially connected to the past, and to all the Serbian women who had come before her. She liked to think it somehow bound her to them in a rather profound, existential way.

"Coffee?" Dušica asked.

"Please." Zora blinked, aware that her sister had caught her daydreaming.

Zora's breath caught as Dušica set out her coveted Blue Willow coffee cups, with their whimsical bridges and willow trees, that Sava had brought over from England. Putting out her treasured china was meant to make her feel significant and caused her chest to swell. "Thank you," Zora said, as her icy fingers wrapped around the steaming cup of Srpska kafa, enjoying the warmth that spread through her fingers. She needed this time alone with Dušica. "Again, my apologies for last night."

"Don't worry, we'll try something else."

Zora stood and moved to the window overlooking their street. Words weren't always necessary. They understood the beauty of silence.

"I'm going to make the beds," Dušica indicated, leaving the room.

Zora surmised Dušica was allowing her time to sift through her raw emotions. Evaluating her marriage, she realized how little Peda had contributed or supported their family. As she worked tirelessly at her day job, she was often called out during the night because she was also a healer, helping people whether in sickness or an injury. Nevertheless, they struggled to make ends meet in their hardscrabble life. Peda's rigid rejection last night stung.

Dušica reappeared, and Zora reached for her hand. "I, ah—the situation with Peda…it's beyond anyone's comprehension."

"How were the kids when they awoke?"

"Despite being the target of his father's anger last evening, Goran awoke and remained cheerful and eager to spend the day with Jelena."

"Do you think he might ask Jelena for her hand in marriage before he leaves?"

Taken aback, Zora struggled for words. "What…? Goran has his whole future ahead of him," she spluttered. "He's bright, athletic, and a born leader. I had hoped…"

"Want my advice? Talk to him before he leaves, to discover his intentions. You might be surprised by what you learn."

"How could I have missed it?" Zora murmured, her voice quivering. Her hand covered her mouth as a breadth of emotions churned in her belly. Was Goran contemplating marriage or ready to shoulder the responsibility of a wife and family? She exhaled, blowing out tiny puffs of air. "I need to start the laundry."

Peda's recent unkempt appearance had not gone unnoticed. His clothing, frayed and disheveled, hinted at something else. Could illness be plaguing him? His washed-out appearance deepened her concern.

**

Goran's friends came to say goodbye. Each visit offered a brief respite and an enjoyable distraction for his dejected siblings, who were genuinely upset by his departure. Aco and Čedo rushed to greet any new guest with a wobbly tray of slatko that Zora and Stana had made over the summer with fresh fruits, quince, crushed rose petals, and sugar. The boys handed each guest a customary teaspoon of slatko, a glass of water, and a shot of rakija. Watching their brother's friends choke down the near one hundred proof homemade whiskey brought a fleeting moment of levity.

The family sprang to action readying Goran for his departure, rummaging for old sweaters and darning socks. Zora headed to the Dormition of the Most Holy Theotokos Serbian Church, seeking divine protection for Goran. Soaked in the lingering incense she'd known since childhood, she waited her turn to speak with Father Cvetić, their parish priest. In her hand was the silver coin Goran had discovered in the Česnica that she hoped he would bless. Leaving church, she went to the market, where she purchased a pair of long underwear. Pulling out her change purse, it dawned on her how short they would be for the rest of the month.

***

Suddenly, it was Thursday—Goran's last night. Everyone, including his girlfriend, Jelena, gathered upstairs for a going-away dinner hosted by his aunt and uncle. Marko walked in carrying a large package wrapped in newspapers that was dripping on the floor.

Goran's eyes grew. "My goodness, Čika Marko…are you kidding?"

Smiling broadly, Marko unwrapped the newspaper as the tantalizing scent of mouthwatering barbecued lamb had everyone oohing and aahing.

"Čika Marko, I cannot believe this—what a treat!" Goran's eyes glistened. Marko had surprised them all with a delicacy no one expected.

Patting his nephew's shoulder, Marko said, "You're welcome, Goran. My father, brothers, and I roasted it for hours over the open spit on the farm. It smells heavenly, right?"

From the oven, Dušica carried a steaming pogača to the table. "Wait for a few minutes until the bread cools."

This bittersweet moment of joy was evident. "Thank you, both," Zora said, moved beyond mere words.

The moment the bread cooled, the family surrounded the wooden table and began eating small pieces of pogača with the savory slices of lamb. Zora watched the cheerfulness play across her family's faces at this unexpected pleasure. She also watched Jelena Vranešević, clinging to her son, eating little.

***

Shrouded in mist, they said their goodbyes. Before releasing him, Tetka Dušica held her nephew tightly. A bereft Lenka sobbed as she hugged Goran until Zora stepped in, asking her to take Vuk, Čedo, and Aco inside, their faces sullen.

Peda firmly gripped his son's shoulder. "Stay safe, Goran." With a quick nod, he turned and went inside, leaving Stana and Neven with their mother.

Goran bounced from enthusiasm. "What a fantastic meal last night! Čika Marko's the best."

Neven nodded. "I agree, but listen, Goran." He tapped his brother's arm. "Be careful out there."

"Ahh." Goran pulled his brother in for a firm hug before patting his back. "Mind your studies, man. I can't wait to see you as a professor."

Stana's tears fell upon her cheeks. "Ohhh, Goran, I hate this and, and…I'm going to miss you so much."

"I promise to write, and I'll be home after training." Looking at his sister, he wagged his fingers in front of her face. "I expect to hear from you, so don't forget to write me; promise?"

"I promise, Goran. I'll write…every day," Stana said, blubbering.

Zora wondered if Goran was attempting to memorize everyone's features the way he was staring at them so intensely. "Goran—"

"Mama, I appreciate everything you've done. Know that I love you," Goran said, pulling her in for a strong hug.

Zora's chin wobbled as she stepped closer. With a callused hand, she gently caressed his elegantly carved face before reaching into her pocket for the slip of tissue paper. Inside was a tiny Serbian Orthodox cross on the thinnest silver chain, which she fastened around Goran's neck. She whispered to him what her baka had taught her: "Always remember how much you're loved, and if at any time you feel lost or afraid, invariably turn your body around and head east."

And just like that—he was gone.

CHAPTER FOUR

SAVA

Belgrade, the Kingdom of Yugoslavia
February 1941

WITH HER LONG HAIR whipping around her face, Sava struggled to see where she was going. The chill bit into her, prompting her regret for not donning the scarf Stana had lovingly knitted for her last Christmas. Approaching the bus stop on her way to work at the university, she mused over Vlado's irritation with her preference for public transportation over being chauffeur driven to work. Wasn't it her effortless grace and insouciance that had drawn him to her over fifteen years ago?

Plunging her fingers into her pockets, she felt the seven train tickets and the unsent note to Zora she'd forgotten to mail at the posta in her hurriedness this morning. "Darn," she murmured. The thought of hosting her nieces and nephews in her home for a weekend, offering them a glimpse into a lifestyle they were typically unaccustomed to, warmed her heart. As their tetka, Sava relished the opportunity to spoil them, her love for them driving her to ensure they had sturdier boots and warmer clothing.

She reflected on her first encounter with Vlado Ivković as a university first-year student. Sava could scarcely have believed she would one day end up living in the prestigious Dedinje. Pulling her tweed coat closer, she longed for the warmth of summer days she and Vlado had spent exploring the magic of Topčider Park's rolling hills and soaring oak trees. Dedinje, with its spacious homes and lush hedges, offered both privacy and proximity to Beli Dvor, the Royal Compound of the Karađorđević Monarchy, and the current residence of Prince Regent Paul Karađorđević and his wife Princess Olga of Greece and Denmark.

The impending threat of the dreaded Tripartite Pact that Hitler had continued to press Prince Regent Paul to sign, and its implications, weighed on her mind. Alongside that was the fragile hope that Princess Olga's royal bloodlines with England might offer some leverage, although Sava recognized most monarchies now wielded negligible power.

As she boarded the bus, Sava fumbled with the fare before finding a seat, her thoughts wandering to her family. The fourth daughter of Zoran and Mima, she had carved a fulfilling path as a scholar and professor, a passion that defined her. She had been christened Jelisaveta, but her sisters had quickly shortened it to Sava. She grew up admiring her sisters, though their lives had diverged significantly before she entered high school. They were all married, with Nada living in McKeesport, Pennsylvania, a town bursting with Eastern European immigrants.

As much as Sava enjoyed being a professor and a historian, she also loved spending time with friends, singing and dancing in the kafanas sprinkled throughout Belgrade. Balancing her academic life with the social obligations of being the wife of a wealthy industrialist, she found comfort in Belgrade's vibrant music scene. Theater outings and sumptuous dinner parties for the privileged bored her, yet at one of the opulent parties she had met and befriended an American woman close to her age. The effervescent Josie Whitney-Shaw, seated next to her at one such dinner, explained how unfulfilled she had been living between Paris and London prior to the war. While traveling with her English photojournalist beau, Richard Warbly, they had attended a royal wedding in Albania and decided to explore Yugoslavia. From what Josie shared, the Yugoslavian people had captivated them from the moment they first arrived, leading to Josie's decision to stay.

As the bus rolled forward, Sava's mind drifted to Vlado and his discontent over her refusal to relocate permanently to England, where his business had expanded. Deep down, she knew Vlado indisputably felt challenged by her youth, more so since battling lung disease; at sixty-four, he displayed difficulty keeping pace with her.

Arriving at her office in the History Department, Sava felt a presence behind her. Whirling around, she exclaimed, "Jesus, Toma, you startled me. What is it?" The concern in his face sent a jolt of worry through her.

"Nothing alarming, so let's try this again." Toma smiled. "Good morning, Doctor Ivković."

Managing a weak smile, Sava sighed. "Despite my pleas, you've persisted in testing my patience, and you're not funny."

"Why not take pride in your PhD? You worked hard for it."

Something was amiss. She *knew* Toma Tatalović as well as she knew her sisters, and there was a noticeable crease between his flawlessly shaped eyebrows. Then, there was his overly serious demeanor as he pulled her office door shut.

"Oh boy, what's wrong?"

Since meeting as seventeen-year-olds at the University of Belgrade, Toma had been her closest friend. His intellect and passion for Yugoslavia's tumultuous history had captivated her instantly, and she adored him, like a brother.

Pressing a finger to his lips, he said, "You have been invited to an SKK meeting tomorrow evening."

"The…Serbian Cultural Club…?" Sava stared at him, her forehead etched into a frown of confusion. Five years ago, an effort had been launched to bring together the most formidable intellectuals and successful businessmen to preserve their rich national culture, and today it was hailed as the most respected organization in Serbia. She had longed to join this organization, but she was puzzled why they would invite her, when women were not permitted to join.

"You cannot be serious? I thought women weren't allowed in."

Holding up his hand, Toma said, "I am, and so are they. However, before you start interrogating me, I have no knowledge of how you were invited. Possibly someone high in the organization recognized your spirited cheekiness," he said, grinning as he squeezed her shoulder. "So, tomorrow, say six o'clock?"

Speechless, she fixed her gaze on him as a lock of his unruly hair fell across his forehead. He was nothing like the classic-looking college professor; women at the university clamored for Toma's attention.

"Ah…the secrecy that men maintain."

Toma walked over to his desk and picked up a folder filled with papers. "I need to get to my class."

Seated at her desk, Sava began to sift through the grim files involving unspeakable beatings and rapes of Serbian women during the summer of 1914. The statistics she'd gathered for her paper on "The Genocide of Serbian Women by Bulgarian Troops" reflected that over eight hundred women had been beaten, and one hundred and fifty were sexually assaulted by Bulgarian soldiers. The unthinkable acts of violence had her pressing her fist to her mouth as she considered how her peers, all of whom were men, would view this paper.

***

Listening to the sounds of laughter from the restaurants they passed, Sava motioned to Toma. "Could you slow down? It's a bit tricky navigating these streets." The clickety-clack of her high heels on the wide cobblestones should have been indicative enough of her struggle.

"Well, why did you choose those shoes?"

Elbowing him, she said, "You're not funny." But Sava knew why she wore the navy-blue suede shoes. They looked terrific with her fitted wool suit and thick belt with a gold buckle.

After they walked past the impressive Parliament building on Aleksandra Boulevard, Toma turned. "Right behind Tašmajdan Park and Saint Mark's Church, you'll see the kafana. The SKK has its own building, but we typically gather here when there's more people."

The esteemed Professor Slobodan Jovanović, President of the Royal Academy of Sciences and known internationally as a preeminent historian, greeted them at the bottom of the stairs. With a twinkle in his eye, he warmly clasped Sava's slender hands into his own. "Ahh, Doctor Ivković…I have waited a long time to meet you. Welcome." Sava noticed him look her over, his eyes lingering. "My dear—you are exquisite." Turning, he kissed Toma on one cheek, then the other, followed by a third kiss.

Surprised to see the unexpected familiarity between the two, Sava suddenly faltered. She had long admired this man and now could barely utter more than a "Good evening, Gospodine Jovanović. Thank you for having me."

"It's our pleasure. Now follow me, dinner's waiting." The professor's meaty hand guided her to the private dining room.

Glancing over the sea of heads, Sava swiftly calculated that the room was teeming with the best and brightest from a microcosm of Serbia's intellectuals and thinkers, representing some of the greatest minds in all of Yugoslavia. Toma led her to a table with two empty chairs. She was grateful to be seated, not sure her wobbly legs could hold her any longer. Normally, she enjoyed this type of event, conversing with scholars and like-minded people, but her stomach thrummed with butterflies. Her idols were in this room, men she had long admired from textbooks and newspaper articles. The room overflowed with brilliance. What could I offer them? she asked herself.

Toma's dazzling smile reflected his perfect white teeth. "How are you holding up?"

"I had no idea…"

"About?"

"The width and breadth of their membership."

"Really?"

"Yes, really. This room's overflowing with the brightest minds in Yugoslavia."

The meeting began with a discussion about the threat of Europe becoming a powder keg if action wasn't taken against Hitler. They questioned whether the British Envoy, Ronald Campbell, had the power and wisdom to convince Prince Regent Paul not to sign the Tripartite Pact, but the conversation about the extraordinary number of intelligence agents in Belgrade, some posing as journalists, captured her attention.

Mesmerized by the theater of voices, she hung on every word, dismayed to learn several intelligence officers had already infiltrated certain sections of Belgrade. This group was confident it was the Abwehr, Germany's military intelligence organization. Sava listened to the unease about Dr. Vladko Maček, the head of the Croatian Peasant Party, who had recently sought outside support from the Fascists in Italy. They feared his actions could likely bring about a vastly different Yugoslavia. The growing tension had been percolating long before 1939 when Prime Minister Dragiša Cvetković agreed with Dr. Maček to create the Banovina of Croatia.

She leaned over. "It's considerably complicated, isn't it?"

Nodding, Toma agreed. "It's a lot to absorb."

Continuing to sneak unobtrusive glances around the room, Sava watched Professor Jovanović take the podium. "Everyone, it's time to split up into your assigned groups. There's work to be done. The success of our organization has never wavered, and we must outline our objectives for our country, now more than ever, against the growing dissatisfaction sweeping across the Kingdom."

Sava found herself with the professor and two others.

"Dr. Ivković, we've read your papers and trust you would satisfy a wonderful spot in the Sloboda Freedom Organization. Organized years ago, Sloboda has stayed in the background; however, with the heightened European events, your recent paper aligns well with their organization." Dr. Jovanović cleared his throat. "If war broke out, you might be one of their strongest assets. May I put you in touch with these gentlemen?" he asked, scratching his white beard.

Her jaw dropped as they shared what they wanted her to do. "Ah...yes."

Despite the meeting ending, Sava felt energized and was not ready to head home. "Toma, let's go to the Question Mark Café."

He lifted an eyebrow. "Don't we have work in the morning?"

"Yes, but Vlado's not home, and I feel like dancing."

Deciding to brave the night, they walked to their favorite kafana on Kralja Petra Street near the old Kalemegdan fortress. The café's sturdy structure was situated catty-corner from the Patriarchy Headquarters of the Serbian Orthodox Church, and as soon as they crossed the street, she heard the harmonica.

Toma stuck an arm out before they walked in. "Tell me again your thoughts."

Lifting her chin, she offered him a brilliant smile. "Truthfully, I was floored." In a giddy moment, she performed a quick kolo on the slanted sidewalk. "It...was incredible. Their discussions and opinions intrigued me. So, yes, I'm thrilled to be a part of Sloboda Freedom Fighters, but I'd love to get Josie involved in it, too. She has experience aiding resistance efforts in both England and France, though to what degree I am uncertain." Her feet and hips swayed to the rhythm of the bugarija.

"Really?" He stared and an eyebrow lifted. "By the way, it's the Sloboda Freedom Organization, though, not the Freedom Fighters," he said with a chuckle.

"Right; well, c'mon." She tugged his arm as her grin expanded, allowing her dimples to pop. "I'll be stuck with Vlado's cronies all weekend, so this will be my only fun."

"You're certain they will ask you back?"

"Oh, I'll be asked back, my friend."

Inside, Toma joined friends at the bar. Sava bolted to the dance floor and joined hands to dance the energetic c'est kolo in a large circle that was snaking its way across the room. Each dancer held the person's hand next to them as they did quick, accentuated steps.

Suddenly, someone broke in next to her, squeezing her hand. "Lovely to see you, Sava," said Olga Alkalaj, a former classmate of hers and Toma's, who'd become an outstanding attorney.

An expression of pleasant surprise made its way across her face, and between breaths, she puffed out, "Olga, so nice to see you." Once the dance ended, Sava wiped the sweat from her forehead as she waited for Olga.

"What brings you here tonight, Sava?" Olga wiped her own sweaty face with a paper napkin.

Sava regarded her friend's short, compact figure. "We were at a meeting and weren't ready to call it a night. You?" Knowing Olga was a Sephardic Jew, seeing her here, dancing Serbian kolos, seemed odd. In their university days, Sava was well aware of Olga's involvement in the League of Communist Youth of Yugoslavia, and she wondered if she was still active.

"How ironic. I, too, attended a meeting earlier." Olga beamed, stepping in for a hug. "We should have a toast—it's been what, five years since we've seen one another? How's the university world treating you?"

"Ah, no changes there, but I adore the research part of it."

Laughing, Olga reached for her hand. "Sava, I've read every one of your academic papers, and what you've written about women. You have uncovered an array of facts no one has ever brought to the forefront. If you would *ever* be interested in discussing a better way forward for our country—the Communist way—I'd be delighted to have you join us. You have one of the freshest, most impressive female minds in Belgrade. Change is coming, my dear friend."

Humbled, Sava embraced Olga, recognizing that, strangely enough, the two of them were headed on vastly divergent pathways. So, it *was* true. Olga had evidently moved up the ranks in the Communist Party of Yugoslavia. Well, well…

***

Early the following morning, the shrill bell of the ringing telephone awakened Sava.

"Darling," Dušica's voice chirped, bursting through the phone lines.

Pressing her fingers to her eyes, Sava prayed for the room to stop spinning. She also vowed never to drink shots of slivovitz with Olga again, especially not *seven* in a row. What was she thinking? "Morning," she croaked, her raspy voice layered with sleep.

"Oh, are you sick?"

"Not exactly." Her head felt like a jackhammer was banging against it.

"Then what is it?" Dušica asked.

Sava heard her sister's voice laden with concern, so she hesitated. "Maybe too much singing and dancing last night."

"Was Vlado with you?"

"No. He's due back from London tonight." Sava recognized the tone. Even though Dušica was trying hard not to react, Sava knew she could not help herself. She pulled her body into a fetal position; she needed more sleep.

"Sava…" The implication was laid bare. Her sister's inflection gave it away and Sava heard it—loud and clear.

"I know, I know. It looks bad for a married woman to be out without her husband," she parroted her sister's words reiterated to her before. Pressing her palm on her forehead, she felt another storm in her belly. "But…I was with Toma, and other friends," Sava reasoned.

"It's not me you have to convince. It's anyone who saw you out with another man who's not your husband. Think about that for a moment, dušo. How many of those people could spread false tales about you? This isn't why I've called, though—we've heard from Goran."

"Really? What did he say?" Sava's heart quickened. She adored her nephew, who had grown into a decent young man.

"He's well. He wrote Stana, indicating he'll be granted a three-day leave soon. These phone calls are expensive, so I must cut this short."

"Oh, my goodness; what wonderful news," Sava whispered, her head falling back on her pillow. Even though she hoped to go back to sleep, her mind raced. Dušica's words hinted at the truth. When she and Vlado were first married, he had given her ample freedom, and their marriage had flourished. It had only been recently Vlado had pressured her to resign her position and move with him permanently to the United Kingdom, which had created an unbearable strain in their marriage. Not wanting to move, Sava had dug in her heels, but each time he returned from England, she felt the noose tightening.

CHAPTER FIVE

ZORA

Kragujevac, the Kingdom of Yugoslavia
March 07, 1941

ZORA AND DUŠICA FINISHED the laborious task of cutting and grinding the ashwagandha root, an essential ingredient Zora used in her medicinal tinctures. It came from India and it was a rare find discovering it today, at the market. Zora also boiled rusomaca roots, which she planned to mix with the ashwagandha, and a sprinkling of gospina trava. Following in Baka Cveta's footsteps, Zora embraced her role of a travarka, locally known as a healer. Her grandmother's influence on her was so profound that growing up, Zora had dreamed of one day becoming a physician.

During those summery months of her youth, tagging along with her grandmother as she cared for the sick had left its mark. Without a physician or nurse nearby, her grandmother was often called upon to assist. In her minuscule kitchen in the village, she boiled a profusion of herbs that she'd collected in the countryside to make her formidable batches of potions. Baka had healing tinctures for pain, earaches, coughs, and fevers. With her grandmother's help, Zora developed a passion to heal with these natural remedies, and her home was filled with the legacy of Balkan herbal wisdom as she produced her own assorted concoctions.

There was a chest in her cozy kitchen with a collection of notes and recipes with various formulas from her baka, linen pouches for her dried herbs and twine, and bottles in varying sizes—Zora was meticulous in labeling each bottle. She kept this chest locked. Lingering over a cup of coffee, Zora rubbed the back of her neck. "Would it be terrible to admit I'm relieved not having Peda here?"

"Certainly not. How long will he stay in Montenegro?" Dušica brushed a knuckle over her sister's hand.

The pause was long before Zora forced a smile. "I'm not sure. Originally, he planned on visiting his family for a good two months, hoping to find a local job. Some of his siblings he hasn't seen since his brother's funeral."

"I'd forgotten; how long has it been?"

"Twenty-three years, and I—" Zora paused as tears rolled down her face. "Ohhh, I didn't see that coming."

Dušica pulled her in for a hug. "Something tells me you're upset; why not tell me about it? Holding it in takes more energy."

"I'm not sure what's to come of our marriage," she said, sighing heavily. "Peda's not a good husband and not always a kind father. I have often wondered if it was how he was raised. But after so long, how do I continue making excuses for his poor behavior? I will say it's been nice not having him around, or having him yell about something minor, like forgetting to pick up an extra bottle of milk." Shaking her head, she revealed, "Unfortunately his blind rage has turned our children, and me, into frightened rabbits. I'm ashamed to admit life has become a dangerous dance with Peda's volatility." Zora stared at her sister with tear-stained eyes, partially relieved and partially embarrassed to admit what she had worked hard to conceal.

"So, if I understand this, are you hoping he doesn't return?"

Curling her shoulders inward, Zora admitted, "I'm not sure what I want, but I can tell you what I don't want." With Peda gone, she'd had time to reevaluate just how unpleasant their lives had become. "The fundamental question I beat myself up over every day is, why have I allowed my children to be raised in an environment of bitterness, browbeating, and intimidation? They're petrified around him, Duš. They're frightened they'll do, or say, the wrong thing, and then BOOM—he'll explode."

Nodding, Dušica said, "I've seen a difference in them from the moment Peda left. They're indisputably more confident."

"Even though I don't have many choices in life, ultimately, I've got to better protect them. It's my job as their mother."

"I hate to ask, but...has he ever hit you, or any of the children?"

There was a sharp intake of breath before a pained expression made its way across her face.

"It's all right; don't say anything. Living in the same household, upstairs, I've already garnered a guess."

"No, no; it's just—" Zora's hands flew to her face. "It's really, really hard. He *has* hit Goran, and he has not acted kindly toward Neven. Peda's treatment of Neven has been, well, it's downright mean."

"How so?" Dušica's unblinking eyes stayed trained on her sister's face.

"Sometimes Peda has these weird notions about Neven. One day he remarked about the way Neven acted, saying he appeared to act…*sissified*, was the word he used. Frequently, he's commented on him being, ah—different." Zora shuddered. "Remember, Peda didn't grow up like we did, surrounded by books and libraries. His family came from peasant stock, and there's nothing wrong with that, except his family's worldview happens to be less cultured than others." Lowering her eyes, Zora said, "Nevertheless, he's convinced our son might be a…homosexual."

With a choked cry, Dušica uttered, "That's absurd."

The implications were clear as Zora rubbed her hands together. "He produced this notion months ago." She was dipping into a topic seldom discussed in Yugoslavia, or anywhere in the Balkans.

With her eyebrows bent in, Dušica posed another question. "Could Neven's behavior be due to nervousness when his father's around? Kids sense things, and out of all of yours, Neven's your brightest and most perceptive, so maybe he's just a bundle of nerves around Peda? If someone made me uncomfortable in their presence, I know I would act differently."

"Hmmm; makes sense. I have often wondered if Peda ever realized he won't get a second chance at raising his children."

Feeling a heaviness in her chest, Zora considered her unattainable position. If she defended her son, it meant going against her husband. If she aligned with her husband, she risked losing her son. She knew this much: if her son was a homosexual, it was going to be a grim time for him. All across Europe, Hitler had conducted raids, arresting homosexuals. Having an inkling of how badly her husband's hands and words had already bruised her beautiful boy, her decision would be an easy one to make.

The back door slowly opened to reveal Neven and Stana coming in from work.

"Jeez, Mama—you look like you've seen a ghost. What happened?" Neven asked.

Panicked that he might have overheard the tail end of their conversation, Zora searched his face for clues. Neven's spectacles were steamed from the quick temperature change, but nothing else seemed awry.

"Oh, we just finished and were relaxing over coffee." Patting the vinyl chair beside her, she suggested, "Come sit with us."

Looking at his sister, Neven beamed. "Tell them."

"Tell us what?" Zora asked.

Neven offered a knowing grin and pointed to Stana. "We Brkovićs have a budding star on our hands."

"Stana?" Zora's brows arched.

Stana hesitated, and in that moment, Zora witnessed Neven's pride in his sister. "Stana sang tonight at Paligorić with Conductor Matić's Orchestra Šumadija. You should have seen the crowd and heard the applause. People were on their feet, Mama, clapping and shouting for more." Neven's eyes burned bright. "The way they clapped for our Stana—"

She needed to hear from Stana how she felt about singing publicly for the first time, and she turned to her daughter. Zora knew Stana adored her brother; however, right this second, he was embarrassing her. She was on the verge of womanhood. Men were already beginning to stare at her daughter's beautiful face, lean torso, budding breasts, and the longest pair of legs—Stana was indeed a beauty.

"Tell us more," Zora prompted her.

Stana's rare green eyes sparkled as they dropped down to her hands. "Um, well, Conductor pulled me aside at practice to say I was ready to perform in public, and because his band was playing at Paligorić, he asked me to sing with them."

Zora grasped the enormity of tonight's outcome for her talented fifteen-year-old. "Oh, Stana. I wished you'd mentioned it." Squeezing her daughter's hand, Zora bit down on her lip. "I would have tried to have been there."

"Well, I was concerned about having Dunja think I was not doing my job, so I sang during my ten-minute break, but then—"

"Then what?"

"I never got to eat, and…" Lifting her head, she admitted, "I'm actually starving."

Before Zora could say they had nothing left from dinner, Dušica's hand shot out. "I have leftovers from dinner tonight. Would you like that?"

"Of course." Stana stood, grinning ear to ear.

"Well, c'mon, upstairs, and Zora, bring your coffee," Dušica said.

After devouring Tetka's garlic-flavored beef stew poured over steaming bowls of polenta, Stana and Neven leaned back in their chairs. Zora could tell they were sated. Neven pushed his floppy hair back. Nearly as tall as Goran, Neven appeared ganglier than Goran's more substantial frame. Zora believed Neven, Goran, and Stana most resembled Peda, with classic Montenegrin cheekbones inherited from the Brković side of the family, whereas Lenka and the others took after her family's side.

Beautiful, thick eyelashes lay on the outer rims of Neven's dusty brown eyes as his hand moved to slide his glasses up his nose. Not forgetting his manners, Neven said, "Tetka, thank you. We were starving, and it was perfect."

With a mouthful of food, Stana's head bobbed in agreement.

Zora's eyes found her daughter's. "Were any of your friends there tonight?"

"Yeah, Biserka and Jasna stood in back by Gospođo and Gospodine Lazić, but the Wehrmacht crowded the kafana."

Neven yawned. "Don't forget to tell them about the tall, blond-haired German who couldn't keep his eyes off you. What's his name?"

Growing still, Stana gaped at him.

"Stana, c'mon." Neven stretched his arms across the table to grab her wrists.

Scowling at her brother, Stana could not hide her annoyance. "His name's *Officer* Kord Webber Gerhardt."

Looking for clarification, Zora's eyes moved from Neven to Stana's. "Would one of you like to tell me what's going on?"

Zora could see Stana was frustrated with her brother.

"Really, Stana? Mama's bound to find out from her eagle-eyed friend anyway, so spill." Neven's palms faced outward.

"Neven, sometimes you're…you're incorrigible!" Positioning her body toward her mother, she said, "Last month, this German came into Paligorić with some other Wehrmacht officers. Dunja seated them in my section, and when Kord ordered his food, he rattled it off in perfect Serbian.

Now when he comes in, he asks to be seated in my section, and speaks to me in Serbian." Breathlessly, she continued, "He's cultured and worldly and speaks four languages."

Dušica stared at her niece. "You called him by his first name?"

"Tetka…he insisted I call him Kord and not Officer Gerhardt. But I address him as Officer Gerhardt whenever I work up front, greeting customers."

Zora placed her hands into a steeple and pressed the tips to her lips.

"When I finished singing tonight, I raced to the kitchen to pick up the platters of food for my customers. Kord's order was there, so when I delivered his food, he said it delighted him to hear me sing, and with a voice like mine, I should not be stuck in a backward place like this. He explained the importance of training under a classical voice instructor in places like London, Vienna, or Paris."

Zora read something more in her daughter's account. Is this what Stana was yearning for? Or was she falling for the crap this Kraut was filling her head with, believing her family would somehow have the wherewithal to send her abroad to study music when they could hardly pinch together enough for food? Surely Stana was not thinking untoward thoughts about this man, or was she…? Not wanting to make her daughter feel "less than," but in no way wanting to shine a light on a Wehrmacht officer involved with her daughter, Zora did something she seldom did. She reached behind for the red pack of Morava's and tapped out a cigarette. "Neven, what do *you* think of Officer Gerhardt?"

"He's fairly young to be an officer, and quite tall, fit, good-looking, and well read."

"How'd you discover he was well read?" Zora questioned, fighting off a swell of worry.

"Clearing the dishes from his table one night, I overheard him discussing the books he's read, and guess what? Most of what he mentioned were identical to the books Luka and I had checked out of from our Kragujevac library." Neven glanced across at Stana. "Do you think he's good-looking?"

Zora's heart plummeted. Please say no, she thought. "How old did you say he was?"

"Maybe twenty-five?" Neven said. "Refined, too."

"He's an officer in the Wehrmacht, therefore a follower of Hitler, for goodness' sake," Zora said.

Stana flinched.

The last thing Zora could ever imagine would be for one of her children to fall for someone who admired Adolf Hitler. It trumped every belief she held close…except for communism. Barely able to keep her eyes open, she asked, "Could you describe his personality?" Zora was trying to picture the man attempting to win over her daughter.

Neven leaned his head back and answered instead. "It's more his mannerisms, and the way he speaks. It's like those older friends of Čika Vlado's, the way they looked down at us when we visited Tetka Sava in Belgrade." Neven fidgeted, then smoothed down his clothes.

"Cultured," Zora said, as her stomach clenched. Her eyes connected with Dušica's, intuitively knowing her older sister understood that a conversation might be necessary with Sava.

Stana turned to her mother. "If we didn't need the money, I'd quit Paligorić tomorrow. But Mama, I have done nothing wrong, and I promise to be careful. Dunja has me scheduled for work the same nights as Neven and Luka, so they'll be there in the kitchen, clearing tables and watching me, hawk-like. And so will Dunja, after you've spoken with her, so please, don't worry; nothing will happen."

Clasping his hands behind his back, Neven grinned. "My little sister. Two guys sweet on her."

"What?" All three heads snapped to attention.

Neven held his hands up. "Whoa; sorry, perhaps I'm outta line."

Stana's eyes flashed. "Jeez, Neven, what the heck's that supposed to mean? Two guys…?"

A flush spread across his face. "Sorry, I—ah, I couldn't help noticing the way Luka's unable to stop staring at you. He hangs on your every word, Stana. And, anytime you're not with us, he brings your name up constantly. So, I think he's afraid to say anything for fear you'll reject him."

Crossing her arms, Stana faced her mother and aunt. "What were you and Tetka talking about when we walked in earlier? I know something happened because your eyes were red."

How perceptive this daughter of hers was, effortlessly shifting the focus away from herself, and onto her. That required a specific skill. "Oh, that?" Zora said. "Well, folks at work have been discussing if Hitler were to attack, what would happen here. Most feel that Hitler would call for the immediate takeover of our Military Technical Institute. It's no secret he covets our ammunition and would love to get his grimy hands on our factory."

"And if that happened, would you and Tetka lose your jobs in the office?" Stana tilted her head to one side.

Zora glanced at Dušica. "Yes. The men from the Sokol society have been preparing for war by stocking up on food and essentials." Zora squeezed her eyes shut for a second, realizing how ill-prepared she and her family were. "But yes."

"So, the Sokols feel an attack's inevitable?" Dušica leaned forward, eyebrows scrunched in.

"They do, same as the articles written in *Glas Šumadije* and *Politika*." Thoroughly exhausted, her eyes began to close.

"I have a silly question," Neven jumped in. "If the Third Reich invaded Yugoslavia, would Croatia stand alongside us?" Elbows on the table, Neven brushed a lock of hair from his forehead.

Zora's eyes popped open. "That's an interesting question. I don't know, but if Croatia did *not* stand with Yugoslavia, not only would it crush your baka, but we could not survive against the Third Reich unless we were wholly united."

CHAPTER SIX

PEDA

Žabljak, Montenegro to Kragujevac, Serbia, the Kingdom of Yugoslavia
Mid-March 1941

PEDA'S DEPARTURE FROM ŽABLJAK was tinged with an awful feeling of self-regret and reproach. As he began the grueling journey back to Serbia, he reflected on his poor behavior toward his sister Seja. Could he have been a more despicable guest? Each step haunted him as he weighed his actions the morning of his untimely awakening.

***

Someone shook him awake. "No, no, let me sleep," he growled into the sofa.

"Peda, wake up; it's time. It would be best if you returned to your family in Serbia," Seja whispered, bent over him.

"What did you say?" His head felt like mush as he grappled to understand her words. Bleary-eyed, he rose from his little sister's uncomfortable, soiled couch, squinting as he checked the time. One o'clock in the afternoon. How in hell...?

With her hands placed on her hips, Seja confronted him. "We've tried, Peda, but it hasn't been easy having you here. It's been an extra mouth to feed. It was fine a night or two when you first arrived, but it's been over a month, and you haven't offered or contributed anything. Did it ever occur to you the hardship your stay has been for my family, not to mention the amount of rakija you stole from my husband's stock out back?" Her words, heavy with the strain of raising five small children, cut into his conscience.

His hands were folded under his armpits and he hopped from foot to foot on the cold flooring. "I, ah, I'm at a loss for words."

"Since you haven't apologized, I'll assume you don't regret taking advantage of us. Jovo wants you gone before he gets home from work today. He's boiling mad, claiming you're responsible for repaying us for every bottle of rakija you drank without his consent. We trusted you, Peda. Jovo intended on selling that rakija. We desperately needed that extra money to make ends meet. We've been sinking and behind paying our bills."

Lowering his eyes, Peda said sheepishly, "I am sorry, Seja. I'll repay you."

"How, Peda?" As she shifted her heavy baby from one hip to the other, he saw the strain of having five of them underfoot. "How do you intend to pay us back?" Her gaze locked on his.

Deflated by the harsh truth, Peda swung his hands in the air. "It was only a little nip here and there. Honestly, I wasn't aware I had drunk that amount." His feeble attempt at justification and the awkwardness of his apology were evident in his sister's face.

"Oh, Peda…" She bit her lip; Peda could see her tears on her eyelashes. "Stop being in denial. You drank bottles and bottles of it—that's plenty more than a nip. I gave you extra time to sleep in this morning because I know you will be walking for a long time."

"Thanks. I'll pack up and be gone soon." He was embarrassed by what he had done. His sister was such a sweetheart.

"It's broken my heart to witness the way our brothers' and sisters' lives have unraveled because of the destructive choices influenced by alcohol. Last year, I decided to wash my hands of it."

"I know, I know." He clenched his jaw because he could see she was not done.

"Your visit brought me right back into this crazy family. The way you drink, Peda—it's reminiscent of our childhood. Our parents' treatment of us made me hate them. While I grew up, I rarely spent time with them; then you arrived, and it gave me hope. I believed you'd created a unique life for yourself in Kragujevac, unlike the others, so it hurts me to say this, but you're just like our parents."

He was embarrassed; Seja's poignant clarity had laid bare their troubled and complex childhood. Peda had always grappled with his parents' destructive behavior and wondered if what she had just said was true. Was he mirroring their habits?

***

The following day, on his solitary journey home, his thoughts were centered on Zora, thankful her family had never learned the reason behind him losing his job.

A warning would have been better, but they'd fired him on the spot for being caught twice drinking while working because of the amount of ammunition in the factory. They had strict safety orders against alcohol or smoking on the job.

He had been walking for six days and could feel the blisters popping inside his scruffy socks. The squishy, watery substance burned against the cuts and sores already on the bottom of his feet. Each step pained him, but Kragujevac was still a way away. He found himself wishing a kind soul passing through on a wagon might offer him a ride, but no such luck. His boots had long since ripped apart, the soles separating into nothingness.

As the road narrowed into a curve, he stopped to rest near a pasture where he could make out a giant of a farmer tilling his land. Peda leaned on the white rickety fence with its paint peeling off.

The farmer shouted, "We have no food; sorry."

Peda cupped his hands around his mouth and hollered back, "No, no, just resting."

"Whaddya say?"

"I've come from Žabljak and am heading home to Kragujevac." Peda sat on the thick stones piled near the fence and pulled from his pocket a grubby handkerchief to wipe the sweat from his face and neck. His heart tipped, remembering how Zora had rushed to hand him the snowy-white handkerchief before he'd left home. Glancing up, he watched the farmer move closer, his stride purposeful.

"Ah," the farmer said, nearing him. Now he saw him close up, Peda could tell that the farmer was actually younger and rangier than he had imagined.

"The number of people desperately begging for food

has been overwhelming. Hundreds of them. Initially, my kindhearted wife tried to help as many as possible, but we had to stop. We have little ourselves. Have you caught any word about what's going to happen with Prince Regent Paul and the Tripartite Pact?"

Peda pressed his lips together. "I haven't heard a word." His fatigue left him with no interest in discussing the politics of Yugoslavia. He just wanted to get home.

The farmer pointed his finger. "It's no wonder, the way our people have been deprived for so long. It should be a question directed to the men in our Parliament. Even though our people are starving, the newspapers have continued to display images of Cvetković, Prince Regent Paul, and the Princess luxuriously clad in furs. Doesn't seem like our system cares about us out here." Pushing his hat back, he continued: "Why can't we balance those scales, help those struggling to put food on the table, and stop fighting every war?" Peering more closely at Peda, he asked, "What's being said in Montenegro?"

"Not much, but I've seen a lot of families packing up and leaving."

Wiping his forearm across his forehead, the farmer said, "The prince's intentions have been unknown. Believe me, if they have the chance, those Germans will crush us."

Peda gaped in wonder. How did this farmer, stuck in the middle of the woods, have such a firm grasp on the politics inside of Parliament? Even though his limbs and muscles were aching, and he was thirsty, he didn't want to debate with this animated farmer he'd begun to grudgingly admire. Peda decided it was pointless to argue about the greatness of the Karađorđević Monarchy, so he chose to ignore any discussion about its shortcomings.

The man produced an apple from his pocket. "Here… take this."

Peda's chest grew lighter.

"No, no; take it. It's a gift. Everyone else has asked me for something, but you haven't."

Peda brought his hands together, with his palms touching and fingertips facing up. *"Hvala Vam."*

An apple. In thirty-six hours, it would be the most he'd had to eat. He wearily stood and gazed at him. "I won't forget you. You're the best surprise I've had on this trip. People from the city would be shocked to learn someone like you has such educated opinions. How did you acquire such extensive knowledge?"

The farmer laughed. "Farming was never the career path my father envisioned for my brothers or me."

"What changed?" Peda asked, wiping the sweat from his brow.

"My father's sudden death while I was in my third year of university studies. Since my brothers were studying in France, I had to quit and return home." Looking down at Peda's feet, he declared: "Your shoes, my friend. Hopping on a train would be a wise choice for you."

"Believe me, I have tried. Each one has been stock full of passengers, some clinging to the side rails in fear. Each one packed. I witnessed the same fear on the faces of burdened peasants, carrying their lives with them." Peda stood. "It's been a pleasure."

After he had gained a mile or so he asked himself, "Why did I open up to a stranger, someone I just met?"

This journey home had been a revelation, reminding him of how he longed for Zora and his family and the need to transform his life. Find a job. Work on being a better person, father, and husband, and stop drinking. He recognized that he had the potential to give his family a better life than what he had accomplished thus far.

Suddenly, he was back at the edge of Žabljak, searching for his brother Sasha and sister Snezena, taking in the filth and disgust. Out of nowhere, two small heads emerged from beneath a makeshift tent before his brother stuck his head out, gawking at him in complete shock.

"Sasha, it's me, Peda, your brother."

"Ah, don't you...don't you live, ah—somewhere else?"

"Yes, but I came to Montenegro to see all of you, even though I live in Kragujevac. Seja suggested I come here, but where's Snezena?"

Sasha has his children with him, here in this filthy dump, Peda realized. He's barely coherent, and who knows if he's recognized me.

It was difficult to discover how far his brother had slid into degradation.

Blinking, Sasha quickly grabbed the paper sack containing a glass bottle and took a sip from it, before he bent his head.

Casting his eyes downward, Peda immediately sank to his knees, trying to rouse his sister. "Snezena...wake up."

Upon opening her eyes, Snezena squinted, before glancing upward, her messy hair tangled and oily. "Who?"

"It's Peda, your brother," he whispered, leaning closer until he caught a wave of her stink. "Snezena?"

It was evident she had no clue who he was, nor displayed any desire to find out.

Assuming she'd had too much to drink, Peda suggested to Sasha, "Let's grab a cup of coffee and something warm for your children to eat."

Sasha shook his head and climbed into the tent, the paper-wrapped bottle still in his hands. "See ya later."

Shaking his head in disappointment, Peda left.

Nearby, Peda shouted at a stray passerby, who'd bumped into him with what looked to be a heavy sack. "Hey, watch where you're going."

"Please; any spare change for food?" the stranger asked.

Grunting, Peda questioned, "Do I look like someone with money to spare?"

"Forgive me." The man placed a hand over the chest of his unclean jacket in what looked to Peda like a conciliatory gesture.

After going a distance, Peda felt remorse for being so harsh with a man who had meant him no harm. What's wrong with me? he thought. Plagued by physical discomfort as well as the emotional turmoil with his sister and losing his job, the reality of his situation was clear. Pausing to estimate the distance to Kragujevac, he reached for a pack of cigarettes.

"Dammit."

Out of cigarettes and entirely out of money, he glowered, but not before catching sight of a grassy field of bushes and a Lipa tree. Zora would love to have more of the flowers and branches from the sturdy Lipa for her magical potions. Without spotting anyone, Peda retrieved his trusty knife from his back pocket and thought, I'll only snip a few.

***

He was home. With a heavy limp and long overdue for a bath, he leaned against the back door jamb. Inhaling the homemade pogača and vegetable soup, he was engulfed in the warmth and cleanliness of his home. Feeling overwhelmed, he was close to tears.

"Anyone here?" he called out, glancing around in disbelief. Where was everybody?

Lenka and Neven hastily headed in, and Peda observed the surprise spreading across their faces.

"Tata, you're home…so soon? How was Montenegro?" Lenka asked, hurrying to help guide him to a kitchen chair. Looking down at his feet, she asked, "What happened?"

"Ah, my feet. With all the walking I've done, my shoes didn't last."

"What can I get for you, Tata?" Neven asked, his eyebrows raised.

"Water, please, and food." Peda tried sitting upright in the chair, but the throbbing in his legs and the ache in his middle back screamed in refusal. He saw Neven move away from him, discreetly lowering his nose and mouth. Am I what smells so bad? he asked himself. He wondered if the awful stench came from his body or his feet. Having been unable to bathe for weeks, he felt increasingly uncomfortable, and soap, a luxury most Yugoslavs could not afford, had been unavailable at Seja's.

Neven placed a generous, steaming bowl of soup and a tall glass of water before him. "Mama warned us not to touch the pogača, so I'll see if we have any crackers in the cupboard. How far did you walk, Tata?"

He was unable to get the spoon into his mouth fast enough, and he knew he was slurping. With closed eyes, he relished every bite. After eating, he felt a surge of energy. "If I had to guess, I'd say about eight days. The trains were so overcrowded I couldn't get on, so I walked the whole way." He was too ashamed to admit he had no money for train fare or food.

"The entire distance? That has to be over two hundred kilometers." Lenka's face worked its way into a frown.

"Closer to three hundred." Peda recognized that look and knew she was on the verge of tears. Drinking his water in a gulp, he stretched his arm out to Lenka for another glassful, then shrugged. "There were no other options. In addition, the streets and trains were packed with too many people. It felt like a sudden rush of them fleeing from their residences. They came from Croatia, Kosovo, Bosnia, and Montenegro. It felt like the entire Kingdom had descended into madness. Our people—" Peda shook his head.

"What do you mean?" Neven cocked his head.

"Like I said, people, everywhere, appeared afraid. They've left their homes, but who knows where they're heading?" Brandishing his spoon, he shared his thoughts. "I'd imagine they're looking for an escape."

"How was Žabljak and your family?" Neven asked.

"Different from when I grew up. The addition of ski resorts has caused it to increase in size. Nevertheless, I'd forgotten its beauty. Montenegro still has the most beautiful locations in all of Yugoslavia."

"How so?" With a finger, Neven readjusted his glasses from sliding down his nose.

After devouring his soup, Peda passed the empty bowl back to his son, eager for another serving. "Well, the Durmitor Mountains possess an elegance, but there's a bunch of hotels and restaurants at their base. Don't get me wrong, it's still beautiful country, simply different. Nonetheless, the place I love most was still there. It's where the raging Tara River flowed beneath the towering, rugged cliffs. Žabljak used to be a vast open land for miles, but now it's full of moneyed people who want to ski on the slopes."

"Wow, Tata. Were any of your siblings involved in the ski business?" With her face turned upward, Lenka looked at her father.

"Only one, a younger brother." Peda had forgotten the length of time that had lapsed since he'd last seen them. His life seemed dull in comparison, especially after witnessing Sasha and Snezena's reckless life. "I stayed with my youngest sibling, my sister Seja, and her family. Remember her?"

Neven asked, "Has she ever been here?"

"I don't believe so. Seja has a bunch of toddlers and little babies. I even managed to secure a job fixing cars in the village through one of her friends."

"Really, Tata? That's excellent news, because the money will come in handy. Mama had to—"

His father cut him off. "There's no money," Peda said. "I worked a measly eleven days before parting ways with that stingy owner. Besides, jobs were not easy to find in Žabljak." Despising any talk about money, his shoulders slumped. He neglected to inform his children of the part about losing his job and Seja telling him he could no longer stay with them. "Where's your mother?"

"Oh, she's working." Neven rubbed his collarbone.

Peda's eyebrows shot up. "Someone sick?"

"Not exactly." Neven sucked in an ample breath before inhaling. "After you left, we had no money for food, so Mama went to Dunja, who gave her a job waitressing three nights a week at Paligorić."

Peda stiffened.

"It has been a challenge, Tata, trying to rustle up enough food, so we decided to forgo eating lunch, so Vuk, Čedo, and Aco have enough to eat. Mama said their growing bones needed the most nourishment."

He squeezed his eyes shut. There were times when his intelligent son lacked the awareness of when to stop talking.

Sometimes Neven overexplains, he thought, but how did I allow this to happen, the depth of my transgressions? What's wrong with me? Feeling an enormous weight on his shoulders, he rested his elbows on the worn tabletop, drumming his fingers.

"Dunja's?" His voice rose. "Of all people, for crying out loud." Dunja was someone he disliked. Why did she call her right after he left?

His wife and Dunja had been best friends since childhood. He knew their story well. According to Zora, she was the gentle one; easy to manage, whereas Dunja was strong-willed and had a hot temper. From their first encounter, Peda realized he and the sharp-tongued Dunja Lekić would never have a meaningful friendship. Never shy about offering her opinion, Dunja detested him the instant they locked eyes, often saying Peda was too brash for his own good.

With narrowed eyes, he said, "Your mother better not be parading around in front of those German leches."

"I don't know, Tata, but we have school in the morning." Neven's face reddened as he faltered.

"Wait." Peda gestured, his hand pointed toward the branches near the back door. "How does your mother manage the drying-out stuff?"

Neven explained that she hung them upside down on wires to dry out.

Peda nodded. "Good, you do it."

Lenka quickly came to Neven's aid, gathering the solid branches and moving them to a dry spot in the corner of the other room. After Lenka finished, she said, "*Laku noć*, Tata."

The feeling of being home was incredible, with a real table, utensils, running water, and a proper bathroom. Things he had once overlooked. Not anymore. He tightly shut his eyes, unable to block out the agonizing images of Sasha and Snezena and the overpowering stench of their unwashed bodies huddled together. His last memory was of Sasha chugging the bottle of rakija down his throat.

***

Peda was awakened by the sound of a door creaking open. It was past midnight, and he had already bathed, changed into clean clothes, and located the coffee can Zora stashed in a cabinet above the stove. It was where she kept extra coins. Unfortunately, it was empty—no money for cigarettes or rakija.

CHAPTER SEVEN

ZORA

Kragujevac, the Kingdom of Yugoslavia
Mid-March 1941

ZORA'S ONLY THOUGHT WAS collapsing into bed as she followed Stana in through the back door. Every inch of her body screamed exhaustion. Despite her deep appreciation for her older ones' help, she was often bone tired. Trying to support their family since Peda lost his job, Zora now juggled three jobs: the secretarial position in the office of the Military Technical Institute, her healing work, and waitressing at Paligorić, all of which took an exceedingly grueling toll on her body. With a mountain of laundry and the endless concern over the unpaid bills piling up, she couldn't help but feel overwhelmed.

"Zora?" Peda's voice pierced through the darkness.

For a moment she went completely still. "You're...home?"

Turning on a light, Zora's shocked face glimpsed the exhaustion carved across his face, although the puffiness under his eyes and the heaviness around his middle had seemingly disappeared.

Stana glided past her mother. "Tata, how was your family?"

Peda patted the empty spot on the couch next to him. "Come and sit, while I explain."

Zora heard the exertion in his voice. Hesitating in the doorway, she watched him and Stana share a welcome connection. She hadn't seen this side of him in a while. It was evident Stana glowed in his adoration. Zora hoped it was not ephemeral.

"Zora?" Peda patted the other side of the couch.

"Sorry, your arrival took me by surprise, and I—we hadn't expected you so soon. You mentioned staying a good two months." She did not have the heart to admit his arrival concerned her. It meant another mouth to feed when they had so little, mainly because he consumed the most food. What would she do? Zora sat on a chair facing him and promptly smelled something strong and overpowering. Catching more of a pungent whiff a second time, she watched Stana bury her face in her shirt, presumably to avoid the stink.

"People crowded the streets and were walking everywhere. It was unusual. Abandoning their homes, they appeared terrified. And the trains… I had no choice but to walk."

"Y—you walked the entire way?" Stana's eyes searched his.

"Look—even my boots fell apart." Peda tugged off his socks to show them.

"Ugh!" Stana shrieked, rearing back and away from the pus-filled sores on his feet. Her slim fingers covered her mouth.

"Peda?" Zora grimaced, forcing her eyes away. Clear his feet carried an infection, her voice was strong. "You must soak them in warm water with Epsom salts right away. I'll add drops of my tinctures, but honestly, Peda, Doctor Milković should see them first."

Shaking his head, he cried, "We don't have money for doctors, so you fix them."

A sound came from her throat as she tilted her head.

"What's that mean?" Peda asked. His lips contorted into an angry frown, revealing his growing annoyance with her.

"I'm going to bed," Stana said. Zora knew her daughter acknowledged the sudden shift in the atmosphere in the room as it grew taut.

With an air of growing frustration, Zora's patience wore thin. Drawing in a formidable breath, she managed to stay calm. "Peda, the pus oozing out is an indication of an infection, something you never want to ignore. I'm not equipped, nor do I have on hand a remedy potent enough to ward off this type of infection, but I'm happy to clean your blisters and smaller wounds."

He gestured toward something near the back door. "I got those for you."

His erratic behavior threw her off balance, leaving her unsteady. One moment anger, the next acting contrite. "I'll grab the bucket." Her voice shook as she saw the branches, flowers, and leaves from the cherished Lipa tree, which would undoubtedly provide a profusion of prom-ising homeopathic benefits from their natural properties. "Thank you," she whispered.

"Sure," Peda groaned, falling back against the couch, his hand pressed to his forehead.

Alarmed, Zora approached, gentler this time. "Do you have a fever? Does your head hurt you?" Upon closer inspection, she noticed his pained expression, yet no smell of alcohol. "I'll be right back." It dawned on her that getting him healed rested on her shoulders, a task that would involve little sleep for her. Somehow, someway, she *had* to get Peda moving... Then she would broach the delicate subject of their finances, hoping to avoid an explosive reaction.

***

The sun finally shone through the milky clouds, and Zora couldn't wait to be outside. Wrapping up her duties at the Military Technical Institute, she donned her coat and left work. Crossing the Old Stone Bridge, her mind was on Goran, wondering about his well-being. She knew his ambition was to be on the front lines, and conversely, it was what gave her nightmares. Nevertheless, her concern heightened with Hitler's demands and the question of whether Yugoslavia was next on his list.

The air was thick with tension, exacerbated by the newspaper's shocking news of Prince Regent Paul's recent trips to meet with Hitler and his high-ranking officials in Berchtesgaden, Germany. The frightening question on everyone's mind was: would Prince Regent Paul succumb to Hitler's demands and sign the dreaded Tripartite Pact with the Axis Powers, which would drag their country into Hitler's clutches? The uncertainty of it all weighed on her mind as she made her way through the bustling streets, the shadow of impending doom closer.

Suddenly, someone shouted her name. Zora pivoted, and in that moment, her breath caught.

Winded from dodging vehicles, Kosta Lazić burst forth sputtering, "Hello, just give me a second." He placed his hand on his chest.

He hadn't changed. Kosta carried himself with an effort-less grace, born of a life unburdened by financial strain. The Lazić family had always lived a life of comfort, and their wealth granted Kosta a natural way of carrying himself, like those comfortable enough to pull it off. Having *more* gave him confidence.

"Leaving work early?" Zora asked, on tenterhooks. After selling his father's business, Kosta had been appointed the new superintendent of the Military Technical Institute. His position at the top meant their paths seldom crossed.

"Yes. I was craving sunshine," Kosta replied, his touch fleeting on her elbow. "It's been too long, Zora. How have you been?"

A shiver raced down her arm, and she stumbled over her words. "Ah, ah…good. And you?"

Her foolish pride, that night long ago, haunted her still. Their last day of high school had set their futures on diverging paths. A confession never made, a trust never extended, and a misunderstanding that took root. The regret of not revealing the truth to Kosta, of not trusting him with her circumstances, tore at her insides.

He ran his fingers through his thick, coppery hair that swept past his collar, and locked gazes with her. "Not well," he confessed.

Zora felt a blush of warmth as old feelings she thought long buried surfaced. "What's wrong, Kosta?"

He hesitated. "It's my sister, Iva."

This kindhearted and beloved man in Kragujevac, whom she once imagined in her future, was struggling with some-thing. "Is she ill?"

He shook his head and spoke with misery in his voice. "She's vanished, along with her family. No word…I—I haven't heard from her in months." Swallowing hard, he said, "If you've got time, I'll explain."

"I have time," Zora assured him; even though she should be home cooking dinner, this was too important to ignore. Hopefully Stana, or Neven, realizing their mother was late, would begin making their meal and helping their younger brothers with their homework.

"It's a tale of displacement and horror. Last summer the SS forced Iva and her family from their Berlin home into a ghetto, condemning them to live amidst squalor reserved for Jews."

Zora stood frozen, absorbing the gravity of the situation.

Rubbing the back of his neck, he recounted Iva's insights into Hitler. "Early on Iva saw through Hitler's façade. Her research, her readings had alerted her to the dangers long before the world caught on. She knew the implications of his hatred toward the Jews."

As Zora listened, she heard the strain in his voice. "That got her attention, not only because her husband was Jewish, but their children were half-Jews."

"Meaning what?"

"Well, Iva once mentioned a proclamation concerning Jews. If someone were only part Jewish, in Hitler's eyes, they were still a full-fledged Jew. Because Iva had complete access to all his press releases, articles, and rants targeting Jews, she feared one day she and David would meet a similar fate and—be starved to death."

Zora's hand instinctively covered her wide-open mouth. "He's a lunatic, Kosta." Looking into the same sapphire-blue eyes he shared with his son, Luka, she whispered, "The agony of this, and what you must be going through—it's unthinkable."

"It was years ago when she first learned about him, but she *knew* he was a complete and hellish monster." Shaking his head, Kosta squeezed his eyes shut.

She winced, seeing the agony move over his face. "Kosta, I'm so sorry for what you have been enduring. I cannot imagine the agonizing ordeal this must be for your family. I'm surprised Stana or Neven mentioned nothing to me."

His face softened as he lifted his shoulders. "We urged our children not to talk about this with anyone, that's why. Fear's a funny thing and I didn't want it to mushroom, nor did I want to impart unnecessary fear among our teenagers. They create enough theater on their own. Do you mind if I walk alongside you, since I'm heading in the same direction?"

Zora nodded, her insides knotting. "Kosta, might there be something I could do to help your family?" She questioned whether his wife, Marija, proffered any support.

He squeezed her hand tightly. "Having someone like you, who knew Iva well, has been valuable. However, beyond listening, there's little we can do except pray for her and her family. I started becoming suspicious in November when Iva stopped corresponding with me. Before that, I used to mail boxes of food to them twice a week. Unfortunately, the SS pilfered through all the boxes and took what they wanted long before it got to Iva." He sighed heavily. "Her telephone was also turned off."

"I can't believe they opened her boxes. Is there not a law against that?" Her eyes locked onto the grayish clouds forming in the sky, and she hoped she'd make it home before it rained.

"Not in their world. During a sleepless night, while the Luftwaffe bombed Glasgow, London, and Buckingham

Palace, I was awake listening to the BBC on my shortwave. In any case, the announcer brought up a name—Auschwitz. He proposed that the Nazis were using cattle trains to transport an unprecedented number of Jews to concentration camps in a place called Auschwitz. That name stayed with me, and I've often wondered if it might be where those monsters sent my beautiful sister and her family."

"I am so sorry."

In slow motion, Kosta tenderly pulled her nearer, as if by a magical string. Captivated, she observed a tiny bead of water, possibly a tear, shining on his eyelashes before trailing down his flawless face. Zora was taken by surprise as he abruptly pulled her closer; sooo close she felt the entirety of his hardened body pressed up against hers. Lightheaded, she instantly whirled away, as if touched by fire.

"Kosta, no." Placing a hand over her wildly thumping chest, she inhaled a sharp intake of air before whispering, "I, ah, I don't know what to say." Her face burned with shame and mortification.

"Zora, no; please, I beg your pardon," he said with a brittle laugh. "It was such a natural feeling, I suppose I got carried away in the moment." His voice was strangled, and he, too, stepped back, his hands dipping into his pockets. "I apologize sincerely, Zora. As you can see, my emotions got the best of me."

Zora glanced nervously along the bustling Knez Mihaila street, looking for witnesses. *My goodness…a married woman with seven children and nearly locked in an embrace with a man who is not her husband. What is wrong with me?* Not knowing what else to say to soothe her nerves, she faltered. "I—I'll burn candles for Iva…in church," she stuttered.

Kosta's eyes brightened. "That's kind of you, but what about your family's exciting news?"

Puzzled, she asked the question before realizing he was trying to defuse the situation. "What do you mean?"

"Stana's singing. Marija and I heard her the other night. She was remarkable and poised. I wished you could have seen the crowd cheering her on, it was rather spectacular."

"Really?" Hearing Marija's name was like a splash of freezing water on her face. Kosta was a married man, and she had absolutely no business cavorting with him on the sidewalk like this.

"Yes; even though Stana's not mine, I was bursting with pride."

Blinking, she felt a rush of emotions. Kosta consistently supported those around him. He did that in his role at work, too. Lifting her chin, she beamed. "That means so much. Stana's often remarked how she would not survive without music in her life. It fills her somehow, you know?"

"I do know. Remember how we used to love singing and dancing together? Speaking of Stana, are you aware of a romance brewing between our two?"

Zora nodded, sensing a greater sense of control. "Neven mentioned it."

"Well, I can share from my perspective that Luka's downright smitten." Kosta's luminous smile showed off dazzling white teeth, something Zora seldom saw in Yugoslavia, dental care being only for the rich. Despite knowing it was wrong, she was relishing her time with him.

After parting ways at the intersection of Knez Mihaila and Andre Marinkovica, Zora realized something. It wasn't his chiseled cheekbones or his well-defined build; what made Kosta Lazić appealing was his intrinsic goodness.

CHAPTER EIGHT

ZORA

IT WAS WELL AFTER dinner before Zora made it upstairs to enjoy a cup of coffee and Dušica's warm walnut-filled palačinke.

Dušica leaned across the table. "I—there's something important I must share with you."

Zora studied her sister's ashen pallor. "Are you unwell?"

"No, no. Nothing like that," she reassured her. "It's Martha..."

"Martha Levine, your friend?"

With a nervous bite on her lip, Dušica nodded. "Yes. The Germans have been surveilling her and her husband. Martha has sensed the prickle of eyes on her, and recently, these fears have intensified. She believed them to be German soldiers, but, in fact, they're spies of the Abwehr Military Intelligence. Two days later, Martha confirmed the same two had been the ones skulking outside their apartment building, which housed a considerable number of Jewish residents."

"Oh...I was unaware of her heritage; not that it matters, I was just saying...Jesus, why am I rambling on like this?" Zora asked.

"It's all right. May I finish? After Martha graduated from school, her parents and siblings moved back to Berlin, their main residence. Despite the distance, Martha stayed in close contact with her parents regularly…until they inexplicably disappeared."

"Vanished?" An icy shiver quickly turned to goosebumps. "Dragi Gospode—that's the second time today I've been told about loved ones disappearing. It's more than a coincidence, isn't it?" Zora felt the landscape shifting beneath her feet.

Dušica's confused frown prompted her to elaborate. "I bumped into Kosta earlier. Iva's story's oddly reminiscent of Martha's, perhaps due to their both residing in Berlin?"

"Most likely and quite tragically, for their families. Martha's anxiety over Hitler advancing into Yugoslavia has spiked, yet she has remained resilient, and determined to follow through with her plans. Martha's husband, Andrew, on the other hand, has tended to wallow, refusing to believe Hitler will attack Yugoslavia."

"Is fleeing Yugoslavia an option for them?"

"Although she has the ability, Andrew has declared it nonsense. He's refused to budge. It's a shame, really, because he's in complete denial and has turned a blind eye toward anything about the war in Europe. He goes as far as denying the possibility of similar events occurring here. Despite our attempts to persuade him, he's remained obstinate, leaving Martha to make alternate plans involving Marko and me."

"How so?" Zora felt a cold dread pressing in on her.

"Long ago, Martha and I made a pact to care for one another's children if something went amuck. Now that promise looms large…"

Standing, Zora suddenly swayed and clutched onto the table. She blew out a great burst of air, the gravity of the situation taking hold. She asked rather emphatically, "You cannot be serious? To harbor two Jewish children, in our midst, and with the German military at our doorstep in Kragujevac? Why, it's beyond daring—it's madness." Pacing, Zora felt too restless to sit. Running her fingers through her hair, she really looked at her sister. "What of the risks to you and Marko…and to our entire family? Have you truly considered the consequences?" Zora touched on her final question. "Have you and Marko truthfully considered every aspect and ramification that could occur if you brought them into our home, notwithstanding how it will impact your lives? Because that's one helluva big ask."

Dušica's face began to crumple. "I know, I know, but she has no one else. Marko and I…we're like family. We're the only family Martha has, and I'm the closest person in her life. We've always been like sisters. I could never abandon her, or her children."

"I understand your dilemma, but we're not Jewish. There's got to be a more practical solution for her children. In times of trouble, wouldn't the Jews seek assistance in their synagogue, much like we would look to our church in time of need? Let's think this through, with every possibility, in order to solve this, while still protecting you and Marko."

Throwing her hands in the air, Dušica sounded exasperated. "We've gone over this repeatedly. Martha has warned us, should Hitler invade Yugoslavia, a decree would mandate that all Jews must register, which would signify a major shift for our Jewish friends in the Kingdom."

"Register? I'm not following what you mean." Confusion was evident in her strained voice.

"Hitler has already mandated in Germany that all Jews register with their local officials. Moreover, he's required them to outwardly display their Jewishness in public by wearing yellow armbands or the Star of David on their clothing. In the newspaper, Martha discovered that Hitler imposed this same measure in Poland and France. It's his method of tracking every Jew."

Blowing out a substantial portion of air, Zora asked, "What's your plan?" She could not fathom the depth of Hitler's hatred toward the Jews, or the extent of his deplorable actions against them.

Dušica's abrupt, jerky movements caught Zora's eye. "Our initial step would be to convert them to Serbian Orthodoxy by baptizing them in church. Father Radovan would give them Serbian names, effectively making them our children. It all depends on whether Father will agree to this. I know it sounds risky, but…"

"How could you possibly explain such a thing to friends, neighbors, and everyone who knows you're childless?"

"We've considered that angle, too. Marko's younger brother Ivan, who lives in Novi Sad, has been burdened by his wife's severe illness, and he cares for their four young children. We would simply say we visited Ivan, and to help him we brought back his two youngest boys. No one would suspect a thing. Our truth would be known to only a handful of family members."

Zora sat back, her mind racing with concerns over the colossal risk they could end up undertaking—a prospect she considered alarmingly dangerous. "What if someone uncovers the truth? Or someone recognizes Martha's sons and accidentally leaks your or Marko's information to the Germans? Wouldn't that be tantamount to signing your death warrant?" Exhaling, Zora shut her eyes, bringing to mind the word—*collaborator*. Opening them, she questioned, "So, your plan would be to allow everyone to assume you're caring for Ivan's sons?"

"Exactly. If anything happened to Martha and Andrew, Marko and I would step in."

"So, your plan would be to hide them in plain sight?" Zora felt a disconcerting chill settle in her bones as she reached across the table for her sister's cold hands.

"Yes," Dušica whispered in a panicked voice.

CHAPTER NINE

SAVA

Belgrade, the Kingdom of Yugoslavia
March 24, 1941

IN THE SUNDRENCHED FOYER of her refined home,
Sava's hair cascaded in gentle waves, catching the light.
As she spoke with her husband, she leaned close, her
stance resolute. "Vlado, you're aware I can't just abandon
my duties mid-semester." Feet planted, arms crossed, and
jaw set, she was not budging. Her academic obligations
and commitments at the university were not things she
could simply set aside, even though Vlado's departure
meant they would be separated for two months.

She understood his desire to return to England; his
business affairs notwithstanding, being near Surrey
would position him in close proximity to his doctors.
Yet with the ominous cloud of Hitler's influence spreading, it was debatable which country faced greater risks:
England or Yugoslavia. As time passed, Sava noticed
Vlado's growing fondness for their quaint home in the
English countryside, where he felt more connected to
the British culture.

Grasping his wife's elegant hands, he admitted, "By God, you're adorable when you dig in like that. Stubbornly optimistic, I wish I had more control over you, my darling, but since I don't, I'm leaving you in very capable hands." Vlado's eyes twinkled.

"What's that supposed to mean?" Sava raised an eyebrow inquisitively.

In a playful gesture he tweaked her nose, then quickly twirled her around. "Života has agreed to manage our real-estate investments, so he'll be around should you need him."

Života gave a brief wave. "Hello, Gospođo. I'll stay out of your way, but please ring me if you need anything." He excused himself to Vlado's spacious library.

"What the heck, Vlado?" Momentarily flustered, Sava stammered before finding her words. "That's unnecessary. I'm capable of managing on my own, but who'll ensure you take your medications on time?" What was he thinking, offering his standoffish employee to stay here? Absolutely not.

"Don't forget, I have been training my nephew, Jovan. He's coming with me, and he's excited to be returning to England, which makes perfect sense. It'll be an excellent opportunity for him to learn more about the business there."

Sava realized she'd never win an argument against her sophisticated, generous husband, who had always supported her career and ambitions; a fact that left his friends puzzled. In granting her freedom, uncommon for many women in their country, Vlado was well ahead of the curve. Reflecting on her unique position, she appreciated her ability to voice her thoughts and share knowledge with her students. Despite their age difference, Sava adored Vlado's bright, curious eyes hidden behind gold, wire-rimmed spectacles sliding down his large, aristocratic nose. As always, he exuded understated class, dressing impeccably this morning in a crisp, white, buttoned-down shirt casually tucked into navy silk pants. Tall and lean from years of tennis, Vlado could easily pass for someone ten years younger than his sixty-four years.

She wrapped her arms around him, savoring the scent of the woodsy fragrance that clung to him. Taking a cautious breath, she realized how precious time with him might be. She planted a tender kiss across his lips. Vlado deepened the kiss as their bodies melded together, hipbone to hipbone. Heart galloping, Sava felt a tingling down to her toes.

Releasing an audible sigh, he pressed light, feathery kisses along her slim neck. "I hate leaving you like this."

Shivering along with an ache down below that caused her to become breathless, she said, "You haven't kissed me that enthusiastically in I don't know how long…"

Eyes crinkling with a smile, Vlado admitted, "I don't want you to forget me." Pulling her toward him once more, he kissed her swollen lips. "I am sorry, darling—it's those foolish pills the doctors prescribed. They've made me terribly drowsy, and, well…"

Sava exchanged a steamy look with him. "Please don't worry about that, but Vlado, I really will miss you, and I'll be there as soon as the term ends in May. Then we'll have the glorious summer together that we've planned."

His large hands squeezed her shoulders. "Darling, promise me—nothing foolish. If anything goes awry in the coming days, you must leave Yugoslavia straightaway."

Tears threatened to leak, and with a ragged sigh, she agreed. "I understand, and don't forget to check on Delphine. I'm hoping she's still safe."

Sava was worried about her treasured friend, Delphine Cloutier, whom she'd met while on their honeymoon off the Amalfi Coast over fifteen years ago. Ever since, Delphine and her husband, Jules Cloutier, had been close friends with them.

"Don't worry. I'll ring Jules as soon as I'm back. In case I can't reach him, I'll try Andre. However, I should not have to remind you of the horrific events in France last summer when Hitler raised that dreadful swastika flag over Versailles and the Eiffel Tower. I'll never forget how heavy our hearts were that day as we openly wept for our French friends."

"I'm concerned she may have joined the Resistance. Delphine's always been incredibly passionate about France, much like me."

Mouth agape. "You cannot be serious? Do you honestly believe she would run off to join...an underground? Resistance, you say?" Vlado questioned, as he rubbed his ear.

Gazing into the distance, her expression transformed into wonder. "I do, Vlado. Delphine's a lot like me. Truthfully, we're the flip side of the same coin. I'd like to think she's off somewhere, fighting to undermine the Third Reich." Sava knew Vlado could never grasp the intense love Delphine felt for France, enough to fight till her last breath. Nothing in Vlado's or Jules' upbringing called for a cause this great. Vlado's youth, so unlike her own, had lacked a strong conviction to die for one's country, which might be why he connected so famously with Jules. Raised similarly, Jules had attended prestigious boarding schools throughout Europe, and both had childhoods steeped in riding horses and reading Shakespeare and Dostoevsky.

Sava and Delphine had grown up in provincial towns and dusty villages, begging for the right to be educated. Delphine grew up south of Paris, in a four-room shack overflowing with eight family members struggling to survive.

"I'm sure she's safe, my dear. Off to anywhere special this evening?"

Sava smiled, slightly embarrassed by Vlado's perspective on resistance efforts, as she said, "Just a quiet dinner at Hotel Bristol with Josie."

"Lovely place," Vlado said. "You've taken quite a fancy to the American, haven't you?"

At the mention of Josie Whitney-Shaw, Sava grinned. "I have. She's not only fascinating but also fun and brilliant. She discovered a lovely apartment in Dorćol, near the fortress of Kalemegdan, and intends to stay there for an indefinite period. Our people have irresistibly captured her heart."

"You don't say?" Looking quizzically at her, he added, "The gentleman with her at that dinner party, the British journalist—did he stay on with her as well?"

"No, he left to cover a story in Africa."

"Very well, then." Vlado pressed a kiss on top of his wife's head. "I adore you, my love. Please, stay out of harm's way."

"I will." Sava watched him step into the automobile taking him to the airport. An unexpected coldness washed through her. Was it her Serbian folklore sending a message? she wondered. Just in case, she obediently and reverentially squeezed her fingers into Troitsa before making the sign of the cross over her body.

***

Sava sat cross-legged on the rug in the living room listening to Radio Belgrade's broadcast as she combed her hair. The intensity of the protests erupting in Ljubljana, Kragujevac, and Belgrade, opposing any alliance with the Axis Powers, was palpable. And when Života drove her through town later that night, the bustling crowds of students and people flocking to the intersection of Alexandar and Milana Boulevard, two of Belgrade's busiest streets, was not to be ignored—it was massive. The air thick with the resounding shouts of defiance, the protestors wielded homemade signs, their messages clear—the most prominent being *Bolje rat nego patk* and *Bolje grob nego rob.*

"Gospođo, please…what do they say?" Života did not have the ability to turn and look with all the people zigzagging through the streets.

"'Rather a War Than a Pact,' and 'Rather a Grave Than a Slave.'"

Upon arriving at the Hotel Bristol, nestled in the historic Mali Pijac neighborhood, a place once teeming with traders from the Middle East, Sava stepped into the opulent lobby, where she felt a charge of electricity snapping in the air. She couldn't help but stare at the lengthy line of unruly guests pushing and shuffling for a position close to the front desk. Everyone seemed in a rush to leave.

At that moment, heads turned as a stunning woman entered. Josie effortlessly made her way through, dazzling in a green silk gown that accentuated her nipped-in waist and flowed gracefully around her shapely legs. The captivating dress offset her vibrant hair color.

"Sava, Sava, hello." She beamed, reaching up to kiss one cheek, then the other, and a third kiss before extending her small, delicate hand to join Sava's larger one. "You look lovely, darling." With a wave of her hand, Josie said, "Come, meet my friends."

Sava's beautifully arched eyebrows expressed surprise. "Friends? I thought it was just us girls?"

Josie chuckled. "I know, darling, but a couple of friends insisted on joining us for dinner."

Her all-too-casual reply signified the ease of someone used to doing exactly what they wanted. Flinching inwardly, Sava recognized this pattern of behavior was similar in people like her husband, and their friend Jules, where rules seldom applied.

Josie whispered conspiratorially, "Since they're foreign journalists, tonight's conversations will be much more spirited than anything you and I would be discussing."

Upon entering the restaurant, Sava observed three Brits and an American seated at the round table in the corner. She found the lanky, blue-eyed American the most intriguing-looking in the bunch. Their badges hung down, assurance they were indeed foreign journalists. Ray Brock, an intelligent American, was the only other journalist she had instantly liked upon meeting.

"Gentlemen," Josie said. "Please meet my friend, the fascinating historian, Dr. Sava Ivković, who will leave you spellbound tonight."

"Good evening." Sava's eyes sizzled with a mesmerizing smile as the American hurriedly rose, offering her a chair. She watched their four heads swivel as they took her in—the tall brunette in a form-fitting white dress skimming her calves. Prior to delving into deep conversations, she wanted to learn a little about each of them and the publication with which they were affiliated. Josie was right, it promised to be an intriguing night.

The portly Brit across the table, Maximillian Furst, wasted no time. "So, Mrs. Ivković; what's your opinion of Prince Regent Paul? Is he formidable enough to go toe to toe with Adolf Hitler?"

This man had no knowledge of Vlado's close connection to the Karađorđević family, so Sava hedged. "Prince Regent Paul's work has been admirable."

"I apologize for being presumptuous, but with your backs against the wall, I fear time's running out for Yugoslavia."

Instantly repulsed by his arrogant smile and dirty gray teeth, Sava took a sip of her water and decided his insolence did not warrant a reply.

"You sure have one helluva mess on your hands," Maximillian asserted. "We've been working tirelessly over here for months, striving to present the news as clearly as we can, but unfortunately, your Kingdom has far too many, shall we say, conflicting ideologies to be taken seriously." He pointed a plump finger in her direction.

Sava responded with grace and composure, refusing to rise to his bait in his attempt to provoke her. In Maximillian, she recognized a boorish bully who relished having an audience he could belittle. She knew that not responding would only make someone like him incensed; therefore, she ignored him. He wants to tango with me, she thought.

Seated on the other side of her, Josie's fingers surreptitiously tapped hers underneath the table. Was Josie signaling her in Morse Code? Nevertheless, Sava feared the journalists smelled blood. Intrinsically, she knew there was no way out because Yugoslavia was being impossibly squeezed into signing the Tripartite Pact. No matter how Prince Regent Paul or the Crown Council tried to stall, there appeared to be no shades of gray. Hitler pursued Yugoslavia with unwavering determination. She suspected his moves were dictated by time, because Hitler had previously declared his intentions to invade Russia by early May, therefore their proverbial clock in Germany was ticking.

"Mrs. Ivković?" asked the blond gentleman, Willie Callaghan, with the subtlest hint of a Southern twang.

"Yes?" She wondered which part of the South he was from.

"What do you feel the consequences might be of the recent resignation of your three ministers, seemingly in protest?"

A terrible taste rose in her throat. What was he talking about?

Maximillian intercepted Willie's question for Sava and answered it himself, glowering. "You're talking about Čubrilović, Konstantinović, and Budisavljević, right?"

God, I wish Vlado were here, she thought. He's excellent at deflecting people like Maximillian.

Willie agreed with a nod. "Correct, but I specifically asked Mrs. Ivković, not you."

Maximillian blushed yet didn't stop jabbering. "From my perspective, their actions were inconsequential, but they may have inadvertently fueled Hitler's self-importance. Regardless, I believe there's no more Yugoslavia. They will have no choice but to sign."

Another Brit joined in; this one Sava felt desperately needed a haircut. Edward Femsby was his name. "It's a darn shame for a country of your size to have Hitler exerting this inordinate amount of pressure; however, the question remains—what will happen later tonight?"

A serious frown worked its way across Sava's forehead. "Why, whatever do you mean?"

Eyes downcast, Edward hesitated. "I, ah, we heard Hitler gave Prince Regent Paul a deadline for his answer, which is midnight—tonight."

Sava felt a wave of despair as she hurriedly stood.

"Gentlemen, excuse us?" Josie interrupted by standing. "It's time we powdered our noses."

Closing the bathroom door, she placed a small hand on Sava's back. "There you go, in and out, through your nostrils. Breathe slowly and evenly. Sava, my apologies. I had no idea Maximillian Furst was such a belligerent drunk…and a jerk."

Sava sank to the velvet chaise, pressing her fist against her mouth. "I'm astonished at how quickly Hitler's tightening the noose."

"It's crucial we stay alert, and aware of any potential developments. Let's see how much more these men know."

With a slow nod, Sava closed her eyes.

"Hey, I have something I need to tell you," Josie said as she bent, checking underneath each of the four stalls before she stood. "It's confidential."

"Yes…?" Sava's eyes opened, and she blinked rapidly.

Josie's dimples flashed. "Behold, my friend, the first American woman to join the Četnik Resistance."

Sava almost tumbled from the chaise as she sputtered, "W—why, that's impossible, Josie. You're the furthest thing from a Serbian revolutionary, and I might add, the old wartime Četnici were typically brawny, bearded, and bawdy." She teased, "You, my friend, could not be more opposite."

Laughing, Josie pushed her shoulders back. "I know, but Kosta Pećanac, the Četnik leader from the Great War, indoctrinated me. He gave me a uniform and my own šajkača. Trust me, Sava, I'm highly skilled and quite good at what I do. I possess the charisma and charm to disarm others without warning. You would excel too. Listen, I need your help," Josie whispered.

"You're definitely full of surprises."

"That's why I invited these men to join us, to gather information. Journalists have a knack for sniffing out the most secretive information."

Sava's eyes danced. Well, well, she thought, wait until the members of Sloboda learn about this. They will be in for a shocking surprise.

"Ladies, just in the nick of time," said Willie Callaghan as they returned. Sava noticed Maximillian was no longer there.

"Tell me," Sava said, elbow leaning on the table. "Which part of the South do you hail from?"

Willie described his journey. "From Mississippi I went to New York University, where I began my career at *Time* magazine. I traveled across Europe before settling in Budapest as Assistant Chief of the Eastern European desk."

Intrigued, Sava cupped her chin in her hand to listen. "Your thoughts on Hitler?"

"He's quite succinct; I don't believe he'll stop until he's conquered the entirety of Europe," Willie admitted.

"That's everyone's greatest concern," Sava said softly, an undercurrent of fear rising in her chest.

Willie lifted his old-fashioned, the ice cubes clinking inside the crystal glass. "He wants an ethnically clean Europe—no Jews."

Her stomach lurched.

"Mrs. Ivković, if Yugoslavia does become aligned with the Axis Powers, might I suggest you remain incredibly cautious and wary of whom you trust."

"Because?"

"Patterns are what I study. Hitler's military has adopted remarkably similar strategies in every country he's invaded. Covertly, his Abwehr unit infiltrates and places collaborators in villages and nearby towns. Soon enough, your former friend-turned-neighbor has started spying on you without warning. As money and food tighten, people become defenseless…and vulnerable. That's how he's targeted people—at their weakest."

She looked at the roasted lamb soaking in its savory juices on her plate. The meat suddenly sickened her. She tore the bread into small pieces, hoping that she would be able to swallow them.

"If there's anything you need, I'll be at the Srpski Kraj Hotel for another month."

***

The following morning, Života and Sava sat riveted, paying rapt attention to the crushing news spilling forth from Radio Belgrade's frantic announcer. "Fresh off the press from the Belvedere Palace in Vienna, where Yugoslavian Prime Minister Dragiša Cvetković and German Foreign Minister Joachim von Ribbentrop sealed the Tripartite Pact by signing it."

Sava's slightly raised lips parted. "Nooo…" What would happen to her troubled nation? A horror for every Yugoslav, to be aligned with Adolf Hitler and his Third Reich. She felt off-kilter. "I'm going to ring Vlado."

Gulping down the last dregs of her coffee, she lifted the black receiver and asked the exchange switchboard operator to patch her through to Surrey, England. She was informed that no international calling was available. Fear vibrated in every inch of her body.

"Apparently, all the telephone lines were busy." Reaching for her jacket, she turned back. "I'm going to the university. If Vlado calls or telegrams, please let him know our awful news."

She rushed to catch the bus, her nerves rattled.

CHAPTER TEN

ZORA

Kragujevac, the Kingdom of Yugoslavia
March 25, 1941

IT HAD RAINED CONTINUOUSLY without a break, the heavy storm pounding their roof and windows, adding to the gloomy atmosphere inside. With hushed tones, Zora bent to Dušica. "It's as if the darkest days have been cast upon us, and everyone's shrouded in a thin layer of dread."

Holding the *Politika* in her hand, she perused the headlines once again, reiterating article after article that detailed their signing of the Tripartite Pact with Hitler and the Axis Powers. "Nothing good will come of us being in bed with Hitler." Zora pressed her fingers to her forehead. "In one fell swoop we are aligned with the devil."

The signing left her, her family, and just about everyone they knew utterly dismayed. Nevertheless, Zora's focus remained on how this new arrangement would impact the hierarchy of the Royal Yugoslav Army, particularly Goran. Would the Yugoslav Royal Army immediately unite forces with the Third Reich?

"We must stay positive until we learn more," Zora emphasized to Dušica, but her words were really meant for her children, who were eavesdropping around the corner.

Lenka returned to the kitchen. "All right, Mama; the younger ones are tucked in—even Vuk, who fell right to sleep. What else do you need help with?"

Zora cast a glance at Neven, who had the *Glas Šumadije* and *Politika* newspapers strewn across the table; she knew he was attempting to locate a potential clue as to what might happen next. Her family no longer believed Yugoslavia would be spared.

It was late, but they were wide awake when a knock on the door had them jumping. "Who could be here at this hour?" Cautiously curious, Zora placed a hand over her racing heart.

"Goran," shrieked Stana, brushing past Neven to rush into his arms. He was soaked and dripping water on the floor.

"We've missed you sooo much," Stana cried. "C'mon, let me take your wet jacket off."

Zora felt her pulse flutter. There her oldest son stood proudly in his Jugoslovenske Kraljevske Vojske Army jacket. She noticed his wider shoulders, more angular features, and the newly gained, sinewy muscles. In an instant, Goran had transformed into both a man and a soldier. She drew nearer, breathing him in, as only a mother could, hugging him tightly, never wanting to let him go. But as she inhaled, she smelled a whiff of something, so she ever so gently whispered, "After everyone's settled, I'll draw you a nice warm bath with Epsom salts and my lavande ulje. It will be nice to soak your weary body."

"I'd like that. It's wonderful being home." Goran lifted her in one quick swoop and spun her around.

Enjoying the chance to act silly, Zora leaned her head back, suddenly freer in this moment of lightheartedness.

Lowering his mother, Goran reached for his Tetka Dušica, then Neven and Lenka. "I've missed every one of you."

"How long will you be home?" Zora's eyes glistened with tears of happiness, thrilled to have him back in the fold.

"Initially, it was a planned three-day break, then, ah, there was a last-minute change. I have to meet my unit at the train station tomorrow at, ah, five thirty in the morning."

"Five or six hours—that's it?" Alarm flickered across her face.

Goran nodded sadly. "I'm sorry, Mama. It's out of my control."

Zora found it odd that he avoided making eye contact with her. Fear spread through her belly, and her thoughts filled with conflicting emotions. What was he concealing? With her characteristic pragmatism, she swiftly recovered and clapped her hands. "C'mon everyone, let's make the most of every moment. Our lives have changed so rapidly, who knows when we'll next be together?" Acting with rare spontaneity, she asked Neven to wake his brothers, emphasizing the importance of Goran's arrival home. "I want everyone included because we're blessed tonight. Tomorrow we'll sleep."

Turning to Dušica, she asked, "What do you say we make a big batch of palačinke to celebrate his homecoming, if we have enough eggs?"

"We have enough." Dušica grinned. "Let me run upstairs and wake Marko. I'll bring a couple of eggs and extra flour."

"You're a lifesaver."

Zora had noticed in the past two months that Lenka had become more isolated and emotional since her fiancé Simo had departed for the army. She wondered how long it would be until she peppered Goran with questions about Simo.

It was coincidental, but no sooner had Zora thought this than Lenka suddenly asked Goran, "Have you seen Simo anywhere?"

Goran's mouth turned into a frown. "I haven't, but it's impossible to cross paths with him because we're assigned to different units. His unit's stationed over two hundred kilometers from mine, but Simo's a good soldier, so there's no reason to worry."

The enticing aroma of palačinke filled the air, drawing everyone nearer to the table. Zora turned to watch her children, and in that poignant split second she longed to capture this moment with every one of them, happily content in their togetherness, so pure and incorruptible. She acknowledged her immense riches.

Overcome by a foreboding sensation, she suddenly dropped the spatula she was holding as an icy chill threatened to consume her, making it difficult to breathe. Gasping, she placed her hands on her knees in an attempt to get air to her lungs. But as quickly as it began, it was over—leaving her momentarily baffled.

"Jeez, Goran; you're gobbling up mine, too. Stop; are you really that hungry?" Stana shouted playfully. It was this exchange that pulled Zora out of whatever fog she had been in.

"Goran, when have you last eaten?" Zora asked her oldest, realizing he may not have eaten in a while.

Once more, Goran avoided making eye contact with her as he fidgeted in his chair. "Two days."

Zora observed a flush creeping up his neck. What's he hiding from me? she wondered. She grew increasingly concerned as things got stranger and stranger. She shot her sister a worried look, as if to communicate her lack of food.

"What about a bowl of kupus bean soup, and pogača from dinner?" Dušica suggested.

Goran's face spread into a grin. "Ohhh boy, yeah."

Dušica instructed Lenka, "Please help me carry a pot of soup from upstairs."

After he'd finished eating, Goran entertained them with amusing tales about the Royal Yugoslav Army's journey through the Kingdom of Yugoslavia.

"What was your favorite?" Stana inquired, seated on the cold floor with her legs crossed.

Goran's face broke into a slow smile. "The Bay of Kotor, because they have little sleepy fishing villages dotted along the coastline, adding to the charm of the area. The Montenegrins enjoyed chatting with us over coffee and cigarettes. The residents were warm and friendly, and unbelievably, not a single person in Montenegro was employed."

"You still remember those jokes?" Zora laughed before turning to explain to her children that for centuries there had been a running joke between the Serbs and Montenegrins about who was the laziest.

Goran's eyes shone. "Mama, you've often said how much you wanted to see the coast."

Zora placed her hand over her heart. "Yes." This son of mine has a memory that never fails him, she thought.

"We also checked on two of our bigger monasteries, even though both were perched high in the mountains. Going up to Cetinje in Montenegro was the real killer."

"Why?" Neven asked.

"It's a dizzying drive to the top. You have to snake around while you're climbing. The hairpin turns in our trucks upset my stomach and made me so dizzy. I wasn't able to look down, or I would have gotten sick."

"Why?" Čedo asked, mimicking Neven.

"Why, you silly goose? Because my belly flipped and flopped like a little goldfish," Goran said, standing quickly to pick up Čedo before turning him upside down and shaking him by his feet. Laughing, Goran asked him, "How does your belly feel now that you're upside down?"

Letting out a loud chuckle, Čedo whooped and hollered.

Seated, Goran continued his story. "We convoyed up to Slovenia and down through Šibenik until we circled the cliffs to Monastery Ostrog." He looked across at his mother.

"You got to Ostrog?" Her hands clasped together, Zora's smile opened. While she was tickled to hear about Ostrog, something niggled at the back of her neck. Why was the army interested enough to check out their monasteries? It made her curious. Unless…? No, she was just being silly. Facing the others, she explained, "When your aunt and I were young, we visited Ostrog, a wonderful healing monastery at the top of a mountain, which left a lasting impression on us. We witnessed far too many sick people, even lepers, sleeping on the steps leading to the monastery, their hopes hinged on a miracle." Clapping, she jumped up. "All right everyone, it's time for bed."

***

Zora talked quietly with Neven and Stana until Goran finished bathing.

"Wow, I feel like a new person," Goran exclaimed.

"So...the bath was good? Be thankful we still have soap; that's a credit to Tetka Sava."

Goran grinned. "It felt like heaven."

"How will your army handle taking orders from Hitler? Have your higher-ups mentioned anything?" Neven asked. These questions had also crossed Zora's mind, and she was interested in hearing Goran's thoughts.

"Listen, stay close to Čika Marko's shortwave radio tomorrow, or the following day, and be sure to tune into Radio Belgrade." Tilting his head, Goran continued, "I wish I could tell you more—unfortunately, I can't." He lifted his hands before shrugging.

"Well, what has your captain said?" Neven asked.

"He's said little."

"Hmmm." Neven pushed his glasses up his nose. "And where might you be headed tomorrow, dear brother o' mine? Something tells me you're covertly involved in a dangerous deed?"

Goran's face and neck took on a multitude of red and purple tones, but he said nothing. Not a word.

He's obfuscating because he's not permitted to say what's about to take place, Zora realized. Inhaling a shaky breath, she studied both sons. Something terrible was about to happen, she felt it in her bones, and she understood Goran's refusal to look at anyone earlier. While fretting about her oldest, she admired Neven's ability to delve into and comprehend the intricacies of the complicated political situation unfolding. Both boys, despite their immense differences, were perfectly in sync.

As she gazed at them, the back door creaked open, and in waltzed Peda.

"Goran!" Peda exclaimed, one hand on the wall for support. "How's it going, my big army guy?"

Zora watched Goran stand and force a smile as he clasped his father's hand. "Tata, good to be here. And yes, it's going well."

***

At 4:30 A.M., Zora and her family gathered outside in the misty darkness to say their heartfelt goodbyes, blowing kisses and waves of love.

With a final wave, Goran turned at the end of Gružanska Street and vanished.

"Every part of me will be praying for his safety." Zora inhaled a voluminous amount of air.

"Don't, Zora. He's young and he's strong. You've got to believe that he'll be safe, or you'll make yourself crazy," Dušica said, offering a "tsk, tsk," as she glanced at her wristwatch. "C'mon, if we don't dress soon, we'll likely be late for work."

Walking back inside, Zora sighed dismally. "I have the feeling deep in my gut, he's involved in something perilous."

"Let's discuss it on our way to work." Dušica bounded up the staircase.

***

Goran and a select group of Royal Yugoslav soldiers were on the train to Belgrade for a top-secret mission. No one except his captain had any of the details. Goran had only been told to head straight to the Yugoslav Air Force headquarters in Zemun. General Borivoje Mirković, the no-nonsense Brigadier General, second in command to General Dušan Simonović of the Yugoslav Air Force, would offer them specific instructions.

CHAPTER ELEVEN

PEDA

*Kragujevac, the Kingdom of Yugoslavia
March 27, 1941*

BARELY AWAKE, PEDA SAT at the table with his hair rumpled and his face creased from the marks made by his pillow. As soon as he took his first sip of coffee, he heard it. A subtle moan. It prompted him to stand, and he spotted Neven outside of the back door, struggling to breathe. Taking three giant steps, he shouted, "Breathe, Neven. There you go; in and out…Whatever it was, you can tell us later. Let's make sure your breathing's back to normal first."

Peda saw the newspapers tucked underneath Neven's arm. His son typically ran five or six miles every morning to get the paper, so why was he breathless this morning? Listening to him panting, Peda grabbed his arm. "Let's get you inside and on a chair."

Several minutes passed before his breathing returned to normal. "Last night, Tata…there was a putsch. A military putsch," Neven squeaked.

"You cannot be serious?" Peda rubbed his fingers under his chin.

Coming into the kitchen, Zora could tell by the looks on their faces something serious had occurred. Looking again at her son, she placed her hands on her hips. "Will one of you tell me what's wrong?" Once Peda explained, she picked up the newspaper and scanned the headlines. "Peda, our military took command of our government— *Bože Sačuvaj*. Was this the secret mission Goran could not discuss with us?" Lifting a hand to cover her mouth, she asked, "What are the odds Goran's unit was involved with this coup?"

Peda shook his head in disbelief. Lighting a cigarette, he said, "I—I don't know."

Tugging on her threadbare coat, Zora looked intently at Neven. "I've got to leave for work, so while the others get ready for school, please fill your father in on the crucial news. And make sure Stana informs Čika Marko."

Peda felt the slight whenever she asked Stana or Neven to read to him, even though he knew she didn't mean to be patronizing. Illiteracy had never been a concern in his family until he relocated to the industrialized city of Kragujevac and married Zora. Here he felt "less than." All the Nikolić sisters had an education and loved spending hours at the Kragujevac library, burying themselves in books. If that wasn't enough, Sava and two of his brothers-in-law, Marko and Vlado, had university degrees.

Not one of his siblings, even Seja, whom he thought was smart, could read or write. His parents had prioritized visiting every tavern and kafana in Žabljak, neglecting their eleven children's education.

Neven lifted the newspaper and began reading aloud. "'In response to the news of the putsch, Hitler was filled with such rage that he violently tore apart the Tripartite

Pact. Tata, he wants to punish us, doesn't he? He wants blood, Serbian blood." Squinting, Neven stared at his father.

"Son, you're just seventeen," he said, stretching his arms in the air. "By the time I was your age, I'd already spent a year fighting in the war, while you have been getting a fine education, and now know everything. Do you wanna know my opinion? Hitler would be a fool to challenge us, but he's too damn eager to get his hands on our bauxite, copper, and chrome." He expressed frustration by throwing his hands in the air. "Yeah, continue."

"Here's one. Hitler directed the invasion of Yugoslavia at the same time as Greece. As he said, his intention or plan was to annihilate us."

Peda's brow furrowed. "That's impossible."

"It's what's written." Neven winced.

He was still unconvinced, even though Neven was an excellent reader. Peda did not believe Neven was making any of this up, but it was just too hard to swallow.

Pushing his floppy hair off his forehead, Neven said, "Tata, there was a book written by Adolf Eichmann called *The Madagascar Plan*. Ever hear of it?"

Peda crossed his arms, offering an insolent air of defiance as he stared at his son. He knows I can't read, he thought; why the hell is he asking me about this ridiculous book?

"Eichmann's book suggested that Germany relocate their entire population of Jews—that's over four million—to Madagascar, in the Indian Ocean. Hitler not only adopted the book's logic, but he also turned it into his own mission, calling it the 'Final Solution to the Jewish Question.'"

Peda's bloodshot eyes narrowed. "Hold on; that can't be right," he said, shaking his head. "Neven, you've got it wrong."

The paper fell from Neven's hands, causing him to rub his eyes. He picked up the newspaper again and read another article. "Oh, boy. They have ousted Cvetković, Cincar-Marković, and Prince Regent Paul from the Cabinet."

"What?" Peda twisted around. "That can't be right." Feeling tetchy and irritable, he tried to open one of the jammed kitchen drawers.

"Tata, what do you need?"

"Matches." Peda continued scrounging in other drawers but wound up empty.

Neven found a pack of matches and handed them to his father. Lighting a cigarette, Peda felt altogether frazzled and unable to accept the jarring news. "Who pushed the Monarchy out? Who did this?" He reflected on what the Karađorđević Monarchy had stood for all these years in Yugoslavia. He was certain King Alexandar's shift from a monarchy to a dictatorship had brought unity among the Yugoslavs. Peda believed that unity would see them through. Had he been mistaken?

Glancing at the clock, Neven interrupted his father. "Five minutes until I have to leave. Is there anything else?"

"Yeah, give me a minute." Feeling queasy, Peda chugged a full glass of water and unexpectedly thought about his mother's obsession with the Monarchy. Was it really respect that she had for them, or more a fascination because they were royals? It brought to mind the day King Alexandar was assassinated in Marseilles and his cousin, Prince Regent Paul, had to step in because Prince Peter was only a child of eleven.

Neven fidgeted with his glasses. "Here's one about Dr. Vlado Maček, the Peasant Party leader, who has shared his frustration regarding the putsch. Want me to read that?"

"Not really, but it's still odd." Peda closed his eyes, hoping to quell his mounting nausea. "Why would Maček be upset? Wasn't he the one who'd insisted on the enormous Banovina for the Croatian people, supposedly to solve the unhappiness the Croatians have felt for years?"

"The Cvetković-Maček Sporazum?"

"That's it." Peda snapped his fingers.

"Yes, well, here's another article talking about how Maček's considering the position of Deputy Prime Minister, offered by our new government."

"You're kidding…?" Peda slapped the table with his hand.

"Tata, you'll want to hear this one from the United Press Association, because it's a message from our new King Peter II. It was a military coup that took place early this morning. He's saying that all Serbs, Croats, and Slovenes must rally around the throne because he, his army, and air staff with General Simonovich ,will lead the country."

"Hmmm, I cannot believe a seventeen-year-old would speak that way."

"He is the exact same age as me. Doesn't he attend a fancy boarding school near Surrey, England? Maybe that's why he's sounding so proper. Or perhaps top military personnel involved in the coup wrote it on his behalf?"

Rubbing his shoulder, Peda wished he had drunk less last night. "What about Goran? Any mention of his unit's involvement?"

"No, nothing."

"Anything else?" Peda asked, more animated after downing his second cup of coffee.

"I've got to get to school, but I'll read this last one. They're inferring the Brits might have been behind the coup. It's proposed that the British whispered into the ears of General Dušan Simonović, the Commander of the Air Force, and Brigadier General Bora Mirković, in hopes of bringing governmental change. A Major Ivan Knezović's mentioned too."

His father reared up, eyes bulging. "So…let me get this straight. You're saying *our* Yugoslav Air Force, Yugoslav Army, and Royal Guards took part in this mission?" Peda inhaled the smoke from his unfiltered Lucky Strikes, his nostrils flaring.

"Not me, Tata, the individual who drafted the article; it's his opinion. Our military seized control of various government buildings in Belgrade, including the offices of Cvetković and Cincar-Marković, our police headquarters, the bridge over the Sava River, and other ministries' offices."

"Dammit, I need a drink before my head explodes." Peda released a powerful gust of smoke as his heart pumped wildly in his chest.

The words slipped out of Neven's mouth. "But…it's not even eight o'clock in the morning."

Peda lunged across the room, grasping his son's throat in his large hands. His eyes transformed into spools of black, and spittle dripped down his chin as he shouted in Neven's pale face: "Don't *ever* question me." He wrenched his hands away but not before he smelled his own rank breath, which he knew filled Neven's nostrils. Snatching his jacket from the hook, he slammed the back door.

***

Neven's body slumped down to the ground.

"Neven!" Stana shouted, emerging from behind. She kneeled, her brown hair cascading over her face. "Where does it hurt?" she asked, her voice cracking. Stana turned to Vuk, who was on her heels. "Hurry, Vuk, bring me a warm washcloth." Leaning over his face, Stana whispered, "How did this happen?"

Neven responded hoarsely, "I didn't mean to, I—I just asked why he needed a drink so early in the morning, and he immediately flew at me...Then everything blurred."

"Ohh, Neven, why does he treat you like this?" She picked up his eyeglasses. "Let's make sure they're not broken." Stana carefully checked for damage, then wiped the lenses clean with the edge of her shirt. "We've got to tell Mama about this. She's under the impression he's getting better. But he's not..."

Neven stammered, "Please, Stana...don't make trouble."

***

The shame was a hard blow to his gut, making him want to run and hide, but he continued to walk. Feeling panicked, he sucked on his cigarette and held the smoke in his lungs for as long as possible, until he began to choke on it, coughing. He never should have reacted so violently. Christ, Neven was a good kid and didn't deserve that sort of response. The scariest part, though, was how quickly it escalated, with him metamorphosing into someone he did not know.

He had to get to Stara Srbija, but the second his feet touched onto Knez Miloša Street, he heard the cheering. Crowds and crowds of people were everywhere in the streets, celebrating, laughing, and singing joyfully. Swept into their festive vortex, Peda observed major streets teeming with farmers, sheep, factory workers, and students, all electrified by the news of the coup. Swiftly downing several shots, he witnessed the galvanized people of Kragujevac thumb their noses at Hitler.

He accepted his last shot before heading to the kafana, where he met Đuro. Taking a seat next to him at the bar, he sat riveted, listening to Winston Churchill address the Yugoslav people from the BBC in London:

> Early this morning, the Yugoslav nation found its soul. A revolution has taken place, and the ministers who yesterday signed away the honor and freedom of the country are reported to be under arrest. This patriotic movement arises from the wrath of a valiant and warlike race at the betrayal of their country, by the weakness of their rulers, and the foul intrigues of the Axis Powers. The British Empire and its allies will make common cause with the Yugoslav nation, and we shall continue to march and strive together until victory is won.

Peda shut his eyes, unable to come to terms with the news that Prince Regent Paul was in custody. Was it true?

Tapping his arm, Đuro said, "Mark my word, we'll be at war sooner than we anticipated. What about you, will you fight?" Đuro asked, the upper half of his body turned toward him.

In annoyance, Peda slammed his fist on the bar. "I defended this country two decades ago, and I doubt this old broken body could take any more battering. But it's the ones inside that never quite heal." Tapping his heart, he explained: "I lost two brothers in the last war. My oldest brother, Bojan, taught me so much about life, including the value of demanding work. His death shattered something inside of me. Brothers, we'd fought side by side, and…to this day, I wish I had taken the bullet—not Bojan. So, no, I'm not particularly interested in fighting."

The passage of time had done nothing to diminish being forced to march through the muck of freezing rivers and streams and trekking across ridiculously narrow pathways over the slick mountain ranges, where several of his friends had slid to their deaths. He understood the struggle of dysentery from rotten food and foraging for dead animal carcasses in the woods, hoping for leftover meat. No, he had no desire to return to those horrid trenches, not unless his country greatly needed him.

"Who knows what the Monarchy will do? Miško, another?" Peda pushed his shot glass to the edge of the wooden bar.

Đuro frowned. "Have you not heard about Hitler's newest directive? *Glas Šumadije's* headlines explained it."

"What?"

"Hitler issued his Directive Number 25: 'Yugoslavia must be destroyed as quickly as possible.'"

Peda was openmouthed.

Finishing up, Đuro stood. "It's time. He's aiming for us, whether you want to believe it or not. But if I were you, I'd have that lovely wife of yours and your children fully prepared. See you tomorrow."

Scowling, Peda double-tapped his shot glass on the bar.

***

March 30, 1941

Walking through town, Peda was unable to ignore the motorcycles, vehicles, and trucks crowding in on the street with the sheep, horses, and peasant carts. The vehicles and trucks carried young men, soldiers readying themselves for the Royal Yugoslav Army. On the corner, he watched families bidding farewell to their sons, offering jackets and scarves. Soldiers streamed in from surrounding villages and nearby selo, and he wondered where each one would end up, before his thoughts turned to Goran's whereabouts.

At the kafana, Peda overheard various customers talking about a recent broadcast from the BBC. Plunking down on the stool beside Đuro, he asked, "What did I miss?"

Filling him in, Đuro said, "Listen up; here's the BBC announcer again. Maybe he will repeat the message."

"War is around the corner for Yugoslavia," the radio announced.

Stunned, Peda responded, "What nonsense…How would a Brit know anything about us Yugoslavs?"

Laughing, Đuro said, "Based on today's *Glas Šumadije*, there's a good chance they're going to call up older guys, because the army might need more men."

Peda placed his fingers on the bridge of his nose. "There's no way, Đuro; we would slow them down."

"You can't be serious?" Đuro questioned as his gaze fixed on him. "I was unaware of the stark difference in our views on fighting and war, Peda. But I'll tell you this: if there's a need for someone like me, I plan on signing up." Đuro puffed out his chest.

Chugging his drink, Peda shook his head.

CHAPTER TWELVE

SAVA

Belgrade, the Kingdom of Yugoslavia
April 06, 1941

THE CONSTANT RATTLING JARRED her awake from her exquisitely rare dream. Kicking off her blankets, Sava rubbed her eyes and wondered what was causing that noise. At first, she thought it sounded like thousands of bees buzzing about, but the hum of a louder vibration made her think differently. Jumping from her bed, she rushed to the window, and in that split second, a deafening roar brought everything into view as she saw multiple planes above. "What in the world?" She blinked, fingers touching parted lips.

Just then, Život poked his head in, shouting, "Gospođo—hurry. We're under attack."

Unable to hear above the thunderous noise, she was startled by a flash of movement from the periphery of her vision. Tearing her eyes away, she acknowledged him with a swift nod, spinning back around. Mesmerized, her eyes stayed riveted on the planes—one after another. "None of these are ours, are they, Život?"

Standing erect, he paled. "Afraid not, Gospođo. It's the Germans' Luftwaffe."

Realization hit. Swallowing, Sava gripped the window sill to brace herself, as a sourness made its way up to her gullet. "W—we're being attacked?"

"Yes, and it's crucial you move away from those windows, Gospođo. It's not safe to be standing in front of them. Please, come downstairs."

Throwing on some clothes, Sava grabbed her boots in her hands and sprinted down the circular staircase to her well-loved kitchen with its soaring ceilings and full-length windows.

"Ohhh." She stopped in her tracks, her mouth falling open as more planes flew in perfect formation past the kitchen windows, the rattling enough to cause her to grit her teeth. "They are so close…and so low…"

"They're German Stukas, better known as Ju87s. They purposely built them to fly low. Listen, I promised your husband if something like this happened, I'd do everything in my power to keep you safe. Right now, you're making it rather tricky. Vlado built a shelter in his study in case of war, and that's where we need to hunker down."

"I—ah, I understand, but could I have a minute to gather myself?" She needed to call Vlado and her family in Kragujevac…Gripped by the onslaught of aggression, her mind swirled in several directions as she looked at the clock. "Why six thirty in the morning, and why today? Why would Hitler attack us on…" Realization smacked her in the face. "That cagey sneak." With a finger poised above her lips, Sava paused. "I wonder if he was mistaken?"

"Who?"

"Adolf Hitler. He must have thought today was our Easter—that's it." As she snapped her fingers, she had another thought. "He might not have known today's only Palm Sunday for us; either way it seems like a stupid error on their part for not checking."

"So, you think—"

Sava didn't allow him to finish his sentence. "I wonder if he thought today was our Easter. Or perhaps he's too ignorant to know that we follow the Julian calendar instead of the Gregorian, like most of the Christian world uses."

"I would doubt Hitler even believes in a God."

Her raw emotions built to a visceral rage. Spots of red swept across her cheeks. "How dare he?"

Before Života could respond, the entire house reverberated. To support themselves, they grabbed hold of the heavy marble kitchen counter, hanging on tightly. Heart hammering in her chest, Sava closed her eyes, imagining herself elsewhere, possibly at a romantic dinner with Vlado, or along the Montenegrin coastline. She ran back to the windows after the house steadied itself. "More?"

"Gospođo, you've got to move from those windows before one of them explodes."

"All right," she said, although she refused to budge.

A loud, thunderous roar forced her to jump way back as more Stukas and medium bombers rushed past at breakneck speed. Their screeching, high-pitched cries filled the air, jolting the very foundation of her home. She covered her ears; the shrieks grew louder as they inched lower, dropping insidious metal that she knew was piercing her beloved city.

Pivoting, she bolted upstairs to her bedroom, where she had a wider view of the city. It was here she made out the lettering and the numbers on the enemy planes, which Života had previously pointed out to her. There were Ju87s and HE 1 medium Heinkels being escorted in by the larger Messerschmitt aircraft. Coincidentally, one flashed by with a Yugoslavian insignia. Sava valiantly saluted this one, murmuring, "*Hvala bogu.*"

Coming from behind, Života clapped his hands. "That's one of ours from our 451st Fighter Group out of Zemun. Gospođo, please step away from the windows."

Hearing the authority and firmness in his tone, Sava walked away. This man was no accountant. There's much more to his layered story, she realized.

Suddenly, glass was shattering and she felt a blast of wind whipping through.

"Downstairs, now," he commanded.

Feeling chastised, Sava followed him to the study, watching while he tapped a code into the back wall, and voila, it slid open, revealing a comfortable room with chairs, a sofa, and cabinets stocked with lamps, food, and candles.

"Well, well." Sava grinned, studying it all, her hands crossed over her chest. "My Vlado's full of surprises."

"He's prepared well, Gospođo." Clearing his throat, he looked up at her. "I'm sure you've now guessed why I am here?"

"You're military, correct?"

"I was. Your husband's a wise man. He knew he wouldn't be able to withstand something like this." Shaking his head, he pressed his lips together. "His lungs; they're too fragile."

Choking back a sob, Sava hung her head. What was wrong with me? she wondered. Why didn't I leave my job and go with him, as a dutiful wife would?

Života fiddled with the radio dials until a cracked voice from Radio Belgrade broke through. Sounding panicked, the announcer began:

> With no apparent warning, Operation Punishment has begun. The German Luftwaffe unleashed hundreds of bombs across Belgrade, destroying homes, buildings, and structures in its calculated path of destruction. This morning, German Stukas and German Heinkels invaded Belgrade's air space, continuing its persistent hammering of brutal bombs on innocent citizens of Belgrade as they scurried to find shelter. Hitler's goal was to crush Yugoslavia purposefully. We hear sounds from the anti-aircraft guns, explosives, bombs, and the hissing of fires ravaging Belgrade. Fires thick with smoke, chunks of glass, concrete, metal, and glass fly as we watch it unfold. Blood is everywhere. Bodies are dismembered, sirens roaring, buildings collapsing before our eyes, entire streets suddenly wiped out! Houses are ripped apart from the bombs."

"Ohhh, no." Shaking in disbelief, Sava choked out a moan as a swift surge of nausea forced her hands to cover her mouth.

"Deep breaths, Gospođo, deep breaths. It's a lot to take in. I'll be right back; there's something I must check."

Slumping to her knees, she whispered, "*Oče naš, iže jesi na nebesjeh…*"

Života lowered his head until she finished reciting the Lord's Prayer, then crossed himself and hurried out.

After some time, Sava tiptoed toward the kitchen, only to hear a thunderous roar, followed by a hefty group of single-engine bombers whooshing by, leaving a trail of white smoke. Unfortunately, that smoke metamorphosed into clouds of curling black smoke, and as she glanced above, she spotted a Yugoslav plane climbing before it unexpectedly burst into flames, igniting their sky. "God, no," she screamed, her fist flying to cover her mouth. Exhaling sharp gusts of air, she felt an inexplicable foreboding.

Života came running in but stopped short to look. "Dragi Bože!" Sava saw the concern marking his face. "I'm afraid this aerial attack's just the beginning. They've already summoned the Wehrmacht's ground troops to advance toward Belgrade. In fact, we caught word the German Twelfth Army was already positioned in Bulgaria, although we have no idea whether they'll pounce on Greece first, or us." Rubbing his thick neck, he said, "Want my opinion? They're marching here, from every corner. Our largest concern will be whether our military had enough time to secure our trains or waterways."

This man was a fount of knowledge, but something niggled the back of her neck. "I'm surprised by the scope of your military strategies."

"Um, I was in the Royal Yugoslav Army."

Sava folded her arms. "There's more to your story, Života, and I've got no time to peel back the layers of an onion, so please, tell me who you really are? It's crucial I reach Vlado, and my parents in Kragujevac." Sava lifted the black mouthpiece perched on Vlado's mahogany desk, but she was unable to raise an international operator no matter how often she lifted the mouthpiece from its cradle.

"They've either scrambled our signals or cut the lines, therefore we're unable to make telephone calls. Don't worry, I called England the moment the air raids sounded at dawn. Vlado was still asleep, but I managed to speak with his nephew Jovan, explaining the situation."

Sava cocked her head. "Why didn't you tell me sooner? Never mind; let's return to your background. I'm curious—my father and brothers-in-law fought in the Great War, yet not one possesses your astute military expertise." Sava's almond-shaped eyes peered at Života, enough for him to wither and turn away. "Who are you really?"

"I served as a Yugoslav Army officer and, ah…conducted intelligence operations. I am also good with numbers."

"Did my husband hire you because of your intelligence background or because you're good at managing his money?"

"Likely a little of both." This time, Života's smile reached his eyes.

"Are you familiar with a young gentleman, Duško Popov?"

Turning his compact body toward her, he rubbed his forehead. "I am. He was a student of mine, at the Military Academy."

Incredulous, Sava simply stared at him. "Duško Popov… was a student of yours…? Well, well," she said incredulously. "Now it's becoming clearer. Duško must have been the conduit between you and my husband."

The room fell silent, and it was Života's turn to stare.

Standing to her full five feet eleven inches, Sava explained. "My husband and Duško's father, Milorad, were old friends and business partners. We have spent time recently with the charismatic Duško; in fact, we stayed at his family's grand villa in Dubrovnik. Is Duško still in London doing…government work?" Her green eyes sparkled. She detested anytime men talked *around* her, to avoid telling her things. Vlado sometimes did it, especially with Duško or Života, but she always figured it out.

The air-raid sirens interrupted them, indicating more planes approaching. As they dove, it felt like a wind tunnel, as every piece of furniture shook in their path. The screeching pierced her ears, but it was the destruction from the bombs dropping that troubled her most. Fear laced her throat; she imagined the terror her friends must be feeling in the center of town. Josie, Branislav, Toma, and Milica all lived close to the university. My God, she thought. Toma. A wave of nausea caused her to run to the bathroom, where she heaved and hurled until there was nothing left.

When she emerged, sweaty and unsteady, Života handed her a cool rag. "Maybe a piece of toast to settle your stomach, Gospođo?"

"In a bit, thank you." Still shaky, Sava wiped the perspiration from her forehead and went to lie down. "I ache for Belgrade," she said, pulling her knees to her chest. "It's too much, this pounding on our small city." She shuddered as another wave roiled in her stomach. This time, she resolved to breathe through it. "What are the odds of our Air Force holding off the Luftwaffe?"

"We're not holding them off." Lowering his eyes, he pointed to the window. "You've seen the number of Luftwaffe planes. How many Yugoslav planes have we seen? Two, maybe three?" Clearing his throat, he said, "I'm not confident in how well-prepared we are."

Dabbing the wet rag over her face, Sava's eyes narrowed. "What do you mean? I thought we had plenty of soldiers.

According to the newspaper, we have approximately 1.2 million first-line troops."

"That's just it; they're figures." Cracking his knuckles, he grimaced. "They're distorted and misleading and our people deserve better. We have far fewer."

"That's impossible. How much fewer?" She sat up.

"Well, a good portion from Croatia never showed up for duty, and on March 31, the leaders of our Supreme Command communicated with our army to mobilize War Plan R-41. This meant we were under enormous pressure because we could not mobilize fast enough."

Her stomach clenched, but she had to know. "W—why hasn't anyone mentioned this before?"

"I'm not sure, but it takes a herculean effort for any army to marshal its soldiers and equipment, not to mention food, weaponry, and ammunition. Imagine transporting a tank. That takes time and skill. The Germans have massive trucks to transport their equipment. We do ours by sluggish oxen carts. A reliable military source told me that the preponderance of our equipment was old and outdated."

"I cannot believe the implications…" Sava's thoughts immediately swung to Goran. "How could we have allowed ourselves to be in this situation?" Feeling better, she rose to make herself a slice of toast.

"Who knows? We're an impoverished country, Gospođo. We haven't had the means to replenish most of our equipment. A few tanks here and there…that's about it."

"What about the leaders of our Supreme Command?"

"Too much pontificating and too little action."

"I'm numb with disbelief." Sava bit into her toast, barely tasting it.

"My concern has more to do with the significant divisions in our country. And how those divisions could widen, likely causing the death of Yugoslavia."

"You can't be serious?" Her eyes reflected pain. "Surely we can come together for the good of our country?"

Rubbing the back of his neck, he blew out a substantial breath. "I'm not so sure. Our religious and ethnic differences have broadened too far to reach a middle ground."

Sava turned toward the windows. "Hear that? They've stopped!" Feeling a jolt of energy, she swung her head around. "I need to check on my friends; will you come with me?"

"Whoa…not so fast." His eyes slid to his wristwatch. "I doubt they're finished. It's likely they're refueling in either Bulgaria, or the Rumanian airfields in Ploesti. I'm sorry, but we cannot risk leaving quite so soon."

Sava paced. "I'll go outside to check for damages."

"Hold up." Života waved his arm. "I'll handle the outside perimeter, but let's eat breakfast first."

Blowing out a large burst of air, Sava cursed under her breath before stopping mid-stride. "You know, you're really something, Života." Realizing this man was doing everything possible to keep her safe, she let down her guard, mouthing, "I appreciate your being here."

Života drew a half smile. "We should eat while we can. I'm afraid this could be a long day. Times like these, it's hard to know what'll come next. I understand your concern for your friends, but let's weather this next storm first, all right?"

Nodding, she whisked eggs, flour, and milk together to make palačinkes in her crepe pan. When she was done, she added a few slices of ham and sliced an apple. She placed the plate before him and smiled. "*Prijatno.*"

While they ate, Života shared with Sava a recent conversation he'd had with two German diplomats stationed in Belgrade. "They said Hitler's focus had not changed—he was still concentrated on Operation Barbarossa. I'm confident today's attack here has them flabbergasted."

Sava enjoyed her coffee. "Or they're talented actors. It's disheartening because our people were celebrating in the streets, and now this. Josie shared that the old Četnik leader, Kosta Pećanac, led an impromptu parade, with his veteran Četnik fighters wearing their old uniforms, marching to hear Patriarch Gavrilo's empowering speech."

"About that parade. It may have further fueled an already inflamed Hitler. Unfortunately, only a few of our higher-ups in Parliament grasped the impact of Pećanac's actions that day."

"That's preposterous. Why would an event with a few hundred old-time resistance fighters marching toward Saborna Crkva and the Serbian Orthodox Patriarchy provoke Adolf Hitler? Josie was there, and she indicated it was quite celebratory." Sava's cheeks flamed.

"Gestapo and Abwehr agents, German Military Intelligence for the Reichswehr and the Wehrmacht, similar to Britain's MI6, were also in the crowd that day, watching and listening. Who knows what they passed back to German headquarters?"

Hands clenched, Sava expelled a massive breath.

***

Minutes ticked by, and only silence. Running a hand through her hair, Sava looked to the windows, wishing the Luftwaffe gone. They'd returned two more times, hammering Belgrade more substantially than before. The German air attack was beyond her harshest imagination. Frozen with fear, she knew she wouldn't remember each minute's detail, while some would haunt her forever. Thinking about her family in Kragujevac, she wondered if they were being pummeled too. While ignorant of the truth, she could no longer ignore the darkness encroaching on Yugoslavia.

The tenacity and speed with which Adolf Hitler had pounced on the Kingdom of Yugoslavia was disconcerting. Squeezing her eyes shut, she hoped the room would no longer be blurred when she opened them; however, it blurred before it came back into focus.

"Has enough time passed, or will they again return?"

Looking at his wristwatch, he shrugged. "I wish I knew, but it'll soon be dark, so I'd say they might be done for the day. Let's wait one more hour. If they haven't returned, we'll head to town and check on your friends."

"That's fair," she said, nervously biting her lip. "I've got to make certain they're alive. Toma, Milica, and Branislav have been family to me since I first arrived in Belgrade. Josie, too." Choking up, Sava clenched and unclenched her hands. "The magnitude of what we've witnessed today, and the damage it has to have incurred, I cannot imagine…"

Života flinched. "I'm not impervious to your concern for your friends, Gospođo. In fact, I find it admirable. Again, I'm focused on *your* safety, especially after listening to the radio announcer describe the number of buildings that have collapsed. It may be difficult navigating our way in."

***

Cautiously, Života maneuvered the automobile over trees and other debris on the roadway. He and Sava watched all sorts of vehicles, from beat-up Chevrolets to luxurious limousines with diplomatic plates, and rickety carts on the verge of losing their wheels, trying to squeeze into the congested street hurrying out of town. Amidst all of this were sheep, horses, and people carrying their lives on their backs. Stunned, Sava witnessed the exodus of Belgradians walking through the chaotic cluster of traffic as truck horns blared and individuals shouted above the cacophony, juggling their bags and threadbare suitcases in their haste to depart.

The scene ahead prompted a momentary pause. Billowing black smoke swirled from the rooftops of countless homes. With a quick scan, Sava observed fires breaking out in multiple neighborhoods.

"My goodness, it's frightening." Her voice was thick with dread.

"The white smoke's from their ack-ack guns," Života added.

Sava blinked rapidly and her breath caught as she breathed in the smoke and dusty gravel. Inside the car, the granules crept into her nasal cavities, causing her to sneeze. As she looked for tissues in her pocketbook, she tasted the grit in her mouth.

"Do you want to continue, Gospođo?"

"Forgive me, Života, but yes; we've got to try."

Inching closer, she rolled down her window, mistakenly hoping to draw in a bit of fresh air, but no sooner than she did, a woman clad in a black babushka rushed over to Sava's car window, yelling at her, "Leave now, don't wait."

A putrid smell, akin to burnt rubber, filled the car. "Oh, brother." Sava sniffed before shoving her hands over her mouth. The stench, mixed with the dust, sent them into a coughing spell. Why didn't I bring something to cover our mouths and noses? she chided herself.

"It's impossible to go further. The rest we will have to do on foot. We're the only ones coming in."

Riveted, Sava couldn't avert her eyes from the flood of people leaving, their lives perched heavily on their shoulders. Loaded with their valuables, hundreds of families in rattletrap vehicles departed Belgrade. Filled with shock, Sava pressed her fingers to her lips. "Where will they end up?"

Forging through the debris, they encountered more panicked strangers offering advice. A disheveled woman in blood-soaked pajamas, pushing a cart, asked, "My Lazo; where's my Lazo?" Two ashen-faced men sprinted by, and in a British accent shouted, "Turn around—don't go any further—too bloody awful."

"Gospođo?" Života clutched her elbow. "Perhaps we should heed their advice?"

Sava wasn't ready to give up. "What could be worse than what we've seen?" she said as she stumbled on a piece of metal. It was tricky scaling the mountain of wreckage flung in complete disorder. Her throat, chest, and lungs burned from the mixture of grime and smoke.

When they made it to the center of town—Trg Republike—Sava saw the brunt of the Führer's fury. Many of the streets were blocked; others had simply vanished. Some apartment buildings were shredded, while others were damaged beyond repair. They observed a living room left dangling in the breeze and an apartment disintegrating before their eyes, collapsing to nothingness.

Hotter and thicker air from the buildings' particles caused tiny pops of explosions. Tucking her face inside her shirt, Sava tried to prevent more smoke from seeping into her lungs. Why had I not better prepared? she asked herself again. Sirens blasted. Ambulances buzzed by. There was a car flipped upside down with a man still sitting in the driver's seat, his eyes vacant, apparently killed on impact. Bloodied bodies, some torn, others shredded, lay dead in the streets. Horns blasted, people screamed, and Sava wanted to cover her ears from the earsplitting sounds of desperate mothers' howls, searching for missing children. I am not brave enough to continue, she realized.

"I—I can't believe they've…" Struggling to find her voice, she said, "Never have I seen…" Wild-eyed, Sava scrutinized the total obliteration. "The rubble, the bodies." Emotions flooded her senses.

Walking again, Života instantly pulled her out of the way. "That was an explosive we just sidestepped. Be careful and watch where you're walking."

Sava's breath came in panicked gasps.

"Gospođo?" He whipped around. "Let's slow your breathing." Pressing his hands on her shoulders, he said, "Nice and easy; that's good. Now exhale through your nose." Pulling a pressed white handkerchief from his back pant pocket, he handed it to her. "Here, wrap this over your mouth and nose, like those American cowboys, and c'mon; let's find your friends."

Adrenaline spiked in Sava as she maneuvered through the maze, but only until her eyes grew with disbelief. "My God, these poor people…lying in heaps in the streets." Sputtering, she looked around as comprehension sunk in. "It's been hours, and we've still got our dead unattended in the streets, bloodied and dismembered?" Sava momentarily closed her eyes, weeping. "What they have done to our people…it's unforgivable. It will be impossible to erase this from our minds."

Turning away, she saw him—the tiny boy lying alone and lifeless in the middle of the street. As she sank to the ground, Sava gathered him in her arms, pulling him close. He was bleeding from what she assumed to be a traumatic head injury, and she rocked him back and forth. Choking back tears clogging her airway, she pleaded, "How could they have been so ruthless with these little guys?" Her body swayed as she hummed to him.

"Gospođo…" Života murmured, dropping to his knees. "It's time you let this little one go." Taking great care, he removed the boy's stiff fingers from Sava's and lifted him from her arms.

Consumed by a profound sorrow for her courageous community, something welled up inside, making her want to sing. She pictured this sweet boy frolicking with his family in the grass somewhere, a swing nearby. Her voice grew stronger as she sang the words to the hauntingly fitting "Gospodi pomiluj, Gospodi pomiluj, Gospodi pomiluj," from the Jektenija za upokojene. Suddenly, a veil lifted, and people, survivors, began to slowly emerge from behind the bombed-out buildings, listening.

Moving timidly, Sava watched them solemnly mouthing the words. As her voice swelled, Sava heard the agony in their voices as they sang along to the omnipresent Liturgy for the dead. Humbly, she placed her hand over her heart, hoping her singing might somehow bring these people a small measure of comfort. And out of nowhere, an evocative memory of her childhood priest performing a funeral surfaced. Sava had ingrained his parting words: Give rest eternal, in blessed falling asleep, O Lord, to the souls of thy servants, departed this *life, and make their memory eternal. Večnja pamjat.* Bowing, she crossed herself and wordlessly slipped away.

"My word, Gospođo, your voice…" Shaking his head, Života declared, "These people will never forget how you made them feel tonight."

"Thank you." Heat rose on her cheeks.

As they walked down the hill, she pointed. "There's the Srpski Kraj Hotel, where all the foreign journalists gather to file their stories. I need to run inside to send Vlado a telegram to let him know we're safe. Who knows what he may have heard on the BBC News about the attack?" But before she took a step further, she shouted, "Oh, it's moving." Dropping back, Sava watched, openmouthed, as the grand imperial hotel tipped dramatically to one side as people rushed out, yelling and shouting.

After pushing Sava further back, Života approached a nearby gentleman. "What happened?"

The man explained, "Earlier in the day a bomb struck the hotel, leaving a gaping hole in the middle of the roof."

Not caring to see this wonderful landmark collapsing in front of her, Sava turned herself around, setting her gaze instead a few meters down to where her university building stood, it too hit by a massive bomb. Her insides were shaking. "I—I cannot imagine the damage and carnage inflicted on us," she whispered, before fear struck her cold. Never could she have imagined building after building pulverized into oblivion.

In her sadness, she reminisced about the countless moments spent exploring her university's cultured hallways with her colleagues and talented historians. Would anyone ever discover the old, treasured books she had stacked against her office wall, nearly grazing the tall ceiling? Toma's office was next door to hers. Tears falling, she glanced through the crowd before finding Života. Clutching his arm, she said, "We must find Toma."

Meanwhile a small figure approached Sava from behind saying, "Sava, Sava, wait."

"Josie?"

An impish grin broke through the white ash covering Josie's face and body.

Sava reached for her friend. "Are you all right?" Sava observed a bloodied gash on her friend's chin, the bruised hands, and their noticeable trembling.

Života slipped his jacket over Josie's shoulders.

After the women embraced, Josie explained, "When the bombing started, I hurried to the hotel to wire England a message before any of the lines were severed. But the first bomb struck so quickly, while I was in the hotel. Jesus, was that ever frightening." Josie's teeth started chattering, and her voice sounded tinny to Sava.

"For the love of God…Josie, you made it out alive." Hugging her slight frame, Sava emphatically said, "*You* are coming home with us tonight—a hot bath and a clean bed, and I will not take no for an answer. But darling, have you seen Toma, Branislav, or Milica today?"

"Branislav and Milica were at the hotel with me, but I didn't see Toma."

"We've got to find him."

Sava turned, nearly colliding with a colleague. "Ljubo?" she asked, reaching out to steady him. She again tried asking after Toma, but Ljubo's eyes never settled on her. Instead, he looked from left to right, abruptly changing his direction.

Yelling over his shoulder, Ljubo spurted, "My family—I can't find any of them."

"He's in shock," Života observed.

As her fear grew, Sava took a deep, resounding breath. Darkness skirted around the edges of Toma's neighborhood, but still no Toma. Sirens wailed as they circumvented streets with overturned carts and naked children in soiled diapers crying, their shrieks piercing her heart. Mothers cried, searching for missing children. Everywhere they looked were clear indications of disorder and hysteria.

Toma's street had experienced severe damage. Rocks, stones, and chunks of steel were scattered all over the street. An icy shiver crept down her back as Sava looked about.

Života touched her elbow. "It's getting late, Gospođo. We must take every precaution against the Germans. Hear that rumbling? It's likely their Panzer division rolling in."

Stubbornly clinging to hope, Sava was not ready to give up. "Just a few more minutes, please." She knew she was testing his patience, and suddenly she saw something.

"Wait—that's Toma's fancy brown-and-white leather shoes sticking out of that pile of mud and bent steel," Sava hollered, feeling encouraged as she pointed. "He's got to be inside."

Jumping in, they clawed through sharp, mangled pieces of pipe, beams, and crushed metal, undaunted even when their hands were cut and sliced. They persevered, digging as best they could, discarding fragments of steel and metal into a chaotic heap.

"TOMA," Sava hollered when she found him. Gently patting his face, she yelled, "Toma, can you hear me?" Sava's heart pumped wildly as she awkwardly cradled his blood-splattered face.

"Let's check for a pulse," suggested Života, bending over his unmoving body. Picking up Toma's limp wrist, Života boomed, "It's weak, but he's got one. Let's gently lift him up—careful now."

Fortunately, Josie had already jumped from the pile and, whistling, somehow secured a man in a dilapidated pickup truck by offering him a fistful of dinars.

The driver agreed to drive them to the hospital, and after loading Toma on the truck bed, they wrapped their coats around him.

Outside the hospital, the driver hurriedly spoke. "I urge you to leave town right away. I saw those filthy Germans advancing toward us."

Inside, Života assumed control, instantly commanding everyone's attention. "I must see the head surgeon, right away."

Surprised by his unusually aggressive demeanor, Sava blew out short, wispy breaths until a tall young man in bloody scrubs emerged from a room marked "Surgery."

When the surgeon saw Života, he lowered his mask and broke into a huge grin.

"Ladies, my sister's son, Dr. Rade Šeran." Grinning, Života hugged his nephew, before quickly filling him in.

Dr. Rade bowed. "We're overwhelmed and have thousands injured, but I promise to work on your friend, Gospođo. I will do everything possible. You have my word." In a respectful gesture he placed the palm of his hand over his heart. "But you must take leave straightaway. We caught word…"

Života's hand jetted out to stop him. "We already heard, and we're leaving." Kissing his nephew thrice, Života pivoted. "Let's go."

Sava was taken aback when they saw the old truck still idling outside.

***

Sava guided an exhausted Josie up the staircase of her home to a private suite, with its own bath. Sava quickly bathed and put on fresh clothes before running downstairs to catch the tail end of Radio Belgrade's announcement:

> Hitler's Blitzkrieg method of attack took Belgrade by storm. The Luftwaffe's systematic air strikes flattened Belgrade, taking a good portion of the Royal Yugoslav Air Command. Our Air Command attempted to fight back, but it was not enough, for the small Royal Air Force was overpowered. The dead and wounded lay amidst the rubble. All international phone lines have been cut.

Drawing in a sharp gasp, Sava questioned how much longer Radio Belgrade would be able to broadcast the news and play the Serbian music that so many enjoyed hearing. The radio station was also the way many received their news. Would the Germans also silence that? If it stopped broadcasting, Sava was aware it would be their final link to the outside world.

"I'm not sure I thanked you enough for what you've done today, Života. You're full of surprises."

"That's my purpose here, Gospođo, to watch over you."

Bending her head, she whispered, "How could I ever thank you?"

"You have already."

"The images of lifeless bodies, some with their hands cleaved from their bodies and carelessly flung in every direction, bloody and alone, will stay with me forever." She rubbed her hands together. "It was complete devastation—how many more of our people will Hitler try to erase?"

CHAPTER THIRTEEN

ZORA

Kragujevac, the Kingdom of Yugoslavia
April 09, 1941

EVEN WITH THE TELEPHONE lines down, Zora believed Sava would find a way to reach her. Four excruciating days had passed since Hitler's brutal assault on Belgrade, and still no word from her sister. Little news trickled out, and what had described tales of horror, leaving thousands dead amidst the rubble. Gripped by fear, Zora and her family envisioned the worst probable outcome. Please let us hear something about Sava's whereabouts, Zora prayed. Could she possibly be trapped in a building somewhere? Their mother was hanging on by a thin strand of hope.

Compounded by her family's fear surrounding Sava, this morning Zora was also uneasy about the risks associated with baptizing Martha Levine's two sons into Orthodoxy. Entering the Cathedral of the Holy Assumption Serbian Orthodox Church brought about a feeling of familiarity and peace. The intricately designed Byzantine narthex reflected a beam of light streaming down through the upper dome and offered a little brightness on an otherwise nerve-racking day.

Spotting Dušica in conversation with Father Radovan, Zora moved toward where you could burn candles. With her three fingers pressed together in Troitsa, she crossed herself while offering prayers for both of her sisters and breathed in the powerful scent of incense hanging in the air, long after Father Radovan had censed the inside with his censor. The smell, combined with the monks' chanting, allowed her to remember so many moments when she and Sava had sung together in this very church. As she recalled those memories, Sava's extraordinary voice echoed in her mind, causing her heart to flutter. In a hushed voice, she whispered, "Please spare her."

A coldness instantly washed over her body, and with it, a strong premonition her sister was alive. Zora's hands shook as she gripped the metal candle stand, afraid she might knock it over. Bathed in sweat, just as quickly as it came, it left her. Inhaling deeply, she immersed herself in the familiar scent of incense and candlewax, which evoked memories of her ancestors. She asked herself if it was the strong scent that reminded her of Sava, which was why she had this premonition. Unsure of how or why these occurred, Zora knew they were becoming all too frequent.

Nevertheless, she was convinced Sava was alive. Wiping the sweat from above her lips, she glanced down the aisle, where the priest was about to begin the induction service for Martha's Jewish sons, Andrew and Steven, to be baptized. Unsteadily, Zora approached the altar.

Father Radovan clearly understood the necessity and urgency of rushing the boys' baptism by granting them an emergency dispensation. The sudden arrival of more Wehrmacht troops into Kragujevac had heightened the unpredictability of war and, with it, more Jewish round-ups. The top priority for Dušica and Marko was to have the baptism done immediately, and in absolute secrecy. If anyone had discovered Dušica and Marko hiding Jewish children in their home, there was no doubt they would face frightening consequences, likely being marked for murder. Different names, Serbian ones, were assigned to the boys: Stefan and Andrej Blešić. Steven and Andrew Levine no longer existed.

Teary-eyed, Dušica held Andrej in her arms. "We're overjoyed to have Father Radovan as our priest." Fraught with emotion, she shifted the cherubic one-year-old from one arm to the other. Both sisters stood and watched as Stefan broke away and started to run through the church. Zora hurried after him until she caught him by the arm.

Stefan clung to her hand as he tilted his head to stare in wonder at the vibrant frescos that adorned the church walls, before unexpectedly releasing her hand and taking off, screaming, "Mama…I want my Mama."

Marko's and Father Radovan's smiles froze in place hearing Stefan's piercing screams. Thank God the church is empty, Zora thought as she searched her sister's eyes. "He's still doing this?"

Nodding, Dušica wearily responded, "It's been rough, and I'm worried he will act like this while we walk through town on our way home."

"Don't worry, there's a lot to distract him; but Dušica, you need to act as though they're your kids. Everyone, including the Germans, needs to see you and Marko with them as a family. And the easiest way to establish yourselves as a family unit would be to not hide. Let others see you with your sons. Your survival depends on this."

"I—I hope you're right, but…the Germans, they're seemingly everywhere with their mean glares and their hobnailed boots with the noisy metal scuff plates."

"Just try to act like this is your family. I'll take Stefan outside now to play."

Zora guided Stefan to the grassy area by the side of the church where the flowers were blooming. She watched his eyes track a colorful butterfly as it hovered over a pussy willow, swaying in the gentle breeze. When he stooped to sniff the pussy willow, it tickled his nose and he fell backward onto the grass, as peals of laughter rang out from his belly.

Zora's mind could not stop swarming with the complicated task involved with hiding and sheltering Jews. She worried Dušica would be stuck in limbo, unsure if the Levines would even make it back. Perhaps the most intricate piece in all of this would be if, years later, they came back for their children. Would that break her sister's heart? Whose children would they then be? Having no solid solutions, Zora watched Dušica whisper to Andrej, and she prayed that life would offer them compassion.

Zora watched Marko come outside and lift Stefan. "You're a natural." The sun shone brightly, and in that brief, captured moment, Zora heard the lyrical ring of a child's laugh, which pushed the thought of war to her rearview mirror. Regret consumed her today. Zora longed to possess the resilience and determination her sisters had, but she lacked the strength and assertiveness, especially in confronting Peda. Being afraid of one's husband was not a wonderful way to live a life. Zora vowed to do better by becoming more of an advocate for herself and her children.

"This one's an absolute dream." She indicated the sleeping Andrej.

"We hope by changing their identities it will increase their chances of survival," Marko said.

Zora noticed Dušica was uncommonly moved, with her head lowered. "I prayed today for Sava and…for Martha and Andrew's survival."

"Do you think they've made it out of Yugoslavia?"

"I'd like to think they did…but who knows." She lifted her shoulders.

The sisters started walking home. "It's a situation none of us hoped to ever find ourselves in. Have you seen the disturbing posters aimed at the Jews, that the Germans plastered all over town? And the way they've begun checking everyone's papers?"

Dušica blinked twice, scanning left to right before she answered. "I haven't, but they've already gathered any remaining Jews left in Kragujevac." Reaching instinctively to rub her neck, she said, "Martha was so prepared, with two sets of identities. Her family kept her well-informed about Hitler's appalling acts perpetrated against Jews. She had a powerful sense when things began to shift. She knew when they were closing in on her and Andrew."

"How?" Zora's hand rubbed her breastbone.

"After following them, they started to circle and taunt her and Andrew. Martha said it must be how hunters tracked animals."

After observing Marko ahead of them, Zora tapped Dušica's hand. "See? They even resemble one another. Dušica, I know this might sound like I'm judging you, and I'm clearly not, but being a mother —you've got to learn how to relax, because kids pick up on it."

Dušica nodded, but a fat tear slid down her cheek. "The guilt has nearly done me in, and in church, I became even more fraught over what we're doing. It nearly crushed me."

"Oh boy…You cannot allow those thoughts in."

"The speed at which this happened caught us completely off guard. I've been plagued by guilt, as if I had taken Martha's children from her. It's made me feel just awful." She pressed the baby closer to her chest.

"Dušica, she wanted you to have them, so they'll be safe. Today was an enormous first step, and an extremely poignant time for you both, and likely saving their lives. I look at you as heroes for what you're undertaking. There's something else I'd like to mention. Right after I burned candles, I experienced another peculiar sensation."

"Nooo. What happened?" Dušica bent her head closer.

"It's strange when it happens. It's as if I'm floating underwater and then, something comes over me. I feel shaky and dizzy, followed by a coldness, then it's over. But this time it was followed by the most powerful sense of Sava being alive."

"Really? I still wonder if you're clairvoyant, or something. You are a healer, Zora, and you've done some incredible work nursing people back to health."

Shrugging, Zora bit her lip. "I have no idea, but it's eerie all the same."

Marko was waiting for them in front of Ljubica's Bakery, with Stefan next to him, eating a sugary doughnut. "What took you girls so long?"

Marko's mouth hung open while Zora explained the premonition. "Wait—you'll not believe what Father

Radovan just shared with me. Remember Stana's choir director, Conductor Matić?

"Of course, why?" Zora studied his face.

"Well, he lost his parents in the Belgrade bombing. Desolate, he was stumbling around at the site where their building collapsed, searching for any remnants of childhood possessions. He was on his knees when he suddenly heard the most beautiful voice singing *Gospodi pomiluj*, over and over. He shared with Father Radovan that this woman's angelic voice might have saved him. Yet, funnily enough, when he looked up, her face bore an uncanny resemblance to Stana."

Zora blinked back tears. It was true...

"Of course, Father Radovan instantly put it together."

"Were they certain it was her?"

"Yes. Conductor described to him that Sava had a short, barrel-chested guy accompanying her as they tended to the wounded in the streets."

"That would be Života," Zora hurriedly announced, feeling a lightness in her chest.

"By the way, Kosta and Luka are heading to Belgrade later today. Before Father told me the wonderful news, I had intended to have Kosta go to the police station to check on Sava's whereabouts."

"That's decent of you, Marko, thank you. Why in all the turmoil would they be going to Belgrade?"

Marko faltered. "His wife Marija and daughter Radmila have gone missing too."

"Oh, no."

"There's few details, but the week before the invasion Kosta and Marija ultimately separated. She moved back to live with her family in Belgrade, taking Radmila with her."

Zora rubbed her collarbone.

***

Thankful she still had laundry detergent, Zora was pleased to see Lenka had washed the dirty clothes and they were now hanging on the clothesline outside to dry. Neven sat in the kitchen with his sisters, crunching numbers. "Hello everyone," Zora greeted them.

"Oh, hey Mama," Neven said earnestly. "We're trying to pool our earnings to help out. Although it's not what we'd hoped, we'll manage. Here's enough to at least pay three bills, with a little left for the market."

Grasping the table's edge, Zora clung to it, shutting her eyes. How did I miss how low we've sunk? she thought. Opening her eyes, she fixed them on her children. "It's your father's and my responsibility to pay these bills, and I cannot—" She bit her lip so hard she tasted blood and was petrified by how quickly they'd slid downhill after Peda's job loss. With her now out of work at the Technical Institute, when she saw her children taking on the responsibility that should have rested on their parents' shoulders, something broke inside her. These children of mine should not be burdened by paying our house bills, she said to herself.

"Mama? Do you remember the story Baka told us about the mothers at the end of the Great War? She said they were upset over not having enough food to feed every one of their children. Baka said they were so desperate, they had to sell some of their children, so the others could live." Lenka choked on her words. "C—could that happen to us?"

As she crushed Lenka to her chest, Zora's voice sounded thick. "Never, my darling Lenka, never. That happened a quarter of a century ago, and under unusual circumstances." What she didn't share with her daughter was how this conversation twisted her insides.

Trembling, Lenka still looked frightened.

Turning to Neven, Zora said, "A quart of milk, eggs, and some flour would help a lot." I will not cry, she told herself. I'll find another way.

Glancing at her insightful children seated at the table, so doggedly determined to help, she once again realized how fortunate she was. Since Hitler had commandeered the Military Technical Institute, Zora had lost her full-time position, so the only money came from her waitressing at Paligorić. Caring for the sick offered little in the way of compensation. Still, it pained her to have them shoulder the responsibility that should squarely rest on their parents' shoulders.

"We're almost adults; besides, we wanted to help. Lenka's engaged to be married, Stana's turning sixteen shortly, and in October I'll be eighteen," Neven said, brushing his floppy brown hair away.

Overwhelmed, Zora was also unexpectedly filled with pride. She thought about her baka's infamous words—*Children teach you how to live.* Baka Cveta had said those words to Zora and her sisters so often they'd been imprinted in her mind. The impact from her grandmother's words was a gratifying reminder of the enduring familial bond passed through generations.

A soft knock pulled her from the memories. "Come in," Zora yelled over her shoulder. "Marko, what's wrong?"

"I won't keep you, but could I have a word?"

Looking at her grown teenagers, she made a swift decision. "These three have convinced me they're adults, so you can talk freely."

Lifting his palms, Marko half smiled. "Kosta's home already. Marija's entire family has been declared dead in the attack, including their daughter, Radmila."

Neven, Lenka, and Stana sank back in their chairs, stunned.

"My God; she was only thirteen." Zora's neck prickled with fear.

Marko lowered his voice. "There's confusion surrounding Marija's whereabouts."

"Is there anything more terrible than losing a child? Wasn't Marija in her parents' building when it collapsed?"

"That's the puzzling piece—no one knows. Frustrated, Marija's brother from Novi Sad drove here to explain to Kosta what he knew. Here's the strange part: apparently Marija went to her brother's in Novi Sad the day before the attack, indicating she was to meet a friend. This friend and Marija left for a dinner gathering…in Belgrade."

"The woman has no decency." Folding her arms over her chest, Zora raised an eyebrow.

"Kosta's in pain," said Marko.

"Čika Marko, how can we help Luka?" asked Stana.

Marko rubbed the back of his neck and his mouth twisted. "I'm not sure, but it's a lot for Luka to absorb. He will definitely need his friends by his side."

Another knock had them all jumping. Since it was late, Marko opened it. He exclaimed, "Sava…it's really you?"

Zora's heart leaped. "Sava!" The sisters embraced, hugging one another for what seemed like forever, simultaneously laughing and crying. Zora's fingers touched her sister's face. "I was so worried about you."

"Could you ever forgive me? I got so caught up in helping the hundreds of injured lying in the streets that I lost all sense of time. No telegrams, no phone service, no trains running…I regret putting all of you through this. Please, forgive me?"

Breathing her in, Zora said, "You're here now, that's what matters, so hug my kids, and then run down to Mama's, so she and Tata know you're alive."

Joyful, Zora half waltzed into the kitchen, but she could barely believe the change that had come over Stana in such a brief time. "What happened?"

With a sheepish expression, Stana said, "I'm ashamed at what an awful friend I've been to Luka. I didn't know anything about his parents' situation because I was distracted by our own problems."

"Stana, no regrets. Each of you will face challenges in your lives. Trust me when I say no one escapes pain and suffering. There's no denying the cruelty of war, but our strength lies in staying united. To survive each day, we must summon our inner strength. Understand?"

Stana burst into tears.

Neven wore a pained expression and blinked rapidly in response. Zora knew Neven hated seeing his sisters cry.

Zora had to ask, "What am I missing?"

Stana responded in a serious tone. "I acted like a huge jerk. They always appeared to be the perfect family." Inhaling an enormous breath, Stana said, "If I'm truthful, I envied Luka's life, their beautiful home, furniture—the whole thing. I'm horribly ashamed."

"Stana, they're just things. Just be mindful of how you treat others and how they treat you in return. Now, off to bed you go." Zora hugged them to her chest.

***

Four nights later, she found a note underneath her door. It said Goran was alive and safe. Zora asked herself, how do I know this handwriting?

CHAPTER FOURTEEN

PEDA

Kragujevac, the Kingdom of Yugoslavia
Mid-April 1941

AWAKENED BY A LOUD screech, Peda opened his eyes and squinted at the light pouring in. Suddenly, he heard it again: a screeching sound, followed by a whooshing, then a sobering jolt that rattled their home.

"What the hell?" he grumbled, yanking on his pants, his once tall, muscular frame now flabby. Not knowing what caused the vibrations rattling the windows, he went to check. He saw Neven, Stana, and Lenka already up and looking out the window. "Everyone all right?" His words came out as a shout.

"That...noise, Tata—what's going on?" Lenka's eyes were enormous, and her hands were pressed to her ears. "I'm late for work, but should I stay or go?"

Peda understood how easily frightened his oldest daughter became, yet she never, ever missed work, so when he saw her hesitation, he knew whatever it was must be alarming. "Lenka, for right now just stay put. I'm going to check outside."

Peda had stepped less than thirty feet outside before a Stuka zipped past him, edging toward the center of town, blowing wind in every direction. "You're too damn low," he shouted, with frantic gestures at the plane, before he went back inside.

Opting to soften the truth instead of lying, he said to his children, "It's the Luftwaffe, making their presence known by dropping a few pleasure bombs."

He saw the prompt fear on their faces, before another boom caused them to jump. He shouted, "Hurry, drop to the floor."

The noise brought Zora and the younger boys running in. Above the high-pitched sound, she asked, "German planes?"

He nodded vigorously while glancing out the window. "Yes, the Luftwaffe."

Another plane zoomed past, causing a loud, buzzing sound followed by a piercing screech. Simultaneously, there was a new vibration, shaking everything inside.

"It must be their German tanks rolling by. Everyone, stay low; they're advancing, likely from their Panzer division."

Twenty minutes later, Peda glanced at the clock. "They've stopped. Before anyone moves, let me go outside and check."

"Tata," Lenka asked with shaking hands, "do you think they're planning to shoot all of us? Is that why they're here?" She was gasping for air.

Peda's eyes pleaded with Zora. "No, they'd never murder an entire town of people." Tired, he rubbed his bloodshot eyes. He needed more sleep. He was so distracted he could hardly concentrate. He also needed coffee badly and was unable to cope with any more burgeoning questions. Why did I finish Đuro's entire bottle last night? he asked himself.

"Will they bomb us like they bombed Belgrade?" Lenka persisted. Peda could see where this was going. She worriedly fidgeted with her feet, moving them back and forth in a repetitive motion. Whenever she was uneasy about something, Lenka asked hundreds of questions.

Zora moved toward Lenka, wrapping her in a heartfelt embrace. "Shhh, it's all right, dušo. We must stay quiet until we know more."

Wild-eyed, Marko rushed in. "Is everyone all right down here?"

With joy, the boys shouted, "Yes," jumping up at the sight of their dear Čika Marko.

"Good, good. Listen; c'mon upstairs. I've just turned on the radio; hopefully we'll catch the BBC News with some information about what's happening. Dušica's put on the coffee."

Zora and the children hurriedly climbed the stairs behind Marko, while Peda went outside.

Not finding any enemy planes overhead, Peda lit a cigarette and gazed at the smoke-filled sky. After stubbing out his cigarette, he walked up and down Gružanska Street, checking to make certain their home and street appeared calm. What a strange occurrence, he thought.

Returning home, he mounted the stairs, his mouth watering from the yeasty scent of bread. He trailed in with a cigarette dangling between his fingers, but his eyes missed little. Seeing Stefan and Andrej playing quietly on the floor, he shook his head. He knew you could not just change someone's name and poof, like magic they'd become someone else. How was she going to pull this off, hiding Jews in plain sight, and not getting any of them killed in the process?

Marko was on his haunches, scratching his head. "That's odd—a mere moment ago, I had a radio signal. Now, nothing."

Neven fiddled with the dials. "Maybe they *purposely* scrambled our signals? I—ah, overheard some officers bragging at the kafana about the dirty tricks they've been playing on us. Maybe this is one of them?"

"Really? What have you heard?" Marko rubbed his eyebrow.

"For starters, they have brought more units up from Leskovac because they want a powerful presence in Kragujevac." Neven fiddled with the buttons on his shirt. "They also discussed the failure of our Yugoslav Army, and predicted the war would soon be over. And they make jokes about our lack of preparedness for battle, ridiculing us for our lack of proper uniforms, ammunition, and decent footwear for combat." Neven paused while his gaze stayed on his uncle.

Zora's hand flew to cover her mouth. "My God, I don't…"

"Were they speaking in Serbian?" Marko asked, his voice elevated.

"No, no," Neven said. "I—I understand German."

Peda leaped in, interrupting his brother-in-law. "It's good my son's fluent in five languages. He's smart, no?" Peda poked his chest out.

Marko blinked twice. "Yes, Peda." Squaring his shoulders and hips toward his nephew, Marko asked, "Have they mentioned a surrender?"

"They have." Neven lowered his eyes.

Peda's eyes widened. "Wait a second. The Monarchy wouldn't send our men to battle unprepared like those idiots suggested—that's just cheap talk." Peda swept his arms in the air.

***

The Germans began their invasion in Kragujevac by shutting down almost all businesses, including every school. Only a few businesses they deemed essential remained open. Thankfully, these included Paligorić Kafana, the bakery Ljubica's, where Lenka worked, and the market across from the boys' high school. Paligorić kept their doors open well beyond curfew due to the Germans' love for Dunja's cooking. On a night like tonight, when Dunja made her delectable podvarak with sauerkraut, smoked kielbasa, sauteed onions with Hungarian paprika, and garlic and bacon, the kafana overflowed with German officers who loved this dish.

It was after midnight by the time Zora finally made it home. Peda was in a washed-out gray undershirt in the kitchen, smoking.

"You're still up?" she asked, surprised.

"I was waiting for you because your aunt phoned."

Zora froze completely. "Tetka Boja…from Croatia? How did she manage to reach us when the phone lines have all been down?"

"I don't know, Zora, but your mother's letters forced her to telephone us. She also warned us not to allow Mima to go to Croatia, emphasizing that no one should step inside Croatia right now because it's too dangerous."

"Dangerous? How?"

Peda shoved his hands in the air. "I…don't know. She indicated something involving a 'Call to the Poglavnik.'"

Christ, she asks a lot of questions, he thought. How does she expect me to know everything?

Frowning, Zora asked, "Whatever does it mean, Peda?"

"I'd imagine it's a roundup of sorts, although it might be a roundup for all Croatian blood to rise." Peda looked at his wife, whose face was a mixture of doubt and confusion. "Boja said her mail's been opened, likely by a group of fascists calling themselves the Ustaše, who have gained a good portion of control in Croatia and apparently are doing wretched things to our people."

"This hatred...I fear our country's being ripped apart, and we're headed for disaster." Shutting her eyes, Zora started, "Those summers in Croatia on Baka's farm with Tetka Boja and her family were magical. Did I ever tell you how peaceful it was with the tranquil forests, gorges, and old stone monasteries?"

"Many times." He lit another cigarette and sipped his drink, knowing his wife was rattled.

"I remember so clearly the smell of fresh-cut grass." A tear slid down her face and she tried to explain, "I vividly remember every villager in my mind's eyes, especially the grandmothers in their babushkas and heavy black clothing, too hot to be worn in the summery heat, yet there they were, picking vegetables and tomatoes in the fields, sweat streaming down their weathered faces." Zora started to cry. "The scent of Baka's fresh spearmint and her goats in the barn that we milked every morning. Those were the smells that have stayed with me and will always remind me of Kušići." She wrapped her arms around herself.

Peda rubbed the back of his neck, at a loss for words. Their childhoods were so enormously different. His parents chose liquor every day over their children.

"Since the attack, all my mother's spoken about is how much she wants to go home to Croatia. I think the Luft-waffe scaring us the other day might have been the coup de grâce for her, although it was awfully clever for Tetka Boja to call warning us, never mind the expense."

"Your mother's pretty strong-willed."

"Peda, I've got to get to bed. I'll talk to my sisters about this tomorrow."

Lifting his glass, he said, "Good. Keep me out of it." Finishing his rakija, he wondered about job opportunities in a town greatly affected by German closures.

***

Another note appeared under her door. The following morning, Zora fingered the slip of worn paper and exhaled a gigantic sigh of relief. Goran was safe and headed to the mountains.

Peda entered the kitchen, massaging his forehead. "Coffee?" he asked.

"None left." She slid the note into the pocket of her apron.

"Dušica?"

"I can't keep depending on my sister for handouts."

"Seriously?"

"It's not right to keep asking."

Shoving his chair aside, Peda jutted his chin forward, his brown eyes glinting. "God dammit, Zora, she's offered."

"My sister's offered because she's seen how little we have. Trust me, that doesn't make it right." Aiming her thumbs inward to her chest, she said, "It's you and me, Peda. We're the ones responsible for feeding, clothing, and providing a safe home for our seven children—no one else. We brought these children into the world, and it's our responsibility to put enough food on the table and clothe them."

Running his hands through his sleep-dented hair, he hissed, "Dammit, Zora, you've constantly criticized me." Irritable, Peda asked, "Where do you suppose I find work when Hitler's carved up our country for ripe picking? He's shut down just about every business in town. Where do I find work—you tell me?" he shouted, as dribbles of saliva dripped onto his chin.

"And before?" Zora asked, stepping back. "You lost your job at the end of December, but every night you went to the kafana, spending money we didn't have…Whether you care to notice, Peda, we're sinking."

"Dammit to all hell, Zora, how dare you question me in that tone? I'm the man of this household."

"Mama, Tata," Neven called, rushing in, and out of breath. Peda could tell Neven was unaware of interrupting a nasty fight between his parents. Neven squealed, "You won't believe the latest news. May I read it to you now?"

Both parents offered quick nods. Neven read aloud:

On April 14, King Peter and his staff were escorted out of the country. Yesterday, Prime Minister Simonović and his Cabinet members were flown out of Yugoslavia from the Nikšić airport in Montenegro.

Peda sank in a chair, dumbfounded. "Please tell me you're kidding me, Neven? The King's gone, and left his people…and Yugoslavia?" His face contorted as his voice rose in volume. "That's impossible and does not make a lick of sense." Agitated, he flexed and unflexed his fingers. "Why would he abandon his people?"

Zora placed a steady hand on her husband's shoulder. "Peda, let him finish."

Neven opened the newspaper. "There's this." He pointed to a photograph above an article. "Churchill sent a telegram to King Peter the day before he left Yugoslavia."

"Yes, read that." Peda pointed, leaning over Neven's shoulder.

> Churchill's telegram to his British Envoy and Minister Plenipotentiary, Ronald Campbell, said he didn't understand why the King, or the Yugoslav Government, would leave their country.

Peda smacked his hand on the table. "I can't believe this stuff. Churchill knew our King planned to leave, yet none of us did. Perhaps Campbell didn't have time to travel to Nikšić and warn the King?"

"How many hours does it take to drive there from Belgrade?" Neven asked his father.

The shock of the King leaving his people flattened Peda. He felt like a deflated balloon, and he stood up, hunched over. "Maybe five hundred kilometers? Unless they encountered roadblocks, I'd say a nine-hour car ride."

"There's something else." Neven folded the newspaper before looking over at his mother.

"Mama, I know the strong attachment you and Baka have for Croatia, and I'm sorry."

> Many Croatians failed to show up to fight in the Yugoslav Army, and our army has been severely

affected by the lack of soldiers. There are serious conversations about a surrender.

Peda shoved his hands in the air and blew out a substantial breath. "What a colossal mess we've made." Suddenly, it hit him. "Zora, maybe your tetka's phone call was a warning? When she mentioned the 'Call to the Poglavnik,' I wonder if she was trying to send us a hidden message or warning, about them failing to show up to fight?"

***

Peda woke with a hell of a headache. Coffee crossed his mind first thing, prompting him to meander to the kitchen upon rising. Seeing no coffee, he realized everyone must be in church; it was their Easter. I could probably steal some from upstairs, he thought, when Đuro's face appeared through the glass on the back door. Motioning him inside, he greeted him. "*Hristos Voskrese!*"

"*Vaistinu Voskrese*, my friend. First, some friends need our help, then we'll have an Easter toast."

Rubbing the overgrown whiskers on his chin, Peda's strapping six-foot-four-inch frame towered over his stout friend. "Hold on. What kind of help, and why, in God's name, on a holiday?" Peda never worked on holidays.

Đuro looked around. "Please, Peda, could you bring a shovel and come with me?"

Thoroughly confused, he asked, "What exactly are you asking me to do, Đuro—bury dead bodies?"

Bouncing from one foot to the other, Đuro grinned. "No, not at all." Lowering his voice, his eyes glanced around. "Some of our soldiers have snuck back into town, but they've got to get rid of their weapons since Hitler's new edict demanded everyone turn in their weapons and radios within twenty-four hours. So, our former military has requested we help our young soldiers by digging holes deep enough to bury their weapons out in the Žeželj Forest. Others will come later to fill the holes."

Whistling, Peda patted his chest. "I'd be honored to help our men…as long as rakija's involved."

To Peda's surprise, Đuro pulled a tall bottle from his coat pocket.

***

Spring was in the air, and the woods abutting the mountain range soared with pine trees that almost reached the sky. Wildflowers poked through the broken branches, while dead leaves blanketed the forest floor. Peda watched the squirrels and foxes as they roamed the ground slick with dew. Drenched in sweat, he rested against the shovel. "Are we done?"

"At present," Đuro agreed with a nod. "Who knows when we might need these weapons to protect ourselves?"

Cupping his hands to light a cigarette, Peda frowned. "I'm not turning mine in. Christ, the Third Reich has forced us to assign over just about everything else. Now, they're demanding a portion of our food. What's next—our blood?"

"Careful, Peda…I don't want them storming your home."

As they descended the mountain, they caught the sound of whispers and rustling in the foliage. Glancing at Đuro, Peda jutted his chin toward the noise.

Đuro placed a finger to his lips.

Again, he heard it—whispered voices. He rotated, wishing he'd brought his gun. Feeling unsettled, he muttered, "Someone's nearby." Suddenly, right below him, he saw a narrow path overflowing with refugees quietly walking, their backs laden with their possessions.

"Whoa, I wonder where, or what, they're running from?" The expression on Đuro's face displayed complete astonishment.

"Likely everywhere. Montenegro, Slovenia, Croatia, Bosnia, and Kosovo. Everyone's running scared."

***

The following day, Stana and Neven updated their father on more unbelievable events occurring in their rocky country. With the *Glas Šumadije* in hand, Stana professed, "Tata, yesterday, the Kingdom of Yugoslavia *unconditionally* surrendered, so we've signed an armistice and the occupation has begun." Groaning, Peda watched her lower her head to read further. "This one indicates that our Yugoslav Army has positioned itself in Doboj, in Northern Bosnia, and has refused to surrender. But another article said they fled to the hills, so I'm unsure which one's the most accurate."

Surprise registered on Peda's face. "It's remarkable… we're fighting back."

After hanging clothes, Zora came inside. "Could Goran's unit be one of them?"

Glancing at her father, Stana replied, "We haven't received any letters from him since he was last here in March, so it's possible his unit was captured."

"What the hell's wrong with you, Stana?" Peda clapped back.

Dropping the newspaper, Stana jumped back, but the scowl on her face remained. "Me, Tata? You're asking what's wrong with me? Nothing; it's what everyone else in Kragujevac has been talking about, wondering whether their son or brother might have been captured. The newspapers claimed over eighty percent of our Royal Yugoslav Army was captured and sent to camps in Germany, so that's why, Tata." With her hands on her hips, Stana glowered at her father defiantly, all five feet eleven and a half inches of her.

Stunned by the alarming percentage and at Stana's anger toward him, he felt a surge of uncontrollable rage. "You know nothing about war—you're...a girl." Peda's eyes drilled into her.

In a quick motion, Neven placed himself between them. "Tata, check this out." Neven pointed to a photograph in the newspaper.

Hands clenched into fists, his rage swelled. If he didn't leave the house, he feared he might punch something, or someone. Snatching his jacket off the hook, he stormed out the back door.

Zora swung Stana around, searching her eyes. "Stana, look at me. Your brother's safe. Someone slipped a note under our door last night, but...are you all right, my darling?"

Stana's eyes lifted to meet her mother's. "He makes me sooo mad, but yes. I'm fine, b—but how do you know about Goran? Did he write you a letter?"

Placing a finger to her lips, Zora pulled the slip of paper from her apron pocket. "See?"

***

Every morning, Neven ran without fail to pick up the paper, but today there were none. "The Germans have taken over the newspapers, Mama," he yelled, coming inside their home.

Washing dishes in the sink, Zora hollered back, "In here, Neven."

He waved a flyer and passed it to her. "Here's another one of Hitler's edicts."

OKH Field Marshall Walther von Brauchitsch, chief of the German High Command, dictated that the German Military Regime would install and maintain law and order, safeguard the railroad line from Belgrade to Salonika, and control the Danube River's shipping route.

Zora dried her hands with a tea towel before waking Peda. He had been lying crosswise on the bed, napping. Gently shaking him, she relayed the news.

Taken aback by his wife's unexpected anger, he scooted back, leaning against the loose wooden headboard, which he'd forgotten to tighten.

"Things have escalated with the Germans; they're boxing us in. Today we've lost our newspapers, which will severely limit our access to credible news." Blowing out a tremendous burst of air, she blurted, "They're despicable… every last one of them." He saw her eyes burn with fury.

Lighting a cigarette, Peda paused, trying to discern what else, outside of the newspaper, might be bothering her. "What has you so upset?"

Looking away, she massaged her neck. "Deacon Jovan pulled us aside in church this morning."

"And?" Peda was not an ardent church person. He had little use for it, but he had tried. God, how he'd tried, after they had married, but his past had bruised him too significantly.

"The Gestapo arrested Patriarch Gavrilo."

"You cannot be serious?"

Chewing her bottom lip, she lifted her hands. "I wish I weren't. The Germans found him at Monastery Ostrog and arrested him. They beat his chief of staff and forced the patriarch, the poor man, to disrobe and walk outside for hours in the pouring rain. Deacon Jovan vividly depicted the utter degradation." Infuriated, Zora moved to the kitchen, where she slammed the pots and pans; Peda knew she was reacting to the unspeakable acts committed by the Gestapo and the SS against their patriarch.

CHAPTER FIFTEEN

ZORA

Kragujevac, Serbia
May 1941

WITH A TRAY OF sarma in her arms, Zora felt her mouth go dry as she watched her daughter escort the confident Wehrmacht officers to a corner table. Her head swam in confusion. It couldn't be him again, could it? After serving Dunja's tantalizing stuffed cabbage cooked to perfection to the young men in green tunics of the Third Reich, Zora stood transfixed. It was him, the handsome officer who continued coming to Paligorić night after night. Were his intentions noble? Absolutely not; he wanted to lure Stana into something untoward. Zora did not like Officer Kord Webber Gerhardt, nor his determination—not one bit.

Behind her, Dunja murmured sternly, "Stop being so obvious, and get in the kitchen." Plastering on what Zora knew was her fake smile, Dunja wiggled her hips as she snaked them between the crowded tables and chairs, making her way to the kitchen.

Shame made Zora's cheeks redden as she anxiously twisted her hands. "That was him, Dunja. The cocky German who's been trying to get close to Stana. Every time I lay eyes on him, I want to wipe that smugness off his face." Blowing out a stream of air, Zora continued her diatribe. "Whenever Stana steps away from her table to attend to another patron, his sneaky eyes trail her every move. He's…coveting her."

Dunja latched onto Zora's wrist, her jet eyes boring into her. "Never do that again, Zora. Promise me—never stop and glare at any of them, or we'll be in big trouble."

She stammered, "Dunja, Jeez; I'm sorry. I just—" Zora couldn't say another word. Her dearest friend had just gutted her and had spoken to her in the harshest of tones, which left her speechless. Holding on to this job and her friendship with Dunja was paramount to her existence. What's wrong with me? she thought.

"Believe me." Dunja spoke bitterly. "Those Germans will slit your throat in a second. Be. Extremely. Careful. Zora. If you're caught watching or listening to their conversations, it's the end. Keep a safe distance. Don't forget the troublesome leaflets they recently dropped from their planes, warning us to comply with their rules or face the consequences. I don't need to remind you about their consequences, do I? And please refresh my memory: you're still fluent in German and French, correct?"

"I understand, and yes, I'm fluent in both languages. Once again, I'm sorry, Dunja. I had no intention of causing any harm to you or your business with my actions."

Resting against the shelf, Dunja lit a cigarette. "Just get a grip on your emotions, Zora. Follow these tips: keep your shoulders back, don't hunch, and avoid staring at them, and everything will be fine. I adore having you here, but the way you react, well, you must learn to be less reactive. I sensed something from your expression. My concern was that Gerhardt noticed you glaring at him, because I definitely did. Know that we have *friends* watching, so don't make trouble. Our entire Paligorić operation could fall apart."

Zora looked startled. "What operation?"

Dunja moved to the stove. "After I've finished spicing this muškalica, I need to get back out there." Zora watched Dunja's orange lipstick wobble before she left. Nice avoidance.

Making her way into the dining room, Zora noticed Gerhardt casually holding a cigarette between his elegant fingers, seated across from two distinguished-looking officers, their jackets adorned with a profusion of medals and badges. Zora kept busy, attending to her customers, tidying tables, and taking the smudged dishes and glasses back to the kitchen.

When she walked in, Neven and Dunja were both drying a massive pot at the sink.

"Feeling better?" Dunja asked her.

"Yes; again, my apologies." Fear pricked at her sweaty scalp. It was important to set things straight with Dunja, but how could she articulate the experience of calmly observing this disgraceful enemy attempting to seduce her naïve fifteen-year-old? Lifting the bottom of her apron to wipe the sweat from her face, Zora questioned if she could ever adequately articulate the intense emotions a mother had when she sensed her child in danger. Uncertain Dunja could ever understand, she chose to sidestep this conversation; instead, she tenderly squeezed her friend's hand. "I heard about the killings…in Gudovac."

Dunja's tears fell before she looked away. "My father grew up there…and has two brothers in a nearby village he hasn't been able to reach." Sighing loudly, she lit a cigarette. "We haven't slept since we first heard." Dunja was unable to control her muffled sobs.

"There, there," Zora said, hugging her. "You have got to be exhausted, and then the stupid thing with me—?"

Using her apron to wipe her tears, Dunja said, "Why so much hate in this corner of the world? All these innocent people slaughtered like this. It's unthinkable…"

"I know. Has anyone come forward and admitted their actions? If it wasn't the Germans, then who?"

"A fascist group in Croatia, calling themselves the Ustaše." Dunja's voice grew soft. "I shouldn't have scolded you like that, and I apologize, Zora. I haven't been myself without sleep—"

Zora interrupted. "No, no, I was in the wrong." She remembered what Peda often told her. It was consistently her fault. She was the one who instigated the issues in their marriage and she was the one who should be blamed.

In a sudden gesture, Dunja pulled her close, her powerful arms around Zora's frailer ones. "You're family, like a sister to me for the past thirty-five years. I could never hold a grudge against you. But I'm concerned because you're carrying far too much responsibility on that thin frame of yours, and that husband…"

Squaring her body, Zora put a hand up. "I understand, really I do." She could no longer listen to any more negativity about Peda's laziness or lack of holding down a job. Completely drained, she had no strength left to protect her husband. Ever since they'd first met, Dunja and he had been at odds with one another.

Setting aside the spoon, Dunja gestured toward the bowls she'd just filled. "Here; take this muškalica to table fifteen." Before the occupation, Paligorić had enjoyed a prosperous business, but since the Germans had come to town, Dunja's business had exploded.

Delivering the bubbling pork imbued with peppers and bacon to the table, Zora overheard Officer Gerhardt flatter Stana with an elaborate choice of words. As she watched his stark blue eyes rake over her body, she again wondered how to protect Stana from this fiend. Gerhardt seemed captivated. Zora feared he would not stop until he got what he wanted. If only they weren't so desperate for money.

As she approached the swinging doors, someone accidentally bumped her elbow.

"Pardon, Serb lady," uttered the older German, who moments ago was seated across from Gerhardt. His hold on her forearm was unusually tight and he stood too close. In abysmal French, he recited words difficult to decipher. "You, lady, you help."

Zora stood stock-still and responded to him in French. "Sir, how may I help you?"

He had a sharp nose and wafer-thin lips and peered down at her from under coarse black eyebrows, his hand inappropriately sliding from her shoulder to her wrist. "Allow me to introduce myself. I am Field Marshall Walther von Brauchitsch. Remember me and bring me your best cognac." Stepping closer, enough for her to catch a pungent whiff of his sour meaty breath, he switched to German. "I see where your daughter got her beauty. With proper grooming and the right clothes, some might consider you stunning." With a click of his jackboots, he spun around.

Despite the warmth in the room, Zora shivered as she scurried to the bar. In a hushed tone, she explained to Jovo what she needed.

Returning to the Field Marshall's table, Zora handed him the bottle of Rémy Martin. His lips twitched into a lazy smirk, and he nodded at her in appreciation, while his gaze lingered on her longer than necessary. "You're good."

Zora moved to the next table and quickly stacked the greasy platters on a tray before heading to the kitchen.

The stocky cook, who'd grown up with her and Dunja, had witnessed the exchange. "That damn Nazi pig, touching you like you're nothing more to him than cattle. I despise every one of them," Miško said, swinging his large chopping knife through the air. "I swear, one day when I'm making a big vat of soup, I'm going to put something good in their bowls, just to make them sick. Not too much, just a perfect amount to keep him on the toilet for three, maybe four, days."

Zora giggled. "Ohh, Miško, what a thought, but really, you must be careful."

Relief flooded her when Field Marshal von Brauchitsch and his disgusting trio exited the kafana. Shortly after, she untied her apron and waited for Neven to finish counting tonight's money with Dunja. Stana and Luka had their heads bent in conversation, and Zora recognized how grief-stricken Luka had been. Thank goodness he had her two to talk with. Luka had poured his heart out to Neven and leaned on him. As much as she wanted to reach out to his father to offer her condolences, she couldn't, not with Peda's insatiable jealousy.

"Ready?" Neven stood, pulling the collar of his jacket up. "I'm sure someone will be following us."

"God forbid if we had a misstep. We don't want to end up like those people in Belgrade, hanging from a light pole," Luka said rather gloomily.

With a gentle touch and reassuring words, Zora said, "Luka, I understand what you're speaking about and I'm so sorry."

Stana's body froze. "What do you mean?"

Luka clamped his hand over his mouth. "I'm sorry, it just…slipped out." Turning to Zora, he pleaded, "Gospođo Brković, please accept my apologies."

Something felt tight in her chest. "Luka, what you witnessed…"

With a massive sigh, he hung his head as his voice cracked. "I saw men hanging from light poles in Trg Republike. I'll never be able to unsee that."

Zora ached for him. At seventeen, he still needed a mother's tenderness. "I cannot imagine how difficult it must have been, Luka. Can we talk more once we're home?"

But Stana insisted. "Who does this? What people would raise children to become monsters?"

Zora wanted to say: It was someone just like your acquaintance, Officer Gerhardt, and his band of German officers at the table tonight; that's who.

Instead, she yelled out a good night to Dunja, who lived upstairs. "Remember, ears will be listening." She worried about these three, on the cusp of adulthood, yet already experiencing life's cruelties. We wouldn't be having these concerns if Peda had allowed Neven safe passage to America, she thought.

***

Everyone's supplies had dwindled, yet Dušica and her mother were baking for their patron saint day—slava. Dušica brought down enough coffee for a full pot, and the woodsy aroma drifted through her downstairs. The Đurđevdan celebration on May 6 was a massive undertaking for the Nikolić women and a day their ancestors had taken their first step into Serbian Orthodoxy. Serbs everywhere who'd chosen Saint George as their patron saint joyously celebrated. Special foods, fancy desserts, and drinks were served to all their invited friends.

Nowhere was Đurđevdan embraced more than in Kragujevac. Yet, this year it was causing Zora angst because she was unsure if the Wehrmacht would allow them to celebrate. She and her sisters had decided to forgo their customary larger celebration; instead they would quietly honor slava in the privacy of their home with only an exceptionally, small group of family and close friends—ones they could trust.

"Where's the boys?" Zora asked Dušica, a confused look on her face.

"At the farm. Marko's father needed help fixing their fences. The Germans stole most of their pigs and goats and broke their fences when they hopped over."

"That's…preposterous." Zora paused, coffee cup suspended midair.

"I know. Look, Mama's here." Dušica stood, welcoming her. "How are you?"

Mima's smile wobbled. "I've been worried." She looked around, her eyes not meeting her daughters'.

Zora assumed her mother was concerned about the war and lack of food. "Mama, come sit." Zora patted the empty seat beside her. "I was listening to Dušica explain about the theft on the farm." Turning toward her sister she asked, "Can the Živkoviće stop them from stealing more animals?"

"You're joking, right?" Dušica's thick eyebrows arched. "They've taken so much from us already, but they're in power, so there's no stopping them." Sighing, she rubbed her forehead. "They'll take whatever they want; but listen, I heard something likely pertaining to Martha and Andrew."

"Yes?"

"A person admitted that a truck driver who worked for the Germans told him over drinks about escorting a group of frightened Jews from here to a camp run by the Gestapo…in Poland." Trembling, Dušica continued. "The man remembered the truck driver saying the name over and over as Auschwitz."

Zora's heart sank for her sister. Standing, she wrapped her arms around her shoulders. "There, now. You have nothing to feel guilty about. What you've done with the boys has been remarkable, Dušica. It's more than a childhood pact. You and Marko will give these boys an opportunity to live. It's the most generous commitment, and you're the bravest person I know."

Mima crossed herself, but her elbow bumped into her coffee cup, sending it careening off the table, where it splattered on the floor. "Oh, dear." Her chin trembled.

"I'll get it." Zora sprinted to the sink to retrieve a rag. She couldn't help wondering if something else was troubling her mother. Hoping to draw her out, she asked, "Mama, why don't we mix the dough for pita while we're chatting?" Pulling out the ingredients, she said, "So far, we've been lucky and I pray it stays that way."

Lifting her head, Zora asked, "Have you ever wondered why other parts of Yugoslavia have withstood such horror, violence, and destruction?"

"I don't have an answer," Mima said, looking down. "Lately, no one in town will even make eye contact or engage with you. Except for the shoeshine boys, who still laugh and haggle over prices on their street corner. Even at Ljubica's, where I go for fresh bread, there's long lines of people, but strangely enough, no one talks anymore. I guess everybody's afraid."

"I think you might be right, Mama. For me, I miss the smells in town."

"How so?" Dušica asked, a frown inching its way between her brows.

"Remember how it used to smell when we walked to the market? The smoky scent of meat cooking on the grill, combined with the sugary scent of cinnamon. Even the stink from the automobile fumes blended in, but now it's eerie because it's all gone." Zora took a sip of her coffee and then exhaled. "I pray something dreadful doesn't happen here…"

Clicking her tongue, Mima wagged her fingers near Zora's face. "Don't wish for trouble, missy."

"Sorry, Mama." Zora kissed the top of her mother's head, noticing a few wisps of gray had snuck in. "I overthink. Do we have enough flour?"

Mima turned to face both daughters. Her face suddenly brightened for the first time today. "I brought some, but Zora, I have the most wonderful idea. Why not invite poor Kosta and Luka to our slava? They'll be completely alone, and no one should be alone during slava."

Zora's eyes sought her sister's. "That was unexpected." Hesitating, Zora asked her mother, "Can I think about it, Mama?"

"What's there to think about? Invite them, or I will." Mima stood. "I have to go home."

Bewilderment spread across Zora's face. She clasped her mother's firm hands in her own. "You just arrived… what's going on?"

With her eyes squeezed shut, Mima emitted a half sigh and half sob. "It's your father. He hasn't been himself. He's constantly complaining about being tired, but then he spends all day sleeping." Mima cocked her head. "He doesn't seem right to me, so I—I need to be home, to watch over him."

Unwilling to admit anything could be wrong with her strong father, Zora moved to unlock her medical cabinet. "I'm sending you home with a powerful herb to boost his energy, but I feel I should check him out first."

"Nah, finish baking. Your father's just getting older and slowing down. We will be here early on slava to help you out. *Ako Bogda*." Crossing herself, Mima repeated, "God willing, we'll see you in two days. I'm still practicing my English. When I visit America and my Nada, I will blend in like an Amerikanka."

May 06, 1941

Dušica flung open the door to greet her Sava. "You made it—*Srećna Slava*. Any roadblocks or problems along the way?" Dušica had been anxiously awaiting her parents and sister so they could start their Đurđevdan festivities.

Inside, Sava happily greeted everyone. "*Srećna Slava*." Towering over her sisters and nieces, she said, "Everyone, meet my friends: Mrs. Josie Whitney-Shaw from the US, and this guy's Vlado's assistant, Života Pavlović."

Stana offered them a spoon to taste their customary Đurđevdan dish. "Please try our koljivo."

Josie lifted a spoonful of koljivo, her eyes twinkling. "It's delicious; what's it made from?"

"We boil the wheat for a long time, and after its completely dried out, we mix it with sugar, walnuts, cinnamon, and other spices."

Turning to Zora and the rest of her family, Josie announced, "I'm honored to be here today for your slava. These are for you." She handed Zora two bags filled with food, candies, and wine.

Zora's mouth fell open. "Why, thank you, but…it's too much."

"Nonsense." After taking another hefty spoonful of koljivo, Josie lifted her shot glass. "Živeli!" Her dimples popped, and she nearly choked on the homemade liquor, burning its way down her throat.

"Živeli!" everyone echoed back to her.

Zora nervously glanced at the clock, finding it altogether strange her parents had yet to arrive. She also wondered where Josie found these hard-to-find items, since nearly every business was closed. One thing was for certain, Josie knew her way around the Serbs. Tickled her mother had invited Kosta and Luka, Zora realized that having intriguing people like Josie and Života in attendance would be enough of a buffer to keep Peda fully engaged.

Sava bent to Zora's ear. "Everything's lovely and as always, you've outdone yourself, but where's Mama and Tata?" Sava's thick eyebrows were knitted together. "Shouldn't they be here by now?"

Zora tried brushing the fear aside, but an uneasiness enveloped her. They were never late. Leaning against the wall for support, she whispered, "C—call…them."

"There's no answer."

Zora was visibly pale. Sava stared at her. "What just happened to you?"

Waving her hand away, Zora shouted as an ominous sense of foreboding nearly knocked her over. "Neven, Vuk—run to Baka's now. Something's terribly wrong. Call me from there. Hurry."

"Yes, Mama." Zora saw the fear in Neven's eyes.

Sava looked her sister over from head to toe, her hands resting on her hips. "What just happened? And don't avoid answering me, Zora."

Too weak to stand, she slid into a chair, and in a breathy voice she said, "A premonition. It was about something dreadful taking place."

Suddenly, the phone rang. "Neven? Nooo…" With anguish, Zora spoke into the telephone: "I'm on my way." Turning to Sava, she said, "It's Tata. Mama cannot wake him."

Pulling Života aside, Sava whispered something before saying to Zora, "Grab your medicine bag, Života will drive you there."

Her father was already cold by the time she got there.

"Mama, I'm sorry, but Tata evidently passed away in his sleep."

"Noooo…Zora, NO," Mima screamed before falling to her knees. Shaking her head, Zora saw the pain slashed across her face. "He was just taking a nap; please, try waking him again."

Sighing heavily, Zora crouched next to her mother and grabbed hold of her hand. "Mama, I understand your distress, but Tata has already departed this world—he's gone."

Shaking, Mima broke into a sob.

***

Three days later, the Nikolić sisters stood shoulder to shoulder inside their Serbian church, Mima propped between them. As Stana sang Mokranjac's moving rendition of *So svjatimi upokoj*, the parishioners filed past the open casket in single file, offering their final goodbye to their friend, neighbor, and kumstvo, Zoran Nikolić, whose heart gave out on the day of his slava. After he was laid to rest at the Varoško Groblje Cemetery, the family held a dača luncheon in his honor. Zora and her sisters walked alongside their mother until they reached her home. It had been an emotional, tear-stained day.

"Now I can go home," Mima cried to Zora, who was helping her mother undress in her bedroom.

"Ohh, Mama, it's impossible to go anywhere in Croatia. We've been over this before. You've had a rough couple of days, so why not try lying down?" Zora pulled back the flowered quilt Mima had made a dozen years ago and helped her into bed.

Mima wiped the tears streaming down her face with her trembling hands before rolling over. Once Zora heard her light snores, she tiptoed out, throwing a blanket over Sava, who'd fallen asleep on the sofa. Never had she experienced such exhaustion in her entire life. Walking home, her feet felt leaden. It was an effort to take the next step. When she finally arrived home, she was greeted by a whiff of something powerful. Taking off her coat, she saw it was grah i kupus, the magical sauerkraut and bean soup. "Ah…thank you."

"Sure." Neven glanced up from the sofa where he was sitting with Stana and Luka. "Mama, you won't believe what just happened."

"What?" Zora sagged. Disconsolate after her father's death, she was unable to absorb any more unwelcome news, but Neven's eyes sparkled enthusiastically.

"A Yugoslav flag was hoisted on Ravna Gora…the Resistance has begun."

A giddiness she hadn't felt in months sprung forth. There might be hope, after all. But what would this mean for Neven and Luka, frighteningly near fighting age? "A Yugoslav Resistance, eh? That's terrific, but I won't have any more of my children going off to fight. Please, no." A prickle of fear made its way down her spine; she had to know. "Neven, if you were called to fight, would you go?" Please, say no.

With fingertips pressed to his forehead, he said, "I've no interest in fighting and hope I don't have to. I really want to finish this last year of school before attending a university."

Relieved, Zora sank into a chair. Emotionally spent, she allowed her elbows to rest on the table. "And you, Luka?"

"Ummm, I—I'm not sure. I've always wanted to protect my country, but after losing so much of my family, I don't know. Like Neven, I want to complete high school and go to the university in Belgrade. It's been my dream."

Zora watched the energy drain from Stana's face, and in that moment she recognized, long before Stana, that her daughter was already half in love with Luka Lazić. She knew also that one swift decision could irrevocably change the course of their young lives.

CHAPTER SIXTEEN

SAVA

Belgrade, Serbia
Early June 1941

THE OCCUPYING FORCES OF the Third Reich had effectively prevented every Yugoslav, including Sava, from leaving Yugoslavia. The Axis Powers strategically annexed each territory in the Kingdom. Early on, Sava surmised that Hitler would exact control over Serbia, not because of their 3.8 million population, but because he longed to control their abundant resources, including the Military Technical Institute in Kragujevac. Sickened by how he had succinctly stripped away every freedom once enjoyed, Sava loathed living under these conditions, always tiptoeing around, knowing you were being watched.

By late April, the Wehrmacht had taken over numerous palatial residences in Belgrade, forcing the owners out to accommodate their own officers. Sava helped many of her neighbors, knowing it was merely a matter of time before they took command over her home as well. Several neighbors approached Sava for assistance and were guests in her spare bedrooms. It was difficult having so many people underfoot, but she handled it with grace. Luckily for her, Života had the hindsight to have already taken carloads of her most treasured items, including her clothing, non-perishable foods, and their cherished carpets, to her sisters' home for safekeeping.

This morning's skies promised to be picture perfect, yet glancing from her car window, Sava saw clouds of hopelessness. An ache had settled in, causing her feelings of despair. In a distressing update yesterday, Dr. Govich, Vlado's doctor in England, had informed her that her husband's lungs were beyond repair. The ugly truth was that Vlado's time was running out.

On her way to a Sloboda gathering she was first meeting Toma, who had just returned to Belgrade. Chewing over the excruciating conversation with Dr. Govich, Sava wondered how she could sneak out of Yugoslavia to be with Vlado one last time.

When she'd first met the world-class entrepreneur, Vlado had shared his preference for living in Great Britain. Favoring the British lifestyle, he liked their way of governing. Throughout his childhood, Vlado had been in the company of the Karađorđević children, yet he held different opinions on how Yugoslavia should be governed. When they married, it was with the understanding they would live generous portions of their lives apart in different countries, yet somehow make it work.

Suddenly, she remembered Toma having a few unsavory sorts in his contact book. Perhaps one of them might assist her crossing the border?

Lifting her chin, she requested to Života, "Please drop me here."

Coming to a halt, Života twisted his neck to glance at her. "Gospođo, what time shall I pick you up?"

Grinding her teeth together she said, "Maybe in four or five hours, but I can manage getting home myself." She despised having anyone question her comings and goings and, God forbid, having an escort.

Crossing Bulevar Despota Stefana, too many conflicting thoughts churned in her mind as she inhaled the stinky exhaust from a car backfire, wondering where he'd found petrol. Nearing the National Theater, she flinched as she glanced down at Skadarska Street, where her fondest memories of cozy nights in the charming kafanas, built on Turkish cobblestones, filled her heart with joy. Now, it sat in darkness and obscurity.

The lights were out on Skadarlija, the bohemian neighborhood once comparable with Montmartre, where the vibrant tamburaši filled Skadarlija with an infectious energy night after night. This was where writers like Bora Stanković and Milovan Glišić unleashed their prolific creativity, along with other literary types. Actors and musicians used to flock to Skadarlija, and there was no place during her university days more exhilarating. Straightening her shoulders, Sava ascended the slope to Trg Republike, Belgrade's famous gathering spot. Will he be the same old Toma? she wondered. Sava's frayed nerves over Vlado's health weighed heavily on her, and not leaving with him in March left her feeling guilt-ridden.

Seeing Toma ahead, Sava let out a shout. "My goodness, look at you." Grabbing Toma by his good arm, she said, "You were unconscious and covered in blood the last time I saw you, but now, you look well." She'd never shared with him the likelihood that his survival was due to Života's swift, intrepid lifesaving skills. When they had discovered him that night, trapped beneath a block of concrete, his arm was contorted at an unusual angle, and his pulse was thready. "How does it feel being home?"

Giving her a lopsided smile, he rolled his eyes.

"Different from Takovo?" Delighted to have her friend back, Sava's eyes gleamed.

Toma offered his signature sardonic brow raise. "I'm thrilled to be back. My mother and tetka hovered over me so much, feeding me and fretting over my injuries. It was nerve-racking." A slow smile spread across his face. "Despite my mother's reluctance for me to leave, I was climbing the walls." Chuckling, he quickly winced. "Oww; I forgot." He indicated his arm. "It's difficult to laugh."

Her eyes searched his for pain, and when she saw none the corners of hers curved into a relaxed smile. "I'm so happy for you, Toma."

His life had hung in the balance that week after the invasion. A sharp piece of steel had pierced his right lung and a section of his intestinal tract and nearly crushed his left arm. Nonetheless, two months later—Toma was one of the lucky ones. In her opinion, he'd made the right decision by recovering in his childhood village near Gornji Milanovac. It was clear to Sava that the tender care he received from his family aided greatly in his recovery.

"Despite the gorgeous day, you appear too serious, so tell me, dear Sava, whatever's troubling you?"

"I—ah." Panic suddenly swept over her, leaving her breathless with shock. Her eyes veered upward, while her hands covered her gaping mouth. "No—" she shouted, inching backward. "What have they done?"

Toma's face revealed a combination of bewilderment and outrage as his eyes followed Sava's. "My goodness—what on earth...?"

"I—it's Danilo, hanging from a noose. How could they...?" Sava cried out in horror. Her voice was clear enough of the indignity committed against her friend. A corrosiveness bubbled as it burned its way up her belly until she was bent over the curb, retching until nothing was left. Her clammy hands pressed her thighs as she slowly moved to stand. Inhaling deeply, she used the inside of her arm to wipe her lips, and shaking her head, stuttered, "This—it's unimaginable."

Pointing upward, Toma's forehead furrowed. "How do you know him?" Toma carefully observed the man who hung from the light pole, still dressed in a suit and tie, the tie swaying in the wind.

"He's one of us. That's Dr. Danilo Stepanović, my friend Olga's husband. Remember the letter I sent you about him?"

"Oh...right, he'd just come on board."

"Yes, a little over a month ago. His wife and I grew up together in Kragujevac. I recruited Danilo for Sloboda, he's the doctor who—" She swallowed back tears. "I just remembered something. He called me from the hospital two days ago, excited because he'd discovered a large quantity..." She pressed her fingers under her eyes, hoping to stop them from twitching. "What if the Germans stumbled upon him with the supplies?"

Toma lowered his head. "He found a large quantity of what?"

"Pain medication and bandages, and..." The rancorousness of the Germans took her breath away. "How did I not expect this? I'm to blame, Toma. I'm the one who brought him in." The weight of her guilt pressed against her. Olga had been dead set against his involvement in Sloboda, feeling the work was too dangerous. But—Danilo *wanted* in. He wanted to help the Royalists. "My God, what have I done? What if the Germans suspected his involvement, or perhaps someone tipped them off?" Her mind zigzagged with questions at the horror of it all.

"Sava, Sava, take it easy," Toma said, looking around nervously. "I'm trying to catch up."

As he ran his fingers through his unruly black hair, she couldn't help but notice how badly he needed a haircut. Why does it matter? she asked herself. Sometimes, she could not grasp how people's basic daily needs snuck in, even amidst war.

"Is it possible it was just a matter of him breaking curfew? Maybe someone at Malo Kafana has more information. If so, we'll be able to confirm whether his medical supplies ever reached us." With his breath hitching, Toma looked up once more. "What a heartbreaking situation." In a disbelieving voice, he questioned, "Are you certain you're all right?"

"Yes, but I must first go and offer my sympathies to Olga if she'll have me. But I'll come to the meeting soon after."

On her way to Olga's apartment, Sava encountered streets void of people. Outdoor cafés, previously chock-full of people sharing coffee and laughter, were now abandoned. As she caught a whiff of the burnt smell of tobacco and pipe smoke, memories of her last interaction with Olga six weeks prior resurfaced, and the moment Olga had demanded Sava's departure from their home for good. It was possible Olga might not open the door.

Mulling over possible theories regarding Danilo's capture by the Germans, Sava considered the correlation between a recent skirmish in Pančevo and Danilo's murder. In retaliation, the Germans had returned to Pančevo and savagely killed eighteen innocent citizens and strung them up on light poles around town, for all to see. Shuddering, Sava's vision blurred, as she questioned whether this could be a link to her friend, or if Danilo's situation were more questionable. Nonetheless, the implications reverberated, causing a nagging sensation deep in her gut.

After offering her condolences to an inconsolable Olga, Sava hurried toward Malo Kafana, unable to shake the feeling someone had tipped off the Germans about Danilo providing medical supplies for the underground. He had shared with her, very recently, his distrust of two colleagues. However, Danilo had persisted onward. The Resistance needed him and requested more medicine.

Swollen-eyed and slammed with grief, Sava spotted Josie the moment she entered the kafana. Beautifully dressed in a fitted Kelly-green suit with beige buttons, Josie embodied fashion. Toma and she had brought in their friends and coworkers, individuals they knew they could trust, who wanted to support the Resistance and create change. Today, they planned to assign specific roles to everyone.

"Toma told me what happened, Sava. I'm terribly sorry. These acts…they're unconscionable."

Sava squeezed her friend's fingers before nodding. "Where's Toma?"

"I don't know, but they're about to start, so let's turn our chairs."

There Toma stood, facing everyone. "I'm thrilled to be here, and grateful for your presence in Sloboda. Today, we're here to establish the safest route to transport these medical supplies up the Suvobor Mountains, with an elevation of 2,800 feet. Anyone good on horseback?"

Josie surprised everyone by raising her hand. "I'm excellent on horseback."

Toma cleared his throat while adjusting his sling. "Josie, our mountains, they're unlike anything you're familiar with. The Suvobor and Rudnik Mountains have a reputation for being treacherous and steep. There's no doubt going up on horseback will be quite a challenge. They offer wickedly narrow paths with hairpin turns that a horse might not even make."

Standing, Josie placed her hands on her hips and stared Toma straight in the eye. "I've ridden horseback up mountains twice as high as yours. I'm certain I'll get up *your* mountains easier than anyone in this room. Questions?"

Sava knew Toma would refuse her. He would never choose a woman when a man could do the job, especially not an Amerikanka. That's just how things worked here. Women were never pushy or assertive. They never tried to force their way in, like Josie was doing. It was one of the innumerable reasons Sava cherished her marriage to Vlado. Educated abroad, Vlado had a more cultured view of a woman's role. He loved having an educated wife with an esteemed academic career, even though it laid squarely against most in the Balkans.

Josie whispered to Sava, her cheeks flushed, "They've got to get rid of these old-fashioned ways and catch up with the rest of the world."

"I don't think the U.S. or Great Britain is any better, but please bring it down a notch, Josie."

Firing up a cigarette, Josie spurted, "Why wouldn't they

take advantage of the most skilled individual, regardless of their sex?"

Blowing out a stream of air, Sava squirmed in her seat. "We've learned to work inconspicuously in the background."

"I'm going up that damn mountain to meet Draža Mihajlović."

Sava recognized her frustration; it rubbed at her, too. Josie loathed being dismissed purely because she was a woman. "Men have the power here, Josie. Can I share a piece of advice with you? Tread lightly and with less assertiveness."

Being a member of the Sloboda Freedom Organization, Sava quickly realized her role was guided by the Ravna Gora Committee, predominately composed of staunch military men who'd never worked alongside a female patriot, and for them, it might feel threatening. Sloboda had two important committees, medical and recruitment, and hoped to continue recruiting young, strapping men for the Royalists. Sava had already been successful in drafting several sturdy farmers, striking a deal with them that involved continuing to farm until it became essential they leave to fight.

Seeing Toma nearby, Sava interrupted a conversation between him and two gentlemen. "May I borrow him, gentlemen?"

Toma quietly moved aside. "So, here's what we've learned—Danilo delivered the medication to us two days ago, checking in at eight thirty that night."

Sava slumped against the wall. "Anything else?" She tried gathering herself.

"It doesn't appear we were compromised. His death was believed to be strongly linked to him and other doctors breaking curfew."

Her lips trembled ever so slightly. "Why him, such a decent man?"

An unfamiliar, deep voice from behind surprised her. "I'm afraid we may never know."

It startled Sava to suddenly be facing a tall and extremely handsome man with the most brilliant pair of eyes, which were looking at her in surprise.

"My God, it's you—the woman who sang that night." His hand covered his heart.

Sava's brows wrinkled in confusion as the man scrutinized every pore on her face. In a heart-stopping moment, she stared, three fingers touching parted lips. Who was he?

The man grinned, revealing perfect, even teeth, and stuck out his hand. "Excuse me for not introducing myself. I'm Boško Matić, better known as Conductor." Continuing to stare rather intently, in a deep baritone, he explained, "I heard you singing to that child, the night of the attack. Your voice was magical."

"Thank you. I know this might sound silly, but my niece in Kragujevac has not stopped talking about her choir director, who goes by the nickname Conductor. Would it be possible—?"

Cutting her off with laughter, he said, "Yes, I'm Stana's choir director, and her resemblance to you, well, it's remarkable." Hands splayed, he continued, "It's obvious where she acquired her voice." The conductor gave her another appraising glance before straightening. "About Danilo, here's what we know. The Germans were searching our hospitals for injured Resistance fighters. Just last week they began stalking our physicians."

"You're downplaying it, but the death of a friend's never easy."

He reached down and briefly touched Sava's forearm before recoiling, as if burnt. There was a pregnant pause before he replied, "You're mistaken. I apologize if I sounded cavalier, which was not my intention." Placing his hand over his heart, he added, "I, too, am overwhelmed by Danilo's death."

His touch caused a jolt, bringing a range of emotions, including fear. Sava took a few measured breaths, feeling unbalanced. There was profound sorrow mixed in with guilt for her husband's severe illness as well as Danilo's passing, and that was what should have been filling her mind, but an unsteadiness vibrated between them, until she asked, "Your tone indicated that you've also experienced loss?"

With a faraway gaze, Conductor presented her with a sympathetic smile. "My parents were in their apartment when it collapsed." His throat sounded like he might be choking on his words. Immediately changing the subject, he said, "We used to study together, Danilo and I. No one was more surprised than me when he joined the Resistance."

It was Sava's turn to bow her head. "I understand." Tears formed and she blinked them away. She would hold it in until later, in the privacy of her home. Instead, she reflected on the key moments in Yugoslavia's tumultuous history that had brought her to where she now stood, with a group of passionate revolutionaries who refused to give in to Hitler. When Sloboda invited her in, it was the next progressive step on her journey. Will the Resistance end up being my destiny or my fate? she wondered.

"Gospođo Ivković." Conductor interrupted her out of her reverie. "Would you and Mrs. Whitney-Shaw be available to recruit in the villages surrounding Kragujevac this week?"

"Of course, but please call us Sava and Josie." Waving Josie over, she couldn't help noticing his unusual, dark-blue eyes, tucked behind gold-framed eyeglasses.

Sava knew Josie was watching their volleying exchange with a raised eyebrow.

Rubbing his chin, he stared at both women. "It takes courage to stand up for freedom and be a part of the Resistance. It's dangerous stuff we're doing. We're thrilled to have two intelligent, savvy women in our organization, but this battle won't be easily won. There will be collaborators everywhere, even among friends. We've taken advantage of the Germans being less suspicious of women working intelligence in the Balkans, therefore we must use that to our advantage if it's all right with you. Yet, there's always the chance you'd be arrested, winding up in one of their deplorable camps. Are you ready for that, Dr. Ivković?"

"Are you trying to scare us off?" Josie asked quizzically.

Grinning cheekily, Conductor said, "No, Josie. It's so you're cautiously aware of the dangers associated with the underground. Two of my childhood friends have been active in the Résistance française. They've provided us with useful tools to help boost our units and have briefed us on vital information about the Germans, including various operations, tactics, and antics. Fortuitously, long ago, these friends and I concocted a silly, secret language involving codes, yet ironically, today, these codes have been the safest way to communicate with one another. They've also educated us about never using real names. So, decide on a code name and use it each time we communicate."

"One of my dear friends has been a part of the Résistance française. Would it be possible to ask about her?" Sava saw his wary gaze.

"What's her code name?"

"I…I don't know." Incredulous, she couldn't believe how foolish she must seem, especially after he had explained about never using real names.

His eyes crinkled into a smile. "The Germans write everything down. They keep list upon list. They've compiled lists of every resident in a particular village. It's how they sniff out a person's identity or learn if they've gone missing. Would you be interested in doing more than recruitment?"

Josie pushed forward. "Definitely."

His smile was contagious. "I'm afraid…others have not been so keen on my ideas about women being our hidden strength. After listening to you, Josie, I'd be delighted to have you accompany us on horseback to Ravna Gora."

"Seriously?" Josie's mouth hung open.

With a mischievous grin, he replied, "Yes. I'll give you the details in a few days. You women would be perfect for passing crucial information back and forth."

"So…spies?" Josie gulped.

Sava intercepted by lightly touching his forearm. "We'll need to know more of what's involved before we commit."

"Also, who's the gentleman who started Sloboda with you?" Josie questioned.

Conductor widened his stance. "He's always stayed in the background because he has a family to protect."

Sava was learning how formidable Josie was when she wanted something. Outside of her spiritedness, one of the most fascinating traits she admired about Josie was her knack for never skirting around a question. She drilled right in. Sava wished more people were like that. However, she squeezed Josie's elbow as a signal to slow her inquisition.

"I have a slight wrinkle. My husband's quite ill and I'm trying to get to England straight away. But after I return…" Sava then explained Vlado's insistence on Života protecting her. "Would he be a deterrent?"

"Absolutely not. In fact, we'd be honored to have someone with Života's military knowledge. But getting out of Yugoslavia? I'd say that's impossible."

How does he know about Života? she wondered. This man was not only a mystery, but he also seemed clever and well-spoken yet lacked the savvy worldliness that Vlado possessed. He had his own worldliness hidden behind leading choir practices in church.

"Could either of you solve crossword puzzles?"

Sava thought it an odd question. She also sensed a controlled tension he kept hidden. "I'm not fast, but I know someone with great speed. Why?" Curious, Sava knew no one faster than Neven, but she would need to know what was involved before volunteering her nephew.

"A pleasure, ladies." He quicky turned and walked away.

"That was weird, his hasty departure," Josie said, looking back.

"Methinks he was close to spilling a secret." A laugh bubbled up inside of her, and it felt wonderful to laugh.

Josie folded her arms across her chest. "He needs a code breaker, and he's completely smitten with you, Dr. Ivković."

Shaking her head, Sava grabbed her coat and walked outside, surprised to see Života idling at the curb inside her car.

Rolling down the window, he said, "Gospođo, please come right away."

"Why the urgency?" she mused. After seeing his woeful expression, she sensed something was off. Heart quickening, she asked. "What's happened?"

He got out of the car. "I'm afraid, Gospođo…your husband didn't make it."

Sava's vision blurred, and a lightheadedness swooped in, almost leveling her. That was all she remembered before fainting.

CHAPTER SEVENTEEN

ZORA

Kragujevac, Serbia
Summer 1941

THE DISTANT THUNDER CAUSED her shoulders to slump. Please, no more rain, she thought. It was accompanied by a blistering, oven-like humidity. Exhausted, she desperately craved sleep. Her nights at Paligorić had become increasingly tense, more so when she overheard the Germans discussing a gruesome act they had recently carried out. Sickened, she had to summon every ounce of mettle to deliver their meals instead of shoving them into their faces. Their cruel treatment of harmless people was vindicative and revolting. It provoked a visceral reaction in her, leading to a fear of eventually exploding.

Tonight, their conversation sounded even more rancorous as they bragged about several innocent villagers who'd perished in fires *purposely* set by them. With her skin crawling, Zora questioned her ability to maintain a smile. With a sharp intake of breath, she forcefully gnashed down on her back molars, so hard she feared one might crack.

Unapologetic, these men, draped in the despicable gray of the Wehrmacht Army, were unadulterated evil.

"Mama?" Neven's light touch brought her back. They were walking home from work and his touch halted her, allowing Stana and Luka to move ahead. The heat had been unbearable, and after a sweltering night at the kafana they were still soaked. "Everything all right?"

"Yes." She didn't want to share with him her angst at their world shrinking and growing smaller. The only activity permitted was to walk to and from the kafana and to the market. Hitler's most recent sanctions banned stopping or even conversing with friends on any street corner in town. It mandated purposeful walking.

"I don't believe you." Right behind them marched two German soldiers, watching and listening. It was nearing midnight, and they were blocks from home.

"I'm worn down, nothing more."

A full moon lit their way, and Gružanska was in their sight. Turning to Neven, she said softly, "When they first seized control of us, they prohibited various social activities like going to school, attending dances, watching theater performances, taking part in sports, visiting museums, or using the library. But now, they've prohibited us from socializing…anywhere." Zora suddenly understood what Martha Levine had shared about Hitler forcing and cramming the Jews into minuscule living spaces in Berlin.

Zora walked in through the back, and her mouth opened in surprise to find her sister at her kitchen table, fanning herself. "Dušica, you're typically not awake at this hour; what's wrong?"

"It was too hot to sleep; besides, Sava called. She and Josie will be here later this week."

"How did she sound?"

"All right, but it's never easy to tell someone's emotions over the telephone. You know she's the type to hold everything in, but she explained more about Vlado. During a series of bombings across England, one struck in the middle of the night, forcing Vlado into a damp shelter for hours."

"Ohh…"

"His doctors felt the cold, drafty cellar likely made Vlado's lungs, which were already weak, much worse. He died from pneumonia."

"Vlado, such a good guy."

"Sava asked if you've made plans for Stana's sixteenth birthday. If not, she wanted to help."

Zora squeezed her eyes shut. "I've planned nothing." Sliding into the chair, she lowered her shoulders. She hadn't given any thought to any of her children's birthdays, primarily because she did not have the wherewithal to celebrate any of their milestones, no matter how significant. A tightness formed in her throat. "Life's far too complex. If only I could have spared them."

"Zora, I apologize for misspeaking. I never meant to imply or suggest." Dušica leaned over. "Let Sava help and indulge your children; she adores it. Hey, did you notice the table out back?" Dušica pointed.

"I did. I'm sorry, we got distracted in our conversation, and I never said how lovely it was. And with candles and an old tablecloth draping over the top, it'll be a sweet hideaway on those soft, summery nights." Seeing the wooden slab Marko had brought from the farm, Zora felt a surge of excitement. Someone handy, who looked for ways to improve their lives, was what she longed for in a husband.

She wished Peda were one-tenth as capable as Marko around the house, but Peda took up every square inch of space, providing little in return.

***

After the Wehrmacht trucks passed, Zora was forced to cover her nose from their exhaust fumes. Coming upon the boys' high school, Prva Muška Gimnazija, she scanned it, looking for signs of life, hoping it would soon open. Neven must finish his final year, and Vuk needed to catch up on his studies. Zora believed, as only a mother could, that Neven deserved to attend one of the finest universities in Europe. Her strongest desire was for this war not to impede that, because Neven had a brilliance the world deserved to know.

Amidst the bustling marketplace, she could not believe the desperate scramble for even the smallest scraps of food. Searching for a compassionate butcher who might give her a bone with some meat still clinging to it, all she found were three potatoes and two carrots. As she bent to grab a bottle of fresh milk, someone unexpectedly collided with her from behind. A voice she would always know caught her attention.

"Why, hello there."

"Kosta, what an unexpected surprise; how have you been holding up?" Zora's pulse quickened. In his grief, he still exuded a handsomeness.

Breaking into a smile, Kosta's dimples popped. "Better; I'm finally able to get some sleep. What about you, Zora?"

"Good, good. Have the Germans kept you busy?" It was difficult when he had been named the general manager of the entire Military Technical Institute after selling his father's factory. But luckily, Kosta's office was in another building and their paths seldom crossed at work. Still, she shouldn't prolong this conversation because if Peda ever found out...

Kosta flinched, turning his wedding band on the ring finger of his right hand. "They tried, but I could never work for Hitler. What about you?" His hooded eyes offered her the kindest smile, and in that moment, Zora recalled his wisdom far beyond his years. Blinking hard, she fought back the sudden tears threatening to engulf her.

"Why don't we step outside?" he suggested. "It's maddening in here." With his hand gently guiding her, Kosta quickly used his own ration card to pay for her groceries before he led them to a quiet area behind the market.

His touch unsettled her. Despite her best efforts to ignore it, there was that flicker of familiar warmth. If she were honest, it was also the subtle closeness she'd never felt with anyone, including her husband. Suddenly, the mask she'd long worn now crumbled, revealing the longing she had for this gentleman of a man.

"Zora," he whispered huskily, closing the distance.

"Kosta, move," Zora screamed as a German soldier materialized out of nowhere to whack his thick truncheon down on Kosta's arm, striking him hard. "No...!" Zora hollered at full volume, her eyes piercing the repugnant enemy of the Third Reich.

His black, beady eyes threw Zora a menacing glare. "No public display of affection. Move," shouted the stocky, hardened soldier, showing disgustingly dirty teeth, the buttons of his Wehrmacht jacket stretched to nearly popping over his rotund belly.

In a shaky voice, Zora said, "Kosta...your arm?"

Recoiling, he pulled it close to his chest. "Go to Dunja's; hurry."

Flinging her burlap bag over her shoulder, she took off for Paligorić, panting as she entered. Looking around, she noted two regulars at the bar drinking coffee, the scuffed wooden planks that lined the floor, the chairs stacked on the tables, and, luckily, Dunja behind the bar. "*Hvala bogu*," she muttered under her breath.

"What the hell?" Dunja's cigarette almost slipped from her lips. "You look terrified; whatever's wrong?"

Kosta arrived just as she'd filled Dunja in on what had happened.

"Let me see that arm, Kosta."

Grimacing, he pushed up his sleeve to reveal a large, angry bruise already starting to swell.

"Ah, not so bad," Dunja said, looking at Zora for confirmation. "Can you treat it?"

Zora lifted his muscular forearm with a measured breath as she felt for any breaks or soft tissue damage. "I have something to reduce the swelling, but you should see Dr. Milković to determine if your arm's broken." Flummoxed by how fast it had happened, she admitted, "I never saw him coming."

Lifting an eyebrow, Kosta sighed. "Who knows? Hitler's new edict, I'd imagine. Guess he wanted to send a message to us about not talking or stopping anywhere. I've seen him before, though, and he looks like one mean bastard."

"I've seen him, too—here."

Dunja stared at her, her penciled eyebrows nearly reaching her hairline. "You're kidding, right? In that case, Kosta, I'd suggest you not come in for a while. We don't need any unwanted attention."

Zora rubbed her collarbone. "The next time I wait on him, I'm going to sprinkle some bits of Atropa belladonna over his food, which will give him more than a bellyache."

"Zora?" Dunja and Kosta burst out laughing. Their stunned expressions showed Zora how surprised they were she was the one suggesting a nefarious act with a plant known to be poisonous.

Dunja took a drag of her cigarette. "Kosta, have Luka fetch the tinctures from Zora, instead of you. God forbid if that crazy husband of hers was home and found you at their door."

"Dunja," Zora said sharply, as a maroon flush rose to her ears. Mortified by her unwarranted comments regarding Peda's failures, she wondered what Dunja would think if she knew what he did with his hands.

"Sorry, sorry."

"I'm leaving." Zora sprinted out the door before she said something she would later regret.

Kosta ran after her. "Zora, wait." With a hand in the air, he shouted, "She was out of line, and we've known her rough edges for years. I'm certain she meant no harm. Our friend has yet to be schooled on how to temper her words." Catching up to her, he panted. "I've been wanting to talk to you, so allow me to walk you home."

Zora blew out a tiny burst of air. "Certainly; however, we've got to keep our heads lowered. I'll walk in front."

"Sure. It's about Luka and Stana. They have feelings for each other, which I could see by the way they looked at one another. It's made me question if they're aware of the rarity of what they have, and it evoked thoughts of you and me."

Every muscle in her body tensed. She could not bear to hear this, not when her nerves were so fraught.

"It was like looking in a mirror of you and me at their age."

Holding herself still, she asked, "Was there a question you wanted to ask?"

"For Stana's sixteenth birthday, Luka wanted to ask her on a date; however, it involves a drive, therefore he wanted yours and Peda's permission."

"Are you asking for him?" Zora's eyes danced.

The corners of Kosta's lips twitched. "Not exactly, more a hint. By the way, Luka's a responsible driver."

Turning to look at up at his muscular, six-foot-four-inch frame, she asked, "Where does he plan on taking her?"

Something flashed across his face before his expression softened. "Vrnjačka Banja," he said, clearing his throat.

Zora stopped breathing. Gasping, she took in air…This was impossible. History should not be repeating itself. The Bridge of Love was where Kosta and she went the summer it went so drastically wrong. It was immediately after they had finished high school, and there was an air of promise to their young love. They had stood on that bridge, pledging their love for one another. Oh, how she remembered it so well…standing in the pouring rain with the water slicing across Kosta's face, and the way he shivered because he'd forgotten his jacket. She could see the exact spot where they'd once believed all of their dreams would come true.

When their plans fell apart, Zora was genuinely crushed. Closing her eyes, it all came back, including the hurt and disillusionment. The Bridge of Love—what an ironic twist of fate. Taking a deep breath to steady herself, she asked, "You cannot be serious?"

"Believe me, Zora, I was just as shocked. It's why I wanted to speak to you first, so it's not a complete surprise."

Zora spun around and took hold of his hand, giving it a tight squeeze. "Tell me—will they have a better chance at love than we did?" Her cheeks burned, but she had to know.

Briefly nodding, Kosta slowly smiled. "I wish I had a crystal ball, but I can tell you how infatuated Luka has been with your daughter."

"I believe Stana feels the same, but they're so young, Kosta, with full lives ahead of them, including an education. In my mind's eye, they're studying together in Cambridge or Paris, then having illustrious careers teaching somewhere together. Neven, too."

He expelled a breath. "This war…" Leaning his head skyward, he said, "I just hope it doesn't knock them sideways. They're our most cherished gifts…and he's all I've got left."

Zora felt a wave of sadness for all that he'd lost. "Oh Kosta…I really hope life treats them kindly. Is it possible for Luka to evade the war?"

"I'm uncertain, but I've taken every necessary precaution to avoid it. He's lost so much family already, including his sister. Hopefully, they'll consider that."

"There's something unique about Luka; he's a special young man."

"Should I walk you further?"

Shushing him off, she forced a smile. "No thank you, but I'll get your tincture ready. Make sure to keep your arm elevated."

"I will, and Zora, it was wonderful bumping into you today, even with this." Smiling, he lifted his injured arm.

***

"Peda?" Zora called, entering their home and making a beeline for her cabinet where she stored her medicinal herbs.

"In the bedroom," he shouted.

"W—what's going on?" As she entered their bedroom, Zora saw clothing strewn across the bed. His hair was rumpled, as if he'd just woken from a nap. Alarm registered in her gut.

"I went to the Royalist registration this morning, for resistance fighters. Your sister and her friend Josie were there. Guess what?"

"No...Peda. Please don't tell me you're considering signing up?"

Grinning, Peda saluted her. "Not considering, Zora. I've already signed up." With his shoulders pulled back, he directed his gaze toward her. "You're looking at a member of the Royalist Resistance of Ravna Gora," he said proudly.

Her throat went dry. "No."

"Why?" He gesticulated wildly, his voice climbing.

"Why? We never discussed it. It's what married couples do, they talk with one another and discuss plans together. Your feet were severely injured on your walk home from Montenegro. It's taken months and a lot of care to heal them. We have no money for boots or extra blankets. There's also the challenge of hiking the Suvobor. How will it affect your feet and knees, which you've complained are hurting?" Leaning against the wall, she inhaled, shaking her head in bafflement.

"How dare you try and diminish my plans?" His eyes pulsed with fury and his pupils darkened as he grabbed her roughly by the shoulders. "You're wrong, Zora...I can do this, so do not stop me." Shoving her aside, he drew in a burst of air. "I suggest you ask your mother to move in here. This way, she could be your babysitter while you work, instead of me."

Feeling completely alone, Zora tried not to upset him further. "That's a great idea, Peda. I'll ask her, and I'm sorry." As she stuttered out an apology, with a pang of unbearable sorrow, she reluctantly acknowledged her marriage was nothing more than shattered dreams.

CHAPTER EIGHTEEN

PEDA

The Royalist Resistance Headquarters, Ravna Gora, Serbia July 1941

PEDA LEFT HOME WITH a bag containing his cigarettes, clothing, socks, underwear, water, rakija, and a loaf of bread. Luckily, he had some dinars in his pocket, which allowed him to find a seat on a crowded train heading toward Gornji Milanovac. From there, he arrived at the base of the Suvobor Mountains. Much to his astonishment, he discovered two men who had enrolled with him, waiting. Covered in sweat, Peda lit a cigarette, feeling a clarity he had not experienced in weeks. After exchanging pleasantries with the younger men, he began to climb, grateful for the sun's golden hue beaming through the trees.

He sensed them behind him as he curled up the precarious cliffs, clinging to the hardened rocks and pine trees, and berated himself for not remembering a pair of heavy industrial gloves. He swore as he stepped over a mound of pinecones, realizing he'd forgotten to fill his empty jug of water. Despite the gullies and caves, the steep mountain offered little protection from the now blistering sun, its penetrating rays burning through his flimsy cotton shirt.

Desperately parched, he yelled out, "I'm going to stop here." His breathing labored from the steep incline, he turned, but Peda no longer saw the men behind him; he imagined they must have veered onto a smaller trail. Looking over at the vast expanse, the mountains highlighted the grandeur of Yugoslavia—a country worth fighting for. Soon after, he discovered a small cave underneath a copse of trees that looked ideal for the perfect respite. Peda gingerly crept inside and folded himself to the ground, utterly spent.

As he enjoyed the coolness, his thoughts drifted to his recent conversation with his friend Ðuro.

"Peda, I've got something to tell you."

"What?" he said, leaning on the bar, nursing his drink.

"I—ah, I've decided to join the Resistance…the Partisans. I leave tomorrow."

"What in the world…?" His friend had made a complete turnaround, switching his allegiance to becoming a member of the Communist Party. Speechless, Peda felt like someone had thrown freezing water in his face. "How could you, Ðuro? What were you thinking?" Peda felt shaken as he grappled with his friend's betrayal, questioning himself for not recognizing the signs.

"Well, after Churchill's speech, and after the King and members of our Parliament abandoned us, why should I risk my life to fight for the very people who've left us, and Yugoslavia?"

"You have no idea what occurred. Maybe they were forced out by the Germans and had to leave in a hurry.

Our King would never abandon us." Peda was so enraged that he threw a drink in his face, storming out.

He regretted not acting better or trying to convince Đuro otherwise. Still plagued by lingering questions, he wondered who had recruited Đuro. Had he been deceived in believing Đuro's views had been exactly like his own? The Royalists supported the Karađorđević Monarchy, and thus the Serbian Orthodox Church, which clashed with the Communists, who opposed religion and God.

"Phew…what a mess," Peda murmured. "I hope these differences will not rip us further apart." Knowing the situation in Croatia all too well, he lit a cigarette and shook his head. Restless, he tossed until falling into a troubled sleep.

Heavy footsteps roused him awake the following morning. Fearing the hard-sounding footsteps might be the Wehrmacht, Peda peered cautiously around the corner. Not seeing anything, he quickly glanced again, feeling his heart race.

"Zradvo," said a loud voice as a giant of a man appeared.

"Hello," Peda said, sagging in relief. The man's long beard, symbolizing the freedom fighters of the Ravna Gora Movement, was instantly recognizable. The šajkača planted on his curly head, the narrow, V-shaped woolen cap traditionally worn by the peasants and farmers in this part of Serbia, was further proof he was a Royalist.

"Are you a recruit?" asked the strapping warrior.

"I am." Peda's legs still shook. "Initially, I mistook you for the Germans."

"Thank goodness we weren't," he said, smiling. "Why not follow my unit the rest of the way to camp?"

Nodding, Peda gathered his things. He estimated this giant was at minimum six feet eight inches tall, with sweat glistening down his muscular back. He also noted how imposingly the twelve men strode uphill in the clamminess, their loose-fitting woolen pants held at the waist by a rope. Their graying shirts billowed in the scorching wind.

The man offered his thick hand when they took a break. "I'm Jovica Ristić from Niš. You'll spend your first few days in camp learning what we do. We've learned to evaluate everyone before assigning tasks, so you might start by doing night watch or cooking meals in the hut. Our greatest needs will determine the outcome. Any idea what you're good at, Peda?" he asked.

Peda breathed in, not liking what he was hearing. Fueled by a desire for conflict, he was determined not to be bullied or overlooked. "Err…I came to fight."

"Ahh…" said Jovica, grinning.

"My intention was to protect our country."

"Noble. We'll see how it all unfolds. Čiča Draža always knows."

Peda saw power in Jovica, with his lean, ropy muscles. This was not the reception he had expected, nor was he interested in learning new things, especially women's work. As they forged on, sweat trickled down his face and neck. Feeling woozy, he wished he'd remembered to replenish his water.

They passed young oak and conifer trees and fissures in the rocks. When the air got hotter, vultures, eagles, and peregrine falcons swooped down before graciously flying overhead, circling them as they climbed.

"Look in the distance." Jovica pointed. "It's a crested tit."

Birds fascinated Peda. "I've never seen one before," he remarked in awe, tipping his head back. "There's beauty in these mountains."

Snaking their way on a narrow, single-filed path, they bumped into twelve revolutionaries coming down. Squeezing into a tiny clearing to allow them to pass, Jovica saluted them. "*Bog svama junaci.*"

With their chins high, they responded, "God be with you, too, Četnicima."

"Where might they be heading?" Starved, thirsty, and ready to drop, Peda deduced these fighters looked young and energetic. He heard them singing as they wound their way down the mountain:

Marširala, Marširala, kralja Petra garda.
Marširala, Marširala, kralja Petra garda.

He had not heard this enthusiastic song about King Peter's guards marching in battle since he'd fought in the previous war.

"Hard to know." Jovica paused. "They could be going on a reconnaissance mission, or to blow up a convoy of German trucks." Grinning broadly, Jovica explained, "A few days ago, we shot one of the staff cars from the Wehrmacht's 724th Infantry Regiment in Valjevo. Inside was a German commander."

"Whoa; what happened?" Peda's eyebrows raised in curiosity.

"They retaliated by storming every village surrounding the town of Valjevo, surprising our people. They wrenched people from their homes…fifty-two, each executed in retaliation."

Peda's hand covered his opened mouth.

"It's why Čiča Draža has continued being cautious, at every turn. We cannot afford a madcap fighter joining us and blowing up one of our missions. The Germans' retaliatory actions against our innocent have been terribly disheartening, therefore we're forever mindful of our people."

"Zdravo." A seljački from below the ridge waved at them.

The sun dipped low as Peda excitedly waved back, looking downward. "I'm surprised the sheepherders bring their cattle this high up the range."

"The higher they go, the fresher the grass. The seljačke play a vital role in keeping us alive. Without them, we would not last on this mountain."

"How so?" Peda scratched his temple.

"They've provided the bulk of our food. Every spring, they bring their herds to feed on the lush meadows of Mount Maljan. Only a small group of farmers grasped the purity of the soil up here for grazing. Over the years, these seljačke built small, log huts with thatched roofs. Even without plumbing, they have all this." Jovica swept his arms wide. "Feeding so many of us hasn't been easy, but these farmers have done a brilliant job providing enough food for us."

"How much further?" Peda nodded in better understanding, but his cheeks burned in mortification. He had been in such a hurry to leave home, he hadn't given a fiddler's fart about food, bedding, or much else. Stepping over a fallen tree, he noticed the bramble and pine needles cluttering the forest floor.

"Two hours. See that? There's a small stream with clean water to refill our canteens."

"I—ah, don't have a canteen, but I brought a small glass jug, but forgot to fill it." Peda's decision to come had been rather spontaneous. He recognized how foolhardy he'd seemed, just to get away from home.

"Bloody hell, man. No wonder your lips looked so dry. Here—take mine." Jovica handed Peda his canteen, which was half full. "Drink up."

Peda chugged the precious water, overwhelmed with gratitude for this leader's unexpected kindness. He wiped the water from his chin with his sleeve. "*Puno hvala.*"

Continuing upward, they passed lichens, various bushes, and an extensive forest of trees until Peda spotted a rusted vehicle. He smiled—signs of life! Around the next curve, they came to a bivouac with four men dressed in a mish-mash of part Royal Yugoslav Army and part Četnik uniforms.

"These are our guards on lookout duty." Jovica saluted them. "Now, we lower our voices, Peda, because up this high, voices carry."

His heart sped up because he was almost there—Ravna Gora. To be with fellow resistance fighters and possibly his son. A tension coiled in his belly. But then, fear set in, and he contemplated whether he was good enough for this mission. Panic suddenly gripped him with indecision. He needed a drink badly. Maybe he should not have come. No, he had the right to be here.

It was dark by the time they reached the Royalist Resistance Camp of Colonial Draža Mihajlović, and from the looks of it, dinner had long passed.

Smiling at Peda after their arduous climb, Jovica placed a hand on his shoulder. "I'll see what I can rustle up at the cook's hut. See that supply hut over there?" Jovica pointed to a stocky, rounded-faced man staring at them. "He'll fix you up with some bedding. I prefer sleeping under the stars whenever the weather's warm enough, unless someone's spotted a bear. You know our Yugoslavian mountains are home to a substantial amount of bears, right?" Chuckling, Jovica walked away.

Spurred by a boundless enthusiasm, Peda sprinted to the supply hut, but then he skidded to a halt. "You have got to be joking—Božo, is that really you? He blinked in pleasurable surprise.

"As I live and breathe…Peda Brković? What are *you* doing here?" questioned a dazed Božidar Momčilović, his hands covering the top of his protruding belly. "Aren't you too old for this stuff? Jesus, Peda, how long has it been since you and I fought in the big one?"

Joyously thrilled to find his old army buddy up here, Peda broke into unrestrained laughter. "Close to twenty-three years. Man, it's really good to see you." So far, the revolutionaries he had seen or met were all Goran's age. "Can I ask you something? I signed up to fight, that's all I want to do, but Jovica mentioned something about everyone first being evaluated. What's that about?" Peda had begun to pace.

"Aw, Peda; the same old fiery hothead." Božo hooted, his belly jiggling. "You haven't changed a bit." Handing him a bundle of straw and a ragged sheet, he suggested, "Take it easy and learn the ropes. Besides, how will you manage the hills every day? Unless you're young, they're a killer on your knees. I'm not able to fight, but it was important for me to still be part of this mission, so here I am. A bit of advice, my friend. When they ask your best skill, think long and hard before you answer. *Laku noć.*"

Lying on the ground with his hands behind his head, Peda was still awake. The men snoring on both sides of him would require some getting used to, but it felt fantastic being here. It was the right decision. Looking over at the makeshift huts and tables where the men congregated to eat meals, he'd felt an instant connection. It was about the camaraderie and bond with these men, these fighters who knew their time ahead would not be easy. Nonetheless, they were here to fight for God and country, and so was he. Peda wanted to prove something to Zora and his family. Finally…he could breathe.

CHAPTER NINETEEN

SAVA

Vraćevšnica Monastery, Serbia
August 1941

B Y THE END OF July, the Royalist Resistance
had left their mark. Their train derailments and
surprise attacks on the Wehrmacht Army had
provoked Hitler to the point where he wanted them
obliterated. Meanwhile, Conductor Matić and Neven
had created a communication system for the Resistance,
and today Sava and Josie were delivering messages. Perspiring and flushed, they trudged down the center of a
seldom-used country path, with Života trailing behind.
Concealed in their disguises, they made their way through
the forest on the southern slope of the Rudnik Mountains,
bringing supplies to the Vraćevšnica Monastery.

The blistering heat of summer had intensified, and today
Sava noticed Života withering under it. Just as they'd nego-
tiated around the dried-up furrows and fallen trees strewn
across the lane, the ox stopped, refusing to budge. Života
tried to detach the heavy cart attached to it, but it appeared
too cumbersome.

"Please forgive me for packing it too heavy." Sava sighed with regret. "I promise I'll pack less next time."

"Humph," Života exclaimed, gasping for air.

In an instant, Sava's ears picked up the sound of rustling coming from the bushes. Suddenly, two Germans jumped from behind, shouting at them, "*Aufhören, aufhören!*"

Fear coursed through Sava, yet she stayed rooted to the spot. It would be up to her to convince them that she and Josie were Serbian Orthodox nuns, but with two rifles pointed at her, they were making it tremendously difficult. "*Guten Morgen,*" she squeaked.

Sava watched their faces register surprise as she spoke their native language. The shorter, more round-faced of the two aimed his rifle toward the cart. "*Entladen.*"

Waving her hand and trying to appear nonchalant, Sava said, "Oh, it's nothing more than potatoes, oats, and milk jugs for our sisters at the monastery." Internally, she was a bundle of nerves.

The soldier, his face marked with mottles and redness, screamed louder. "*Entladen!*"

Heart jumping in her throat, Sava turned to Života and Josie. "They said to empty the cart right now." Sava prayed she could resolve this before Života fired any shots, knowing he carried a gun.

Once the cart was unloaded, all that remained was a file folder with the sheet music for the *Liturgy of St John Chrysostom* by the famed Serbian composer Stevan Mokranjac. Holding her breath, her eyes darted to the taller man, who moved to reach the file. Unsure of what to do, she instinctively grabbed the folder and opened it. Gesturing toward the sheet music with her finger, Sava began to sing. As her nervousness dissipated, she gained momentum, and her voice grew more robust.

Taken aback, they gawked at her. Sava observed their stiff shoulders loosening into a more relaxed stance. When she finished singing, both men nodded at her, smiling. The taller of the two said, "Beautiful." He then helped her place the sacks of food back onto the cart, and with a click of his dusty heels, he lifted his hand, and firmly stated, "*Heil Hitler.*"

Relief swept through her as she viewed their departure through the woods. She stammered, "How could they have found us…out here?"

Života's steely resolve returned. "Frankly, I think they must have gotten separated from their unit; they were nothing more than snot-nosed kids."

"Quite persistent little buggers, weren't they?" Josie fidgeted with her hands.

"They sure frightened me. Look, my hands are still shaking." Sava understood the enormity of the risks associated with working in the underground, which for her was both exhilarating and dangerous.

"I was convinced we'd be arrested, but you saved us." Josie's eyes brightened. "Sheesh, what's that bloody smell?" Her eyes glanced down before she cried, "Careful, it's animal scat."

"Eek," Sava said, lifting her long black podrasnik off the ground as she attempted to skirt around it. She leaned toward Josie whispering, "Conductor embedded messages on the actual sheet music. If they had gotten hold of it, we'd likely be dead right now. It's why I acted so spontaneously."

"Whoa—whose idea was it to bury the messages?"

"Conductor's. I helped a bit, but it was really Neven who reconfigured the coding by inserting it inside our choir's musical notes. If you look closely at the staff and two particular notes, you'll see it."

"My goodness, that's brilliant. But Sava, you're quite impressive in your own right. I mean that sincerely. Women here are seldom recognized."

Touched, Sava said, "Thank you." Perspiring, she questioned why the sisters she knew never seemed overheated, dressed in black, even on the hottest days. "The only clothing not making me hot is the apostolnik, possibly because it's covering my head and made from a light cotton."

"How much further?" Josie asked, and Sava noticed she too was drenched, soaked.

Josie's eyes tracked two eagles above, their wings spread. "Two kilometers. They're extraordinary, aren't they?"

"They sure are." Sava's upturned face beamed in wonder. "Were you aware that twin eagles graced our Yugoslavian coat of arms? I'd guess the Occupiers may have already altered it to reflect something disturbing, like a swastika."

"How are you holding up, Gospođo?" Života asked, his beefy hand swiping the perspiration from under his neck.

"It's tricky navigating these long-neglected back roads."

Harrumphing, she forged on, finally arriving at the old stone monastery dating back to the fourteenth century. Sava experienced a flood of relief when they passed through the brown gates adorned with hand-painted frescos on each side. She was excited seeing the nuns of Vraćevšnica Monastery lined up to greet them. "Hello, my friends," Sava warmly greeted each nun as they hurried them through the courtyard, vibrant with colors.

"Hmm," Sava murmured to herself, curious about what might have frightened their worried faces.

Whenever she entered the tranquil, majestic white building, it felt like returning home. Equally, she marveled at the head of Vraćevšnica, the Most Reverend Abbess Mother Katarina, and the agility she had for an eighty-year-old.

Turning, Abbess Mother kindly suggested, "Sisters, please bring the slatko and three tall glasses of fresh drinking water for our guests." She then turned her gaze to Sava, Josie, and Života before clapping. "Friends, please come."

Remembering their mouthwatering slatko made from fresh rose petals, Sava nearly swooned. It might possibly be the best she'd tasted, and it all came from their flourishing garden. The reverential sanctuary was thick with the earthy scent of candles and the intoxicating fragrance of sacred incense, inducing fond memories of her and Zora singing. Sava savored the tranquility as time stood still in these hallowed halls. If only she could stay here longer. The tense muscles in her neck loosened, and her pulse slowed.

"There's been some trouble," Abbess Mother mentioned softly.

"What type of trouble?" Sava's body was instantly alert.

"Ah…" Abbess Mother paused before answering. "There was a surprise attack on our Resistance, which ended poorly. It's easier if I show you, but I must warn you—it's gruesome. The Germans showed no mercy."

Sava's eyes moved to Života's, who was leaning against the wall. Her thoughts raced with concern for Goran.

"Unfortunately, the night may be long, so enjoy these refreshments." Sighing, Abbess Mother's hand clasped onto the cross hanging from a long chain around her neck.

Once they'd finished, Abbess Mother led them down a cavernous stone hallway with wooden cross beams on the ceiling. "Our sisters were extremely distraught when they brought the injured men here last night." She continued walking toward the rear of the monastery, which abutted the forest.

"Goodness. I hadn't realized you had this much space; it's huge."

Sava gasped as they entered a sizeable room that reeked of a foul odor. The makeshift cots held eight of their revolutionaries, all brutally injured. Promptly covering her mouth, Sava focused her attention on Sister Simonida tending to an unconscious soldier. "Abbess Mother, how did this happen?"

Heaving a sigh, she first crossed herself. "Our men were doing reconnaissance work in the forest and an entire Wehrmacht unit ambushed them. Despite the casualties and injuries, they couldn't risk bringing any of the wounded here until after dark. Tragically, the delay resulted in the loss of two men, suffering significant blood loss." Wringing her hands, Abbess Mother continued, "Forty-five of our men perished, and another ninety were gravely injured. They brought the worst here. We're doing our best, but having only one nurse has made it challenging. Our sisters also have difficulty *touching*..." Abbess Mother's voice trailed off.

Sava offered a soft smile in acknowledgment of the nuns' apprehensiveness around men. Concentrating on Sister Simonida, she deduced this nun was no more than twenty years old. "Josie and I will follow Sister Simonida's lead, Abbess Mother." Bowing from the waist, Sava wondered how, with little medical training, she would be able to help the men.

While the nuns hovered in the background, after grabbing a pair of scissors, Josie moved to a cot and efficiently snipped away the burnt clothing to reveal the man's naked, scorched body. Sava heard the nuns' collective gasps, knowing they were stunned by his nakedness. This soldier's body was covered in burns. Sava moved closer, instinctively realizing little could be done to save him. Still, she followed Josie's lead because Josie had training and had assisted the medics in the fields of England and France.

"Can we radio a medic?" Josie asked, squeezing her eyes shut. "This one's bad, and we've nothing strong enough to ease his pain."

Abbess Mother stepped in, frowning. "I'm afraid not. We're their last hope."

Josie blinked. "You can't be serious, Abbess Mother?"

"They only have one medic on the mountain; that's why they brought these men here."

With a glimmer of possibility, Sava's face lifted. "There might be a way. May I borrow your telephone, Abbess Mother?"

"Yes, my child. Across the hall, hidden behind the credenza, and against the back wall."

Eyebrows raised, Sava exclaimed. "Interesting."

"We try." Abbess Mother winked.

Clucking, Sava realized there was undeniably more to Abbess Mother. "I have a sister in Kragujevac who's a travarka. Since we have no access to a physician, she might be our best option." Sava followed her to the credenza. "It's worth a try, right?"

Josie entered with bloodied hands, skidding to a halt. "God, yes. Your family's full of surprises."

"Growing up, we spent summers in my mother's village in Croatia. My mother's mother was the local healer who treated everyone in the villages with her medicinal herbs. Zora sat at her feet and absorbed all of it. By the time Zora was ten years old, she had gone from village to village with Baka Cveta, helping tend the sick. Today, we marvel at her capacity to heal."

"How soon could she get here?" Josie questioned, her eyes pleading. "It's doubtful this fellow will make it through the night."

Sava looked past the worry lines sprinkled across Josie's freckled forehead to Života, who'd just entered the room. Catching his eye, Sava asked, "If my sister were available, would there be enough petrol to fetch her in Kragujevac?"

"I believe so. It's about a one-hour drive."

With the receiver in midair, Sava suddenly became frozen with fear. What am I doing? she asked herself. She didn't want to add more pressure to her sister's challenging life; dragging her into the Resistance might be a terrible idea…But Zora was exactly what these men needed. Her sister knew nothing about her role or involvement in Sloboda and the Resistance, nor the dangers she faced daily as one of two stealthy couriers.

Shutting her eyes, Sava placed the receiver back on its handle. "I can't do this. With seven children and a ne'er-do-well husband, who's now with the Royalists, I cannot justify…" She wrapped her arms around herself and closed her eyes, reflecting on the unease of placing Zora in a situation of duplicity and subterfuge. Weighing the odds, she went outside and paced over the smooth stones on the walkway.

Minutes passed before Abbess Mother came to check on her. "What's troubling you, dear?"

Sava's stomach twisted in knots. "I'm petrified about dragging my sister in. Her life hasn't been easy." Sava didn't want to reflect on her sister's shoes that no longer fit or her incredible shame whenever she was forced to accept handouts.

Abbess Mother laid her hands on top of Sava's. "My dear, God never gives us too much to bear. If I assume correctly, someone has minimized your sister's life. Why not give her the power to decide? She may surprise you. Oh, that reminds me; one of the men who came last night said he needed to speak with you. He's expected back tonight, so I've instructed one of our sisters to await his knock." As they walked inside together, the gracious Abbess Mother said, "Good luck."

After a lengthy telephone conversation with Zora, Sava's voice escalated. "My sister's arriving tomorrow." Although conflicted, she choked down her concerns, knowing there would be no turning back once word of Zora's healing got out. Facing Abbess Mother, Sava tapped her heart. "Thank you for your guidance." Moving toward Života, Sava said, "She will be ready at four o'clock tomorrow morning."

***

Time mattered greatly, and the second Zora arrived, the sisters whisked her through the monastery gates, her mahogany hair piled high on her head. Carrying a large worn tapestry bag overflowing with tinctures, bottles, and what looked like branches and rolls of gauze, Zora lowered her head in devotion as she walked inside.

Sava's first impression was how much her sister resembled Mary Poppins from P. L. Travers' book, which she'd read her last time in London. Hugging Zora, she whispered, "They're all thrilled you're here. I gather Dunja understood?"

"Is Dunja part of it?" Zora asked, eyebrows raised. "I hadn't put that piece together."

Dipping her head, Sava attempted to explain. "I'm sorry, love. I wanted to tell you, but I didn't want to have you worry. Our job's to support the Resistance from the shadows—all for the good of saving our Kingdom."

"I should have gathered as much. Tell me, what about Kosta?"

Oh boy. She could tell Zora felt excluded. "Come; let's walk outside." Sava firmly clasped Zora's hand and explained how Sloboda was formed.

Returning inside, the metallic smell of blood and burnt flesh permeated the air, and Zora immediately crossed herself before murmuring, "But by grace." After rolling up her sleeves, she reached into her bag to retrieve her mortar and pestle. She began to mix a powerful combination of hajdučka trava, with rusomaca and vrba ili potočnjak, before lifting out her special potion, which she mixed into the compound. After dipping the linen cloths into the compound, Zora painstakingly wrapped each soaked piece of linen around the man's wounds. "There. Let's hope this will extract the harmful toxins from his body and stop his bleeding," she said to Sava.

Holding her breath, Sava nodded before making her way toward the back, where a man writhed in pain, his gun still in his holster. "You must stay completely still," she said, her eyes fixed on his, as she cautiously withdrew his pistol. Ensuring the safety was on, she laid it on the floor beneath him. Inhaling, she began to irrigate his untidy leg wound. With his body exposed, Sava observed his taut stomach muscles quivering in pain. To soothe him, she hummed an old folk song.

"OWW. That hurts like hell." His stormy eyes darted up her willowy frame. "I like you singing. Will he make it?" he asked, pointing to his comrade that Zora was tending to.

"Let me check." Sava went to ask her sister.

Shaking her head, Zora whispered, "It's doubtful he'll survive the next twenty-four hours. I gave him something to numb his pain; there's nothing we can do without a skilled surgeon. His belly's riddled with bullets." Swallowing, Zora's voice was muffled. "I'm sorry."

She tamped back her ache at the wrongness of war; Sava could never reconcile an ounce of meaning from fighting. Returning to her patient, she studied the lean curves of his face. Reaching inside for strength, she looked him in the eye. "I'm afraid his wounds are too substantial, and there are too many."

He reached for her hand, squeezed it, and in a scratchy voice, admitted, "He's my kum. We grew up next door to one another, like brothers."

Sava's heart plummeted. "I'm so sorry. We tried, but…"

Kumstvo was sacred to Serbians, spanning generations of respect. It was the most incredible honor to be asked to be one's kum. Among Serbs, nothing held more regard.

"Let's see if I can find something to alleviate your pain." Reversing her steps, Sava went to Zora and watched her work. It reminded her of Vlado, who'd extended countless offers for Zora to attend the university for a medical degree because he'd seen such promise in her. If only he were alive to see her now…Blinded by tears, Sava swallowed the lump in her throat.

While caring for these men, Sava lost track of time, until she heard the sweet blend of voices filtering through the room. It must be evening vespers in the monastery, and the enchanting sounds drifting in were from the nuns chanting in melodic reverie to *Slavite Gospoda*, a song she knew by heart. Lifting her face, Sava started to sing harmoniously, her voice rising with the nuns'.

Sava's voice stopped Zora in her tracks. Smiling and with goosebumps, she listened as Sava magically blended perfectly with the nuns. "Their chanting must be their way of offering prayers for the men."

After vespers ended, Zora motioned Života and Sava closer. "I'm sorry to tell you, but it's paramount you're aware, specifically Abbess Mother. These men are full of lice, which could spell big trouble."

"How so?" Sava's eyes rounded.

She pointed to the first man she'd treated. "It's likely he was already suffering from typhus long before he was shot. Humans contract typhus from lice bites."

"Oh, dear." Sava backed away, her green, almond-shaped eyes growing in size. "How did you know?"

"The bloodied bites and the scabbing on his neck, arms, and trunk. His fever was another indicator of an infection. Everyone treating these men must wash their hands, often and meticulously. Also, every instrument must be thoroughly cleaned after each use. Typhus spreads extremely quickly."

Coming in at the tail end of their conversation, Josie's mouth opened. "Typhus? Oh, shit, where's the Epsom salts?" She pivoted; the nuns were right on her heels. Placing her hand over her mouth, Josie turned. "Forgive me for swearing, I meant no harm."

The nuns giggled, staring in awe at the diminutive American.

***

Sava was bone tired. Every inch of her body ached, and the instant her head hit the pillow, she was asleep. Yet, something interrupted her delicious dream.

"Gospođo?" A young nun tapped her wrist.

"What?" Sava asked groggily, trying to open her weary eyes.

"There's someone from the Resistance here for you." The nun backed out of the room.

Sava went to the other cot to awaken Josie. They quickly splashed water on their faces from the bowl on the dresser and ran their fingers through their hair. After dressing, they darted down the darkened hallway toward the front door, the thick stones cool on their bare feet.

"Gospođo Ivković? The tall man quickly rose. "I'm Jovica Ristić, and I'm afraid I've got some bad news."

"Yes?" He had got to the point rather quickly. Sava's immediate concern was for her nephew, and her heart thumped wildly.

"We caught word, and Čiča Draža wanted to ensure you're aware of what's transpired recently in Croatia…with the Ustaše. There's been another atrocity in Glina. We don't have all the specifics, but they locked over two hundred of our people inside ah—a church and butchered them all. The perpetrators bullied them into believing that by converting to Roman Catholicism, their lives would be spared."

"Nooo…" Sava closed her eyes, imagining the families. A lump formed in her throat as she brushed a strand of hair back into her ponytail. "Any other messages?" She stood to her full height, her back erect, but the heaviness of the news weighed her down.

Jovica's thick brows furrowed. "Yes. Čiča Draža advised extra caution about never letting your guard down. Stay close to Života. Last week, three British officers visited Ravna Gora and surprised us by asking if we had a female resistance fighter who's an Amerikanka."

His eyes swung to Josie. "Čiča wanted to make certain you, Gospođo Whitney, were aware of this." Looking at Sava, he asked, "What messages do you have for us?"

His carved cheekbones, Sava noted, were more prominent when his face relaxed into a luminous smile. She handed him the sheets of music. "On our way here, two German soldiers surprised us by jumping from the bushes. They forced us to unload our cart."

"Really?" Jovica stood perfectly erect, but Sava saw the way his alert eyes drilled in. "This…we never expected. None of us realized they'd venture this far into the forest." His eyes raked over her face. "Are you certain you're all right, Gospođo Ivković?"

Josie motioned to the warrior. "We're fine, but only because of this genius. She started singing, from the sheet music, likely saving our lives. Please let the men on Ravna Gora know how wonderfully capable Dr. Ivković is. Would you mind stepping outside, so I can borrow a cigarette, and you could describe the Brit asking about me."

Sava thanked Jovica before sprinting back to their room and tiptoeing over to her cot, hoping not to awaken Zora. Seething with rage, Sava sat with her head in her hands struggling to grasp the unfolding events in Croatia and questioning what could have driven this group to commit such a large-scale killing. What was their ultimate purpose, and how had this hatred manifested itself? On this warm, airless night she also wondered what secrets the old monastery walls held. Tossing, an eternity passed before she finally fell asleep.

CHAPTER TWENTY

ZORA

Kragujevac, Serbia
Late August to early September 1941

IN THE EARLY HOURS before dawn, a heavy mist had descended on Kragujevac. Unable to sleep, Zora lay awake, contemplating Officer Kord Webber Gerhardt's fascination with Stana. He had become more relentless in his pursuit of her daughter, causing Zora to grow more alarmed. After adjusting her work schedule to coincide with Stana's, each time he came in, she meticulously supervised his every move. Gerhardt was trying to lure Stana to Berlin to sing on one of the grandest stages in Europe. Zora found his boldness and arrogance repulsive, and unfortunately, she worried Stana might be enjoying the attention. Apparently, he lived a charmed and cultured life in Germany, aside from being handsome and charismatic.

"Mama." A whisper penetrated the darkness.

"What's wrong, Čedo?" Zora sat up.

"My knees hurt."

"Your knees? Did you fall?" She slid her hands to the bottom of his pajamas to roll up a pant leg and, sure enough, his knobby knees were indeed swollen. "Are you sure you didn't hurt yourself, maybe wrestling with your brothers?" Please let him say yes, she thought.

"No." Čedo grimaced in pain. Zora could see the tears on his eyelashes. Having had his share of sickness, Čedo knew the difference.

"May I lift your shirt to measure your heartbeat?" she asked gently.

"Yeah," he whispered, shivering. "But I'm sooo cold."

"Well, hop on in, my sweetheart." Moving closer, she smelled the stink of sickness coursing from his body and knew he must have been battling a fever. After tucking him in, she sat with her legs crossed, considering the most prevalent illnesses she'd recently seen. She couldn't stop thinking about her initial diagnosis—rheumatic fever. A dreaded illness. Zora contemplated Čedo's symptoms and continued to reconsider others.

"Čedo, have you had a sore throat?"

"Yeah, my throat hurt a lot last week. I told Baka Mima."

"Ah…good. While I was away, what did she give to help your sore throat?" Zora worried about the consequences of her mother potentially becoming infected, too. Despite her previous good health, her mother had visibly aged in the five months following their father's passing.

"She looked at my throat and gave me hot tea and honey."

"Ah, bravo, Čedo." Patting her bed, Zora suggested, "Why not sleep here today? It's cooler and quieter."

After checking his temperature, Zora dressed quickly and awakened Neven. "Please go to Dr. Milković and ask him to come…right away."

Heart pounding, Zora rushed to run some chilly water over the washrags, which she used on Čedo's forehead and chest in hopes of lowering his temperature. After removing the compresses, she placed slices of potatoes across his chest.

***

"Rheumatic fever," Dr. Milković said. Once he had packed his stethoscope, he took hold of Zora's elbow and directed her to the kitchen. "I've said this before, and I'll say it again, Zora, you have overlooked your true calling. Medical school would have been an excellent choice for you. Čedo will require monitoring for the next week or two, but I feel we caught it early, thanks to you."

After the doctor left, Zora let out a substantial sigh. While she was pouring water into the kettle to boil, Dušica came in, trailed by Stefan and a wobbly Andrej.

"Dušica, no—Čedo has rheumatic fever…the little ones."

Taking a step back, Dušica shooed the boys out of the door. "How bad?"

Zora explained the situation.

"What should we do?" She looked frightened to Zora.

"Stay away. If Marko has an extra chicken, would you make a pot of chicken noodle soup? Čedo adores your soup."

"Of course, I, ah…the Germans questioned Marko this morning."

Zora studied her in alarm. "And…?"

"I—I don't know all of it. They showed up at the farm and interrogated him and his father."

"My God, were they asking about the kids?"

"I don't know…" Dušica shut her eyes before her legs gave way.

***

With a combination of medicine, potent herbs, and an old Serbian remedy of garlic and honey, Čedo got better. There was a noticeable improvement in his complexion, and he'd regained the ability to stand and walk independently. Although not entirely out of the woods, Čedo's health had significantly improved, enough that Zora could return to work. Prior to leaving the house, she said to Vuk, "I put his medicine here. Make sure he takes it after he's eaten."

"Sure. Is there anything else?"

"If there's any change in his complexion, or his temperature climbs, call me right away."

"Yes, Mama." Vuk stood soldier straight.

"Don't forget to keep an eye on Baka as well."

"Yes."

"Vuk, I know this hasn't been easy. War does that." Swallowing hard, Zora said, "I know how tough it's been, and I'd like you to know how much I appreciate you." Pulling him in for a powerful hug, she stepped outside where Neven and Stana waited.

Neven asked, "Mama, what have you heard about Milan Nedić?"

"Aside from previously serving as a minister of something, nothing else. Why?" Zora's eyebrows arched.

"Last week the Germans appointed him to lead our new quisling government. Some have labeled it as a puppet government."

"A puppet government, just what we need. We've got bread lines for miles, nowhere near enough food to feed everyone, and no jobs. Our political landscape is enough to make my head spin, but I'm sure we'll hear more about it soon enough. Maybe he'll have the power to open our schools?"

Entering the kafana, Zora caught a whiff of something remarkable bubbling in the large white pot on the stove.

"Wow, whatever you're making, Miško, sure smells wonderful. I hope you saved me a bowl." Stana impishly grinned before tying on her apron.

Pulling her aside, Zora said in a hushed voice, "Stana, never expect a free meal. How will Dunja make money if she gives her food away for free?"

"Trust me, Mama," Neven interjected. "Dunja will never go hungry; she's earned plenty since the Germans arrived."

With a single swift motion, Stana snatched up three hot ćevapi platters and delivered them to a table. Zora observed Dunja warmly welcome in two distinguished German officials, along with Officer Gerhardt. Not him again, she thought. Taking a heavy breath, she watched as Dunja led them to a circular table in Stana's section.

Neven positioned himself on one side of his mother, while Luka flanked the other. "Don't worry, we're watching."

"I do not trust him."

"Sorry to interrupt." Miško nudged her with the readied platters for table four.

Zora delivered the brimming platters of pljeskavice to the short-haired Germans and turned her gaze to the older officers with a profusion of gold-braided insignias on their tightly fitted jackets of the Wehrmacht. Sporting mustaches remarkably similar to Adolf Hitler's, they appeared engrossed in conversation with the younger Gerhardt, whose star shone brighter tonight for some strange reason. Moving toward the kitchen, Zora walked past their table and caught a familiar name. "Neven, does the name List ring a bell to you? Where have I heard that name?"

The color drained from his face as he pulled his reddened hands from the hot, sudsy water. "Wait—Major Field Marshall General Wilhelm List? If that's who you're referring to, he's huge, Mama. One of Hitler's top generals, and in his inner circle."

"My God, you cannot be serious, Neven. You've seen his photograph in the newspaper, right? Let's confirm it's him."

Peeking out from the small, round kitchen window, Neven professed, "Yep, that's him. Major Field Marshall General List is at the table with Gerhardt."

Rubbing her collarbone, Zora's eyes narrowed. What could have prompted a high-ranking member of Hitler's inner circle to come here? Running a hand through her hair, she straightened her ponytail. Despite her head spinning with possibilities, she knew she needed to appear calm.

Miško peeked, then handed her more dinners. "Here; take these ćevapi straight to table ten while they're still sizzling."

The platter's scalding steam burned her arm as someone simultaneously bumped her elbow. Letting out a small yelp, Zora awkwardly tried balancing the platters and came face to face with General List, his silver epaulettes on his lapel, the braided gold shoulder boards, and the scarlet stripe running down one of his pant legs, indicative of the highest attainment in the Wehrmacht Army.

"G—good evening, sir. How may I help you?" she asked politely, ignoring the fact that he bumped into her.

"Well, good evening to you," he remarked gracefully in German, his eyes looking her up and down to the rounded toe of her well-worn black shoes. His intense gaze left her feeling uncomfortably exposed.

He attempted to speak Serbian, but failing miserably, mimed lighting a cigarette. Zora could see he had a sense of humor.

"Ah…matches," she responded in German. "One moment, please." After delivering the platters, she hurried to the bar for a pack, promptly returning to hand him the matches.

"You, my dear, are full of surprises." Lighting his Roth-Händle cigarette, he stepped closer, his expression more serious, his breath rank. "You're lovely."

Zora's stomach coiled. Did they never bother to brush their teeth? "Anything else, sir?" she asked sweetly, through clenched teeth, nearly gagging.

Wagging his finger in front of her face, he said, "You… are definitely one to watch."

Zora's smile remained locked in place until she returned to the kitchen, where she bent over, gasping.

***

The following night at Paligorić, Zora sat in conversation with Dunja and Conductor.

"I heard about your interaction with General List last night. We heard Officer Gerhardt will be joining List as his translator while he tours Serbia and makes necessary adjustments."

"What fantastic news," Zora said with a welcome relief.

"It's good to see you, Zora." Conductor moved to reach her hand, his touch grazing her wrist. "Thanks for treating our men." Lowering his voice because the kafana was beginning to fill, he explained more. "The Partisans and the Royalists will be joining forces to discuss a large-scale attack against the Wehrmacht."

"Any idea when?" Dunja asked, sucking on a cigarette.

"I'm not sure, but the British have been pressuring us for a unified Resistance. Neither side is interested—in fact they've been vehemently opposed. However, we're aiming for a date in the next week. So that you're aware, the Germans have once again begun going door to door, reminding residents to surrender their weapons and radios. Not complying with this second request will be instant death."

Zora's hands instinctively covered her mouth. Paling, she immediately thought about Dušica and Marko, hiding two Jewish children, and of course their hidden radio.

"What about guns for our own protection?" Dunja asked. "I've always kept a loaded gun under the bar in case some jerk starts trouble."

"The Occupiers have made it clear. All residents have been required to turn in their weapons and radios to the municipal office within a two-hour period. Failure to do so…" Conductor shrugged. "Your choice, Dunja. The Germans are angry with us. Our men have made remarkable strides against them. In fact, two nights ago, we blew apart one of their minor camps between Užice and Pozega, so they'll assuredly make us pay. Two weeks prior, a train accident occurred, causing two rail cars carrying German supplies to derail. These supplies, intended for the Wehrmacht Army, inexplicably disappeared."

"Bravo, how were you able to accomplish that?" Dunja's smile deepened.

Conductor fixed his gaze on her. "One of our more recent recruits possesses exceptional technical expertise in the field of train dismantling; we're fortunate to have him. Ladies, we're creating ripples."

Zora knew he was talking about Peda and his abilities.

"Unfortunately, we expect them to retaliate, so we must maintain caution."

"Certainly," Dunja replied. "By the way, some ladies dropped off food for the Četnici. Could you take it with you?"

"No, but I'll let Beba and Mališa know. The work they've done delivering supplies to Vraćevšnica has been noteworthy."

Beba and Mališa? That must be the code names for her sister and Josie. Beba was the nickname for little sister, and Mališa meant small one, which suited Josie because she was barely five feet tall.

Suddenly, in walked a bearded and scruffy-looking Kosta. Zora could not hide her shock at seeing him with a beard.

"Ahhh…my dearest friends all gathered here. And Conductor, great to see you in person. Is my son here?" Kosta planted three cheek-to-cheek kisses on Conductor before hugging him.

"You, too, Kosta. I assume Luka's in the kitchen."

Sliding onto a bar stool, Kosta let out a rugged sigh. "It's getting tense out there. I'd hoped by now either the Brits or the Allies would have come to our aid." Kosta scratched his fuzzy neck.

Adjusting his eyeglasses, Conductor lifted his shoulders. "Honestly, I expected the Brits to do more. Apart from providing Čiča Draža with some liquor and cigarettes, we have yet to see much else."

Zora took in the whole scene. Against the formidable Third Reich, these two founders of Sloboda were making small but impactful waves. With foresight and a deep sense of dignity, these two friends, as young university students, had laid the foundation on which Sloboda rested.

CHAPTER TWENTY-ONE

PEDA

Suvobor Mountains, Serbia
September 06, 1941

THE MOUNTAIN AIR WAS stifling, even though it was barely seven in the morning. It was one of those days where stillness begged for relaxation. Following a strenuous two-day battle with the Wehrmacht, the Saboteurs had just returned. Exhausted, they lay on the ground, their bodies aching and in pain.

Peda's thoughts were on Goran, whom he'd seen only twice in two months. He'd felt an immense sense of pride in Goran's dedication to the Royalist cause. His son had carved out a loyal unit of guerillas, composed of younger, more energetic revolutionaries; regrettably, their paths seldom crossed because Goran's group was based near Valjevo, where a German stronghold existed.

These mountains had done wonders for him and he felt restored. Being a part of something that mattered gave him a real purpose. He had veered off course and lost his way. His ill-fated period of despair had been an abysmal time for him, but now he was more confident. Plagued by falling short as a husband and father, Peda was aware of his past blunders, including the way he had left, so suddenly. If he knew how to write, he would have written Zora a love letter confessing his many mistakes. Unfortunately, that required asking someone to write the letter for him, which he would never allow. Without alcohol flowing through his veins, Peda was clear on the slip-ups in his marriage, focusing instead on what mattered most—his wife and children. Putting his head in his hands, he wished he had been a better man.

Stevan approached his unit. "Guys, any idea what today represents?"

"Yeah, Saturday, our day off," Ranko teased.

"It's September 6, and King Peter's birthday," Stevan said. "Later in the day, we'll take that pile of logs up top to burn and show the world we have not stopped fighting for our freedom, and for the Karađorđević Monarchy. But for now, we're having Divine Liturgy down below in honor of his birthday, so I suggest everyone freshen up. Let's meet in thirty."

Seated on the stump lighting a cigarette, Peda awaited his unit. It had been two months since he'd arrived, shaky and nauseated. During the first week, he'd awoken each morning drenched in sweat and vomiting. Some men looked away or acted like they hadn't noticed, but Stevan, his Saboteur leader, stuck by him. Stevan offered him fresh stream water and coffee, and with a steady hand on his shoulder, Peda slowly recovered. Yes, he'd had a few scuffles, but nothing significant.

His unit appeared and they headed down. Leaning forward, he heard Stevan humming his favorite song about Marko Kraljević, every Serbian's epic folk hero. Growing up, Peda's children had been familiar with stories about Marko Kraljević and his heroic acts against the Turks on his white horse, protecting the most vulnerable.

As the land leveled off, they passed a cluster of oak trees until a plateau appeared. The crowd of about five hundred villagers gathered around a makeshift altar table surprised Peda, but not more so than one of their commanders, abreast a white horse behind two priests. To further set the stage, Peda scrutinized the rushing stream rippling over the rocks and branches that wound through the cliffs. The noise from the water, combined with the smell of burning incense, and the crickets chirping, raised the hair on his arms. Not accustomed to attending church, Peda stood in awe.

After the liturgy, the soldiers closed ranks, their three fingers raised in Troitsa, as the commander led them in a sacred oath of loyalty to the Royalist Resistance. The men then chatted with some teenaged recruits, primarily sons of the villagers and nearby farmers. As they ascended the towering limestone ridge, Peda remembered how intimidated and unsure of himself he had initially been.

When questioned by the commanders about his work history, he had explained his experience, including his military service in the Great War. Following an evaluation, he was assigned to the Saboteurs, a group of fifteen men with skills associated with misdirecting a railway train, setting booby traps, or blowing up trucks. Having had previous experience at JZ, the Yugoslav Railroad, Peda had gained knowledge and training in certain types of equipment, such as unlining bars. Unbeknownst to him, at the beginning of his career, his experience as a section hand, brakeman, and track foreman provided invaluable knowledge in the fight against the Nazis. Resistance work relied heavily on sabotaging rail cars. Peda's expertise enriched the Saboteurs.

***

He sat up. The lice were making their way toward Peda's chest hairs. "Jesus, they're eating me alive!" he shouted, swatting them away with his shirt. "What I wouldn't give for a hot shower." He groaned as he swung his arms wide in the air, agitated.

Ranko rolled over. "Dream on, big guy. Why don't you go roll in the mud with those goats?" He smirked, pointing to the animals below.

Peda often admired the beautiful range they shared with the shepherds. Hopping from one foot to the other, he furiously scratched himself as he observed a farmer in his billowy shirt and comfortable opanci on his feet, steering his flock. Why hadn't he ever considered becoming a farmer?

Right then, Stevan came over. "Just making sure everyone's awake? Breakfast in five, gentlemen. We're heading out soon, so—boots up."

Peda admired Stevan. Well-mannered, he was a succinct young man with an engineering degree who led his unit with integrity and respect.

"Yeah, yeah." Peda grinned as he vigorously scratched his neck and chest before pulling on his ragged boots and crisscrossing the bandoliers over his chest. "Bloody hell, that stings."

"Peda, your chest doesn't look so good." Stevan stared.

Slapping the šajkača on his head, he grimaced. "I'll manage."

"Stubborn mule," Ranko hooted.

Horrified by the images of people burned alive in their homes, their group spoke quietly over breakfast. It was another unimaginable example of the Third Reich's abhorrence in burning entire villages. The scale of Serbian deaths had greatly increased, leaving them more impassioned to fight for their freedom. Being in the Resistance had opened Peda's eyes to the travesties at the hands of the Führer. Hitler's hatred, which he now recognized, had moved to the point of madness, drastically shifting Peda's worldview.

Crowded around the stone table the Saboteurs had constructed, the men observed Stevan. From his pocket, he produced a handcrafted train map and tossed it onto the table. "Gentlemen, familiarize yourselves with this after you have finished eating."

"What's on the trains?" Peda inquired, eyebrows raised. He needed a rough estimate of each rail car's weight.

"A message we intercepted revealed a specific train carrying medical supplies, food, and winter gear for the Wehrmacht. Animals too."

"How many carts should we bring down?" Peda asked.

"I'm working on that now," Stevan replied, jotting notes on his pad. "Listen up, everyone," he said. "The men on horseback will lead, and everyone else follows."

The group on foot stopped to rest. After he had scanned the area with his field glasses, the tenseness in Peda's shoulders dissipated. His clothes clung to him. The forest was indeed toasty. Leaning against a tall, sturdy oak, he struck a match. Lighting a cigarette, Peda asked the men, "Fifteen minutes?"

They nodded in agreement; most were too weary to speak.

"Careful, Brković; you don't want to set the damn forest on fire," Ranko said jauntily, glancing up to watch a golden eagle spread its wings. "Whoa…even at twilight, it's glorious."

"There's enough light for it to soar." Tilting his head, Peda watched Serbia's celebrated eagle fly overhead. He and Ranko had gotten used to crossing themselves whenever they spotted an eagle because they believed seeing one was a good omen.

Taking a substantial drag, Peda asked, "Why do you think we've seen so many Germans lately? Aren't they supposed to be fighting in Russia?"

"Maybe Hitler heard about a fabulous group of Saboteurs knocking their troops on their arses." Ranko broke into a fit of laughter at his own joke.

"You're right. We have done well picking our spots." Peda pulled out his field glasses again. "We're on the outskirts of Čačak. Still a way to go, so boots up, Ranko." He patted him on the back.

Peda and the others began to march single file down a steep, curvy path, humming. Many of their songs tended to be capstones of Serbia's tumultuous history or about heartache or longing.

Adjusting his ammo belts and rifle, he was reminded of his favorite song, "Tamo Daleko," ripe with pain and despair on a terribly sad night. The words, "*There, there, across the sea,*" would forever haunt him, reminding him of the loss of his brothers.

Peda roused himself from the painful memories. Stevan's beautiful Arabian mare was trotting toward him. As the mare circled, Stevan remarked, "This looks like a suitable spot to camp, under that sprawling oak. Spread out, men." Dismounting his silvery horse, Stevan led it to the nearby stream.

Peda wiped his face with a dirty handkerchief, then wrapped his long hair, which grazed his collar, with a slip of rope. After laying his threadbare sheet on the hard ground, he sank down. Someone had already lit a small fire, so he scooted closer to warm himself.

Plunking down next to him, Stevan offered, "Here, try one of these." He passed Peda an unusual-looking red-and-white-colored pack of what looked to be American cigarettes.

Peda examined the label on the package of Lucky Strikes before tapping out a cigarette. Taking a puff, he inhaled. "Ahh, what luxury. How did you get your hands on these?"

"Čiča received a visit from a British delegation last week, and an American lieutenant, part of the contingent, brought an entire case of Camels and Lucky Strikes."

"Really?" Kicking off his boots, Peda looked at his unsightly feet.

Stevan's eyes glanced over. "Please check the supply hut when we return. Those boots of yours won't last much longer, Brković." Leaning closer, he lowered his voice. "The Brits were inquiring about a female in our Resistance, supposedly an Amerikanka." He took a long drag of his cigarette.

"Why were they asking?" Peda's expression flickered in the campfire.

"Methinks you might know her."

Peda's back straightened. His heart sped up, and he was unsure what to say. Was Stevan someone he had mistakenly put his trust in? Zora often reminded him to be careful about revealing too much to someone he'd just met.

He lowered his head, not wanting to give anything away by his facial expressions. "I met her when she recruited me. She's a friend of my wife's sister, from Belgrade."

Leaning back, Stevan took a long pull on his cigarette as his eyebrows rose. "Despite her intelligence and good standing with the British, her sudden departure from England perplexed them. It sounded like she could be a spy."

Peda stared at him dumbfounded and caught off guard. "I, ah, thought she mentioned growing up near Chicago. She must be sharp-witted, though, because she learned Serbian quick. Stevan, she has friends in some pretty high places in Belgrade." Peda crossed his arms.

"Is that so?"

"And my sister-in-law holds a prestigious position as a professor at the university." All of a sudden, Peda felt the same ominous feeling Zora often got whenever she sensed something terrible was about to happen. Why was Stevan grilling him like this?

"Could she be a spy, Peda?"

Gospode, he thought, what does he know? Struck speechless, Peda faked a yawn before rolling over. He had to end this conversation, but what had Sava and Josie gotten themselves into?

***

Two days later, Čiča Draža greeted the weary Saboteurs on top of the mountain, wearing his tattered gray uniform of the Yugoslav Royal Army, and a warm smile. Clutched in his hand was his constant companion, his cherry pipe. "Thank you all," he said, clapping.

Sabotaging the German railcars had been a success, but moving the bulky shipment up the mountainside was a demanding task. Peda was famished and needed a bath badly. His clothing reeked. He couldn't stand himself, so he raced to the stream, tore off his clothing, and bathed in the forty-five-degree temperature.

September 17, 1941

The Reich's chief propagandist, Joseph Goebbels, made an announcement that drew a crowd of Royalists to the radio. After clearing his throat, Goebbels declared:

> Hitler's new Directive Number 312 to Field Marshall General List has ordered him to put down the resistance movement in the southeast, and the Führer has ordered the oppression of Communist armed resistance movements in the Occupied Areas. Issued by the German Armed Forces High Command (OKW) under the signature of Field Marshall Keitel, the Führer's orders specify that for each German soldier killed, one hundred are to be executed. For each German soldier wounded, fifty hostages are to be executed.

"My God, he has lost his mind," exclaimed Stevan.

The announcement stunned all of them, but Peda could not sit idle. "It's time they pay. Those animals want to erase every one of us—Jews, Serbs, Romas. To them, we're all replaceable."

***

Footsteps scuffling in the dark awoke Peda. From where he was lying, he saw a movement of men. Squinting, he watched one of his commanders pull on his boots while another readied the horses. Where could they be going in the middle of the night? Shivering, Peda fell into a deep, troubled sleep. Hours later he sought out Stevan.

Lips pursed together like he had eaten something sour, Stevan explained, "They're enroute to a secret meeting with Marshal Tito, head of the Partisan Resistance in Struganik, to work out details of a surprise attack."

Peda tried to control his emotions. "Whoa, that's one helluva big deal. Why all the way to Struganik?"

"They picked a neutral location, hoping the Germans will not be anywhere close by. It takes time crossing over to the other side, which was why they left early."

"Makes sense." Peda scratched his beard. "But Ranko insisted Tito's headquarters were in Užice, where he's building a school?"

"He's correct, and he's also launched a Communist newspaper called *Borba*. It's a mystery to everyone where he's getting the money to build those schools and buildings, and provide new uniforms for the Partisans, when we're all starving."

"What's your opinion, Stevan? Could we pull it off...a joint effort?"

It took him a while to reply. "Who knows, Peda; who knows?"

CHAPTER TWENTY-TWO

ZORA

Kragujevac, Serbia
October 01, 1941

SERBIA'S UNPREDICTABLE FALL WEATHER reminded Zora of the importance of paying closer attention. Dušica's umbrella offered no defense against the heavy rain, making it hard for her to see. The gusty winds on Knez Miloša had her shivering under her already soaked jacket. Why didn't I dress warmer? she asked herself. Ten more steps and she'd be at the Apoteka.

"Ah, Mrs. Brković, let's get you inside." The chemist extended his arm as he opened the pharmacy's door. "Your son's medicine should be ready in about ten minutes."

"Thank you, Gospodine Prodanović." Feeling uncomfortable for dripping water on his clean linoleum floor, Zora tucked her head in close, trying to appear smaller.

"Please, dear, have a seat, I'll be with you in a moment."

A formidable figure in Kragujevac, Mr. Prodanović was a mystery to Zora, mainly due to his stature and aloof demeanor. But today, deep crevices appeared on his forehead, along with a slight stoop in his posture.

Wrapping her arms around herself, she expressed gratitude toward Milan Nedić for reopening Serbia's high schools. Fortunately, Neven and Vuk had returned this morning to their Prva Muška Gimnazija, and Stana to her girls' high school: Ženska Gimnazija. If only they would reopen the elementary schools, Čedo and Aco could also return. Zora felt an even stronger need for her children to get an education. She didn't want to stew in what ifs, but she worshipped each of her children and wanted them to grow and expand.

He returned with a hot cup of tea, which he handed to her, his unexpected warmth surprising her.

"Why…thank you," she whispered. "How's your family, and your sons?"

"Both of my boys have joined Draža Mihajlović and his Četnici. I heard your husband also went up. Your older son's been there awhile, hasn't he?" He peered down at her from rounded, metal spectacles.

"Yes," Zora said, recognizing their town had no secrets. There was comfort knowing his young sons were also part of the Royalists Resistance. Unfortunately, many individuals in Kragujevac were collaborating with the Germans, making it difficult to find people to trust.

Leaning in, he said, "The Nazis, they're hellbent on destroying every member of our Resistance. Never let your guard down, Gospođo."

Dread caused Zora's skin to prickle. Was he aware of her part in aiding the Resistance, and if so, was this a warning of some sort?

Clearing his throat, he said, "Last week I overheard two of Hitler's lieutenants in here discussing a plan to eliminate every one of us, without delay. So, I sent word to the Royalists."

Her hand shook as she set the saucer on the counter. "Gospodine, was it a directive they were speaking about?" The air suddenly filled with tension. Noticing his anxiety, she glanced around to confirm no one had entered the pharmacy.

Behind his spectacles, his brown eyes were unfocused. "I'll tell you…just give me a minute."

"Could it have been the directive 'One Hundred for One'?"

Snapping his fingers, he admitted, "That's it." Just then, the bell over the door jingled, alerting them to a new customer. Straightening, he said loud enough for whoever had just entered to hear, "Let me check on your order." Turning back around, Mr. Prodanović handed her Čedo's prescription and the bill.

Blanching, Zora reached into her change purse with trembling fingers, ready to burst into tears. "Gospodine, I—I'm not sure I have enough. Would it be possible to pay you a little today and more next week?"

Gospodine Prodanović held himself still until he slowly nodded.

"I'm forever grateful for your kindness, and thank you." Zora half bowed before paying. She bolted out the door, shame and mortification her constant companions.

Arriving home, she discovered her mother splayed across the kitchen table, fast asleep. After she gave Čedo his medication, she heard a loud rumble, causing her to hasten to the window, where she watched more Wehrmacht trucks roaring by. Soon after, Neven and Stana trudged in with Luka.

"Why such gloomy faces?"

"We, ah…heard Lenka's good friend, Lazo, was killed in a battle." Stana's eyes watered and her voice cracked. "He was so young, plus we're worried how Lenka will react after we tell her."

Zora took Stana's hands in her own. "Ahhh, dušo, I'm sorry to hear about Lazo, and you're right. He was far too young, his poor mother…" Zora tsked. "How about you let your grandmother and I share this news with Lenka, all right?" Zora knew she would have to spoon-feed the information to her oldest daughter, bit by bit. With Lenka, it was often like standing on glass; you never knew when it might shatter. Lenka's emotions were even more fragile since the occupation. Stana, two years her junior, was significantly more mature.

"Let's take deep breaths, shall we?" Looking at them, Zora recognized how shaken they truly were. A sudden death of someone their age brought them up short. These three were suspended on a precipice, somewhere between adolescence and adulthood. "No matter how hard it gets, you must never forget how precious life is. Even fraught with sorrow, life is incredibly magical and full of wonder. It's essential you search for the goodness in people—because that's what you'll need to cling to in these challenging times."

✶✶✶

Several days later, a glowing Stana burst through the door. "Mama…Conductor asked Luka and me to go to Monastery Žiča with him tomorrow morning. So, can I go?" Stana had been at Luka's, where they held choir practice in secret, a pleasant reprieve during the war.

"Could you tell me a bit more?"

"He mentioned us helping him deliver documents and boxes. He's allowing Luka to drive his Citroën automobile. Don't worry, he said it would only be about three hours."

Stana spoke so fast Zora wondered when she'd come up for air, but her daughter appeared overjoyed. The emotional angst brought by war was concerning enough; she wanted to allow Stana this small block of joy. "It sounds like a pleasant morning for a drive to Kraljevo."

Nearly jumping into her mother's arms, Stana squealed in delight. "Thank you."

"It's a wonder he found petrol," Zora said under her breath.

***

The absence of soap worsened their already difficult living conditions under the occupation. Zora's inability to maintain her own personal hygiene as well as keep her home and family's clothing clean affected her dignity. Walking along Knez Miloša, she was on her way home, happy to have gotten hold of a delectable meaty bone which she planned to use to make a hearty beef soup. Dreaming about the hearty soup, she came across her neighbor.

"Good morning, Mitza." Zora stepped closer to the curb for fear of smelling badly as she ran a hand through her hair, placing a few strands in her ponytail.

"I—I fear they're plotting something." Mitza's eyes were enormous. "They're planning something. With all the extra trucks and additional soldiers coming in, something's up." Her eyes darted left to right. "And the letter they sent, do you think it was a warning they'd arrest us if our kids don't return to school?"

Surprised flickered across her face. Typically, Mitza was shrewd and unfazed, so to see her truly frightened, it gave her pause. "Is the letter from the Third Reich the reason you're so uncomfortable?"

Wincing, Mitza's eyes flooded with tears. "I don't...It's just a feeling I have."

A roaring in Zora's ears drowned out the noise.

***

Arriving home, Zora was speechless to see Sava and Josie Whitney-Shaw at her table, speaking in a hushed tone with her mother and Dušica.

"Hello." Sava never arrived empty-handed, and today there were two sacks brimming with food and supplies. As a sign of gratitude, Zora patted her hand over her heart.

Sava stood, placing a hand on each side of her sister's lean face. "We were en route to a mission, when a battle broke out near Topola, forcing us to reroute here. We believe the Royalists were attempting to destroy a bridge near one of their camps. The Germans must have heard and counterattacked. Of course, it's supposition on my part. But I love the chance to be here with all of you," she said, beaming.

"That's close to here?" Dušica turned to Sava, seeking clarification through their gaze.

"Less than an hour."

Zora sensed something troubling her sister. "Sava, what is it?"

"Am I that obvious?" Her chin wobbled.

"Why…yes."

"Toma was arrested. I'm afraid he was taken to one of those camps."

Zora focused on her sister, knowing the Royalists and Života would search all over for Toma. Stepping behind for a bottle of her lavender oil, she began to gently massage Sava's tight neck and shoulders.

"Ahh, my goodness, that feels marvelous."

Života entered, breathing noisily. "Pardon, Gospođo, fighting has broken out in Kraljevo. Based on Kosta's knowledge, it's intense." With a stern expression, he said, "I recommend we stay here overnight."

Zora's hand instinctively reached for her neck. "Our men?"

"I believe so. Kosta was trying to find a back way in to Kraljevo, because he caught word they're blocking the roadways."

Sava's eyes blinked. "Života, could it be…?" She lifted her face to the ceiling as if in prayer.

"It might be Žiča Monastery, we're just not sure, Gospođo."

The Nikolić women wore similar expressions of shock.

Sava took the time to explain to Josie, "Our monasteries—they're the ecclesiastical center, and are the very heart and soul of everything we Serbians hold dear."

October 10, 1941

Luka sprinted in, looking like he'd seen a ghost.

"Luka?" Zora asked, with a whisper of dread.

"Žiča's burning…Monastery Žiča's on fire. Stana and I were just there the other day."

Zora believed he was on the verge of becoming hysterical. His eyes suddenly looked too big for his face.

"I—I was home alone when Tata's radio squawked out a—a voice that started shouting orders about getting everyone to Žiča, right away." Looking at her, he questioned, "Do you think it was someone from Ravna Gora giving orders?" Squeezing his eyes shut, he added, "There's more…"

With a light touch on his shoulder, Zora guided him to a chair. "Sit, Luka." She considered how frightened he was; it was likely because Kosta was en route to Žiča. It's no wonder he's so upset, poor boy, she thought.

"All right, tell me." She sat next to him and clasped his enormous hands in her own.

"The man's voice, he mentioned the Luftwaffe and Stukas and large airplanes dropping bombs on Kraljevo and Žiča. He said the nearby buildings were already decimated." His breath came in short, quick bursts. "And…Bishop Nikolaj, who we just met, might be inside the monastery." He started gasping for air.

"Luka, slow your breathing, in and out, in and out…" She observed him and watched until his breathing seemed normal.

"The man shouted about needing every available man they could muster. The voice said the Germans were shelling the monastery with cannon fire. My father left to go there," Luka stammered.

Seeing him so panicked, Zora grabbed hold of his arm and pulled him into a powerful hug. "I understand, and you must stay here with us, Luka. Dealing with this alone, it's too much to manage. Now, go out back; Neven and Stana should be there cleaning."

Zora flew upstairs to alert Dušica and Marko. When she returned, Neven was at the kitchen table, head bent, talking quietly with Luka.

Rubbing his forehead, Neven looked nonplussed. "How could they destroy one of our most sacred monasteries? Are there no boundaries for their excessive hatred?"

"Luka, who do you know with some petrol that could drive us there?" Zora asked.

Luka sprung up. "Are you serious, Gospođo?"

"Well, you're both strong enough, and I'd like to help our injured."

Neven pushed up his glasses and his face became alive. "What about Kutz Osmajlic? He's got a truck, maybe he'd let us borrow it?"

"Oh, I don't think so." Stana raised an eyebrow, coming inside. "His father's passionate about communism, so no; he wouldn't be interested in helping save a monastery."

"Thanks, little genius." Neven chortled, pretending to punch her arm.

Redness spread across Luka's face as his eyes sought Zora's. "Gospođo, my apologies. I'd forgotten, Tata had a message for you and Dunja. He said to tell you it's likely the Germans will return to Paligorić to gloat and celebrate afterward. So, it's crucial to remind Dunja to double up on their drinks."

Zora replied with a grin on her face, "Your father's a brilliant man, Luka Lazić."

Neven and Luka visibly relaxed their shoulders, and Stana's sigh of relief was heard by her mother. These children of hers and their dear friend Luka had been on eggshells since the attack and subsequent occupation. She understood the overwhelming, chaotic nature of life during wartime, and despite her best efforts to manage what they heard, it was merely an illusion.

CHAPTER TWENTY-THREE

PEDA

Ravna Gora, Yugoslavia
October 10, 1941

THE GOLDEN EAGLES CIRCLED overhead. They were not only infuriating; their disruptive, high-pitched shrills were driving Peda nuts. He pondered whether a dead wolf or mountain lion were to blame. Rubbing his hands together, he scooted closer to the fire, hoping the noise wouldn't keep him awake. Worn out, he'd begun to experience the toll from hiking and the impact it was having on his fatigued body, especially his knees. The fighting had escalated to where the Saboteurs were being called upon daily, either to derail a rail car carrying supplies for the German Army, or to blow something up.

The Wehrmacht had strengthened their tactics, and their attacks were more penetrating. Despite the persistent throbbing in his knees, and being the oldest in his unit, Peda refused to stop. It had been years since he felt this good. The Resistance provided him with a purpose, making him feel alive. There was only one thing that could relieve the pain—a few nips of good ol' one hundred percent proof, homemade rakija. Leaning back in contemplation, Peda lit a cigarette and watched Božo approach, carrying two tin cans of something steaming hot.

Handing one to him, Božo, not too subtly, plopped down next to him. "I'm afraid the nights will become mighty cold up here. You should move closer to my hut, so you don't wake up with frostbite, Peda." Glancing upward at the eagles overhead he asked, "What's got their attention?"

"Who knows, likely a dead creature. What's this?"

"It's sort of a Šumadinksi tea. Drink up, my friend. It's a remedy for whatever ails you."

Peda peered inside. "Any rakija?"

"No." Božo crossed his arms and tucked his hands underneath his armpits. "But I noticed you limping the other day. It's gotten worse."

"Jesus, you're worse than a woman, watching me like a hawk."

"That's what friends do, Peda. They watch out for one another. I know you are in pain."

With an eye roll and a grimace, Peda redirected the discussion. "I came here because of my strong belief in the King and the Monarchy, and for our freedom. I've always taken pride in what the Monarchy represented. But the Germans, they've carelessly extinguished so many of our people; what do the members of our Cabinet feel or say about these deaths?"

"Speaking of killings, Čiča said we've lost thousands in July alone. That doesn't count our Royal Yugoslav soldiers arrested and sent to camps, and the thousands killed in the April attack no one's spoken about. My younger brother was one of the Royal Yugoslav soldiers in that group, and I worry every day whether he was murdered, because Hitler has nearly eliminated our entire male lineage."

"I am sorry about your brother, and you're right, Božo. I, too, heard they were marched out and sent to something called Oflag XIII-B Camp. Have you ever heard of it?"

Stevan's booming voice interrupted them. "Men; we're moving out in ten minutes. Grab your gear; Žiča's engulfed in flames, and we need all men onboard." Hurrying to wipe down his mare, Stevan shouted, "The Luftwaffe's at it again, but this time, they're bombarding the monastery."

Peda immediately stood, extinguished his cigarette with the heel of his worn boot, and hurriedly sprinted to fill his canteen with fresh water. After reaching for his rifle and knapsack, he crisscrossed his bandolier over his chest. He was ready.

Božo ran after him shouting, "Take these and wrap them over your noses and mouths for protection. And try to avoid inhaling any of that filthy stuff into your lungs."

Peda stowed the cotton strips in his knapsack in astonishment and swallowed the lump in his throat. "You really are something, my friend."

With a smile on his face, Božo stepped back and gave a salute. "I've long desired to become a doctor. *Bog vam pomogo*, gentlemen."

"May God be with you, Božo. After this war's over, we're getting you to the university."

***

The searing heat hit him first. Fires burned in every direction. As soon as one disappeared, a new one emerged. Every member of his unit was in a low crouched position, making their way toward the monastery by duck walking. Peda could see Wehrmacht soldiers scattering in all directions to evade the fire, while his unit moved behind the monastery. Their goal was to save the monastery itself. After passing out the cotton strips to the men in his unit, Peda covered his own nose and mouth.

Twenty minutes later, flying embers scorched his back and shoulder. "Oww! Oww! Someone help get it off me. Help—my back's on fire. Oww," Peda yelled in agony.

"Drop to the ground, Peda, and roll," screamed Stevan. He shouted at the others while he quickly tried to stomp out the fire on Peda by throwing chunks of dirt and ground cover with his bare hands. "Get water."

The pain caused his eyes to water and his legs to buckle.

"Breathe, Peda, remember to breathe," Ranko hollered, his eyes bulging. The water squelched Peda's body with a sizzling noise. Ranko and Stevan half carried him to the grass.

Stevan suggested, "You stay with him, Ranko. You're the one with training. First take off his bandolier and jacket, very, very slowly. It's important to keep his body cool. We've got to assess his wounds." Patting his leg, Stevan said, "Hang in there, Peda."

Many hours later, the Royalists were able to save the main section of Žiča. Despite the Wehrmacht breaking through, the Royalists pushed back more forcefully. The Germans had destroyed multiple buildings surrounding Žiča, but the monastery itself was intact, with Bishop Nikolaj inside. The Saboteurs were moving to a secret location, but Peda was not among them. He was moving through the forest, zigzagging as best he could between the pinewoods on a twisted path, which forced him into a railway tunnel cut into the side of the mountain. When he reached the tunnel, he tentatively soft-stepped it, to ensure no Germans were inside.

Hearing a catarrhal whistle, Peda stopped, flattening himself against the tunnel wall, feeling an excruciating pain in his back from the burns. He took in huge gulps of air, tears sliding down his cheeks. If left untreated, the burns would hinder his ability to fight, so he was heading home, hoping Zora could treat them. They all agreed it was too risky to enter any hospital, therefore his wife was their best hope.

It was Stevan who had suggested Zora. Covered in black soot, Peda hoped the camouflage was enough. After sliding down the final hill, he passed a wooded area full of wrens and blackbirds. He stepped on the slippery moss of wet, green pasture and knew he was less than one mile from home.

Slipping in through the unlocked back door, he exhaled a gigantic sigh of relief, while simultaneously inhaling a heavenly scent of something simmering on the stove. Cradling his arm, Peda swallowed.

"Tata?" Neven spun around, surprise on his face. Peda observed his son's eyes travel the length of his body before stopping at his arm. "My goodness—what happened?" Neven recoiled and quickly covered his mouth.

"What's worse? My stench, the filthy clothing, or the blackened face?" Peda tried making a joke, but it fell short. With a jumpy sensation in his belly, he wondered if the wave of nausea was because of hunger or maybe a little of both. "How are you, son?"

Neven's hands flattened to his sides. "Good…but your face, Tata?" Peda watched his son put the pieces together. "You were at Žiča, fighting the fire, weren't you?" Neven took big strides to reach the sink, where he ran warm water on a dishrag before quickly returning to his father's side. "Here Tata, you can use this to wipe your face and neck while I heat a bowl of soup for you."

"A glass of water too, please. How did you know where we were fighting, Neven?" Peda felt suddenly nauseous. Wincing, he thought he might be sick. "Could you please fetch your mother? And…some rakija."

Neven hurriedly returned. "We don't have any, but here's some tea." Neven poured his father a coffee cup full of tea and went to wake his mother.

"I can't drink any more tea, my stomach can't handle it." Peda pushed the bowl he'd just devoured and the filled cup of tea aside.

Standing in the doorway, Zora looked ethereal in a white nightgown that was too large for her shrunken frame, her russet-colored hair cascading to her waist. "Peda… what happened?" By the way she looked at him, it was clear she was assessing his injuries. He was also certain she smelled the fire that clung to him.

Clearing his shaky throat, he began. "I—ah, I've missed all of you. Our unit was fighting the Germans at the monastery, but the fire…Well, the wind shifted, and I ended up engulfed in flames." Lifting his arm, he said, "My officer suggested I come to you. But how does he know about you, Zora…what have you done?" Before she could respond, he flipped his other hand, signaling her to stop. "First, I must use the bathroom." He was ashamed and didn't want her to see the bites covering his body. Heat rose through his neck. "I'm going to take a bath."

Zora gently stepped in. "Let me draw you a warm bath, Peda. I'll add a touch of healing oils, and a drop of Epsom salts." Steering him to the bathroom, she spoke sweetly. "Neven will hold your arm away from the water, so I'm able to treat your bites. It's crucial your burns don't come in contact with the water or the salt."

"I will not allow my son to see me naked." His back stiffened and his expression turned dark.

"Peda, please…" Her tone grew softer. "Don't worry. I've already seen the lice bites on your neck and hands. It's because of your living conditions on the mountain. Goran had the same bites. Trust me, Peda, Epsom salts will kill them immediately, then I'll tend to your burns."

Scowling, Peda bit his bottom lip. After applying the final dressing, Zora wrapped his arm and shoulder in linen swabs. She covered him with a blanket and planted a kiss on his forehead before tiptoeing to bed. His pain overwhelmed him and he hoped he would be able to finally get some sleep. God knows…he needed it.

***

The following night, pretending to be a peasant, Peda returned to the forest near Kraljevo, retracing his steps. He was exhausted and reluctant to leave his wife and family, but he knew his unit depended on him. Taking comfort in his familiarity of the forest, he knew he was close once he passed the gushing stream and the white birch trees.

In his peripheral vision, he spotted two šajkače floating in the water. Speechless, his mind raced with possibilities. Shaken, but undeterred, Peda continued his climb through the dense foliage of lichen trees until he heard the soft wolf whistle and knew it was Stevan's. Relaxing, he continued following the path as it turned right. Ten minutes later, he'd rejoined his team. After he had briefed Stevan on the scene in the stream, the men made space for him by the fire.

Stevan's expression grew serious as he issued instructions. "Take it easy today, because tomorrow we will embark on our most important mission. We're teaming up with Tito's Partisans for a surprise attack on Germany's 3rd Battalion of the 749th Infantry Regiment of their 717th Division. Through a united Resistance we aim to make a substantial impact with our combined forces. Therefore, we expect all of you well rested and prepared to pounce. So, let's make a sizeable dent in their forces. Questions anyone?"

Peda took a drag from his cigarette before he excitedly admitted, "I cannot wait to squash those bastards."

His crew gave a rousing shout. "Hear, hear." They scattered to find their sleeping spots, while Peda stomped on the underbrush with his boots, packing down a pile of leaves. Throwing a sheet down, Peda settled on top, drifting off to sleep.

***

Near the small village of Ljuljaci, the surprise attack was launched on the German 3rd Battalion, located on the road between Gornji Milanovac and Kragujevac. Peda saw the clouds of smoke spiral from atop the ceramic-tiled rooftops. As the German artillery launched shells of ammo, they were met with the echoing roar of Resistance fire. Gunfire erupted from the Royalists' old German Lugers and machine guns as curls of smoke charged the air. Grenades sailed across the Rapaj Brdo hill before they exploded. Ultimately, this attack left ten German soldiers dead and twenty-six Germans wounded.

In the nearby village of Bare, Peda glimpsed a German lying face down in a puddle. With immense pride, the Royalists assisted their injured comrades onto oxen carts after successfully overtaking the Wehrmacht.

Hiking up the mountain, its edges sharp and rugged, Peda and Jovica carried Lugers, bayonets, and booby traps. Others pulled the weaponry on carts or miniature mountain ponies. Drained, each man hiked the narrow, rutted path, careful of their footing. Jovica surprised everyone by breaking into a beloved, timeless song sung by many before them. Soon they all joined in singing *"Sprem'te se, sprem'te, četnici."*

This grueling battle would be one Peda would never forget. As he stepped over a fallen tree, he paid close attention to the voices reverberating up the mountain, knowing the abundance of Serbian songs focused on themes of rushing rivers, lost loves, or losses from the wars. But these specific lyrics resonated within each one of the men today.

Peda topped the last canopy as Ravna Gora came into sight. Half starved, his eyes locked onto an enormous platter of what looked to be polenta with goat's milk a local woman carried to the table, but before he could taste it, Stevan pulled him aside.

"A commander just intercepted a message over the Wehrmacht airwaves. They're convinced it's the Führer himself." Stevan spilled the details. "Apparently, Hitler's boiling mad, furious, and making serious threats against us. Of course, we'll have to wait until our translators fine-tune his tirade. Meanwhile, Čiča's concerned enough about his threats, he's suggesting for now we all stay put."

"Why?"

Stevan rubbed his chin. "It's predominately his concern for our people. Regrettably, they don't focus on us, but the most vulnerable among us, including women and children. Because of how swiftly and outrageously they react, Čiča , and recently Milan Nedić's quisling government, have expressed concern."

"Wait—are you implying joining forces with the Partisans was a wrong move?" Peda frowned.

Stevan averted his gaze and took a long pause before responding. "I'm not sure, Peda."

Peda stormed off toward Božo's hut. "Please don't tell me this will turn into another bloodbath," he murmured under his breath.

"Whoa, Peda, I heard the battle was really difficult, but what happened to your arm?"

"I got burned."

"Oh, let me check." Deep in concentration, Božo unraveled the gauze.

"Careful, it's still tender. There's ointment in my knapsack, could you grab it? I'm supposed to apply it twice a day. Oww, that hurts, Božo. Please be gentler." Peda's eyes burned, and as he looked at the sky, he pinched them shut. "I'm supposed to keep the wound clean, but ouch, that stings." He watched Božo dab the ointment on.

"That's one hell of a nasty injury, my friend." Checking out the ointment, his eyebrows raised in curiosity. "What's in this stuff?"

CHAPTER TWENTY-FOUR

ZORA

Kragujevac, Serbia
October 17, 1941

WHEN THE THIRD REICH announced they had reopened every school in Serbia last month, the response they received was lukewarm, because looming large in the background was the genuine concern over the safety of their children. Accompanying the Reich's announcement was a letter to every family, the one troubling her neighbor Mitza that insisted each child *must* attend school every day. If not, their parents would face harsh penalties. Prior to the occupation, Kragujevac had boasted a respectable educational system featuring exceptional professors and a rigorous curriculum. Zora had a hunch the educational system under the Third Reich would be less so. And on her children's first day back, her intuition proved correct.

Neven was already bemoaning to his mother the unique challenges and setbacks affecting every student. "The Germans had to combine classrooms because most of our beloved professors were let go, arrested, or sent off as prisoners of war." Fiddling with his glasses, he continued. "They weren't ready for us when we started."

"Whatever do you mean?"

"Well, there was nothing for us to write on, or with. No paper, or pencils, or even chairs for everyone to sit on. And…they had two textbooks for the entire classroom. How am I supposed to study without a book? Our professor said they had to close other high schools, because they were turned into sleeping quarters for the Wehrmacht."

"Really?" Zora's face was a mask of confusion. There had been a housing shortage all over Šumadija, but using schools as hotels or boardinghouses confounded her.

"Yeah, and guess what else?" Fidgeting, Neven bounced from foot to foot.

"I'm afraid to ask." Zora smiled, tousling his thick hair.

"Tomorrow, they plan to bring the students without a school to ours. So, imagine about seventy boys crammed into a classroom that typically holds no more than eighteen."

"Neven, I cannot tell you how disappointed I am to hear this. Besides having a real mess on their hands, I wonder why they'd have everyone return when they're so unprepared? It makes little sense." Zora asked the question, but she quickly realized why. For all the note-taking they seemed to do, the Germans were frightfully disorganized. Groaning, she saw Neven's exasperation on his beautiful face. This was his final year, and he was so close to graduating—now this. If only they could get their hands on a textbook for him.

Considering the merits of an education in a meager country like theirs garnered mixed emotions. Her husband, never formally educated, still felt the shame, making him excruciatingly insecure. Long ago, Mima had shared with her family the awkwardness she'd felt growing up as an unschooled peasant. She described how those in power may have used illiteracy as a means of control to keep peasants in their place, or, quite possibly, to keep them poor. Since most in her village were illiterate, they relied on a neighboring priest or an educated villager who could read a letter or document that came in the mail. Remarkably, when Mima married at sixteen and moved to Serbia, she'd immediately learned to read and write.

Zora was reminded of something else. Early in her marriage, she overheard a friend's biting remark about Peda's inability to read. The careless and persnickety way her friend *lessened* her husband stung something fierce. Ironically, that exchange, years later, served as a life lesson Zora never forgot. Sighing, she recalled that she never did stay in touch with that friend.

At the stove, her mind drifted to the argument she'd overheard last night between three red-faced Germans over the recent skirmish in Ljuljaci—ten soldiers dead, and twenty-six wounded. They were so terribly angry, when their quarrel escalated, they said the most awful words against the Serbs. Refusing to differentiate between commoners or Resistance rebels, they lumped every Serbian together as *common bandits*, whose future was of no concern to anyone.

Entering the kitchen with a black babushka on her head, Mima rewrapped the ever-present black shawl across her body. Even though it was a respectful custom for a grieving family to wear black for one year following the death of a loved one, Zora felt their tradition hindered people. It created an atmosphere of sadness. She knew her father would not have wanted their mother to turn morose, or retreat into herself. Zora kissed her mother's head and added a pat of lard to the frying pan before pouring in the egg and flour mixture, courtesy of Marko's farm. Eggs were undeniably a luxury Zora hated living without.

Devouring her breakfast, Stana leaped to her feet. "We'll take Aco, but where's his jacket?"

"I'll get it." Walking into the boys' bedroom, Zora tapped Neven's arm, signaling him to get his head out of the book.

Standing at the door with a mischievous grin on her face, Stana said, "Neven, c'mon. I don't want to be late."

Amused, Zora knew she was in a hurry to see Luka. Each morning, Neven and Luka walked Stana to the turnoff at the Women's Teacher's School before they headed to their own. Neven and Luka, inseparable since their youth, were kindred spirits who loved to read books and study together, and when Stana had turned six, she slid right in with her older brother and Luka, making them a snug threesome. Teeming with pride, Zora kissed their foreheads. "Be good and learn everything."

"We know, Mama, we know." Neven chuckled. "You've repeated those same words to us every day since we were little." With a twinkle in his eye, he bent and quickly lifted his mother in the air. "You know how much we all love you, don't you, Mama?" he said, spinning her around.

Laughing joyously, Zora exaggerated swatting him on the back with her wooden spoon. "Put me down, silly boy." She giggled before blinking, suddenly feeling a strange rush of tears. Shooing Neven out the door, she made the sign of the cross. "Go with God."

Retracing her steps to the kitchen, she had the oddest sensation. Why am I so emotional today? she wondered.

Once she had gathered all her ingredients, she mixed the yeast and warm water with the flour and salt to form her dough. Yesterday, Marko's unexpected sack of beans, potatoes, carrots, and three eggs had nearly brought her to her knees. She wasn't sure if he understood how few ration cards she had left, but she was incredibly grateful.

Sunday, October 19, 1941

Marko found Zora in her kitchen, bent over the sink, washing dishes.

Seeing his grim face, Zora's pulse quickened. She wondered if his leg bothered him; she had noticed his limp was more pronounced in recent weeks.

"What's wrong?"

"Have you heard the latest news…about the arrests?"

Her trembling fingers found her parted lips. "I had not." She could not bear much more disappointing news. "Paligorić was packed with Germans last night, but I heard nothing untoward."

In a weary tone, Marko imparted the news. "The Wehrmacht has begun their reprisals in Ljuljaci. Dunja called earlier."

"Was she all right?"

"Yes. Apparently, a villager who's a customer banged on her door at five this morning. Petrified, the man begged Dunja to hide his two sons."

In disbelief, she questioned him. "Marko…how will she manage this?"

"You know Dunja…"

"That's what worries me. How…can we protect everyone?" Zora gripped the sink for support, pulling in short bursts of air. Despite wanting to remain calm, her mind raced with thoughts of him and her sister, and the unimaginable risk associated with hiding Jews. Now she had Dunja, hiding two boys, to worry about.

His expression turned serious. "Thus far, they've yet to change their patterns. They return to the same location where their soldiers were killed. Conversely, if something were to go terribly haywire, and we sensed real danger, know our plans remain intact. Duš and I will take the boys to the Rudnik Mountains. You remember our hiding spot?"

"Sort of." Zora rubbed the back of her neck, disregarding the flutter of panic in her belly.

"When the hill levels off, you should see a small pine tree clearing. Take a sharp right. Go off the trail and follow the forest until you pass the tall, spikey bushes to the small cave."

"Thanks." A coldness swept through her. "Since we received the notices from the Third Reich, every parent in town has been extremely anxious, and a feeling of panic has taken hold."

"I'm trying not to scare you, but we're already packed, just in case. If something were to happen, we're taking Aco and Čedo with us. Even if I have to carry Čedo, he's coming with us."

Her heart leaped. "We don't deserve you, Marko."

Dropping his head, he said, "On my way down, I noticed the radio signals were scrambled again. It's never a good sign." He planted a kiss on her cheek and squeezed her arm. "Please be extra cautious on your way to work tonight, all right?"

***

The seasons were changing. Zora detected a lingering warmth in the air as a fog started to roll in. She walked behind Neven, Stana, and Luka as they spoke quietly, her eyes averted but watchful. The sight of boarded-up, shuttered cafés, kafanas, and bakeries filled her with sadness. Hearing about the reprisals in Ljuljaci had left her feeling unmoored.

Without warning, the sidewalk rumbled as heavy German Panzers pounded past, followed by more German trucks laden with soldiers.

"Where do you think they're heading?" Neven asked, lifting his head.

"I'm afraid to know," Luka said.

The moment Zora stepped inside Paligorić, Dunja immediately pulled her aside. "We're in serious trouble. They're shooting our people in the villages near Grošnica, Maršić, and Mečkovačka. Look at this…Someone mistakenly left this on a table last night." Dunja pulled a crumpled note from her brassiere. "I found it cleaning up. Damn monsters. They're making it known we're about to suffer and posted this notice in town."

"Ohhh…" Zora blinked in shock as she began to read it.

We have begun to arrest and shoot people in the villages of Grošnica, Maršić, and Mečkovačka. For every German killed, one hundred civilians will be executed. For every German wounded, fifty civilians will be executed.

Signed, German Command of Captain Fritz Fiddler and the German Command of Major Paul König.

Beads of sweat glistened on her forehead and above her lip. Closing her eyes, she struggled to swallow. After Zora reread the chilling edict a second time, she knew full well the Führer had initiated these words—*One Hundred for One*—and even though Major Paul König had signed it, Zora believed it was Hitler's mark. Sensing Dunja hovering in her peripheral field, Zora smelled her fear. She also knew there was no clear path forward for any of them.

Dunja pulled hard on her cigarette and blew out a large plume of smoke as she shakily exhaled. "We've got to be extremely careful. One wrong move…"

Zora leaned back, allowing more air into her lungs. A visceral rage grew in her bosom. Hitler's tactics of preying on the most vulnerable disgusted her sensibilities. He played dirty. Spinning around, she saw Neven and Luka watching her falter. My God, she thought, how am I able to keep them all safe?

"Mama, please be careful…" Neven stepped closer.

Luka's eyes were enormous circles. "Yes, please, Gospođo."

Monday, October 20, 1941

Zora awoke with a staggering sense of foreboding. It was that terrifying dream she'd had about her family being murdered. Remembering the Wehrmacht's notice, she swung her legs over the side of the bed and noted the time. "Oh, dear."

Scurrying to the kitchen, Zora saw her mother happily cooking breakfast for her children. "Mama, forgive me," Zora pleaded. "I cannot believe I overslept." She sheepishly shook her head.

Ever pragmatic, her mother said, "Your body's telling you something, Zora. Don't ignore it." Mima often preached the restorative powers of one's body healing itself, and holding her spatula like a professor at a lectern, she said, "You never get enough sleep."

"Morning, Mama," Stana chirped, leaning against the back door. "Neven already left to meet Luka at school. It's because of that science project they haven't stopped talking about. When Vuk woke later, he rushed out to catch Neven and missed his breakfast."

Stana latched on to Aco's hand for his first week of school and waved goodbye.

Shuddering, Zora murmured, "I don't know what's wrong with me, but I should have kept them home today." Her stomach clenched with a rising panic, and she steadied herself before pulling out a bowl and beginning mixing ingredients for making bread dough.

By lunchtime she had arranged the dough on a pan to rise when a persistent knock at the door startled her. With sticky hands and a niggling at the base of her hairline, Zora opened the door.

Mitza stood white-faced and trembling. "Zora—the Germans…I've just come from town. They're yanking men—boys—students—young and old, whoever they can find, from their homes or work, and taking them away."

"No, no…" Zora vehemently shook her head as her stomach flipped.

"I saw them…removing men from the butcher shop, the cleaners, even the courthouse." Mitza peered into Zora's face. "I even watched them drag three judges from the court. And at our church, they forcefully grabbed Father Radovan by the neck. It was bloody awful." Mitza's pitch rose. "Hurry, Zora; go get your boys, because they're taking all the males away on big trucks." Breathless, Mitza's cadence sounded disjointed, as if she were struggling to form her words. "They've blocked our roads…No one in or out."

Zora placed her hand against the doorframe to steady herself, not wanting to believe what she was hearing. "Were our boys taken…?"

Mitza had already run next door, but she turned around. "Hopefully not, but I'm going to the school to get my boy."

Closing the door, Zora hurriedly raced upstairs to alert Marko and Dušica and to ask Marko to run and fetch Aco at school. After imparting the shocking news, she rushed to pack Čedo's medicine and clothing and handed them to her mother. "They're taking Čedo and Aco with them to hide in the forest. I need you to stay and wait for the others. Burn your candles, Mama, and pray. Pray with all your strength. I'm going to the high school to find Vuk and Neven."

Zora sprinted toward the Prva Muška Gimnazija, praying she wasn't too late. The moment her feet set down on Knez Miloša, she felt a charge in the air. There was a flurry of activity as the steely, contentious Wehrmacht Army spread across the street, their jeeps mounted with machine guns blocking most entrances. Panic rose up in her throat as she whizzed past them, hoping they wouldn't stop her. The smell of fear and the growing sense of dread were palpable.

She heard the screams from a man being pulled from his home. The screams made her freeze mid-stride, and out of nowhere, she chanced upon the volunteer soldiers of the Srpski Dobrovoljački Korpus, loosely known as the Ljotićevci. Wondering why they would be here, Zora could not rationalize why, unless they were collaborating with the Germans? Under enormous strain, she questioned whether she might be mistaken. Help me understand what's wrong with this picture, she thought—Serbs working with Germans?

Zora pushed through her mounting fear and continued her pace until she reached Daničičeva Street. Slowing down, her gaze fell on the large and imposing beige brick building of the First Men's Real High School, diagonally across from the market. She wondered what secrets it held. There was nothing alarming on the school grounds, and from the outside, it appeared normal, like any other school day. Lungs burning, she sprinted up the raggedy stone steps, her forehead slick with sweat. Opening the school's main doors, she felt her skin prickle from a peculiar, unnerving silence. Shouldn't a high school with all boys have a little noise? The squeaking of a chair? The sharpening of a pencil? Or the muffled voice of a professor speaking to his students in their classroom? Why was it so quiet?

Vuk's classroom was on this floor, so Zora flung open every classroom door. She found each empty—bereft of any students or professors.

Mounting the staircase to the second floor, where Neven and Luka's classroom was located, she assumed the professors had gathered the entire student body here. Terrified, Zora's fingers clutched the tiny Serbian Orthodox cross that hung between her breasts. They had stripped each classroom of its students and professors. She felt cold, so very, very cold. Was she shaking?

As Zora hurried down the steps, she heard moaning sounds that she soon realized were coming from her throat. Someone had cleared the principal and secretaries from their offices. No one was inside the high school. My God, she thought, what have they done?

Outside, the clouds gathered as she gasped for air. She'd forgotten her coat, not that it mattered. What mattered was finding Neven and Vuk to take them home. Her boys.

Hearing a rustle, she pivoted and was less than a foot from the pair of soulless gray eyes of a Wehrmacht combat soldier. He wore a green tunic with his pants stuffed into his jackboots. On his head was the ubiquitous German coalscuttle helmet worn for battle.

Pulling his gun from his holster, he hollered, "Go. Go off street." His voice sounded pinched and high-pitched, more a whine.

Zora thrust out her chin and said, in a strangled voice she didn't recognize as her own, "What have you done with my boys?" Feeling emboldened and no longer caring that she was standing in the belly of the beast, she inhaled. Zora was unwilling to heed his warning until she got answers. She was ready to roar. "Where are my sons—where did you take them?"

Something flickered before he averted his gaze. "All gone. Barracks." He stepped back and positioned his gun to her chest. "We shoot. Go NOW!"

Zora watched tiny dribbles of saliva slide down past his chin. Her field of vision narrowed, and her chest expanded as it drew more air into her lungs. Her eyes twitched as reality flooded in. The Germans always meant what they said. Time mattered greatly. When he pointed his gun at her a second time, Zora understood she had two options: to flee or be killed. With those insane odds, Zora whirled around and sprinted away, utilizing her long legs to her advantage as she ran as fast as humanly possible.

Sailing past a sea of smug soldiers closing in on the Old Stone Bridge, she did not slow her pace until she neared the iron structure of the Kolonija Gate. Her legs and thighs burned, and in front of her home, Zora slowed down. Placing her hands on her shaking knees, she tumbled to the ground like a broken doll. "My sons," she wept. "My sweet, sweet boys..."

Stana hurried outside after seeing her mother from the window. "Mama, what happened?"

In the silence that followed, Zora attempted to sit upright. Avoiding her gaze, Zora's fingertips touched her opened lips.

"Where? Are? They?" Stana's questions punctuated the air.

Zora could not get the words out. The weight of the news was too great to bear, let alone say.

"Wait—Baka said you went to get Neven and Vuk." Hands on her hips, Stana's face twisted, and her eyes narrowed. "Where are they?"

Stana's anger punctured her already shattered heart. A small piece broke off. "I tried, Stana, believe me I tried, but no one was at their school." Thick with grief, Zora wobbled, before standing and following Stana inside. "I fear someone took them." Instantly, the words on the note Dunja had handed her last night came back into focus. God, no. She squeezed her eyes shut.

"NO...not Neven and Vuk." Stana unleashed her rancor. "What about Luka?" All the air seemed to flow out of her as she fell to the sofa, weeping.

After a time, Stana sat up with tears running down her face. "Mama, I am sorry I screamed at you. Forgive me? But where could they be?"

She studied her daughter's face. "Stana, I searched everywhere but I couldn't find them. The Germans were spanned out, everywhere. There was an apparent roundup today. A soldier stuck a gun in my chest, forcing me off the street."

The front door swung open to reveal an unsteady Lenka, her hands tugging at her braid. "The Germans; they've rounded up every male in town. Th—they came to the bakery, shouting and waving guns in our faces and, and… they took Ivan." Unsteady, Lenka covered her mouth with her hand before pitching forward. Hearing her emerging panic, Zora guided her to a chair. "Sit, Lenka."

"Mama, wait. Where's the boys, and Neven and Vuk?" Lenka's head swiveled. "Are they missing?" Zora could surmise the panic lapping at her heels. "They took everyone, d—didn't they? I saw them, Mama, pulling Father Cvetić from our church. They're insane." Lenka's hands shook, and her face shaded gray.

Stana sprung up. "I've got an idea. I'll run to Luka's, maybe they're hiding there?" Stana's wet eyes turned to hope.

"No, Stana, leaving's not an option. If you go outside, they will shoot." Looking poignantly at Lenka, Zora asked, "Please telephone the Lazić home." Zora was desperate to engage Lenka in something to prevent her from falling apart, and her breath hitched.

After attempting to dial them three times, Lenka shook her head. "Nothing." Placing the headset on its base, she said, "The Nazis must have cut the phone lines."

CHAPTER TWENTY-FIVE

ZORA

Kragujevac, Yugoslavia
October 21,1941

ZORA SPENT THE ENTIRE night in the kitchen, feverishly praying. As dawn approached, she found solace by laying her head on the cool kitchen table, unable to bear the silence. Suddenly, she heard it—the crack of a rifle in the distance, followed by a rapid rat-tat-tat of multiple shots being fired. One after another, in quick succession, the sounds smashed through the first rays of light. Jerking her head up, Zora froze. "Oh, no…" She shuddered as the bone-chilling gunfire echoed and the room tipped. "*Sačuvaj Bože…*" she murmured, holding her head in her hands. Who were they killing?

Everything shifted on that dark Tuesday morning—a day Zora would never forget. Hurrying to open the front door, she was shocked by the number of the Führer's military forces clogging her street. Effectively trapping her and her neighbors in, they had closed the Kolonija Gate. A piercing cry, followed by a heartbreaking wail, were quickly drowned out by the noise of gunfire. Her own tender heart ached, and as her hands wrapped around her middle, she sensed an imminent threat that every mother feared. Inhaling, Zora knew her community was in peril. Who were they shooting?

As the menacing machine guns continued firing shot after shot, Zora doubled over, as if taking in each bullet herself. Shaking, she slammed the door as her body gave way, sliding to the floor. The sounds were too loud. There was no way she could mask the sounds, and she hoped somehow her daughters and mother would be able to sleep through it. She covered her ears, but the gunfire intensified, and it was accompanied by the moans and wails of the people.

Flinching, Zora cried, "My boys…where are my boys?" Pulling her knees to her chest, she sobbed the heart-wrenching sobs of despair, rocking back and forth. "Please dear God, please keep Neven and Vuk from harm."

Awakened by her daughter's cries, Mima padded in and kneeled. "Shh, shh, my dušo." She caressed Zora's face. "Come; let's light a church candle and pray. Maybe they will release our boys after realizing how young they are? We must pray, Zora—for life. C'mon, remember today's Neven's eighteenth birthday." Crossing herself, Mima continued, "Let's pray for our Neven first."

"Lord no, what kind of mother forgets her dearest son's birthday?" Zora shouted. The raw pain caused her face to crumple.

"Please don't torture yourself over a date." Mima became instantly transported in prayer. "*Molim te Bože*, protect Neven and Vuk in your strongest light, and keep them safe from harm. Lord have mercy."

The reality of hearing her sons' names in prayer hit Zora front and center. Her stomach lurched as she rushed to the sink, feeling the sour, acrid bile rise in her throat, causing her to gag. Bracing herself, she vomited into the sink, green, slimy bits. Blinking rapidly, she turned her head.

"No, Mama, NO. I won't pray, and won't ask God for his help. Not after this. If your God is so divine, why is he allowing this to happen? They're executing innocent young lives." The veins in Zora's neck protruded as tiny beads of sweat formed on her forehead. "If something happened to them, I fear I will not be able to carry on."

Mima took command, firmly grasping Zora's shoulders. "Zora, Zora, do you realize what you are saying? We must keep hope alive. Never speak against God."

Zora's piercing scream echoed throughout their home. "Do you not hear the thunderous noise of the rifles and machine guns? Who do you think they're shooting? It's the young boys and men they forcibly removed yesterday. By God, Mama—Neven and Vuk were in that roundup."

Hesitating, Zora sucked in a breath. "I—I didn't want to tell you this…" she stammered. "But the Germans posted a notice telling us exactly what they were about to do. Dunja showed me the notice, but…we've been too trusting and naïve to believe they would enact something this inhumane. Every day, we Serbs have lived in denial, refusing to believe that something so atrocious or despicable could happen here, in Kragujevac. Well, guess what, Mama? It's happening, right this very moment."

Mima held her throat and her eyebrows shot up. "Please, Zora. Help me understand what that means?"

"It's Hitler's method of retaliation." Zora stopped, attempting to swallow her sob. "This was a direct result from what occurred last week because our two Resistance groups banded together in a surprise attack against the Germans in Ljuljaci, and we killed and injured some of their soldiers." She wasn't sure she should continue, so she shut her eyes.

She was numb. Mima's voice sounded muffled, as if underwater. "As soon as it's over, we'll search for the boys. We'll search everywhere, Zora. We won't give up until we find Neven and Vuk. I'll tell those awful Germans to take me instead, if they need another body for their damn quota," Mima declared passionately, her voice snapping with emotion.

"Mama, no." Zora's tense muscles flinched in reaction to another round of earsplitting machine-gun fire, this the most strident. "I—I won't lose them, or you." Standing, Zora went to her, and mother and daughter held tight to one another as their world shrank.

Mima said, "I need to check on your girls. They were inconsolable last night, crying for hours on end. They were awake for hours and Lenka was extremely anxious. They're frightened, Zora, but we cannot ignore Stana. If something were to happen, I—I cannot bear to imagine." Catching her breath, she asked, "Are you certain Luka's with Neven?"

Looking at her mother, still in her nightgown with her chestnut-colored hair tumbling down in waves, Zora squeezed her swollen eyes shut before nodding. "Luka *would* be with Neven, and you're right, if something were to happen, without a doubt, Stana would be most affected." She pressed her fingertips on her forehead; it was suddenly too much to bear. Swaying, Zora dropped her head onto her chest. "Please don't let this be true."

Two hours later, she bravely opened the door to view the soldiers still standing guard. Craning her neck, it was difficult not to be plunged into the thick gray clouds of smoke pervading the air. She was reminded of the familiar stench from a German Mauser used by their Resistance. Wrapping the sweater snugly across her drawn body, Zora cocked her head, not knowing which was worse: the terrifying gunfire, or the muffled cries seeping from the homes of the desperate mothers and wives and girlfriends and sisters and bakas crying for their loved ones, ruthlessly torn from their everyday lives by an evilness permeating their closeknit community.

Aged twenty years in two days, Zora was wrung out. Deep shadows dogged her eyes, giving them a hollowed appearance beneath her translucent skin. Devoid of the ability to feel the never-ending stream of tears rolling down her face, she entered the house and sank into a chair at the kitchen table. Lowering her head, she liked the feel of the cool Formica tabletop against her forehead.

***

Oddly enough, by midafternoon, the noise stopped. Mima answered the knock at the door.

"Mima." Mitza's small eyes were red. "We're quite sure they've finished. Don't ask me how, but my brazen kid sister snuck through Šumarice early this morning…and watched. The Germans and Ljotićevci were seen leading men and boys from the old barracks on Stanojve down the long stretch of road into Šumarice. She said they were using Šumarice as a killing field." Mitza punched out her words, her tone and inflection monotone.

"My God, Mitza, you're shaking," Mima said, her brows knitted into a frown. "Why don't you let me make you a cup of hot tea?"

"I—I have to find my son…my Boban." Mitza's voice changed pitch. "He's likely still at the barracks and we're going to find him."

"All right, Mitza, thank you," Mima said quietly. "After we put on our shoes, we'll be right behind you." Closing the door, Mima went to wake Zora, who had finally fallen asleep.

***

Zora and Stana tore down the hill, turning onto Bulevar Kraljice Marije. They were sprinting side by side, mother and daughter, heading straight toward Šumarice. Zora had made the decision to leave Lenka at home in case someone returned. Mima was behind them, walking with a few of their older neighbors.

The Third Reich's armed forces were positioned across the vast, open entrance to Šumarice. Zora saw countless soldiers running about in the choked-filled air, shouting commands as their pack radios squawked out orders in German. Witnessing the sheer number of soldiers in one location was overwhelming. Zora took in a giant amount of air, and that's when she smelled it—the coppery, over-powering scent of blood. With each blind step, her nose picked up the stench from unwashed bodies, a foulness from the open latrines, and an acrid, sulfuric smell of gun-fire. Lifting her eyes toward the crowd gathering, Zora heard women shouting and questioning why they were not letting anyone through. One questioned why the guards were pushing them back. Seeing the Ljotićevci conversing with the Germans, Zora again shook her head in disbelief. "Please tell me they're not working with Hitler?"

"Hush, Mama." Inching closer, Stana, the taller of the two, pulled her nearer. "Let's move to the front. I can't make out what they're saying." Latching on to her mother's arm, Stana said, "I know Neven and Luka must be together, and Vuk with his classmates. C'mon; maybe we'll see them."

Another wail cut through their senses and Zora saw Stana recoil. So naïve and unassuming. Zora closed her eyes. Please, dear God, she prayed, let us find them and I will never ask you for more.

Mother and daughter moved together seamlessly. Every fiber of her being was on full alert as her eyes flicked back and forth, pulse racing. Suddenly, they were in the front, facing a commanding line of soldiers in their pressed, green tunics standing shoulder to shoulder, their Mausers cavalierly flung across their backs.

Staring at her from underneath the lids of his cold, insolent eyes, one of them stated, "Kinder, Küche, Kirche!"

Zora winced at the ridiculous alliteration of Nazi empowerment, meant to describe that a woman's place was supposed to be in the kitchen.

"Ma'am, no one's allowed any further," said a baby-faced, blond soldier, stepping nearer to Stana.

"Please…" Zora said, barely above a whisper. "I must find my boys. Can you h—help me?" Unadulterated fear laced around her throat, making it sound as though she were being strangled. Suddenly, she recognized him, this young German she had waited on countless times at the kafana. Why she remembered him was because he was one of the few with good manners.

Something momentarily flashed in his eyes before he faltered. "I—I…"

Seizing the moment, Zora begged. "I know you from the kafana. I've brought your food and always treated you kindly, like your mother would if she were here. You may have recognized one of my sons who also worked at Paligorić." She pleaded in a shaky voice, "Could you please help me find him? His name's Neven and today's his birthday, and they mistakenly took him and my younger son yesterday. One's only fourteen, and the other—"

"Stop," yelled a thickset, older German with the cruelest pair of blue eyes, pushing through with a Karabiner 98k slung over his shoulder. Brazenly brushing the young soldier aside, he flipped his action rifle horizontally, using it to push Zora and Stana back. "No. None of you Serbs—no one comes in." He sneered.

"Where are they?" Zora hollered defiantly, unafraid. Meeting his meanness, she glowered right back at him.

Taking two steps back, an unkind smile swept across his face. "Digging today." He pointed behind him. "You no can't…go. Leave."

"Digging graves?" The sting of his words blindsided her.

Staggering, Zora held her stomach while she moaned. The raw pain was profound. It slashed at her heart the same as if he'd taken a large knife and severed her chest. Everything slid into place, causing her to let out a resounding wail. "Noooo. No. NO." The walls crashed as she collapsed, heartbroken.

***

"Mama, please. We've got to find them. Please, get up." Stana attempted to pull her mother up but couldn't. Turning her eyes, she saw the familiar face of Lieutenant Kord Webber Gerhardt. "Kord, over here," Stana called. Their eyes *had* connected. Stana was certain of it. Kord had seen her first, and he quickly looked away. Stana yelled his name again. "Kord, please help me find Neven and Luka." He didn't answer, and for the third time, Stana yelled and waved. "Please, Kord, help me."

Openmouthed, she watched him quickly turn and move in another direction. Baffled, Stana swallowed, searching for her grandmother. "Baka Mima," she called out. "Over here." Stana towered over most of the women and finally spotted her grandmother. "Hurry; it's Mama."

With a strength unusual for her age, Mima pressed through the crowd. Quickly dropping to her knees, she cradled her daughter's head. "Zora, you must get up before you're trampled. Come now, my love. The Germans; they're watching you."

***

Slowly lifting her head, Zora said raggedly, "Something terrible's happened. They told us they're…digging." Shutting her eyes, Zora grimaced, before a primeval pain forced her onto all fours. She let out a high-pitched, mournful cry, a mother's sorrow amidst unimaginable loss. Hearing her, the other women and bakas in their babushkas suddenly pushed through the jumble of sadness, their grief too strong to be ignored. They, too, began to moan. These broken-hearted mothers and women collectively mourned together, their loss so far-reaching, it was impossible to ignore.

Mima could not breathe. Gasping, her hands shot up, rubbing underneath her chest in an attempt to get air into her lungs.

"Baka, my goodness, slow down. Breathe slower. Good, now breathe out. There you go," Stana instructed, her hand resting lightly on her grandmother's thin wrist.

"Let's go to our church," Mima said. "There's a chance they'll know more than these bastards, who won't tell us anything."

Bracing her grandmother on one side and her mother on the other, Stana began the long walk to town.

***

A woman stood outside the Dormition of the Most Holy Theotokos Serbian Orthodox Church, where a small crowd had gathered. She held a clipboard in her shaky hands, and Zora could see that the woman appeared frightened. "Blood spilled this morning, and innocent people have been killed, all due to the German act of reprisal. They're calling what they have done '*One Hundred for One.*'"

Reeling, Zora asked in disbelief, "Do you have any names?"

Sadness stretched across the woman's face. "Was it a husband or a father, perhaps?"

"No, no; my two precious boys…they were in high school. One is just fourteen, and the other, well, today's his birthday, Neven would—" Zora stumbled over her words.

The woman clutched her throat, and in a gentle tone she said, "I am so deeply sorry, but the Germans took every student and professor from all the schools: the Prva Muška Gimnazija, the First and Second Gymnasium, the Teacher's School, the Military Technical School, the Craft School, and the Civic School. They told us they released a few prisoners who were being used to dig graves today."

It took incredible strength, but Mima bravely spoke. "Were the students from the Prva Muška Gimnazija digging?"

The women paused for an interminable amount of time. "I, ah, Gospođo…" Three generations of Nikolić women waited in anticipation.

Looking at Mima, the woman said, "Gospođo, I am terribly sorry, but I'm afraid those students and their professors—they did not make it. Regrettably, they were among the first to be executed by a firing squad early this morning."

"*Mili Bože na nebesima!*" Mima cried out, shaking her head back and forth.

"NOOOOOO!" Stana roared, crushed under the weight of it all.

With grief snaking its way into her soul, Zora shut her eyes. "There's nothing more for us here."

CHAPTER TWENTY-SIX

SAVA

Kragujevac, Yugoslavia
October 21, 1941

IT WASN'T UNTIL THEY reached Route 149 Tuesday morning that traffic came to a complete standstill. Sava tapped her fingertips as her eyes darted over to Života's. "Now what?"

"I think everyone has the same idea. They're all in a hurry to get to Kragujevac. Unfortunately, unless we're on horseback, or on foot, there's no other way."

Tapping her foot in frustration, Sava questioned, "What do you think happened down there?" Fear lined her flawless face.

Lighting a cigarette, Života paused. "I'm not sure."

Irritated by not knowing, Sava refused to tell him just how petrified she'd been since the moment Josie went missing. Arrested, they'd said, for spying. Shortly thereafter, the SS and Abwehr agents had also captured Conductor and Kosta. She felt they were systematically plucking out her inner circle. She also had a feeling Germany's counterintelligence was watching her.

Offering her a weak smile, Života asked, "What's raised your alarm?"

"Well, it's unsettling…being the last from our original group: Toma, Josie, Conductor, and Kosta all taken." Sighing, she unlatched the car lock on the Mercedes-Benz and climbed out. Walking on the highway's narrow shoulder berm, she saw others getting out of their vehicles and doing something similar.

Once night fell, they took turns sleeping in the car. Sava appreciated Života's last-minute act of bringing blankets, pillows, and sheets.

Twenty-four hours later, the Germans reopened the Topola–Kragujevac Road, and Života inched forward. When they approached the outskirts of town, he suggested, "Let's roll down the windows; perhaps we'll hear something." But outside of an occasional baa from the sheep milling near the roadway, there was only silence.

Entering Kragujevac, a microcosm of a town steeped in Serbian history and culture, the smell hit them first—gunpowder and smoke. Holding herself erect, Sava's breath caught.

Without warning, they heard the subtle cries from women weeping. Unnerved, she felt a cold sensation wash over her, signaling something dreadfully wrong. "What in God's name?" She closed her eyes, wanting to block out the soul-wrenching cries which tore at her nerve endings. "Hurry, Života."

The moment they arrived in front of 7 Gružanska, smoke hung like a dark cloud over her family's home.

Pinching her nostrils, Sava raced from the automobile to the house, leaving Života to tend to the sacks and luggage. Wild-eyed, she glanced around. "Mama, Zora, anyone here?" Fear niggled at the base of her neck. "Zora…?" Sava heard her voice growing louder.

A soft moan had her whipping her head around to see her sister shuffle in, looking considerably older than her thirty-eight years. Zora's eyes were haunted, causing her to stop short. Heart thumping wildly, Sava touched her sister's arm, but Zora immediately recoiled, as if burnt. Paralyzed by the anguish on Zora's face, Sava needed to know. "Please talk to me. Zora. Let me in."

Sinking to her knees, Zora swayed, letting out a fevered cry. "Nooo…"

Icy chills raced down her back. Sava kneeled next to her, laying a soothing hand on her back, but once more, she shrugged it off. Terrified, Sava sat back on her haunches, never having experienced Zora quite this distraught. "Darling, please talk to me. What happened?"

Lifting her head, she shrieked, "No. No one can help me, my sons—they're gone. They took Neven and Vuk, and, and shot them by a—"

Sucking in a huge burst of air, Sava gasped. "Ohhh… my God, no." Her heart galloped and she leaned against the wall for support. How had this evilness seeped into her very family? Trying to steady herself, Sava softly said, "Zora, are you certain it was Neven…and Vuk?"

"The lady told us. Our boys were the first ones executed yesterday morning." Zora sobbed, and through her tears and frantic movements, she slowly explained, wrapping her arms around herself. "It hurts too much—nothing can bring them back. My precious Neven…and Vuk…gone. Why?" Pitching forward, she continued crying.

Sava fought back her own tears, and after a time, she lifted Zora from the floor. "Come, sit." Sava patted a kitchen chair. "I'm making you coffee and something to eat." Sava unpacked the sacks Života had left on the table. Hanging on for dear life, Zora would have to bear the enormous weight of losing two children.

"Zora, were you there yesterday?"

Unfocused, Zora did not respond.

Sava tried again, this time lowering her voice. "Zora, please tell me where you were yesterday?" Glancing around, she wondered where her mother and the rest of her family were. It was peculiarly quiet, and odd that no one else was there. Noticing the milk she'd unpacked must have spoiled on the way down, she hurriedly checked the other items, before making Zora a plate of scrambled eggs and toast. She understood how certain moments could drastically change a person's world, and Sava believed her sister was experiencing this right now. "Go ahead, take a bite."

Stone-faced, Zora sat unmoving. Sava lifted Zora's hands and wrapped them around the warm coffee cup. Nothing. No movement. A knot formed deep in her belly as she decided to give her more time. But perhaps she should telephone Dr. Milković who worked closely with Zora? Maybe just give her more time? It had been the most shocking news a mother could ever hear.

Washing the dishes piled in the sink, Sava sank into the loving memories of her nephews when, out of nowhere, Zora suddenly shouted at her. "Roads blocked. Germans everywhere. Street locked. Boxed in. Terrible time. Mitza came. Ohhh…" Zora moaned, before she bent forward, pressing her forehead on the table.

"No, no, love. It's not your fault, darling, none of it." Sava quickly moved to place her hands lightly on Zora's shoulders. "Please, do not beat yourself up." Trying to understand why, for whatever insane reason, Zora apparently felt guilty, she whispered, "There, there…let's try to sleep, now." Lightly, she rubbed her sister's shoulders and neck until she was confident Zora had indeed fallen asleep.

She found her mother, curled on the bed, sleeping. "Mama," Sava breathed, kissing Mima's forehead. "May I talk to you?"

Mima's eyes slowly opened, and the look she gave was chilling. Bursting into tears, she clutched Sava's hand and tearfully explained.

Leaning back on her heels, Sava blew out a tortured breath. "*Bože, Bože sačuvaj*, a grisly massacre?" With her fingers touching parted lips, she was unable to come to grips with what had occurred. Stammering, Sava said, "A brutal bloodbath, including children? No word in their language could capture the evilness of it all. It's too much for any mother to bear. A tragedy of epic proportions."

"Let's not forget our poor Stana," Mima said, her face wet with tears. "Our little dove just lost *two* brothers and a boy she's madly in love with. Were you aware Luka took Stana this summer to Most Ljubavi and asked her to wait for him?" Mima's hands trembled as she wiped her face. "There's no doubt Luka was with Neven. And Zora's so broken-hearted, I can't even remember how I got her and Stana home. They were both inconsolable. I—it was the worst day of our lives."

Blanching, Sava sucked in copious amounts of air. "This sorrow—it knows no bounds. I wish I could somehow take it away…" She shook her head. Zora had fallen asleep at the table. She hadn't touched any of the food. "Might you encourage her to eat, Mama? She'll need her strength in the coming days. Meanwhile I'll check on Stana and Lenka."

"All right, but if Stana's asleep, let her be. She's exhausted and needs sleep more than anything right now." Shoulders sagging, Mima folded her face into her hands and wept.

Since Stana and Lenka were asleep, Sava went outside in search of Života. After filling him in, she handed him a written note. "Please make sure this gets to Ravna Gora, right away. Goran and Peda need to know what happened. We need them here. Zora needs them desperately."

Života stared at her in complete disbelief. "Bastards. You would not believe the amount of Germans swarming about. Once night falls, I'll arrange for someone on horseback to go up the mountain. Who provided your mother with the details about the casualties?"

Gazing up at the sky, Sava felt chilled. "She said it was a woman at our church, which is in the center of town." Feeling confident Života would take care of her message, she went back inside and watched her mother spoon-feed Zora.

"I—it's too much, Mama. How will I ever find the strength to go on?" Zora clawed at her neck. "And… Goran? We haven't heard from him in weeks. Nothing. I don't know whether he's alive or dead." Under her breath, Zora said words to herself that made no sense, until she unleashed another torrent of emotions. "It feels like someone's stabbing me with a sharp knife—my insides hurt. Ahh, God—just take me."

A cold prickling sensation ran down Sava's spine. There was nothing more painful than hearing her sister admit she had given up on life. And even though she was unable to comprehend the true agony she must be feeling, she still had five other children to care for and nurture and love.

Sometime later, Sava whispered soothingly to Zora, "I'm here as long as you need me; I'm in for the long haul."

The rippling effects of a loved one's death left a tremendous void, and she knew it would be a lifetime before her sister would be able to put her grief aside.

"There's no reason to live. I have this overwhelming hatred." Zora gasped. "And…where has God been…in all of this? How could he have allowed those God-awful monsters to shoot my children…my boys?" Zora's anguish flooded her face.

Mima sat at the table with her head in her hands, saying over and over, "Dear Lord, please help us."

"I cannot bear to go on. It feels like I'm standing in quicksand and sinking fast. I cannot wake up without having my boys." Zora cried.

There was so much raw pain in Zora's words, it took Sava's breath away. She went into the bathroom to run warm water for a bath as her mother came over.

Mima choked out her words. "Let her cry it out; eventually, it will help her heal. God bless her."

"Come, Zora," Sava said, holding her hand out to guide Zora to the bathroom. "I've made a warm lavender bath for you to soak in before bed. Tomorrow, we'll sort everything out. Come, my love."

***

Sava was woken by the subtle squeak of a door opening. Sitting up, she glanced at the dials on her wristwatch, which reflected three thirty in the morning. "Who's there?"

"Sava…you're really here?" Dušica's face showed confusion. She was holding Stefan in her arms, and behind her was a filthy Marko, holding Čedo. Aco brought up the rear, carrying blankets and sacks. Despite looking harried and unsettled, they were here, and alive.

Seeing them with twigs stuck in their hair was a most comforting sight. "You made it back…all of you?" Sava watched Marko gently lay Čedo on his bed, before returning to lift Stefan from Dušica's arms.

"Yes." Dušica looked fearful as she clutched her throat. "We heard the shooting, and the rifle fire, and the smoke and explosions. It was horribly frightening for the little ones." She tugged Sava's arm. "Tell me…did something bad happen in town? Because its packed with German military of all kinds."

Sava observed Dušica's knitted forehead and clenched jaw, recognizing their lives would never be the same the second she unloaded the weight of her words. Hesitating, she coughed to clear her throat, knowing these few minutes would be the last time her family would know serenity. "My love, what I'm about to tell you is the most devastating and horrendous news you'll ever hear. Dušica, you may need to sit down because it's unimaginable, and heart-shattering—Neven and Vuk were executed yesterday."

Dušica's hands flew to her mouth as she backed away. "NO, no!" Forcefully shaking her head, she cried out, "No, Sava—you've got it wrong. Vuk was with us."

Sava was suddenly off balance and placed a hand on the wall to steady herself. "What are you saying? Are you one hundred percent certain, Dušica, because Zora was told a firing squad murdered Neven *and* Vuk…?"

"No, I mean yes, Vuk is with us. But Neven—?" Reeling, Dušica staggered before righting herself. Bending over, she breathed in large gulps of air. "Please, no." After a few seconds, and with a tinge of sadness, she explained, "Walking to school the other day, Vuk bumped into a friend, who shared what he'd overheard the Germans discussing. Vuk immediately decided not to go to school and instead ran to the woods, where he knew about the cave. He decided to hide in the cave and found us there too. But…Neven?"

"You're saying Vuk was with you and…he's alive? B—but where is he?" Sava's jaw dropped. She could not seem to process this miraculous news amidst the sorrow.

Dušica looked behind her before insisting, "He'll be here. When Andrej started to become fussy, Vuk offered to take him. I would imagine he's ten minutes behind us. It was complicated attempting to make our way through the woods behind town, especially with the amount of—"

Cutting her off, Sava said, "Duš, I didn't mean to insinuate. I understand the riskiness." If her sister only knew what she'd been doing for the last five months…"It's because of you that Vuk's safe, and that's extraordinary." The news about Vuk being alive was a miracle handed to them on a platter, which she hoped would be bittersweet for Zora.

"And Zora?" If Sava hadn't reached out her arm, Dušica likely would have fallen over. "I cannot imagine the depth of her sorrow. How's Mama holding up?"

Sava tried tamping down her emotions to explain. "It's a frightening time, but Mama's all right. Zora's been vacillating between anger and shock. I must warn you though, when she starts railing against God, well, it's loud and not pleasant to hear." Biting her lip, she said, "Go take your bath, and when you're finished, I'll have breakfast and coffee ready for you."

Sava deliberated on whether she should let Zora sleep or awaken her with the news. In either case, it would carry a deep emotional impact. Reaching into the cupboard to make her family's favorite breakfast, krofne, a sob escaped her throat. Pressing her lips together, she pushed back the overwhelming sorrow threatening to engulf her and began making the doughnuts. Mixing the dough for their favorite comfort food, she stirred the bowl, not paying particular attention to the tears dripping into the batter.

"Tetka?" Vuk tiptoed in.

Her breath caught as she whirled around to see her sweet nephew before swooping him into a massive hug. "My goodness, Vuk, what a blessing it is to see you. I—we thought…"

Lowering his eyes, Vuk nodded, his face smeared with dirt. While Andrej slept in his arms, she saw that his green eyes, so much like his mother's, burned with questions. "How's Neven and Luka? Were they able to make it out of school all right?"

Her throat thickened. She could not speak. With two fingers pressed to her lips, Sava softly shook her head.

Vuk squeezed his eyes shut. "How, Tetka…how did it happen?" He glanced toward the bedroom where his mother slept, tears filling his eyes.

She laid her hand on his tender heart and said, "When your aunt and uncle return, I'll explain all of it. For now, why don't you get cleaned up? Meanwhile, let me get this little one upstairs so Dušica can bathe him."

Thirty minutes later, they were seated around the kitchen table, as Sava tried to assemble the tumultuous events leading to yesterday's despicable horror.

Dušica moaned, "It's too much—we failed them. We should have insisted everyone come with us." Shaking her head, she squeaked out, "I feel horrible we survived and Neven didn't. We should not have left anyone behind."

With great tenderness, Sava drew Dušica in. "There was no way to anticipate what was to come. None of us could have predicted this. Moreover, every parent was feeling scared because the Germans insisted that every child must attend school or face the consequences. Therefore, every parent was left with zero choices. I'll lay odds on every child having been in attendance at school on Monday, October twentieth. Everyone except our Vuk." Sava tousled his hair.

Dušica's hands shook. "Zora's pain must be unimaginable. How will she survive this monumental loss? It's too—"

"Look," Sava said, pointing to the clock. "Why don't we try to sleep for at least a few hours, because when we awaken, we're taking Zora to search for Neven's body at Šumarice and prepare his funeral. It's crucial we keep an eye on Stana, too. She lost a brother and her boyfriend in one swoop. She's decimated, and inconsolable." Making a guttural sound, Sava rubbed her throat.

"My God, Luka." Dušica's hand rubbed her slim neck. "How could I have forgotten?" she whispered as she glanced at Marko. It was suddenly too much.

"If only," Vuk said. "If only Neven and Luka hadn't been so determined to work on their science project and had foreseen not going to school. Or if someone had warned them, like my friend, maybe they'd be here now."

My God, Sava thought, he was also berating himself. "Vuk, I think you should go in and wake your mother. Your being alive will be a glorious gift for her."

***

It was Stana who finally located her dear brother lying in a mass grave, his arms intertwined with Luka's and countless other classmates of theirs. Sadly, their bodies were tangled to such a degree they were unable to separate them. Zora would not be able to have a funeral inside the church without a body. Whoever had dug these graves had done a poor job. Sava suspected animals must have brushed aside the thin layer of dirt to get to their bloodied bodies.

Around them were other families consumed by grief: mothers, grandmothers, aunts, and sisters, all weighed down by sorrow, much like her family. Sava watched Zora kneel on a wet clump of dirt, attempting to get a closer look at her darling Neven.

"How could they? Even in death, they torture us like this. The way they murdered my son and these young boys has made it impossible for us to have a church funeral. Neven loved our church and our music…so much. What will I do?" Zora said in a strangled voice.

A woman kneeling nearby said softly, "It doesn't matter, anyway."

"Why would you say that?" Zora's face showed alarm. "I want to properly bury my son."

"I understand," the woman said. "But since they killed Father Radovan too, along with many other priests, we have no one to bury our boys. That fascist Marisav Petrovic, he's responsible, that's who."

"Who?" Zora's head lifted.

Sava listened to this exchange with interest.

"He's some commander of the Fifth Regiment of the Ljotićevci, but he grew up not twenty kilometers from here. Most locals never cared for the crazy ideas he often spouted off about fascism. He's a disgrace to our people. But could he have stopped the Germans from shooting our boys? Who knows, but he must pay for allowing all of these innocent children and priests to be murdered."

Stunned, Sava questioned who this man was. One day, she would make it her mission to learn more, but now she needed to help her family through this unimaginable loss. Research and finding the truth were a part of her very fiber. Sava would not rest until she uncovered the truth.

Standing, the woman said with her hands trembling, "The lady at the church told me some of the victims had been given paper and pencil to write a message to their loved ones b—before…they were killed. I'm going there now, to see if my Ivan might have left me a message." The woman began to cry.

"Thank you." Zora held her heart.

Walking out of Šumarice, two German soldiers, who looked familiar to Zora, approached her. "Ma'am? Ma'am, we must remind you that no ornaments, decorations, flags, or Serbian crosses will be permitted on this site. Do you understand?"

Zora spit. It landed on the toe of his shiny boot.

CHAPTER TWENTY-SEVEN

PEDA

Suvobor Mountains, Yugoslavia
October 24, 1941

After reading Sava's devastating note, Peda wanted to lash out at someone. Instead, he grabbed his rifle and stomped off toward a section of the forest, which was dense with thickets of brush, overgrown bushes, and fallen branches.

"Why are you letting him run off like that, half-cocked and with a gun?" a distressed Božo questioned.

"I'm not." Jovica rubbed the sides of his thick beard. "I plan to keep a close watch on him. I'm going to follow him from a safe distance. Losing two kids in a brutal massacre has to be gut-wrenching. It'll take a herculean effort for him and his wife to recover from this staggering blow. Don't worry though, we're looking out for him."

Just then, Stevan came over. "Good gracious, I just heard, and to make matters worse, the Germans captured Goran's unit near Valjevo."

A peculiar expression appeared on Jovica's face as he glanced at the sky. "How much more can one man take?

How about we hold off telling Peda about Goran? I fear it's too much for any father to bear."

Božo's eyes watered. "Something like this has the power to break a person."

"Agreed. Peda's in a lot of pain. I hope to prevent him from falling into an even darker spiral, so let's try to get him back to Kragujevac and to his family," Jovica said.

***

Peda could feel the fog moving in, but he forged on, the fine mist clinging to his face and hair as he made his way deep into the forest. He needed this time alone, and away from everyone. Huffing, he stopped, pressing the tops of his fingers onto his eyelids wanting to staunch the flood of tears. With his heart ripping apart, he released a massive sigh that sounded more like a howl and rocked back and forth, finally releasing the sobs which he'd been holding in. "Why?" he screamed. "Why have you taken my boys?"

Awakening sometime later, Peda had no sense of time. In a sudden jolt, he found himself upright and confused of his whereabouts. Filled with fear, he remembered his horrifying dream about the German Army shooting all seven children, repeatedly. Standing, he raised his fist to the sky, the forest's canopy obscuring his view. "Damn you, Hitler. I'm going to make you pay."

Jovica lowered his field glasses and from behind a cluster of bushes approached Peda from forty feet away. "Peda," he said, " I'm here to bring you back to base camp. Nighttime poses great danger in this section of the forest area."

Peda's raw eyes widened in surprise as he glanced around in a panic. "No, Jovica, I'm not leaving. There's nothing left.

Don't you understand I need to be alone? It's agonizing, and I—I have to be with my family. They need me…"

Jovica approached with his palms raised. "I know, Peda, I know. I'm terribly sorry. No one knows how you feel, but we all understand loss." Pausing, Jovica said, "This might be difficult to hear, but my orders from the commanders were clear—you must return to base camp. Unfortunately, no one's permitted off the mountain until we've completed our surveillance. Trust me, Peda; this massacre has unmistakably affected everyone. Our losses have been too severe, and a great many Četnici have suffered family losses, but that in no way will diminish yours."

Back at camp, Peda found a peaceful spot away from the others where he could stare off into the distance and mourn. It was down the mountain a bit and right underneath the lookout area. There was a strange heaviness weighing him down, pressing on his shoulders and chest, which made it difficult to breathe. Try as he might, Peda could not rein in his emotions, which vacillated between wanting to shoot someone or turning the gun on himself. He also thought about his family, wondering how they were coping with the grief that was swallowing him whole. Unsure how any of them would be able to recover from this tragedy, he was also unsure of where he belonged anymore.

Suddenly, he heard one of the guards above him boasting about the ease of smuggling in bottles of his uncle's fresh-made rakija.

"It was simple," the guard said. "I brought them up on a cart at night and buried them right there." The guard pointed to the ground close to where Peda sat. "It's where Čiča, or one of those old commanders, won't find it. I can drink all night when I'm on duty."

Foolishly, Peda sought out the young guard.

***

Intoxicated, Peda weaved sideways, arguing with two of the young patriots. He shouted, "I don't care, no one's coming to save us, or Yugoslavia."

"Stop what you're saying, Peda. That's incorrect, the allies will come and the King will come, and—"

"The King?" Peda shouted. Their voices rose to a fever pitch as another revolutionary tried quieting them down. Drinking for hours, these men had lost count of the number of shots they'd consumed. Restless, with pent-up anxiety, and fueled by alcohol, their argument quickly turned to a full-fledged fight. Someone swung at Peda and several others joined in, fighting one another in the pouring rain. In an attempt to catch Peda from falling down the mountain, several of the Saboteurs tumbled in the dark.

When the men above heard the commotion, they immediately skidded down the slippery mountain to quiet them. Unfortunately, the fight had mushroomed into a full brawl. "Peda, quiet down. Stop screaming like that, or you'll land us in hot water with the Wehrmacht." A fellow Saboteur tried to restrain him, but Peda fought him off.

"Get your hands off me."

Others flew down the cliff, just as floodlights appeared from an overhead plane. All of a sudden, lights shone down on the intemperate Royalists, making it easy for the Wehrmacht ground crew, who had quietly been monitoring and listening from below, to race up.

"Holy hell," shouted a Royalist. "Hurry; it's the Germans. Get up the mountain, now." Some were able to escape by briskly climbing back up, but the German authorities swiftly apprehended the rest, including men like Peda, intoxicated and less agile. Fourteen of Mihajlović's men were forced into a covered wagon, their bodies bound in chains.

November 1941

Peda awoke to a pungent stench of decay as it all came rushing back. The massacre. His sons dead, and the altercation with his fellow fighters, followed by the arrest on the mountain. With a groan, he became startled as thoughts spilled out, including the sensation of being flung about on a cold, wet metal truck as it maneuvered unnaturally, then nothing. "Where am I?" He tested his voice. He could make out a dank, crowded room with bars on it. Was it a cellar? It appeared larger.

Turning, he tried sitting up, but gagged. "What's that smell?" he murmured, before immediately vomiting all over himself.

While adjusting himself, Peda's attention was drawn to a pair of deep brown eyes, sunken into a skull, and excessively pronounced cheekbones. "I apologize for this." Peda pointed to the mess on his lap. "Where are we, friend?" He had to find a washroom or a basin of water to wash the stink off himself.

The man stared blankly.

"Pardon. Do you speak Serbian?" Peda asked.

The man slowly nodded.

"Where are we?"

Again, the man nodded.

Frustrated, Peda sought another, but the clomping footsteps prevented him. A stern guard opened the door so two men could drag out an enormous can that sloshed around... The can emitted an odor, and it suddenly hit him.

Jesus, I'm in a prison cell, he realized. But where?

The prisoners stood and hurried to form a line. Peda watched as they walked through a chilly, concrete corridor, stopping in front of the central bathroom. As he got in line, he noted the burly looking Gestapo with his heavy eyebrows and sour face who had begun to separate and pull certain prisoners out of the line. Tapping the man in front of him, Peda asked, "Where are we?"

"Banjica Concentration Camp, in Belgrade, but technically Dedinje. The Gestapo run it. Shhh; no talking."

"Why?" Peda knew Dedinje. It was the ritzy neighborhood of Belgrade, where his sister-in-law Sava lived. Thank goodness she was nearby and would rescue him.

"If you're caught talking in line, they'll break your fingers."

"I have one more question: why were those men pulled out of line?" Peda asked determinedly.

The prisoner replied quickly. "The Gestapo randomly interrogates people upstairs in separate rooms. Alternatively, they might execute a prisoner by shooting them out back."

"Whoa." Peda's breath hitched, then he offered a tentative smile. He had taken note of a constant stream of inmates being singled out. But the only sounds he heard were boots scraping and keys clanging on metal chains. He'd heard dreadful stories about the Banjica Concentration Camp and the sadistic torture methods of the Gestapo: starvation, repeated beatings, and poor sanitary measures. Jovica had shared with him how frequently the Germans relished capturing and sending any member of their Resistance, especially their commanders, to Banjica.

Peda didn't get his turn in the restroom. Their line was called, and they were returning to their cell. He raised his hand to ask the guard, "Excuse me, but I didn't get my turn to use the bathroom."

"Is that so?" answered the round Gestapo with a bad complexion and teeth too crowded for his mouth. "Come with me," he said, after locking the others inside.

***

Beaten raw, as daylight faded, Peda crawled down the cool hallway. In the basement, the guard saw him coming and quickly unlocked the cell door, allowing Peda to shimmy through, on his belly. When the guard walked away, a gaunt-looking man stumbled toward Peda, handing him something.

"I—thank you…" Peda could barely speak, feeling as if a few of his teeth had come loose in the exchange upstairs. He was chilled and shaking. Wooden truncheons had been used, causing a concentrated pain in nearly every part of his body. Struggling, he used hand motions to thank the man who had given him the tattered blanket before he fell back.

***

A week later, he started to heal. The swelling in his eyes had dissipated, and his facial pain lessened; the headaches, not so much. The pain in the back of his head made focusing difficult. He found no help or support as he grappled with the loss of his sons. Many times, he would suddenly wake in the middle of the night, crying, which disturbed those around him. One night he had awoken during a violent dream and shouted aloud. The guards dragged him upstairs. This time he returned with a broken hand and wrist. Luckily, Dr. Miloš, a renowned university medical professor and physician who happened to be his cellmate, helped him. With some ingenuity, Dr. Miloš devised an arm brace from torn pieces of cardboard and a few strips of yarn.

Banjica housed a diverse group of individuals: resistance officers, judges, aristocrats, physicians, academics, painters, bankers, and artists. During his once-a-week walk outside, for thirty minutes, Peda met two female prisoners who were the military wives of Čiča's inner circle. Due to the Gestapo separating the male from the female prisoners, Peda instantly searched for Josie. Prior to his arrest, Jovica had shared with him that Josie had been arrested for delivering an important message from Čiča. A source close to Čiča later confirmed that Josie was taken into custody on a train as it crossed into Bosnia. She was believed to have been sent to a camp in Germany; however, no one knew for certain.

Peda formed a close relationship with Dr. Miloš, who had been instrumental in his recovery. "What about those peasants? Have you seen how they've been tortured? Have you seen their toenails? It looked like each one had been ripped off with rusty pliers. I saw the guards making fun of the way they're walking. They're heartless." Sighing, Peda said, "They'd beaten them mercilessly for two days; it's a wonder any of them survived."

"I hate to say this, Peda, but you'll get used to it."

"I never want to get used to their wicked ways."

"Well, I've been here since last summer, and these dungeons down here, they use them for what they consider their worst prisoners. And their guards, and block leaders—they're the vilest human beings I've ever encountered."

"I believe you. But you're a doctor—what led to you being arrested?"

"I was accused of providing medical supplies to the Royalists. A close friend of mine, another doctor, was murdered because of it. It happened last June. They shot him and then hung him up in Trg Republike as a spectacle, for all to see. All this time I've been puzzled as to why I've been spared."

"Were you guilty?" Peda could not stop scratching his neck and shoulders. The lice bites now covered his body.

Looking up at Peda from underneath hooded eyebrows, Dr. Miloš suddenly winked. "But of course. I, too, was supplying medical supplies to Ravna Gora."

Suddenly, the loudspeaker blasted with a standard announcement of a new prisoner being checked in. "You are now entering the Command and the Territory of the German Army Military Command and the Government of the National Salvation. You shall follow all our rules while under arrest. Is that clear?"

"Lunchtime." Peda jumped up. It was the only meal he had been able to force down. The guard brought in a large liquid bucket filled with potato soup and doled out one measly thin slice of bread to everyone. Holding the bowl to his face, Peda sighed. "I never knew potato soup tasted so good."

"It isn't. It's quite horrible." Dr. Miloš spit his out. "I'd give anything for a piece of lamb or a slice of burek."

Peda nearly cried as he brought the bread reverentially to his nose. "Every time I smell this, it reminds me of my wife and family back home."

***

December 1941

Weeks passed and Peda felt his world shrinking, growing infinitesimally smaller. It consisted of trying to stay alive in a damp cell with several hundred people squashed in one room, many with a fever or pneumonia, or typhoid.

As they shuffled in line through the icy corridor toward the bathrooms, a tall Partisan suddenly smirked, shoving him out of line.

"Hey, you," the guard hollered before grabbing Peda by his armpits, where he was dragged upstairs. Another Gestapo pushed him into the interrogation room. A split second later, Peda's eyes tracked a sudden blur of red hair in his peripheral vision. Quickly rotating his head, Peda was certain it was Josie being interrogated across the hall from him. Squeezing his eyes shut twice, he quickly reopened them to refocus to ensure it really was her. There was serious bruising on her neck, face, and hands, and a startling cut, like his, above her darkened eye. What had they done to her?

"Sit," lambasted the hefty Gestapo with a thick belly and a mustache mimicking Hitler's, who shoved Peda into a metal chair. Josie lifted her eyes to stare at him from across the hall, before blinking twice. Was she trying to send him a message? He believed she knew it was him, and he wondered what type of hidden message she might be conveying.

Returning his eyes to the guard across the table, Peda answered, "No, I saw no plans. You have the wrong guy. I've told you this before: I've never been involved in decision-making."

"You in charge of blowing up trucks, Wehrmacht trucks?" The interrogator aggressively pounded each question, his fists slamming against the table.

Peda leaned closer, noticing his watery blue eyes and hawk-like nose. What an ugly bastard, he thought. "Like I've said before, you've got the wrong guy. My help was limited to carrying supplies up the mountain. I got fired from my last job, and it's clear I'm too old to serve as a soldier."

The German slammed his file on the desk and left the room. Good.

While Peda waited in the room, he listened to the scrawny Gestapo across the hall say to Josie, "You and other lady—you Yugoslav spies. We know you spy. British knows too. We send you away to camp for women spies. You see what trouble you in, you bad spy lady," he hissed at her in horrible Serbian.

"A spy? Holy hell." He let out a powerful gust of air. Then they forcefully pushed Josie out of the room, well before Peda had a chance to speak to her.

***

The rain hadn't stopped. The chill in the basement matched the gloominess inside in the cell. Peda was eager for news about Zora and his family, realizing the burden must be overwhelming for his wife. He also wondered if he had compromised their Ravna Gora location by his yelling, which had alerted the Wehrmacht.

Cross-legged, Peda observed Dr. Miloš meticulously picking the lice off his arm, when a guard suddenly approached, unlocked the cell door, and yanked the older gentleman out. Startled, Peda quickly stood and questioned the guard. "Hey, you're mistaken," he said, glaring at him. "He's a good man, and a doctor."

Smirking, the guard replied, "Is that so, Brković? Well then, as you wish." Peda was also pulled from the cell and led, with Dr. Miloš, toward the stairs.

Rounding the corner to the front and the stairwell, Peda could see them checking in a new group of prisoners. Communists. One of them looked familiar. Turning, he surprisedly said, "Đuro…my God, is that you—Đuro Grubičić?" Peda looked at his old friend's now lean face. "How'd you end up here?"

Suddenly, a door flew open and out strutted SS-Hauptscharführer Willy Friedrich, the head of Banjica, who had evidently overheard Peda's exchange and flung a hand in Peda's direction. "Who in the hell do you think you are, the greeting committee for God's sakes? Get the hell outside," Friedrich barked before the guards pushed Peda and Dr. Miloš out back.

Dr. Miloš began to recite the Lord's Prayer: "*Oče naš, iže jesi na nebesjeh…*"

Something stirred in the pit of Peda's belly, causing him to shake uncontrollably.

Friedrich came out, lifted his pistol, and shot Dr. Miloš between the eyes.

"You cruel bastard," Peda screamed. "What the hell are you thinking? You just shot—"

Friedrich raised his gun once again and shot Peda once in the head and once in the chest. And as Peda lay dying, the last words he heard were Friedrich's instructing his staff: "Load them up and take them over to Šajmište. Burn them with the Jews. Leave no trace of evidence behind."

CHAPTER TWENTY-EIGHT

ZORA

Kragujevac, Serbia
December 1941

IN THE DAYS THAT followed, the excruciating grief nearly drowned Zora. Not able to imagine a life without Neven, she was not confident she could carry on. The days began to run together as she and her mother stumbled through as best they could, making meals for the children while mumbling brief, incoherent responses. But it was the nights that caused the most searing pain. Zora sagged under the weight of it all, and when darkness crept in, the memories of Neven were so sharp, she could not help but wonder—why him? Her guilt quickly rose, and she felt powerless as a mother who was unable to save her son. It ate away at her insides, along with her ability to think or even function properly.

Shivering in the small bedroom, she tucked the blankets tighter around her mother and went to check Čedo's temperature. Finding it normal, Zora let out a sigh of relief.

An early knock on her door startled her. Reaching for her mother's shawl, she quickly wrapped it over her fading nightgown and cautiously opened the door. In front of her stood a mountain of a man, heavily bearded and shabbily dressed in an odd assortment of rumpled, mismatched clothing.

"Gospođo Brković," the man said with a hand over his chest. "Excuse me for interrupting so early, but I've come a distance with an urgent message from Colonel Draža Mihajlović." The man pulled a crumpled paper from his pocket and handed it to her.

Clutching the note, Zora squinted. "Haven't we met before, Gospodine…? I feel like I know you from somewhere." Her hand lightly touched her neck.

"Ah, yes, Gospođo, it was at Vraćevšnica Monastery last fall. I'm Jovica Ristić, Čiča Draža's assistant. You're the wonderful travarka who helped save many of our men." Clearing his throat, he said, "I—ah, worked closely with your sister, but she's not why I'm here."

"I remember." Lowering her eyes, she read the message.

> Dear Gospođo Brković,
>
> Please accept our sorrow for the untimely death of one of our most trusted guerilla fighters, Peda Brković. The Gestapo executed him several days ago at the Banjica Concentration Camp. I apologize that we have so little information to provide to you.
>
> *Bog da mu dušu prosti,*
> Draža Mihajlović for the Royalist Resistance Četnici of Ravna Gora.

"No…" she cried, the paper floating to the floor. "I—it's just not possible." Turning pale, Zora felt her throat close up and she was not able to breathe. Her heart was racing fast. Vlado, her father, Neven, and now…Peda? This cannot be happening, she thought. Grabbing her neck, she made an unusual, gurgling sound.

Jovica immediately understood what was occurring and lifted her up. He carried her to the kitchen, where he set her on a chair, while his eyes swept the kitchen. Filling a glass with water, he handed it to her, saying, "Drink, quickly."

She gripped the table for support as the water soothed her throat. Once her breathing returned to normal, Zora said, "Thank you. I—ah, it's been a tough year. We have had so many losses, nearly every adult male in my family. Could you explain to me what happened to my husband and how he ended up in Belgrade…and…Banjica?" With arms folded across her chest, Zora didn't mention to him the rocks in her chest, weighing her down.

Jovica paused, tugging his beard. "Gospođo, please accept my condolences. These have been the most painful messages to deliver. This one in particular greatly saddened me. In the short months I had gotten to know your husband, I'd grown to love him. I first came to meet Peda when he was alone, frightened, and shivering in a cave in the lower Suvobors."

As she listened, a lump lodged in her throat.

Just then, Dušica popped in, glancing at Jovica before her eyes settled on her sister. "Hello. I'm Zora's sister, and you are?"

Shoving out a hand, Jovica stood. "Good morning, I'm Jovica." Lifting a brow, he asked, "Another sister?"

Dušica pulled out the kitchen chair for him. "Yes, I'm the oldest. There's four of us, but one's overseas. Let me make you some coffee." She boiled water for the barley coffee and returned to the table. Dušica said, "I'm ready."

"Peda's technical skills made him an asset in the Saboteur Unit. I'm sure you're aware that in a different life, Peda could have easily become an engineer. He excelled in our Saboteur Unit," Jovica declared. "All of us, including his commander, Stevan Radulović, send their regards. Please know, his good friend Božo was with him on the mountain."

"Božidar Momčilović was with him?" Zora suddenly sat up in her chair. "I can't quite believe it." It reminded Zora that even in a storm, her husband had not been alone.

Grinning, Jovica said, "Yes. Any free time Peda had, he spent by the fire reminiscing with Božo, who ran our supply hut."

Dušica's mouth hung open. "Wait—what am I missing?"

"Peda was murdered by the Gestapo in a concentration camp in Belgrade." Zora shuddered, handing her the note. "Jovica was just about to explain." A hundred questions leaped forward in her mind. Was he drunk when he was arrested? How could she bear telling her children of another death, and how would they ever find the resilience to move past another ghastly tragedy? Inhaling, she berated her husband one last time for not accepting the offer to send her boys overseas.

Hesitating, Jovica glanced between the sisters. "Your husband was distraught after receiving Sava's note about Neven and Vuk's passing. It nearly killed him not to be with all of you. But Čiča forbade anyone from leaving the mountains until our intelligence felt it was safe."

"Wait—Peda was under the impression that two of our sons had been shot?" Zora leaned across the table, her mouth hanging open.

Jovica looked at her, while Zora noticed the confusion sprinkling across his face.

"Vuk wasn't killed in the massacre; it was Neven. Why… did my husband—Ohhh, no." Zora's troubled eyes met Jovica's. "Please tell me Peda didn't die believing both of our sons had been executed. He…never knew differently?"

"No, so, Vuk's alive…?" Scrubbing his face with his hands, Jovica looked down, his face a picture of puzzlement. "But Sava's message was clear. I read it t—"

Zora cut him off. "The day after the massacre, a woman at the church told us that all of the boys from the Prva Muška Gimnazija were the first to perish, which was likely why Sava's message reflected that. I—I'm incredibly sorry, I never sent word to Peda clarifying that only Neven died. Had I known, despite the confusion and chaos, I would have…" Zora blew out tiny puffs of air.

"Gospođo, please. You've been through far too much, but allow me to share what we know," Jovica said with a wretched smile.

His compassion and gentle demeanor nearly undid her. "Could you first help me understand where Goran might be? We haven't heard from him in months." She wiped the tears sliding down her cheeks with the back of her hand.

"Of course." Folding his fingers into a steeple, he let out a huge sigh. "During a skirmish near Valjevo, the Germans surrounded Goran's entire unit."

"And?" A range of emotions played across Zora's face, mainly sadness and fear.

"According to our intelligence, Goran's unit was taken to a prisoner of war camp in Germany. Nonetheless, we intercepted a German radio message revealing his unit was in Austria, approximately seven hours away."

A sudden fury bubbled inside of her. "I need answers, Jovica, and I need them now. My family's shrinking. So many in our family have played an integral role with the Četnici, including my son, my husband, my sister…and myself. I left my job at the kafana to rush to care for your injured revolutionaries. Now my husband is dead, one of my sons is dead, and the other's missing—don't I deserve some damn answers?" Unsure of how much more she could take, Zora slammed her hand on the table. "It's crucial I learn where Goran's being held."

Dušica's eyeballs nearly popped from her head.

Jovica stared for a long time, and the silence was alarming.

"Despite our best efforts, Gospođo, it's impossible to get a lick of information from the Germans, but we believe he's being held at the Dachau Concentration Camp, in Southern Germany."

"Thank you." Zora let out a massive breath.

"If you ever want to leave Serbia, please know it would be our sincere pleasure to help you and your family safely across the mountains to the coast. Assisting Peda's family to safety would be an honor."

"Thanks, but we will not be leaving."

Dušica interrupted. "Pardon, could you tell us how Peda died?"

With a nod, Jovica began. "In late October, he and thirteen other Royalists were captured by the Wehrmacht and taken to the Banjica Concentration Camp in Belgrade. Some of our men were killed right away; however, others, like Peda, were detained inside the camp. Sorrowfully, we caught word that Peda was shot by the prominent Gestapo, Willy Friedrich, who's head of Banjica Concentration Camp."

"Had he been drinking?" Zora held her breath.

An irrepressible smile escaped from his lips. "Peda stopped drinking the moment he arrived atop Ravna Gora. Yet in his grief, he gravitated to a few younger, irresponsible men who had foolishly snuck in bottles of rakija."

Letting out a sigh, Zora asked, "Why would the head of the concentration camp shoot my husband? Is that frequent practice?" Her insides were threaded with knots.

"What we know is that Peda died a hero, bravely defending Dr. Miloš, a well-known physician and head of our medical university, who happened to be his cellmate. When the Gestapo yanked Dr. Miloš out of the cell, Peda jumped in, questioning the guard. What occurred afterward we will never know." Fingering his beard, Jovica said, "An intriguing detail, though. Dr. Miloš was a close colleague of Dr. Danilo's, who was killed last summer for helping the Royalists."

"Dear God, he was Olga's husband," Zora said. "Sava grew up with Olga and they were close friends in Belgrade. Had Peda made the connection?"

"With Dr Miloš ? I do not believe so, but we Serbians are so very connected with one another, no?" Shaking his head, he added, "Nonetheless, your husband died a hero."

Dušica asked, "My husband, Marko Živković, and my father-in-law were taken two days ago. Would you have any information on their whereabouts? Also, Kosta Lazić, and Conductor Matić, too?"

"I'm astonished at how intricately connected your entire family has been in all of this. Your deep ties to the Royalists will not go unnoticed; I will certainly pass this on to Čiča Draža." Rubbing the back of his neck, he said, "I'm well acquainted with Boško, er, Conductor, and Kosta: both honorable, intelligent men."

Slack-jawed, Dušica slid her chair next to Zora's.

"Were they executed?" Zora fought to keep her tone neutral, but her chest was about to implode.

"We don't think so, Gospođo; in fact, our intelligence believes Kosta's imprisoned in Mauthausen, and likely alive because he's physically strong. Our assumption would be that the Germans marked him for work in the labor camps. But we surmise that Conductor just might be with your son and our Patriarch Gavrilo at Dachau. We've gotten word that Dachau is where they've been taking the clergy. One of our commander's wives was recently released after being held for five months in Banjica, and provided us with valuable details about the beatings and starvations. Mistakenly, she was first sent to Mauthausen, then Dachau, and then Banjica. Through her we've obtained firsthand information about the camps, how they operated, and who was being held there." Briefly closing his eyes, Jovica's demeanor changed. "I'm afraid I'm the bearer of an additional bit of bad news."

Zora and Dušica shifted their gazes toward him. "What?"

"The Abwehr arrested Josie Whitney-Shaw. We assume she was initially sent to Banjica, and her time might have overlapped with Peda's, but our most current information has her somewhere in Germany." Wiping a hand through his long, tangled hair, he said, "The Abwehr made allegations against Josie, claiming she was a spy."

"Whoa...hold up." Zora lifted her hand. "The Germans—" Realization hit her square in the face. The implications. "What then, about Sava? Everything our sister and Josie did for the Resistance has been done together." Tapping her forehead, Zora tried to remember something important. "Let me make sure I understand this correctly. Sava began working underground with Toma, Josie, Života, Conductor, and Kosta. And with Života's recent arrest, who's working with Sava?" Zora felt her heart clanging inside her chest wall. "Who's protecting our little sister?" The color drained from Zora's face. "Everyone that was close to Sava…"

Dušica laid a hand to steady Zora. "We fear for our sister. What steps have the Royalists taken to ensure Sava's safety on these dangerous missions?"

He offered them a feeble smile. "We're doing everything possible…"

Rising from the table, Zora was categorically angered. His words pretty much revealed the truth: no one was protecting their sister. "Unless you can fully protect our Sava, I think she should stop running missions. I greatly fear for her safety." Trembling, she moved to the stove where she lifted a pot and slammed it on the burner harder than necessary.

Dušica walked Jovica out, pressing a slab of bread into his hands, and whispered, "Zora bears burdens beyond our capabilities."

Jovica put his hand out to shake hers. "I understand. Please let her know we've relocated to a safer place in Brajići. If she ever needs to reach me, have her go through Dunja. God rest Peda's soul."

"Despite this tragic news, we're grateful you made the effort to come. It shows every sign of respect. *Hvala Vam*, Jovica."

***

Sitting with her mother and Dušica, Zora sipped the

putrid-tasting barley coffee. Grief-stricken, life seemed impossibly difficult. Every smile pained her. The arrests, the duration of internment, and the senseless loss of life were all too much to bear. Peda's murder presented a cruel paradox, and as a mother she was unsure how to explain his death to her children. "I'm hesitant to tell them the truth, especially Stana."

"Even though it's difficult, you must tell them the truth, Zora. It'll hurt, but this war has toughened even the weakest of us." Mima sighed, crossing herself.

CHAPTER TWENTY-NINE

SAVA

Vraćevšnica Monastery, Gornji Milanovac, Yugoslavia
January 07, 1942: Božić

NO MATTER HOW HARD she tried, she could not take away her sister's anguish. All she could do was offer a loving hand to guide her nieces and nephews through those early, catastrophic days, which gave Zora the space to grieve. Sava stayed with Zora for one month until she noticed the younger ones becoming more independent and readying themselves for school.

In addition to the innumerable losses, the aftermath of the massacre created a destructive divide between the two resistance groups. Locked in intense disputes, their tensions culminated in vicious fighting, and now it had become a three-sided war: the Germans, the Royalists, and the Partisans.

On a cot in the monastery's chilly dormitory, Sava flicked open her eyes. Even with the wind rustling through the lush trees in the forest, today was warmer than normal, causing the melting snow to trickle down the mountain. Vlado's passing had left Sava with an uncertainty about where she belonged, but here, at the monastery, she found comfort. After hastily putting on her clothes, Sava stepped outside before entering the rear of the church.

The sisters were already assembled in the nave, so Sava quickly lit candles in honor of her lost family members. Crossing herself, she breathed in the intoxicating Athonite scent, created by the finely ground essential oils, frankincense, resin, and fur. Fighting back the tears in her throat, she relived the memories of her precious family singing and enjoying Christmases past as the candles flooded her senses. Once the nuns began to sing, Sava was swept up in the poignantly sweet moments when they were still alive. Lowering her head, she reflected on her trusted friends and comrades, captured and carted away, especially Života.

Noticing that every candle in the sanctuary was lit this morning for Božić, Sava took her place beside the nuns to sing, her mind overflowing with the horrific German propaganda targeting the Royalists. While battles intensified, Sava's workload had multiplied, and messages were stacked high. With no petrol available, she had to rely on finding transport either by horse or on foot, unless by luck, she found a train working.

Sister Simonida squeezed in next to her. "*Mir Božiji,* Jelisaveta."

Smiling with her eyes, Sava gave her hand a warm squeeze. "Merry Christmas, my dear." Ever since Sister Simonida had learned her real name, she used it in every conversation. While she sang, Sava was preoccupied with her plans to be with her family in Kragujevac by late afternoon. However, she'd been told to wait for a Royalist to come with an important message, and he'd yet to arrive.

After liturgy, she followed the nuns to a long wooden table adorned with fresh kajmak and Česnica. Following lunch, Sava planned to have a private conversation with Sister Simonida regarding the growing issue of typhus within the Četnik ranks, as well as the influx of refugees from Kosovo, Croatia, Macedonia, and Vojvodina into Serbia. It was important for her to learn more about dis-infection and quarantine techniques, such as haircutting or available medicines, but she couldn't find any information at the nursing school on Deligradska Street in Belgrade. Due to the severe damage caused by Nazi bombings, it was hard to access relevant resources or locate any nurses. Just as Sava was about to sink her teeth into her first delicious bite, one of the sisters tapped her shoulder.

"Gospođo? There's a man covered in blood at the door, asking for you."

Sava hurried to open the large doors. "Toma? My word, what happened to you?" Over her shoulder she hollered for Abbess Mother or Sister Simonida, as she struggled to prop Toma in the doorway, his heaviness bearing her down.

"Sister Simonida," Abbess Mother clapped. "Please help Sava with this gentleman." Glancing at Sava, she asked, "A friend of yours, I presume?"

"An extremely close friend, Abbess Mother, more like a brother."

"Very well. Let's get him to the back room."

Once they had lifted Toma onto one of the cots, he croaked, "I—I was in a prison for weeks."

Rustling his hair, Sava praised him. "Bravo, Toma. Don't worry, everyone here will take excellent care of you. Nobody can compare to our wonderful nuns. Just close your eyes and relax." Hope, she said to herself. In our darkest hour, that's what we must cling to.

"They held me captive," Toma incoherently mumbled, grimacing in pain.

Reaching for a pair of scissors, Abbess Mother swiftly cut off his clothing, then emitted a squeal. "Lord have mercy, what have they done to him?"

Sava swayed as she saw the angry welts and large cuts covering the entire length of Toma's long body, several already infected. He had an elevated temperature, which she recognized was a direct sign of an infection. To Abbess Mother she said, "Unfortunately, last spring, Toma was gravely injured in the Luftwaffe bombing in Belgrade, rescuing his neighbor's children. He spent three hard months recovering from those injuries."

"Well, my dear, let's begin by praying for him," Abbess Mother suggested, lowering her head. "Now tell me about this man, and his significance to you," she asked, tilting her head.

"He's my closest friend, and like a brother to me." Tears suddenly streamed down her face. She felt a profound sense of fury at this injustice, hoping one day these revolting Germans would be held accountable for the savagery committed against them. "We're both historians and professors at the university. Toma was the one who encouraged me to join Sloboda, which morphed into the Royalists Resistance of Ravna Gora."

"Very well. Rest assured, my dear, we will take safe care of your friend, Jelisaveta."

Sava never made it home for Christmas. She and Sister Simonida alternated four-hour shifts around the clock, turning Toma's weakened body to prevent any additional wounds from becoming infected. Pausing for a moment to enjoy a cup of real coffee, she wondered how her family's first Christmas was with so many loved ones gone. Yesterday, in the monastery kitchen busily preparing the meal for their Christmas lunch, memories had resurfaced of Baka Cveta using starter bread to make the hallowed prosphora bread for liturgy. As far back as she could remember, her mother would wake in the middle of the night to make Česnica for their family and prosphora for their church, because as a long-standing member of the Kolo Srpskih Sestara, the Circle of Serbian Sisters, she dedicated every Sunday morning to make prosphora for their church. Sava recalled her mother's voice: *As long as you have starter bread, none of you will ever starve.*

"Sava?" Toma struggled to raise his head.

"You're awake?" She bent, offering him a sip of water. She thought his fever must have broken because his lips were cracked, and there was an unpleasant odor of sickness emanating from him. "Toma, you had a high fever when you arrived, but now it's normal." With a joyful expression, she shook the thermometer. "It's great having you back, *brate moj.*"

It was a miracle Toma had made it here on foot. Marveling at his resiliency, she knew he would have to stay until he'd gained back his strength. Mumbling under her breath, she said, "I'd love to meet the angel perched on your shoulder."

***

Kragujevac, Yugoslavia
July 19, 1942

Worried about her niece, Sava had been astonished by her downward trajectory. Where Stana had once exuded confidence and joie de vivre, ever since the massacre she had sunk into an awful malaise, preferring to wallow for days in bed. Even with little, their lives before the war, in retrospect, had been idyllic. Without her brother and boyfriend, she was adrift. Today, though, Sava had a plan.

"Hello everyone," she said from the opened doorway. It had taken her hours to get there and she was soaked in perspiration.

"Tetka?" Lenka asked, looking panicked.

"Hello love, where's your sister?"

"Ohhh, um; she's in bed…reading."

Sava noticed the fib right away. When she walked into her nieces' bedroom, Sava's pleasant voice rose: "Happy seventeenth birthday, Stana Brković!"

Stana slowly opened her eyes but fixed her gaze straight ahead.

In that moment, Sava knew she needed to address Stana's behavior with Zora, at minimum to protect her niece from a lifetime of pain and unhappiness. She also didn't want Stana to feel she had lost her only chance at love.

"Stana, my love. I have a birthday gift for you that the nuns made. It's krofne." Bending to tousle her niece's oily hair, Sava gently kissed her forehead before handing her the sack filled with doughnuts.

Stana accepted the bag, setting it aside without opening it.

Blinking in confusion, Sava went in search of her sister. Shockingly, Zora exhibited a similar behavior. She, too, was lying in bed.

"Zora, can you hear me?" Not wanting to disturb her

sister's delicate sleep, she hesitated, but she felt the need to address Stana's situation superseded her sleeping. "Zora?"

"What?" Zora squeaked. Her voice sounded drowsy.

"I need to discuss something with you. I'm worried about Stana's deep sorrow, which I feel has lasted too long for one so young. I would like to help her, but it involves taking her away from here to heal. Zora, would that be all right if we did that?"

Squinting, Zora reached to hold Sava's hand. "Being away from here would greatly benefit Stana, or any of us. The reminders and memories eat away at us."

With a huge sigh of relief, Sava sank back. "The nuns have kindly offered Stana a place to live in the dormitory for three months. I envision her enjoying the fresh mountain air with the lush vegetation surrounding it—a truly promising start. You've been there, Zora, so you're able to visualize how pleasant it will be in the summer months. Do I have your permission?"

Zora slowly gave her a nod. It was the first time Sava had witnessed a normal response from Zora in months. It warmed her heart.

"Sava, you're our remarkable warrior, always going beyond to keep all of us safe. You'll never know how much I appreciate all that you have done for us. And I agree wholeheartedly, it will be beneficial to get our little dove some help. They're singing nuns, correct?"

"Yes."

"Thank you for caring so much, Sava, and for loving my children the way you do. This pain…it's so overwhelming that on certain days, it tightens around my throat, sort of like being suffocated."

Sava sat back, her heart thudding in her chest as she allowed her head to nod in acknowledgement. It was the most Zora had confided in her since that tragic day. Still, it was a solid beginning. Amidst this war there was hope.

CHAPTER THIRTY

ZORA

Kragujevac, Serbia
January 07, 1943: Božić

ANOTHER YEAR PASSED AND the fighting continued, but for the people of Kragujevac, grief inarguably clung to them like a second skin. The horror of the tragedy, and every place people visited, still haunted them, serving as a reminder of their lost ones. Blanketed in despair, Zora and hundreds of other shattered families continued to mourn in the privacy of their homes, where their doors were covered in black. She remained shrouded in black, a mourning custom she had once dismissed as outdated. Wearing black had become a way for her to further distance herself from those who asked too many questions, or the drunken Germans she served in the kafana.

Zora and her mother were busy in the kitchen, preparing a small amount of food for Christmas. Mima layered her secret spices to a pot of sauerkraut and bean soup, while Zora stood at the table, squeezing dough between her fingers, trying to remove the last of the air pockets.

"Trust me, Zora; your children *need* this celebration. It's important we show them how to carry on."

As she kneaded the dough she was making for their Česnica, Zora remained quiet. If she voiced her opinion, inevitably, she and her mother would become embroiled in another intense argument. She understood how difficult it was for anyone to comprehend the magnitude of her anguish. Releasing an exasperated breath, Zora knew her mother loved her, yet could never fully understand the layered and complicated grief she experienced in her daily struggle to survive.

Bending to turn on Marko's radio, which Dušica had brought downstairs, Zora said, "Hopefully, there's a BBC broadcast that'll update us with news about the war."

"I really miss Radio Belgrade. Remember how we used to sing along to the music, especially on holidays?" Mima studied her daughter. "It was as if the tamburaši were here with us, but now we're stuck listening to the terrible OKW broadcasts on the radio. The other day, they played that hideous "Lili Marleen," over and over. Why do they play that so often?"

Shrugging her shoulders, Zora admitted, "Our food and medicine have dwindled to nothing, but all they're concerned about is that ridiculous song. To make matters worse, they've placed German-speaking officials, who speak no Serbian, in our municipal offices. Dunja overheard their plans to tamper with our water supply and electricity."

"What are you saying, Zora?" Mima's eyes grew wide.

"Mama, I didn't mean to frighten you, but they've been using random acts as a way of control. Vuk and I have already filled our jugs and glass bottles with fresh drinking

water to ensure our safety. But there's something else...
They want Čiča Draža and have dropped leaflets and
posted notices in town."

She heard her mother's sharp intake of breath.
"Why?"

"They want his head on a platter. In fact, the Germans
are offering a reward of 100,000 gold marks for his capture—dead or alive."

Zora continued to turn the dials when all at once, a
burst of static shot through the air, startling mother and
daughter as the British announcer said, "We regret to
inform you that Nikola Tesla has just died in New York
City. I repeat, Nikola Tesla is dead."

"Ohhh." Zora's eyes bounced to her mother's. "I'm sorry,
Mama. I wonder what happened?"

"Tsk, tsk." Mima reached underneath her wrist for her
ever-present handkerchief. "Maybe old age? He was the
same age as my mother, who treasured her friendship with
him and his family from the second they moved near her
home. It was in the village of Smiljan, a few miles north of
Gospić, and my mother had just turned seven. She adored
his family. Do you remember me telling you his father was
their parish priest?"

Zora's mouth opened in surprise. "I never knew that."

"Yes. Father Milutin Tesla was Nikola's father. My
mother adored spending time in their home and in his
father's library."

"Really, Mama? They had a library in their home in
Croatia...back then? They must have been wealthy."

Mima grinned. "Not really, but I'd imagine as a Serbian
Orthodox priest, Father Milutin was the only one in their
village who owned books or knew how to read."

"Hold up a second, Mama." Zora grimaced as the announcer's tone changed. "He's mentioning something about Hitler. Let's have a listen."

"It's reported Hitler has forced every Jew in Warsaw into a Jewish ghetto. In other news, the US President Roosevelt, in his State of the Union address, confirmed the US has 1.5 million servicemen overseas."

Confusion lifted Mima's brows. "What does he mean?" Zora watched her mother's eyes move to the Božić candle flickering in the middle of the table.

Crossing herself, Mima murmured, "Promaja…"

Vuk entered, grinning. "That was not a draft, Baka; it was me walking past the candle. *Mir Božiji*," he said, before sliding into a chair.

"Merry Christmas." Zora's voice did not project a joyous enthusiasm for the holiday. She stared at her son. It was remarkable how much Vuk had changed, seemingly overnight, from an easy-going young teen, to a more serious fifteen-year-old. He worked nights with her at Paligorić, clearing tables and washing dishes, like Neven and Luka had previously done. Zora refused to allow Stana near the kafana for fear Stana's unpredictable grief might fuel the Germans. So, it was Vuk and her working nights.

"Are you hungry?" Mima asked Vuk, watching over the stout metal pot of barley coffee percolating on the stove.

Before he answered, Zora tapped her forehead. "I almost forgot." She pulled an envelope from her apron pocket. "It's a letter from Nada. It came in yesterday's Pošta."

"Ohh." Mima lifted her head. It was the first time Zora had noticed the creases lining Mima's face. My mother's suffering just as intensely as everyone else, she thought. Why have I failed to notice this before?

"May I read it?"

"By all means." Mima clapped her hands together.

My dearest sister Zora, Mama, and family.

Since this is my third letter, I hope you have had time to consider my previous offer. Bobby and I want you to join us and live in the US. It would be a wonderful, fresh start for all of you. I know you're in pain, Zora, but your children deserve to grow in an environment of happiness, not in an impoverished, war-torn country. Please pack your bags and get to Italy. We will wire money for you to sail from Italy to New York. Come soon, before this war ends. Our newspapers say there are thousands of refugees in Europe begging to come to the US. Write back soon.

I love you all,

Nada

"What other letters?" Mima looked bewildered before she began to cry. "It's been ages since I've seen her. This might sound crazy, but we should consider her offer."

"Mama, you cannot be serious. H—how could we leave… all of this?" Zora rubbed her neck.

"All of what, Zora?" Her mother's steely resolve frightened her. "The despair, and searching for hours for a few potatoes and maybe two eggs? Is that what you call living?" Shaking her head, Mima recrossed her arms over her chest. "No, Zora, no one should be forced to live like this, with empty stomachs so hollowed out, growing fears, and far too much wretchedness. It's not what I'd envision a good life to be. The Germans—they're animals, with not one shred of mercy." Exhaling, Mima reached for Zora's arm, squeezing it. "It's time, Zora…we're sinking here."

Zora was shocked by what her mother had revealed. With her pulse racing, she said, "I—we cannot leave here. Well, what about Goran…and Neven?" She felt nauseous and a chill passed through her. "What if Goran came back and couldn't find us, or what if…?" Underneath it all was her deep, intractable fear. She dreaded leaving everything familiar, and not being able to visit Neven's grave every day.

With a comforting hand resting on her back, Mima said, "Neven will always be in your heart, wherever you go, my dušo. Although we're uncertain what will happen to Goran, it's vital we maintain a sense of hope."

Zora lowered herself into a chair. Her dark eyes were sunken, and her usually well-groomed hair was unkempt. She hadn't changed her clothes in days, and a weariness had settled in. Everything overwhelmed her. Exhausted, she sensed her mother's sadness for her.

"It's important we talk about this and respond to our Nada."

Vuk, who had been quietly paying attention, shifted his gaze toward his grandmother. "If we went to the US, perhaps I could attend the university with Stana?" Vuk's eyes held such promise it nearly broke Zora.

***

Months passed as mother and daughter continued their disagreement over leaving Yugoslavia. Mima finally said, "I cannot stomach bickering any longer. Will there ever be a chance of having a serious conversation about Nada's offer? It's becoming increasingly dire, and we're suffering more and more. Ever since they arrested Marko and his father, we have had such little food, so what do you suggest we do?"

"My answer hasn't changed—I'm not leaving." Zora stepped back, the weight on her shoulders nearly crushing her.

"What about the good-looking Četnik who arrived last year promising to protect our family if we decided to leave? Didn't he mention his men would safely lead us through the mountains?" Mima's soft brown eyes questioned her daughter's.

Zora avoided making eye contact with her mother, and instead she nervously rubbed her collarbone. "Crossing those mountains on foot would be an absolute nightmare, and dangerous. There's little consideration about transporting either you or Čedo across. Would you be able to climb, Mama?"

"Hold on a second, missy." Her mother's eyes blazed with fury. "Čedo's health has improved, and he's much stronger now, so I wouldn't diminish him. I have a higher stamina than you care to recognize. Besides, I spent my youth climbing, so Čedo and I will get across." As she gaped at her, Mima said, "Zora, Zora, never forget that in the direst of times, one finds their greatest strength. Where is that optimistic daughter of mine, always curious, adoring exploring unfamiliar terrain?"

Feeling untethered, Zora faltered. "She's gone, Mama. That daughter of yours died."

CHAPTER THIRTY-ONE

SAVA

Mountains of Serbia
January 1944

SAVA'S SPACIOUS HOME, WHICH held all of her most treasured belongings, including her and Vlado's unforgettable wedding album, had been requisitioned by the Germans two months ago as part of their war efforts and broader Nazi agenda of dominance. She knew they despised any Yugoslav having more than themselves, and in that vein, they had requisitioned nearly every home in Dedinje in what they called the "military and strategic purposes" of the occupying forces. Giving her less than ten minutes to pack, they had booted her out with a sturdy pair of old boots, four articles of clothing, and her toothbrush.

Desperate for a place to live, Sava had suddenly recalled Josie mentioning an extra key she gave to a neighbor, an elderly woman named Lalić. Sava hopped on a trolley, hoping the neighbor might still be there. Luckily, Mildred Lalić was at home, and she gave Sava not only the key, but a quart of fresh milk, two eggs, and three slices of bread.

Stunned, Sava stammered, "How…?" While she understood the remarkable generosity of Serbs, with the unbelievable diminishing shortage of food, her gift was too much.

Gospođo Lalić's warm smile brightened Sava's day. "Nonsense, my brother's got a farm and comes often."

Despite the impropriety of the urge to hug someone she'd just met, Sava went ahead and hugged her anyway. "I won't forget this generosity—or you."

The accommodation was temporary, yet Sava ensured the doors and bolts were in working order before she hunkered in. Regrettably, when three weeks later she returned to Josie's rental in the Dorćol neighborhood, it was only to find the Third Reich had already requisitioned it as well, indicated by the notice plastered across the front door. Sava observed a rather tall, grim-faced Wehrmacht official off to the side, and she assumed the petite blonde was his wife, standing with their three tow-headed children.

Their eyes refused to meet hers as she pulled the key from her pocket. Sighing, Sava glanced again at the sign on the door. It was the same as the one posted on her own Dedinje door, *Beschlagnahmt.* How dare they? Tossing people from their homes was not only shameful, but it was also one of the most reprehensible acts performed by the Germans. Taking what didn't belong to a person was inherently wrong and went against every fiber of what Sava believed in. Furious, she gathered what little she had and banged the door shut behind her. Offering a terse glance in their direction, with her shoulders pulled back and head high, she whizzed past them. She was on her way to meet Toma at Trg Republike.

In her rush, she luckily sidestepped an enormous clump of animal muck gracing the sidewalk. Disgusted by the mismanagement of Belgrade under the Serbian puppet government of Milan Nedić and the Third Reich, Sava muttered under her breath, "God help us all." Spotting Toma a few blocks ahead, she sped up.

"Are you sure you'll be able to manage living out of a suitcase? I understand you've been doing this for a while, but your sister's home, in Kragujevac? Why, it's far humbler than you're accustomed to, my Sava dear."

Staring back at him, she sharpened her reply. "Please do not patronize me, or make me out to be a snob, Toma. I will make it work, so let's sort out the rest. You will only contact me through Dunja, right?"

"Yeah, and I was only teasing you." Tucking papers inside the pocket of his jacket, he studied her. "Look, I don't think you're…hell; never mind." Waving his hands, he said, "Let's use Paligorić and Dunja as our go-between. Are you sure the Germans don't suspect her?"

"If Dunja lived in Hollywood, she would undoubtedly receive awards. There's no one better."

Toma pulled on his cigarette before stifling a laugh. "I agree, but you cannot be too careful with the Abwehr."

"Has there been any word on where they're holding Života?"

His face clouded. "No, nothing, but I have a question. Have you ever wondered if Peda suspected you were the one who provided the coordinates for their Saboteur missions?"

Blushing, she squinted. "I hadn't." Feeling uncomfortable with the compliment, Sava tried diverting his attention. "Whenever I'm at Paligorić, I intend to assist Dunja by waitressing. Remember the last time I did that?" With a broad smile, she let her shoulders loosen up.

Tugging her ponytail, Toma gave her a serious look. "I will not repeat this, but you must be vigilant of your surroundings."

"I know, I know." Sava pressed her fingertips to her temples.

Looking at his watch, Toma nodded. "Let's get you on the train."

She quickly embraced him. "This war has taken too much from us. Promise me you'll take good care of yourself." After kissing him on the cheek, she patted it. "Please, Toma. I'm tired of mending your broken bones."

"I will, my friend." He squeezed her shoulder and waved.

***

The Royalists moved sporadically, hoping to confuse the Germans. They moved between Serbia and Bosnia via the jagged limestone Dinaric Alps, changing positions on the mountains as often as necessary. Sava stopped and glanced back as she descended the snowy cliff, curious if she would come across any of her comrades today. She was also making certain she was not being followed. The German forces were inching closer. With the rise in battles and skirmishes, no one was available to accompany her today. Again, she was on her own.

***

March 12, 1944

Dressed as a nun, Sava carried her basket of herbs and potatoes through the soft snow. Her eyes darted left to right, making sure she wasn't being followed. The conflict between the Germans, Royalists, and Partisans had intensified, creating many conflicting challenges, although none were more prominent than the violent battle between the two opposing resistance military forces.

Winter had taken a tremendous toll on the Royalists, especially those who'd stayed on the mountain. Sava repeatedly expressed concern about the number of men with lost or frozen limbs, all met with customary Serbian bullheadedness. Frustrated, she watched others simply too hungry or worn down to fight. Overnight, she observed the Partisans begin to gain the upper hand, pushing at them relentlessly. With increased hostilities, their clashes became more rancorous as Sava witnessed brother fighting against brother, and kumovi against kumstvo. Honing her studies at the university, Sava had acquired many lessons on war from her father, but even with the knowledge, she had never fathomed the level of turmoil and complexity a civil strife would bring to her people.

As she traveled from Vraćevšnica to a meeting in Gornji Milanovac, the hair on her neck suddenly stood at attention. Pausing, Sava listened, but before she had the chance to turn around, she sensed someone behind her. Suddenly, a group of soldiers dressed in black uniforms with silver buttons swarmed her.

Roughly tackling her to the ground, they shouted, "*Spionin! Spionin!*"

Spy? Sava struggled to stay calm while her heart beat rapidly. "You cannot be serious; I am no spy. You've got the wrong person," she pleaded. Knowing they would enjoy seeing a powerful reaction from her, she refused to give them one. Pressing her lips together, she closed her eyes for a split second, not allowing them to see a tear glistening on her eyelashes. As they dragged her through the forest's edge, Sava heard them swearing.

Keeping them in the periphery of her vision, she viewed them from her rough position on the ground, until they reached their truck, parked haphazardly in the snow. They lifted her onto the truck bed, shouting obscenities at her. Still unaware she was fluent in German, they grabbed her basket from her and threw the potatoes and herbs away; she knew they were searching for military paperwork or some notes. When they discovered no evidence, she heard the frustration in their voices.

Discarding the basket, they shouted, "Where are messages—you Serbian spy?"

***

Banjica Concentration Camp, Belgrade, Serbia
March 15, 1944

Three days later, Sava regained consciousness. Reluctantly she opened her eyes. She was in a grimy cell that emitted a brackish odor. Groaning, she closed her eyes, grimacing. Her entire body was inflamed from the beatings. After hearing an announcement over the loudspeakers, she knew she was being detained in the Banjica Concentration Camp. How ironic for them to bring her here, the old barracks of the 18th Infantry Regiment in Dedinje, on a hill less than two kilometers from her home. Her former home, she remembered unhappily.

There were about forty incredibly frail, emaciated women, who seemed to have been reduced to nothingness,

staring at her. Was starvation their primary form of torture? Heart thudding in her chest, Sava took a large breath,
knowing she would need to toughen up to survive here.
"Hello ladies, I'm Sava…Ivković. They arrested me a few
days ago while I was walking through the forest."

The room stayed completely silent.

"Why were you arrested?" asked a nervous-looking brunette standing in the back, fidgeting, before crossing her
arms over her chest.

Sava knew the stance well. This room, terribly crowded,
held too many women. She wondered how they'd survived
each day, packed into such cramped quarters. Not sure how
much she should admit, she forced a smile. "Why were any
of us arrested?" Good; that got her attention.

The dark-haired woman persisted. "Are you part of the
Resistance, or had you sympathized with them, perhaps?"

"Why would you ask that?"

"Because you're assigned to Room 38."

"And that means what, exactly?" Her own tone caught
her off guard. It wasn't her intention to sound indignant;
she guessed it was because this woman was irrationally
irritating her.

"They only bring their most serious offenders to this
room. It's the last stop before execution. They refer to this
room as their *Todeslager.*"

Death camp? Sava stood to her full height. Filthy, and
with cuts covering her palms and arms, she pulled herself
erect. Plagued by disturbing thoughts of what the Gestapo
might do next, she quizzed the woman. "Tell me…am I
not permitted in this cell if I do not meet this particular
criterion, or should I ring the guard and ask him to speak
with you?"

The brunette let out a chuckle. "I like your spirit, Sava Ivković—welcome to Cell Block Room 38. We're all here because Adolf Hitler wants to eliminate the 'Serbian problem,' as he calls it."

"Thank you." With an unusual display of transparency, Sava decided to reveal something to these women. "They called me a spy."

Everyone's neck craned to get a closer look at her.

A young, frail woman asked, "Might it be true?"

Arranging her face to exude an air of nonchalance, Sava said, "Obviously not, but we're quite aware of Adolf Hitler's tactics and fondness for intimidation. Hence, we know his soldiers enjoy squeezing information from our neighbors, hoping to dig more dirt on us. They're getting desperate, so who knows?" Smiling, Sava looked at everyone before lowering her voice to a whisper. "I would appreciate your help in explaining how things work around here, and since we're having this lovely pajama party, I'll go first. I'm nothing more than a historian and history professor at the university."

"Oh, my goodness…I know who you are," said a frail woman breathlessly. "You were friends with our dear comrade, Olga Alkalaj. She often spoke of you, highly I might add, *Doctor* Ivković. I've read every paper you've published. It was courageous of you to address the challenges faced by women."

Openmouthed, Sava stared.

"You're with Draža Mihajlović's Ravna Gora Movement, correct?"

After a moment's hesitation, Sava nodded. "Yes, I am."

One by one, they came forward, introducing themselves. Stunned to learn just how formidable these women were in their own right, Sava listened as they shared stories of their fulfilling lives as academics, physicians, attorneys, writers, and artists. Sprinkled in were housewives, resistance fighters, nurses, and university students. Most were also members of the Communist Party, which had morphed into the Partisans Resistance Movement. They explained to her that the best way to stay safe was to remain invisible.

Later that night, she lay awake, wondering why the Gestapo had picked this very location, precisely in the middle of a residential neighborhood. Intimidation was the answer she produced. The Germans often employed this tactic, and she concluded their aim was to instill fear in the people of Belgrade. Being part of the underground, Sava had insider knowledge of the best way to navigate Banjica Concentration Camp. Despite the German propaganda suggesting the Gestapo *and* the local Serbian Guard shared control over it, Sava knew it was untrue. During the autumn of 1943, several Royalist commanders had luckily been sprung from Banjica with the help of the Serbian Guard, making it clear to Sava that Banjica was unquestionably controlled by the Gestapo.

During the initial phase of her stay, the Gestapo took her upstairs for interrogation, and she was beaten regularly. Their torture methods were so sadistic, she was thankful they had removed none of her teeth or fingernails. Trying to break her, these heartless individuals would finally witness the indomitable strength of the true Serbian spirit, embodied by the resilient Šumadijan women.

***

Banjica Concentration Camp
July 1944

Sava found herself upstairs once more, facing intense questioning. They were furious, and they demanded answers. "Where's Draža Mihajlović?"

With a determined gesture, Sava jutted out her chin, squared her shoulders, and gave nothing away.

The red-faced guard pulled out the chair she was sitting on so fast, she splattered to the concrete floor. Kicking his sharp boots to her back and kidneys, he hollered, "We have proof." His sausage-like fingers clasped papers, which he shoved in her face. "Look—this you. You lie to us. No nun, you a Četnik. So, you tell us where Mihajlović camp, you liar. You no fool the Third Reich, you spy for Četnici."

Witnessing the veins in his neck pulsating, her heart sped up. I will not allow them to break me, she told herself. Wanting to appear nonchalant, Sava deliberately yawned, knowing it would serve to further enrage him.

Throwing the papers on the ground, the feverish interrogator shouted, "Take her away. No food, no water, two days. Maybe she ready to talk after no food." He shoved Sava toward the guards in the hallway.

Sucking in voluminous amounts of air, she reached a hand to her lower back, the target of his repeated blows. She squinted, relieved the beatings were finished, but fearing she might pass out from the pain. Hunched over, she knew this time was worse. She felt their rage and their heightened intensity.

In solitary confinement, Sava had ample time to think. She really longed to be informed of the goings-on in the outside world. Unfortunately, she would have to wait until

Sunday. Last week, through a new inmate, she discovered her sisters had been sending her packages of food and warm clothing. She had received no packages. The cunning Gestapo knew Room 38 was marked for execution, therefore they happily seized every package destined for her. Their cunningness knew no bounds, and to gather information on their inmates, the Gestapo frequently moved prisoners to different cells, hoping to find useful individuals willing to collaborate. It was a challenging task, but divulging key details about fellow inmates was a sensitive matter within the walls of Banjica.

Back in her cell, drenched in sweat and feeling nauseated, Sava shakily slumped to the ground, feeling unwell. She knew they were intentionally starving her.

The woman with kind eyes, Milanka Yaksich, crawled closer. She was an American-born Serbian from Minnesota, who had come to Yugoslavia to join the Partisans. She enjoyed conversing with Sava because she spoke English. "My God…Sava, the way in which they've tortured you…?" Taking Sava's hand in her own, she squeezed it to slip her a piece of bread. With the back of her palm, she then checked Sava's forehead. "You're burning up."

Dizzy and fatigued, she shivered as she closed her eyes.

Three days later, bathed in sweat, her fever broke. "W— what happened to me?"

Milanka and several others crowded around. "We were so worried about you, Sava. Here, try a few sips of water." Gently lifting it to her lips, Milanka murmured, "Thank God you pulled through. You gave us quite a scare."

Sava swallowed the sliver of bread and water, incredibly grateful to these wonderful women. Without their help, she might not have made it. These women, members of Tito's rivaling Partisans Communist Resistance, were nursing her back to health. She lay back against her dirty blanket, considering the essential lessons the Yugoslavian men could learn if they had been assigned to Cell Block Room 38. Sava realized her purpose might be broader than that of a messenger. It might be worth considering, provided she made it out of here one day, because she had the ability to demonstrate empathy and a willingness to engage with individuals who held divergent ideologies.

Jovanka, the brunette who had remained elusive from the moment Sava arrived, advanced closer. "Sava, glad to see you're awake." Leaning over her, she whispered, "We should talk. I've caught wind the Germans plan to shut down this place in a few weeks."

There was something about Jovanka that Sava found oddly invigorating. As she lifted her hand, she whispered, "Tell me more." Even though her voice sounded timid, her mind was sharp.

Hesitating, Jovanka looked to Milanka, who encouraged her to continue. "We have to do something. If we come together in unity, we harness a collective strength and power. I've been actively working on a plan because I passionately believe we should not stand idly by while they intend to annihilate every one of us. Despite your alignment with Mihajlović, my comrades not only like you, but profoundly respect and admire you. That speaks volumes to me. Are you willing to stand with us, Dr. Ivković?"

Sava felt a flicker of something, possibly hope…? Her gaze lingered on Jovanka before she finally replied. "I will stand with you," she said, her voice cracking.

Relief swept through Room 38.

CHAPTER THIRTY-TWO

SAVA

Banjica Concentration Camp, Belgrade, Serbia
September 11, 1944

THEIR PLAN WAS IN place. The women of Room 38, knowing they had nothing to lose, formed a suicide pact. Banjica was in a state of mayhem, and in a rush to leave, the Gestapo hurriedly set fire to documents and paperwork in the large bins behind the building, while the guards brought more files from the interrogation rooms. It was Sava's belief they were eliminating all remnants of the unspeakable atrocities and crimes they had perpetrated. Their intensified efforts to rid the camp of prisoners, and the agonizing screams of torture, kept her awake. They released some prisoners with lesser-known crimes and told others they would be released shortly.

No hope remained for Sava and her cellmates. Room 38 held members of Tito's Partisans, including two Serbian-born Americans, and Dr. Sava Ivković from Mihajlović's Resistance. The Third Reich deemed these women too valuable to be set free, as they had played a crucial role in the Resistance, thus were sworn enemies. Following heated discussions, the women did not want to go out without a fight and were prepared to take decisive measures.

They were ready. Jovanka had stolen a key from a drunken guard, and later that night, after a dinner of lumpy potato soup, they were crouched on the ground, ready to launch their attack. Adrenaline surged through Sava's veins, and after the guard made certain the cell door was indeed locked for the night, each woman sprang into action. Without making a sound, Jovanka placed the key in the lock. Each woman quietly slipped out, tiptoeing down the darkened hallway, concealing their handmade tools and weapons under their sleeves. In the lead, Jovanka trod carefully.

Sava was in the fourth spot behind her and peered around the corner until she spotted the sluggish guard, Peter Krieger. Waving her fingers, Sava gave the go-ahead sign to Jovanka, who pounced on Krieger from behind. With two savage swings to his kidneys, he dropped to the ground, but not before letting out a scream. Sava and another held him down while the younger woman attempted to cover his mouth. One of his arms broke free, and it flailed about. Quickly realizing their mistake in not securing the gag over his mouth first, Sava tried to help her, but it was too late. Krieger thrashed and hollered. His shouting alerted the other guards, who were there in a flash.

One of them waved his gun before positioning it. "Stop," he shouted at Jovanka.

Sava screamed, "No…"

As his shot rang out, Jovanka dropped to the floor. The guard repeatedly shot more rounds into Jovanka's chest and head. Chaos ensued as additional guards came running, swinging their truncheons, batons, and bayonets. Armed with fury, they beat the women, over and over, with their heavy truncheons, before pushing and steering them back into their cell. In a frenzy, the guards continued their beating until their arms could no longer lift their truncheons.

During the fight, a guard delivered a powerful blow to Sava, causing her to fall backward, hitting her head on the hard concrete. Despite bleeding heavily, she somehow found the strength to crawl toward the rear of the cell. The rest of the women, beaten to a pulp by bayonets and batons, lay scattered on the ground, their blood streaming like the river Danube. Sava's back burned from multiple wounds and bruises inflicted on her, and she no longer felt the use of her legs. Struggling to get air into her lungs, she felt a cold sweat on her forehead as black dots appeared before her eyes. "So cold," she mumbled, before she lost all sense of focus. A body suddenly collapsed on top of her. Then another. That was when she passed out.

***

Hours later, the beatings and shootings finally stopped—the women of Room 38 had been silenced. Their attempt to escape had failed miserably. At two in the morning, a guard ran to a cell that housed the Četnički male prisoners.

"Go and clean up the mess in Room 38 right now. Throw everybody on those covered trucks out back. Do this NOW. We're calling the gravediggers, so they'll be standing by. Be quick and don't forget to clean the bloody walls." Clicking the heels of his boots, he turned back around, pointing his gun. "Keep quiet or risk your life."

The men nodded in unison. They hurried to gather buckets, mops, and washrags. The smell hit them first, followed by the worst scene imaginable. An older gentleman, Peter, a university professor, whispered, "I think I might be sick," before retching into the bucket he held. Lifting his head, he stammered, "Never have I seen anything so horrific. What have they done to these poor women? It's the worst level of degradation of human bodies I've ever seen." Sighing, he joined the others in cleaning the cell.

After doing what they could to remove the blood and gore, the men carefully lifted the fragile, broken bodies. Gagging and holding their breath from the overpowering stench of death, they expressed shock at finding two women at the bottom of the pile, quite possibly alive. One had a pulse, so they conferred with Peter, not knowing what else to do. One of them said, "You've got a knack for talking to people. Could you go outside and see if there's a kind Serbian guard who would be willing to help? These women desperately need medical attention. The rest surely did not deserve to die like this."

"Yes." Peter went outside, where three German military cargo trucks sat parked. Continuing to look around, he spotted a policeman smoking a cigarette near a Serbian police car. Walking over to him, Peter delicately explained the situation.

The policeman agreed to smuggle the two out of Banjica. "My brother's with the Serbian Guard. He's told me how rotten the Gestapo has been."

Inside, Peter instructed his cellmates on the plan the policeman had suggested of swaddling the women in dirty rags and the blood-soaked towels. The prisoners did so and quickly carried them outside, tenderly placing the women face down on the back floor, before covering them with more rags. Finished, they nodded to the policeman, who immediately drove out of Banjica.

***

Two sweaty gravediggers in the Jewish Cemetery leaned on their shovels, speaking in hushed tones. The older of the two shook his head. "My God, these women...I've never seen people so savagely beaten. Some...had their skulls bashed in. Will you look at this one, so disfigured her family would not recognize her? What do you think happened over there?"

Breathing heavily, the second replied, "I—I'm not sure, but two of the women were mutilated...My stomach lurched just looking at them. Did you see the deep slash marks across their breasts, and the way they were cut... from the bottom up? They must have used either a sword or a long knife. By God, I've never in all my life seen something so hideous."

"I know. When I first saw them, it sickened me, too. I've got three daughters of my own. But their families? Thank goodness they won't see how horribly damaged these women were." Scratching his head, he asked, "What about the body count?"

"What do you mean?"

"Well, the paperwork said twenty-six bodies, but I only counted twenty-four. What do you think?"

Shrugging, the younger gravedigger replied, "Because they came piled on top of one another, it would be easy to miscount, especially in the dark."

Unbeknownst to either of the gravediggers, they had buried an injured woman who still had a beating heart.

***

On the outskirts of Belgrade, a Serbian police car pulled up to an old, yellowed house perched on the rise of a farm. The policeman knocked on the door, and a bespectacled, diminutive man wearing a white shirt with his sleeves rolled up answered.

"Are you Dr. Subotić?" asked the policeman.

The bespectacled man replied, "I am."

"I have a package for you." The policeman reiterated, "It's actually more than one."

Dr. Subotić nodded and pulled from his pants pocket a fistful of dinars. "I believe it's all there."

The policeman counted the dinars, ensuring he'd received the agreed-upon amount. "All right, I'll get them."

"Please, pull around to the side. You'll see the door to my office."

The policeman followed the instructions and dropped the female bodies inside the door. Turning, he said, "Oh, I almost forgot." Running to the car, he quickly returned, handing the physician a small shoebox.

Confusion spread across the doctor's forehead. "What's this?"

The policeman shrugged. "I don't know." He got into his vehicle and drove off.

"*Bože sačuvaj!*" Dr. Subotić exclaimed, alarmed to find a premature baby inside the shoebox, struggling to breathe. "Oxygen, stat!" he screamed. "And get these women onto beds, but first see if they have a pulse before you clean them."

***

In the quiet room, with the soft hum of medical equipment, the air carried a faint scent of antiseptic mingled with the metallic smell of blood. The first light of dawn filtered in through the closed blinds, casting a gentle glow on the two figures lying on the improvised beds. Dr. Subotić had worked through the night, and now he was finally allowed a moment of rest, his eyelids heavy with exhaustion. He pondered the fate of these two women rescued from the brink of death. The premature baby that had accompanied them was now stabilized, a testament to the resilience of life amidst the chaos of war.

But whose child was this? Was it the taller brunette with the elegant bone structure, or the smaller, more compact one with curly hair? It was difficult to determine; he had never encountered anyone in all his years of practice more severely beaten than these two. He had remained on his feet for more than twelve hours, fueled by a ferocious determination to save them. Dr. Subotić was lucky to have had spare blood, because without a blood transfusion, neither would have survived. While sipping his tea, he felt a flicker of hope in his weary body. Perhaps there was some humanity left in this world. Without the heroic efforts of the policeman, neither would have made it.

Throughout the lengthy surgery, he pondered many questions about the brutal actions of the Gestapo, wondering what could have driven them to beat these women so mercilessly that one became unrecognizable. Never in his fifty-eight years had he seen such torture.

***

Sava's mind was a tumultuous sea of fragmented thoughts and memories as she drifted through the dark expanse between consciousness and oblivion. The air carried a faint hospital smell and she could hear something, maybe medical equipment beeping in the background. Echoes of her past mingled with the pain that blanketed her body, a constant reminder something wasn't right, and just beyond her reach. There, amidst the commotion, a light appeared—a distant yet comforting warmth drawing her back in. With an effort that seemed to require an incredible amount of energy, Sava fought through the haze and pushed against the weight holding her down to slowly open her eyes.

She was agitated and confused. The world that greeted her was fuzzy and enigmatic, its shapes and colors melded into an indecipherable fog. The ceiling was unfamiliar, and the greenish walls jarred against the darkness of her recent memories. Oooh, the pain in her head was excruciating. Please...

Where am I? she wondered.

Feeling woozy, Sava closed her eyes, trying to remember where she might be. A rhythmic beeping forced her eyes open enough to wonder if she was in a hospital.

Panic rose when she tried to move, only to find her arms and legs unresponsive, bound by something. A weakness... or an unknown? Her eyes searched the room, which held nothing remotely recognizable. Her throat was parched, each breath a laborious task which left her gasping for air.

The room was silent save for an occasional footstep or the sounds of hushed conversations, but the pain hit her again, robbing her of breathing.

Where am I? The question reverberated in her mind, a stark reminder of the disorientation that gripped her. She had distorted memories of the escape attempt, the brutal retaliation, followed by a darkness that claimed her. They all swirled together to form a plot that seemed both distant, yet painfully recent.

As the initial shock of waking up subsided, a growing awareness of something horrible replaced it. The presence of another, the steady breathing of someone close by, offered her a strange comfort. Yet the identity of the person remained a mystery. Unable to move her head, only her eyes, she surmised that whoever was breathing must be next to her. Shrouded in the shadows, she hoped to learn more.

In this liminal space between life and death, past and future, Sava found herself at a crossroads, her fate intrinsically linked with that of strangers who had become her saviors. Her journey ahead was uncertain, but someone had saved her life, she was sure of it, and it must be someone in the medical field who was impeccably talented.

As she lay there trying to piece together the fragments of her shattered world, the door to the room creaked open and a figure stepped inside.

CHAPTER THIRTY-THREE

ZORA

Kragujevac, Serbia
September 16, 1944

IN THE DIM LIGHT of the kitchen, the Nikolić women found solace in their shared sorrow. Dušica and Zora whispered, their voices barely audible, while Mima's quiet tears described their mutual grief. Ever since Dunja had related the staggering news about Sava and the other women's fatal attempt to escape Banjica, resulting in Sava's subsequent death, they were plunged into a profound period of mourning. Their little sister—gone. An open wound that refused to heal.

Mima's despair was palpable, her voice breaking the silence. "Without a body, it's just another cruel example by the Germans. I can't bear this, unable to properly bury my Jelisaveta." Her sorrow filled every corner of the house.

Zora felt the weight of her mother's torment as she acknowledged the impossibility of their grim reality. "I understand, Mama, I really do. I'm terribly sorry, but there's nothing any of us can do to change the situation."

Mima's resolve hardened as she declared once more, "We must leave here—now."

Twisting her fingers, Dušica hesitated before glancing first at her mother, then to her sister. Gently, she touched Zora's wrist. "Zora, our losses…It's too significant. Every one of us has been drowning in our grief. I'm in agreement with Mama. The time to act is now. For the sake of our future, and the future of our children, we have to leave Kragujevac. If not, we won't have sufficient time to cross the mountains before the heavy snowfall. So, we have got to try, my dear sister—for our children's sake."

Zora's heart, already in pieces, threatened to shatter completely at the thought of leaving Neven and Goran behind. "How could I abandon my sons?"

Straightening her spine, Dušica's resolve was unwavering as she inhaled. "We must move forward, Zora. There's no room for hesitation. It's important to send a message to Jovica letting him know we're prepared to leave."

"Can we give it more time?" Zora asked, flipping her head from side to side.

"No." Mima stood, patting her daughter's shoulder. "We have done nothing but talk about this for the last two years. If we want a chance at living, we've got to leave here—now." She turned to Dušica. "Have you told her yet?"

Zora was confused. "Told me what?"

"King Peter gave a speech on the BBC, right around the time Dunja shared the news of Sava's death," Dušica said quietly. "I believe it has dismantled our Resistance… and our people. It's a confusing time for us, which has me concerned…"

After a deafening silence, Zora responded, "What are you talking about, since I'm obviously in the dark?"

Dušica chewed her bottom lip before starting. "The crux of King Peter II's speech was his announcement telling General Mihajlović, the Royalist Resistance, and all the Serbian people to join Marshall Tito's People's Liberation Army of Yugoslavia."

"You're joking, right?" Incredulous, Zora strove to comprehend the intricate implications of the King's call to unite with the Partisans, a move that threatened to dissolve the Royalists and redefine their struggle. "You're saying he asked Čiča Draža to stop what we're doing, and…join the Communists?" she spluttered, her eyes nearly popping out of their sockets. "Why…that makes no sense, Duš. The consequences alone…"

"I agree; however, both Mama and I were listening. We heard it, and people have been talking. A few women have said that their sons and husbands have returned quite dejected. Others have quickly switched allegiances."

"You cannot be serious, Dušica?" Zora's fingers tightened around her throat, a visceral reaction to the shock coursing through her veins. Overwhelmed, her gaze flitted across the room in a desperate attempt to decode the chaos unleashed by the King's words. Inside her mind, thoughts collided and tumbled as she grappled with his reasoning, all while the weight of his declaration pressed heavily upon her—the enormity of its implications for the thousands dedicated to preserving the Monarchy and Yugoslavia.

Could this speech really be true? If so, where, amidst this upheaval, did honor find its place? Was the King really behind this, and if so, what about the thousands of men, soldiers, whose lives had already been compromised in the valiant defense of the monarchy? This made no sense at all. It would only cause confusion and havoc with their people.

Even though they were a country at war, and the King was living in exile, surely, he would know better. The questions reverberated in her mind, amplifying the turmoil within.

Pacing in her kitchen, Zora admitted, "Joining forces with the Communists would be in direct contradiction to the position of the Monarchy, who opposed any form of communism." Stopping, she closed her eyes and really pondered this, before saying, "I wonder if Churchill, or the Brits, were behind King Peter II, possibly squeezing our young King into making this statement? He's too young to make these decisions on his own." Staring off, Zora recentered herself. "Or someone in the Cabinet wrote the speech on his behalf, but why...?"

"I agree. Although, there's one more thing. King Peter II ordered an act to dissolve the Royalist Resistance and Čiča as its general. It was dated August 24."

As the full gravity of the situation for their country emerged, the truth struck with undeniable force. Zora was overwhelmed by a profound sorrow, a despair beyond mere disbelief. With a voice tinged with resignation, yet carrying the weight of their devastated reality, she spoke softly. "I guess we'd better start packing."

***

September 18, 1944

The day of their departure arrived, their hearts laden with sorrow. They were leaving so much of themselves behind. Zora had prepared for their journey with a practicality born of desperation, baking loaves and loaves of bread to sustain them if no other food was available. They cemented their decision to leave when they heard from Jovica, who assured them he would await their arrival in the forest.

"I—I'm not sure I can go through with this." Zora stared at her mother. "Maybe I should stay behind and meet you… after the war." Tears glistened on her lashes.

"NO. We are all going," Mima stated. "We are all in this together, and we will face whatever comes our way."

***

May 1945

It had not been easy. They had to hide in their family village in Croatia for months, but they finally made it. The path was fraught with hardship, yet there were also moments of pure wonder. Their journey was arduous, and they faced unseen challenges and detours, yet with Jovica and his men's unwavering support, they navigated the ever-shifting landscape together. Their camaraderie became a beacon that guided them, and it helped Zora recognize how wonderful Peda must have felt being alive with this positive group of fighters.

In the spirited mountains of Yugoslavia, Zora found unexpected beauty amid this sanctuary. Beneath the expansive sky, the mountains gently whispered to her, renewing her spirit. And when the first rays of morning light cast an ethereal glow, Zora felt the weight of her sorrow lifting, replaced by a burgeoning sense of her own fortitude, buried beneath the wreckage of her past.

The border between Slovenia and Italy signified the end of their shared path, a threshold beyond which lay diverging futures. The farewell was poignant—a blend of gratitude, sadness, and the tentative stirrings of hope. Jovica had fulfilled the role of protector and friend to not only Zora but her entire family. His bond with them would be indelible. This goodbye was not just to Jovica and his revolutionaries, but to a period of Zora's life that had irrevocably changed her.

The mountains receded in the distance, silent sentinels to the journey that unfolded in their shadow. They had been watchmen to her transformation from one bound by grief to one awakened to the myriad possibilities of what lay ahead. Clasping both daughters' hands in her own, Zora crossed over the border into Italy, with the rest of her family behind them. She carried with her more than just memories but a spirit alight with the promise of new beginnings, new challenges, and the possibility of a kinder, more humane society on their path forward.

AUTHOR NOTES

BOOKS AND STORIES HAVE fascinated me since I first learned to read. When I was twelve, I had the incredible opportunity to work at the Carnegie Free Library for three hours each week, pushing carts laden with books before shelving them. Those three hours helping the librarians were nothing short of magical, leaving me with an insatiable fascination for the emotional impact of stories. They showed me the limitless potential of books and took me on journeys without ever leaving home. Books have helped shape me, and I'm rarely without one in hand.

My growing passion for European history made me realize the immeasurable importance of the past. Yet, regrettably, the echoes of the atrocious acts all too common in the Kingdom of Yugoslavia still have a lingering impact today, over eight decades later, evident in the ongoing events and diminishing glasnost in other parts of the world.

While driving through Serbia with my childhood friends CC and MM over a decade ago, I spotted through the fog an enormously tall, ninety-foot structure of a Saint George Serbian Orthodox cross positioned in the center of a bustling four-lane highway near Kragujevac. Piquing my curiosity, I learned about the painful events of the Kraguje-vac Massacre, which occurred over three days, culminating in the shameful, gruesome executions on October 21, 1941.

Because the Germans could not find enough adult men

to meet their quota associated with their edict *One Hundred to One*, they were prompted to systematically begin wrenching innocent children from their school classrooms. This ghastly horror stirred something within me, compelling me to learn more.

Back in the States, I immersed myself in extensive research after devouring over 154 books. As I began to outline my framework for this long-ignored story, I soon realized I needed a more precise description of what occurred before, during, *and* after the event. I broadened my investigation by dedicating thousands of hours to research in university libraries meticulously analyzing various academic journals and a vast collection of old newspapers, papers, essays, and diaries, which eventually led me back to Serbia, France, England, and Washington, D.C., to conduct even more research.

I worked hard to author this novel inspired by past events while aiming to capture the essence of the Serbian people. By providing you with an intimate glimpse into life in the Kingdom of Yugoslavia and the culture of Serbs, I tried blending reality and fiction as authentically as possible. Please know that Sloboda Freedom Organization is not real, although I love the thought of one existing. To the best of my knowledge, the date of each actionable event is as close to accurate as humanely possible. The list of characters outside the well-known ones, such as Winston Churchill, Slobodan Jovanović, King Peter II, Čiča Draža Mihajlović, Prince Regent Paul, Nikola Tesla, Josip Broz Tito, Bishop Nikolaj, and Patriarch Gavrilo are imagined.

In my early research, I discovered articles pertaining to Yad Vashem's awards given to individuals (many posthumously) who helped hide or safeguard Jews during

World War II . Since 2018, Yad Vashem has awarded the honor of Righteous Among Nations Award to one hundred and thirty-nine Serbians who have helped save Jews in the Kingdom of Yugoslavia, a country where the Nazis enforced the death penalty for assisting Jews. It *was fascinating to stumble* upon an article highlighting Klara Baić, a single mother from Serbia, who'd received both the Women of Valor Award and the Righteous Among Nations Award from Yad Vashem. These honors were bestowed upon her for her courageous act of providing shelter to two Jewish boys during the war despite the danger it posed to her own life.

Klara's story sparked a new perspective in my own story. Combined with my friend Lily's mother's account of sheltering Jewish friends in their Belgrade apartment until the Četnici could move them to safety, my characters were unexpectedly taking shape.

Tetka Dušica's character is loosely based on the goodness of people like Klara Baić and evoked strong feelings about the love and inherent goodness of my very own tetka, my Aunt Ljubica (Louise) Kusić. She made the selfless decision to forgo her education at a young age to help raise her younger siblings, including my mother. This one's for you, Wissie. The nickname Mima (for Milica) is a nod to another tetka of mine who is gone too soon.

Sava, like many other sons and daughters who fought for freedom in her tiny country the size of Maine, was named after my maternal grandmother (my very own Baka Sava Lalich), who I knew *only* through the rich tapestry of familial stories weaved together and lovingly passed down to me and my siblings. Sava's surname pays homage to my dear godfather, my Kum Nick Ivkovich.

Josie Whitney-Shaw shares certain admirable qualities with Ruth Mitchell, a courageous, intelligent American woman who achieved the historic feat of being a Četnik. Ruth Mitchell was described in an Associate Press article dated April 2, 1941 *as having been sworn in as the first American woman member of the Komitaji, a near-legendary group of Serb guerilla fighters who had a history of four hundred years of mountain warfare against the Ottoman Turks.* Accused of spying by the Gestapo, she was court-martialed twice before being sent to prisons and camps in Belgrade, Graz, Vienna, Munich, Salzburg, and the Liebenau Internment Camp.

Remarkably, Ms. Mitchell survived and authored two books, proudly recounting her war experiences and involvement with Draža Mihajlović's Royalist Resistance organization and was passionate about trying to save his life. Ms. Mitchell's brother, Billy Mitchell, founded the U.S. Air Force. Although there were female Četnik 'couriers' it would be fascinating to think they had female spies, but I have no confirmation of their presence.

I must pay tribute to the phenomenal Milanović sisters, Maca, Biserka, and Narandja who helped bring light to the Yugoslavian villages' oft forgotten abilities of natural healing. There were numerous injuries from gunshots, and there were countless frozen and severed limbs. With a scarcity of medical professionals near the villages and mountains of Yugoslavia, it is highly probable the local women from neighboring villages played a crucial role in attending to injuries by using their knowledge of natural herbs. Typhus was quite serious among the Yugoslav resistance, culminating in far too many typhoid deaths.

Since so much of Yugoslavia, including their National Library, was destroyed by the Nazis, I was thrilled to find a few original kafanas still in existence in Kragujevac, and inspired by them, I decided to use their real names. Nothing else about Paligorić Kafana and Stara Srbija Kafana is necessarily true, except for their delectable foods.

During my time in Serbia, I had the pleasure of meeting with knowledgeable historians, including Dr. Bojan Dimitrijević, PhD a distinguished military historian and Deputy Director of the Institute of Contemporary History. I was warmly welcomed to the Institute by Dr. Dimitrijević, and his generosity, expertise, and extensive knowledge of Yugoslav military history exceeded my expectations. I also met with Dr. Boris Tomanić, a scholar at this institute, who authored articles emphasizing key events leading up to the Kragujevac Massacre. Boris helped clarify specific points, and I am profoundly grateful to both gentlemen.

After touring the broad collection of military tanks, equipment, and ammunition used during World War II at the Yugoslavian Military Museum in Kalemegdan Fortress, I had the pleasure of meeting two high-ranking officers in Serbia's current army.

I also want to thank Vladimir Mijatović, Senior Archivist at the Historical Institute of Belgrade, for willingly answering a wide range of questions, particularly concerning the renaming of many streets in Belgrade.

The exceptional curator of the Banjica Concentration Camp Museum, Andrej Ćirić, conducted a private tour of the museum, explaining the untold and ineffable tale of the twenty-six women imprisoned in the Banjica Concentration Camp who resolutely refused to leave without putting up a fight. As he described their courageous journey for liberation, I felt chills and knew I would revise my original ending to include and pay homage to these remarkable women. Their story must be shared by a wider audience.

Written accounts of the daring women of Room 38 were scant, due to the Gestapo destroying nearly every shred of evidence and in leaving mere fragmented accounts from prisoners with minimal views. Additional insightful conversations with Andrej confirmed there was just one woman out of the twenty-six who'd survived, and that was because she was taken away earlier to give birth to her baby daughter. This is where my imagination took over.

Thanks to Narandja Milanović, PhD, and Gary Eagleson, I had the chance to collaborate with Dr. Branislav Cvetković, an outstanding historian with two PhDs. Branislav helped me sift through the vast amount of research I'd gathered, of which a significant portion was written in Cyrillic. I apologize in advance for any errors due to transliteration. Translating can sometimes lead to the loss of subtle meanings in the words. Please know I made every effort to remain as authentic as possible. Any errors are solely mine.

Through Branislav, I gained an introduction to the ethnologist Nenad Karamijalković, the former Assistant Director of the Muzej Kragujevac 21 Oktobar, and the current Director of the Cultural Heritage Preservation Institute. I deeply appreciate Nenad's profound knowledge of history and willingness to assist, advise, and support me in this novel, including reading specific chapters. Despite the numerous emails and challenging questions, he patiently and graciously addressed each one.

I would like to emphasize the emotional depth of my novel is due to my time visiting the extraordinary museum and sacred grounds of Šumarice Park, where I spent hours walking with Nenad. Šumarice Park spans over thirty-two hectares of land and has been transformed from mass graves into dignified monuments commemorating the **2,792** lives lost in the Kragujevac Massacre. I suggest visiting the Muzej Kragujevac 21 Oktobar, designed in red brick to symbolize the blood shed on October 21. Nenad offered a priceless glimpse into the symbolic significance of each monument spread throughout the reflective grounds. One of the notable monuments is the Broken Wings, which commemorates the 301 children who were executed. This monument was eloquently depicted in a renowned poem by Desanka Maksimović, *Krvava bajka*, translated to English as *The Bloody Fairytale*.

Thanks also go to the exceptional Marijana Stanković, Director, and Kristina Jorgić Stepanović, PhD and curator, of the Muzej Kragujevac 21 Oktobar for their outstanding help and contributions to this novel. What a ride it has been, Kristina, especially with the arrival of your precious newborn.

My husband and I journeyed through the hills, up and across the Suvobor Mountains, on our way to Ravna Gora. We were struck with awe as we witnessed the airfield—depicted in the impressive novel *The Forgotten Five Hundred*—constructed by the villagers, U.S. Airmen, and Četnici working tirelessly on their hands and knees to build a runway. Allowing my mind to wander, I pictured the chilly winter weather conditions, which undoubtedly impacted the revolutionaries sleeping on the open grounds. Navigating the miles, I once again pondered how these courageous women and men achieved their missions, all on foot.

Bursting with ideas, my husband and I traversed miles and miles of Paris's extensive streets and boulevards, previously trodden by the spirited women of the Résistance Française. It was on these boulevards and in Toot's Paris apartment where Sava's character first came alive. While considering various options to enhance Sava's role in the resistance, I noticed the scarcity of written information about the courageous women who directly or indirectly supported Draža Mihajlović's resistance movement. Inspired after finding a photograph of women in housedresses and babushkas pushing enormous cannons uphill on oxcarts while the men carried their slim rifles over their shoulders, I fastidiously wrote.

It was a privilege to conduct a portion of my research at the renowned research center at Churchill's Imperial War Museum in London, England, where I explored their collection of exclusive materials, including never-before-seen photographs of King Peter II, diaries, and lesser-known books about World War Two in the Kingdom of Yugoslavia. I am indebted to Zoe Melabianaki and the research librarians and staff for pulling together a cabinet's worth of books and academic works for me at the most wondrous place to work.

The Library of Congress is a writer's dream come true and a glorious place to conduct research. Working closely with Angela Cannon, the talented librarian specializing in Russian and South Slavic Collections, has been a joy. She consistently amazes me with her ability to uncover rare gems I'd never find on my own. You are indeed one in a million, Angela—thank you! Hats off to Zoran Sinobad in the Library of Congress' Film Department for broadening my scope of vision by viewing seldom-seen World War Two films.

I enthusiastically applaud librarians everywhere who work hard to get books into people's hands. The exceptional librarians at the Orange County Public Library deserve my heartfelt thanks for their unwavering determination to locate hard-to-find books for me.

I had the privilege of working with Protodeacon Ivan Gašić at the Office of the Episcopal Diocese of Šumadija in Kragujevac. Our work involved verifying the names of the Serbian Orthodox priests who were executed in the Kragujevac Massacre. In the archives, there were nine priests listed, and Protodeacon was able to confirm six names: Fathers Radovan Cvetić, Živojin Aksentijević, Radomir Savić, Nikola Aleksić, Andra Božić, and Jovan Knežević. Historians verified the names of the remaining priests, which include Fathers Ozren Janošević, Mihailo Radovanović, and Dragi Mijatović. Vjecnaja pamjat.

I am immensely grateful to Father Bratso Krsić for his invaluable advice and assistance with transliterations—far too many to count. I would also like to extend my heartfelt thanks to the sisters of Monastery Vraćevšnica, with a special mention to Nun Magdalina for providing detailed information about Vraćevšnica, Serbian nuns, and the specific monastic clothing they wear. Thank you very much; you have my heart.

I have no confirmation of their presence and Vraćevšnica Monastery was not bustling with activity, and none of the nuns of Vraćevšnica were actively involved in assisting the wounded. However, my research found articles mentioning *certain* monasteries that provided a safe refuge for the Royalist forces for a night. Vraćevšnica became my choice after journeying through the Ravna Gora mountain range and realizing its convenient location.

I applaud and am indebted to the historians, curators, professors, and archivists everywhere, but especially at Yad Vashem in Jerusalem, the Holocaust Studies Program at Western Galilee Academic College in Akko, Israel, the Dornsife Center for Genocide Research, and the Shoah Foundation of the University of Southern California in Los Angeles. Their exceptional survival stories in the VHA Archives, which I have used, help shed light on some of humanity's darkest days. My strong hope is that you continue uncovering truths worldwide.

It really does take a village of elves to help draft a book. In no short order, I'd like to express my immense gratitude to the collaborative team of editors extraordinaire at the History Quill organization in London, England. Words cannot adequately express my thanks to Rachel, Edward, Rachael, Barbara, Naomi, and the extraordinary Theodore Brun, novelist (and tutor) who transformed me into a believer in the effectiveness of outlining. Thank you all.

It warms my heart to have on my team the lovely Rebecca and Andrew at Design for Writers in the UK.

During the early stages of my research, I faced significant challenges. The primary sources I'd gathered consisted of texts written in Cyrillic script, and the process of transliteration required an additional two years to complete. Snežana Ceran Vranjković and Slavica Ristić, two remarkable friends, played a vital role in helping me translate academic documents and books. I am forever grateful to you for dedicating your time and effort to this novel. Jovica is for you, Slavica.

For help with Serbian words and phrases, I relied(heavily) on my Serbian friends, Ivana, Gorjana, Simonida, Michael, Marija, and her tata, Djani, and Dejan Krstić, a former journalist from Kragujevac and fellow author, as well as my dear friend Joanne and cousin Stephanie, whose fathers demonstrated astonishing courage crossing the Suvobor Mountains eighty years ago to unite with the Četnici. It warms my heart having your support.

I am fortunate to have the extremely competent George Pavlovich—whose father, Žarko, was an ammunition expert in the Royal Yugoslav Army—help verify the guns used in Yugoslavia. George's understanding of the weaponry employed in World War II by the Royal Yugoslav Army was indispensable.

Throughout my life, the countless heartfelt stories shared by friends involving their families' struggle for survival, loss, and escape from the former Yugoslavia have stayed etched in my memory. *Each* of you has enriched the narrative of this story by contributing your familial stories.

I would like to express my gratitude to the Muzej Kragujevac 21 Oktobar Museum, for granting me permission to use Jakov Medina's last message, which was an inspiration for my book's title.

Closer to home, thanks go to my sister for dedicating (a lot) of time to reading my earliest, bare-bones first draft and to my dear friend, Dodo, for reading the more expanded version. Thanks also to Piper, the late Bill Eckstein, the late Nick Evanovich, Nush, Toot, Marija in PA., choir mate Dr. Steve for conversations about ancestral trauma, Seka G., Gail, and Danny. To the American-born Serbian tamburaši Kum D and Kum B, thanks for clarifying the rhythm and flow of the effervescent music so many of us hold dear.

Even closer to home is my beloved Watsquad, whom I adore beyond measure. That's you, K.K., and you, SH., for your endless love and tremendous breadth of technical expertise that continually keep me sane.

To my dearest husband—a mere thank you will never describe how grateful I am to have *you* by my side. I will marry you again tomorrow. And, to my faithful little foot soldiers, Zoey and Gracie who patiently sit by my side, waiting for their walk.